COIL

REN WAROM

ISBN (TPB) 978-1-937009-79-3

Apex Publications
PO Box 24323
Lexington, KY 40524

For media inquiries please contact Jason Sizemore (jason@apexbookcompany.com).

This one's for Welsh Byron. With love.

PROLOGUE

He awakes to a hum of pain, persistent as the droning of bees. His skull aches. His throat burns. His mouth held wide as a scream by a wad of slimy stuffing, bitter as chewing pills. His body burns, restricted by bonds so tight they feel like a cage of secondary ribs. The pain is vivid fire, bright and furious, glittering as the voice of glass.

Last time he woke, he panicked, pain and fear driving him to screaming. He's learned his lesson. Screaming makes the pain worse. And so he grits his teeth against the wad, heedless of taste, and rides the pain out until he's able to think beyond it. To feel. And discovers there's nothing else to feel, his body so cold he can't discern where it begins and ends. He thinks he might be naked, but he can't see to tell. There's no light here. Nothing to help his eyes adjust. All he sees is a black, endless vacuum. He could be anywhere. Nowhere. If not for the pain, he would imagine himself dead.

The silence is profound, broken only by a soft, dripping music of fluids and the rush of nasal breathing. He thinks it is his own, but there's a strange echo. Is someone here with him? Watching? The urge to scream rises again, inevitable as the swell of a wave. He trembles with the effort to control himself, determined not to surrender. It's not courage; he can't take that pain again. He's more afraid of it than he is of this darkness, this silence, this cold. The strange emptiness of his head. He can't remember his own name. Can't remember if he even had one. Where all that information should surely reside, there's nothing.

All he has of memory is disjointed. Impressionistic. Feels more like a dream than reality, but it must be real. Mustn't it? He hasn't always been here. Has he?

He remembers, or he dreams, of walking. From where to where is gone. But he was walking, sunshine warm on the top of his head, a counter to the cold biting through his clothing. The crackle of glass, or ice, sounds underfoot. Faint music drifts over distant laughter. The air is cool enough to sear the lungs. No sense in it, no coherence. Memory or dream fastforwards, then to a moment of black. Only a high note remains, a vague awareness of pain pure as the onset of a migraine, and then the world caves in around him. Swallows him completely. A last recollection fleets behind the rest like a mirage, a shadow seen from the corner of the eye: incongruous circles. Bright red.

Red in the white.

CHAPTER 1

*B*lack eyes cold as the icy ground, Stark surveys the Wharf Guard tanks squatted like grey toads in front of Wharf End's imposing tenements. Behind their stolid presence, yellow tape crackles, and grim-faced Wharf Guards hold formation, bulky in winter uniform. Most residents may have left this part of the Wharf, but the gang folk haven't. This is Broken Saints territory. Attack is not only possible, but fully anticipated, and the Guards are a line of tension, fit to snap. Stark can't fault their unease. There's something about this case; a subtle but unpleasant pall of ill fortune, bleeding back through the horrors faced by the victims, the awful isolation of their deaths. And here it is, too, this fucking case, leading him back to where he was born: to where he died. To where Teya's face rises with such crystal clarity, he could reach out and wipe the tears from her eyes.

He believes in coincidence, in the arbitrary nature of life. He's seen all too often how horror arises from the insipid, the mundane. But in this case, right from the beginning, he's been struck by a powerful sense of pattern, of convergence. Past and present colliding. Now here's this body, in this place of all places, and every instinct he possesses screams that this is a message. Twofold. One for him, from someone he never thought to hear from again, and one for someone else. Someone he desperately needs on this case:

Bone Adams, the premier Mort in all the Spires, whose attention to detail and vast array of connections in the Zone are sorely needed here. He's put two formal requests for Bone through his office at City Central to the Notary Board, the Spires governing body, and they've rejected him outright each time, citing cost and logistical difficulty, which is so much bullshit, he could mulch a state farm with it. Bending to lean through the back door of his car, Stark grabs his coat.

"Don't bother waiting," he says to his driver Tal. "This one's an all nighter." Slamming the door, he cracks his knuckles and strides to the nearest private. "Is De Lyon here?"

"No, sir. He called in. Said to tell you to get the Buzz Boys to bag it up and send it to him; there's no way he's stepping foot on Saints territory, not for another Doe."

Stark twitches, his muscles bunching beneath cheap polyfibre, and barely restrains himself from unleashing a tirade on the blameless private. It's not his fault that De Lyon is as inordinately determined as the Notary Board to see nothing in these nameless bodies. To leave them as they're being found: abandoned to die.

"Buzz Boys in then?"

"No, sir. Like I said, that's been left down to you."

Stark nods, biting back a grin. "There's my first good news." De Lyon, the Mort assigned to the case, a man about as useless and self-important as it gets, has gone and handed Stark the excuse he needs to act. He gestures the private aside, impatient. "I'm calling in another Mort to look at this. Send him corpse-side as soon as he arrives."

"Sir." The private snaps a salute.

"I'm not army, boy," Stark mutters. "Not anymore."

He moves on, thickset and gruff, his body like his temper; short, built on a grand scale. Unfazed by the smell, he pulls aside pieces of tape as if they're cobwebs, and steps inside the shattered entrance. This place is a miserable hole, airless, corridors thin as choked arteries and black with the greasy soot of living. Stark resists the impulse to fend his way through. He doesn't like the uncontrollable sense of urgency, the copper tang of remembered fear these conditions spark, memories of a personal history he's worked hard to disown.

By the entrance to the scene the stench of vomit fills the air. A lone private stands, surreptitiously wiping his mouth, flushed with shame. It's obvious this is his first assignment as a uniformed creeper; he has that demeanour suggesting unrestrained cockiness reduced to cinders. Stark claps a hefty paw on the boy's shoulder. The boy rocks and gags. Stark winks, too long at this job to care. What's dead is dead. Not much to do about it. Only the job. Only ever the job. The boy will learn.

"Body?" Stark demands, voice dry and heavy as stone.

The boy straightens smartly and raps out, "Secure, sir."

"Good lad."

Stark pushes past the tape placed around the doorway. Stops just over the threshold, steadying an urge to walk back out triggered by the unexpected lurch of his innards. A woman. It had to be a woman. Pulling his chin left, then right, displacing tension, he wrestles back self-possession by sheer force of will, and gives his attention to the room. To the body at its centre, warped by ropes to near enough the shape of a reversed question mark. As ever, the sight fills him with dull, helpless anger. Fierce determination.

Given the outlandish state of these bodies, not merely the ropes but the bizarre lack of any modifications, Stark's first instinct had been to suspect Bone Adams's involvement, mainly based on the fact of his voluntary freedom from mods, beyond unusual in the Spires. After the first bodies were found, Stark spent hours hunting down everything there was to know about Bone Adams, and, finding a mess of a man who goes between his mortuary and the Zone with nothing more than drinking in between, went swiftly from suspecting him to suspecting that the bodies are meant for him: to see, to solve. Meaning Stark needs him here. Now.

Screw the Notary; this time, he's bypassing fucking procedure and going straight to the source. He snatches out his cell and dials with clumsy, impatient stabs.

"Bellox, it's Stark. I need Adams." Stark's tone is brusque, demanding, allowing GyreTech's Mort Director, who's taken over the late Leif Adams' duties until a new MD is voted in, to know he's not in the mood to be fobbed off.

"I'm very much afraid the Notary would have significant issues with that request, Stark. The cost ..."

"Bellox," Stark interrupts firmly, "I've had costs and logistics rammed down my throat by the Notary vultures twice already. Not interested. It's BS, and we both know it. Just give me the Mort I want. I'll take the heat, if there's any to take. De Lyon's on my last nerve and I'm getting all kinds of twitchy about his incompetence. May have to put in a complaint to GyreTech's Chair. May have to mention your name."

Bellox chokes on that, as Stark knew he would. The GyreTech Chair has a reputation for coming down hard on incompetence. This is his ace card, one likely to get him yelled at by all and sunder, considering his inability to conform to protocol and the trouble it causes, but this is why he does it. Protocol, procedure, achieves nothing but frustration, not only stifling proper investigation but often stagnating it completely. This is how murderers walk free. How crime goes unpunished. How the worst of the world perpetuates all but unchallenged.

He hears Bellox's teeth grinding in the silence, until he bites out with painful reluctance, "That won't be necessary. When do you need him?"

Stark smiles. Grim satisfaction. "I needed him last fucking week, but today will do. ASAP. Site's at Wharf End. He can't miss it, the Guard have a shit-load of tanks bugging up the air."

Job done, he ends the call, jams the cell into his pocket, and turns back to the room. Takes it all in, slow. The first look. The first smells. These impressions are the ones he'll keep at the forefront in the investigation to come. The ones that will tell him the most, if they tell him anything at all.

CHAPTER 2

*H*ungover as all hell, Bone navigates the early morning rush, a flood of heedless human pinballs colliding under blue skies. Across the 'scraper-tops, Canted Cross gangrunners trail in his wake, swift as shadows, their warbling cries carrying clear as bells over the chaos of street noise. For the past two weeks, that sound has followed him everywhere, feeding irritation, pointless paranoia. They're impossible to outpace, the only option is to go underground. Take the Bullet. But meagre, piss-coloured lighting and uneasy proximity to rats are more than he can bear. He may as well dive in the sewer and swim to goddamn work.

Today's not supposed to be work. He's been called in, savage with rage at the imposition. All he wants is to continue drinking until his head is numb. It's the only peace he gets. Stopping in the centre of the flow, Bone narrows his eyes against a spiteful glare of sun to light a cigarette, his hands shaking so hard it takes three attempts. It's well below zero this morning, and the frozen air is a razor in his lungs. The smoke's worse, but he inhales a lungful anyway, coughing fit to snap his neck. Spits on the snow and winces. There's blood in it.

"Fuck."

Smearing the bright stain to pink streaks with an impatient foot, he fights on, willing himself to wake up, buck up. The effort's hopeless. Too many nights of reckless drinking have piled up on the back of the inability to sleep. It's not insomnia, it's dreams. Hallucinogenic, freakish dreams he wakes from disorientated, detached from his body and sweating like a bitch. They're not nightmares. They frighten him more than any nightmare he's ever had, and no amount of willpower can fix the mess he's become enough for him to function this morning or any other. The truth hurts, but smoking hurts worse, so he drags hard on his cigarette and loses himself in the pain. Follows the flow onto the Grand, a wide avenue of tall, whorled spires in black metal, framing rows of blinding glass skyscrapers.

His home, Gyre West, is a tiny island like an off-centre eye in the insane sprawl of Spires City, cordoned off by the river Wern. Like him, this island holds itself separate in more ways than one, but like the rest of the Spires, it crawls with City Officer guards and their gang counterparts—Canted Cross here—a stalemate no one's interested in breaking yet. The tensions between them, wound to snapping point, crawl under Bone's skin and bristle, an array of acupuncture needles incorrectly set. If the troubles on the Spires' outskirts reach Gyre West, small, separate, and therefore insular as it is, it'll fall in record time.

Bone tosses his cigarette to land, hissing, in the snow. Heads for a steel and white square on the corner of Grand and Friar St East: Gyre West Mort. Its uneven roof slips with heaped snow, reflects blinding white, stealing sight, leaving only dazzled red haze in its wake. The smallest mortuary in mega-corp GyreTech's Spires Mortuary network, Gyre West's handles a mere 20 precincts, a fraction of those covered by other mortuaries. Bone's been a Mort here for ten years, Head Mort for eight, and this is the only mortuary he's ever worked, regardless of better offers. His father's decision, that, but one he's stuck with, even though his father, Leif Adams, ex-Chief-Mort of the Spires, has been dead nearly a year now.

Bone's institutionalised. Any mortuary but this one feels alien to him.

Recently, thanks to personal problems arising from Leif's death, he's had to share duties with a deputy: Canard Jute, a recent graduate and the definition of loose cannon. He hates that imposition, but desperately needs it. He hates needing it.

"Better be warmer in here," Bone says to Cyrus, sitting loose-limbed in reception, as he stamps snow off his boots.

Cyrus shrugs. "Depends on your take on warm."

Half-hopeful, Bone responds, "Warmer than out?"

"No such luck," Cyrus returns with a rueful smile.

Bone grunts. "Typical."

"When is it not?" Cyrus couldn't look less bothered; he's a big guy and Bone's never once seen him in a coat. He gives Bone a curious eye. "Hey, aren't you supposed to be off shift till next Monday?"

"No such luck," Bone replies ruefully and heads for his lab.

Down at the lab, Bone slams through white double doors into temperatures so far below zero his fingertips immediately blanch white, his breath plumes out in long, ghostly trails.

"Goddamn it!" He looks over at Nia, who stands grinning by the cadaver fridges. "Heating?"

"Fucked."

"Bellox mention those repairs he begged GyreTech for?"

Nia's mouth twitches, amusement and bitterness. "Told us to light a fire in the trash can."

"Heartless bastard. I'll set fire to his trash can."

"You won't."

His reply is a grimace of intent as he continues to the claustrophobic office at the back, where he stands exhausted, staring into nothing and rubbing a throbbing temple in hard circles.

"So, what do we have that requires my urgent attention?" he calls out. Resentment makes his voice too loud, but the resulting throb in his head feels like excessive punishment.

"Spiral corpse," comes the breezy reply.

"Fucking hell. Like it couldn't wait." Moving fast to avoid freezing to death, Bone scrambles into scrubs and steps from the office, shivering. "Pop it on the table, then, let's get it over and done, so I can go home and thaw out."

"It's already on the table, as I'm sure you noticed," she replies, generous with her scorn.

"Ah. No. Sorry, Ni." Snapping on gloves, Bone strolls to the table and rubs a finger over the concentric, interlocking circles on the meat of the corpse's right shoulder. "So, this is, what, number ten ... eleven? I've lost count."

"Twelve. Moron."

He sneers, childish. "You ask Spaz about it like you promised? Because I'm tired of his insistence that I deal with these fucking things. This is the fifth one that's cut into my time off-shift."

Nia's Uncle Spaz heads the Establishment, the Zone-based gang all other gangs in the Spires defer to. Nia and Bone exploit the connection in situations where Bone's unusual friendship with Spaz yields no answers. This is one such situation. The first of the spiral corpses was brought to Bone's lab four weeks ago, from the edges of Upper Mace. Spaz made it clear at that point, he wanted Bone to deal with any others found. It's not the first time Bone's handled fairly private gang business from out of his constituency, but it's the most curious. Apart from the spiral tag, the bodies aren't anything special; they're only failed gang initiates executed in the normal fashion. Bone and Nia know what it has to be, a new gang, but Spaz refuses to confirm or deny.

"Yeah, I asked him."

Bone raises both brows. "And?"

"Not a peep, just the same as the last time you tried asking," she says. "Gang business, not mine, blah blah blah. He was definitely on edge though, way more so than usual."

"I got the same impression. Intrigu ..." Rising from his lungs in a dry, tickling wave, the cough takes over his whole body, immediately torquing his ribs to a hard knot of pain. He slams a mask to his face, struggling to stop, to breathe between paroxysms. Comes out of it with embarrassing slowness to find Nia's eyes on him, cool and concerned and derisive. She's always seen straight through him.

"Fuck me, Bone. That's one hell of a cough," she says. "You look shitty enough without getting sick. And you're hungover. Again. That's not going to help, especially not considering your beverage of choice."

"And? Off-shift."

She regards him in silence. He can't bring himself to hold her gaze, stares instead at the intricate silver implanted around the curvature of her cheeks and eyes, trailing down her neck and into her scrubs. His narrow face reflects there, gaunt and unshaven. He looks like hell. He should probably stop drinking, but the drink shields him from far worse.

Relenting, as she always does, Nia touches his arm. "Are you okay to continue?"

He nods, wincing as the beginnings of a migraine rolls around his wrecked head. "I'm fine. Fine. Work is better than alone, and it's not like I can sleep."

He wants to talk to her, to tell her everything, tell how since Leif died, he's been fighting this constant, crushing sensation of loss. It's not grief. He hated Leif and Leif hated him. Leif was never a father; he was shackles, containment, control. His death should have signalled freedom; instead, Bone is coming unglued, losing the parameters by which he judges his existence. And then there are the dreams. Dreams of darkness, suffocation. Probably just a cheap, mental metaphor for a life under Leif's thumb, but he's scared to sleep, anyway, scared to face them. And too scared to share. Even with someone he knows will try to understand.

He yanks on his mask. Snaps viciously, "Scalpel."

Nia fits the blade roughly into his unsteady grip. "Your skin matches our Doe here to perfection," she informs him, acidic, taking his attitude personally and making him instantly guilty, because she deserves better than this and they both know it.

Disgusted by himself, as usual, he curls his lip. Cuts. Jerks back as gas hisses and thin, stinking liquid spurts up in a declining arc.

"Shit."

"Not shit. Blood." Nia swabs Bone's nose, the movement oddly prim despite the cotton clasped in surgical tongs, the coolly amused amber gaze. "Seriously, though, you need to get help. Leif's gone. You're killing yourself by degrees and he's not worth it. He never was."

Bone's eyes sting. He grips the scalpel hard in a shaking hand. Beads of fetid blood cling like oil to the blade. He watches one slide and topple from the edge as the scalpel trembles. The mirror-like glow of the scalpel. The flash of dropping blood disappearing into the gaping mess of his first incision. Too deep. Crooked. He can see the dappled rot of subcutaneous fat. The blue-white of bone. Can almost see the heart, still and silent under the ribs. Chambers filled with pools of gelatinous, putrid blood. What can he say? The equation should have been simple, life minus Leif equals peace; how it's become this horrendous fucking mess, instead, is beyond his comprehension. All he wants is to be free of it. Light-headed, longing for the cool burn of a gas-malt, longing for a cigarette, Bone does the one thing that might get him through to that moment: his job.

"Where's this one from?" he asks, knowing Nia will allow the subject change, even if she disagrees with it. In these rooms, she's a professional first and his friend second.

"On our territory, for once. Precinct 17. The canal. They dredged him up this morning. Someone saw a foot in the reeds, turned out to be a whole cadaver. Unusual there, hence his delightful level of degradation."

"Yeah, it is rather." Bone frowns at the corpse, annoyed by its refusal to be simple. "Give me your prelims."

"He's not an initiate," she says. "He's established gang, which means he's Canted Cross, but he's been executed exactly the same as the failed initiates. Canted law for transgressors is exile to Spine Freak territory, weaponless. So, this is a great deal more serious than usual transgression, and it has to be connected to the Spiral." Nia catches his eye. "Which proves we were right."

"Shit." A new gang means nothing but trouble, and some of these corpses have been young Spires lads, trying to become gang-folk. That never ends well. "Reckon he tried to switch affiliation and got caught? An attempted change of allegiance would constitute a more serious response."

Nia looks down at the corpse, her half-sneer telling an epic tale of scorn and gang-etiquette drilled into her from birth, never quite lost. "An honourless death."

"Precisely."

"So why the canal of all places?"

Bone shrugs. "Beats me. Probably wasn't killed there. Maybe someone played 'chuck the corpse?'"

"What if he's not Canted?" Nia says, offhand, busy staring at the corpse.

Bone's horrified response turns into another prolonged coughing fit. When it stops he wheezes out, "You really want for a non-Canted to have been swanning about on Canted territory?"

"No." She grabs the saw, thrusting it across the table. "But check the bolt-pattern, just to be sure. Not like we don't have to empty him out and weigh his organs, anyway, might as well be thorough on all angles whilst we're at it."

He sighs and reaches for the saw, his hand trembling so violently, the fingers blur like fluttering wings. Ignoring Nia's tut of disapproval, he applies the blade in a reckless arc, damned and damning. The clock counts out motes of time. Nia's reproach forms a beacon that Bone ignores, just as she ignores the spray of rank blood painting his scrubs. The saw stutters to a halt. Lifting the sawn section, he exchanges it for his scalpel and severs away, dropping organs, heavy and liquid, into deep steel bowls. Looks into the empty cavity, poking latex-shod fingers up and down each rib shooting right of the spine—a collection of severed branches.

"Well, that's sort of a relief."

Nia's eyebrows elevate. "Canted?"

"No doubt about it." Bone feels around each nub of steel, counting them out.

Nia bites her lip. "A new gang means all types of shit may be gearing up to hit the fan."

"Yup," he says heavily, distracted. His gut is beginning to hurt. He needs that drink he wanted earlier. "So, what do we tell Spaz about this one?"

"Nothing," Nia says, emphatic. "Not enough new intel to bother him with. We file a basic report, off record as required, and forget about it. Deal with any further corpses as quietly and cleanly as possible. Do our job—"

Loud, insistent bleeps from Bone's call-alarm cut her off. He swears and snaps off his gloves with two sharp jerks, chucks them on the scalpel tray. His cell's at home, so he goes for the office phone, dialling with impatient force.

"What?"

"Bone. I'm sorry, but you're needed again."

"I'm not on fucking call, Bellox. I'm off-shift until next Monday. Get that? Mon. Day. Canard's your man till then. Call him." He moves to slam down the receiver.

"Bone!" Almost a shout, an edge to it like glass, and Bone hesitates. "You've been personally requested. By Stark."

"Stark? Fascinating. But he doesn't cover my jurisdiction."

"I know. Look, Bone, I really am sorry to do this, believe me, but Stark made it clear he needs you, right now, and he'll go to GyreTech if he doesn't get you, which I cannot bloody afford to deal with ever, frankly, so get moving. The tenements at Wharf End. There's a blockade. You can't miss it."

Dial tone purrs in his ear. The receiver drops from his fingers and clatters to the desktop. It makes him jump. He peers out at Nia, her hands full of rotting liver.

"I have to go," he tells her.

She nods. "Where've they called you?"

"Wharf End."

"Wharf End? But that's way past River Head, over the Sewer Estuary."

"Way out of my turf, is what it is," he mutters.

Nia's hands tighten, sending rivulets of rotting fluids to spatter the shining white floor of the lab, a Braille of indifferent death. "Bad juju," she says quietly.

"Yeah." Bone starts to peel out of his scrubs. "Real bad juju."

CHAPTER 3

ank exhaust whips the hair of a rat-faced child, slaps it into tails to match her face. Dressed in a tattered tee and filthy shorts, she should be freezing, yet she stands, blank as a brick, oblivious to all but the array of tanks and guards outside the dominating facade of the tenements. It's obvious she's a street kid, but she's a bum note of scenery and her presence tightens Bone's anxiety. His head is still pounding, a swiftly grabbed coffee having made no inroads towards curing his ailments. He's so tired, his eyes are burning coals, searing the sockets.

From the rooftops, the sharp, gull-like cries of Broken Saints gangrunners echo about the street. They're different from Canted calls, which are more like the chatter of starlings, but he understands neither. The girl does, though. She listens for a moment, head to one side, and then pelts for it, her speed in the snow extraordinary. He watches her go. Sunlight ripples, rendering her a dwindling streak of red against a dull, white expanse. When she's gone, he scours the roofs, squinting, looking for the runners. They're impossible to spot, so he walks forwards to the blockade, where a private snaps him a swift salute.

"Welcome to the circus, Mort Adams. CO Stark requested you join him corpse-side on arrival."

Bone frowns. "Thanks."

He hates official titles, prefers his Zone name: The Bone-Man. It's a gang nickname, an honorific. He's the only outsider to ever receive one. Bone was a joke when he was born, bad Mort humour. A gang name for a Mort's son, it caused problems in the Zone when he started training. He had to work ten times harder to prove his worth, but it paid off in unexpected, often uncomfortable, ways—they've come to attach too much significance to his refusal to ornament his flesh. He'd tell them the truth, if they'd listen, but he doubts they'd believe him. They want it to be what they think it is. You can't fight that sort of thinking, so he doesn't try, merely quietly resents it.

Stumbling across rough ground, he enters the tenement, only to find himself blinded by darkness. Panic hits the same way it always does in this sort of sensory deprivation, and he all but screams the detective's name, "Stark!"

"Bone? Here! Keep straight on. Follow the smell," comes back, solid as a guiding rope.

Bone swallows the urge to run, and follows the voice because the smell is everywhere. Slowly, he adjusts to the dim light. There's quiet scuffling in the corners. Rats, their fur heavily matted and grease-smeared. Fear snakes through his lower intestine and he hurries on, desperate to put them behind him. Comes to a door manned by a skinny Wharf Guard private, pale as fish guts.

Bone points. "Corpse?"

The boy nods, and Bone ducks through, cursing the cramped doorway. Inside, Stark waits for him, standing beside her, and Bone falters to a stop. Stares. Blood buzzes deep within his veins. Awe intermingles with the sensation of falling, and everything fades but *her*. Poised in a halo of angelic white light, she's a slowly mottling statue, perfectly aligned. The tang of her rot is acrid and stings his eyes, making them water. He wipes a shaking hand across to clear his vision, needing to see her.

Her skin. It's her skin. As pure and unmarred as his, bar the natural effects of decay. He almost refuses to believe it. There's no one in the Spires like him, no one whose flesh is unmarked. No one else whose natural inclination to alter the self with mods of iron, steel, and silver, or multifarious genetic alterations has been stifled. He's alone. Or at least, he thought he was because now there's *her*. How ironic they should meet now, when their similarities can make no difference to his state.

Squat as a tank next to her alien beauty, Stark holds up a large glove-encased hand and gently strokes her slender arm.

"Ballerina Girl," he says. The low timbre of his voice vibrates Bone's eardrum to the point of discomfort.

Bone's motionless. Fixated. He follows the long lines of her attenuated limbs in a caressing gaze and moves without thinking. Walks a slow circle about her, rising with exaggerated care over the system of ropes crossing the room, intricate as spider's web. She's perched delicately, gracefully even. Ethereal despite the rigid lines of restraining rope and the dappled gnaw of rats. Despite the brightening maroon blush of lividity speckling her lower body, and the animalistic rictus of her face. She's a macabre artwork of flesh and rope.

Her body floats above the denuded toes of her right foot. The left soars in a high arc above and over her thrown-back head. Her arms, too, sweep back. Her naked body twists into a curve so extreme that, were she not held by that torturous formation of knots and pulleys, she would crumple. Her dilemma hits his chest full force. He's overtaken with the urge to reach out and pluck her from the web, rescue her, even though the moment she might have been rescued is long since passed. But those ropes, they make him ache so far inside, he can't pinpoint the location of that hurt with any accuracy.

He steps towards her, reflected in her blank eyes. Up close, the illusion of purity, of mod-free skin, is broken. He sees the scars where mods should be, the evidence—almost invisible to all but Morts and surgeons—of genetic tampering. Those tiny pucker marks by the eyes, the pinprick of white stipples in the irises, the body's reaction to change. He's halfway relieved, but his gut cramps in disappointment, too. Being alone is a burden, and Bone often wishes there existed the option of normality without modification, or that modification felt in any way normal to him after all these years of being denied his own. All he wants, all he ever wanted, is to feel normal.

"Ballerina Girl?" Bone digs in his pocket and snaps on gloves, focusing on the corpse, his job. "She's labelled?"

Stark points to the inside of the leg suspended at a freakish angle above her head and Bone steps around to look. Tattooed in spidery writing, it tangles along her inner calf: BALLERINA GIRL.

"Any work you know?" Stark asks, intense with hope.

Bone reaches out and rubs his finger along. The writing stretches in flesh just beginning to slip. He traces the letters one by one. Delves deep into the repository of Zone scratch names and their accompanying styles stored in his memory, registering only disappointment, frustration, and the beginnings of bewilderment.

"It's not a style I'm immediately familiar with, no," he says, slowly, thoughtful. He turns to Stark. "I'm betting her killer tagged her himself. In which case, with all these mods removed—which is probably her killer, as well—he'd most likely be a surgeon. I'm looking at a fairly impossible task, even with my somewhat larger list of Zone contacts. But I'm guessing you sort of knew that. So, why am I *really* here?"

"Because there are no mods, and I think that means something. I think it means you're supposed to see it. And because Ballerina Girl makes three."

The distant roar of the tanks' exhaust momentarily dims. Bone turns back towards the creature floating centre stage and the precise machinery of her presentation. That elegant layout of hooks and pulleys holds the rope web unyieldingly taut, even to the weight of her sagging flesh. He looks beyond her at the whole room, realising it's no longer slowly corroding ruins but a grotesque stage for the performance of Ballerina Girl.

A coat of deep red paint, daubed on in thick waves, disguises the walls and obliterates the narrow windows, bleeding onto the blackened plas-wood of the floor, into the mould-patched expanse

of the ceiling, eradicating every trace of the room's former function. Whatever perverse impulse has moved the hand of her killer,
there's explicit intent to it. The little light that may have penetrated
this derelict capsule has been blotted. Instead four powerful, solar-
fed spotlights are set into the far corners of the room, angled to
highlight her perfect, unreal curves and mask-like face. Simple.
Pre-planned. Perfectly executed.

Tension coils through Bone in a slow, sick spiral. He's seen
more than he cares to recall, but nothing so careful as this, so delib-
erated. No one in the Spires cares enough to put this much thought
behind slaughter. Violence here is a reflex; effortless as the countless movements a body undertakes in order to function. Ballerina
Girl represents a calculated act of destruction, art as opposed to
aftermath. And there have been two more like her. Three aberrant
artworks, now his to interpret. But how does he begin to interpret
this? Bone rubs at arms stippled with reaction.

"Okay," he says through numb lips, "I'm listening."

Stark takes a seat across from the body on an unsteady pile of
rubble. He fumbles out a thick pad, bound with elastic, and
unsnaps it; flips through, clearing his throat.

"To date, we have the Sphinx and the Crucifixion. Both labelled
the same way, though in differing locations on the skin. Former
found last Wednesday, latter two days ago. Both tied with the same
double braid rope, same pulley system holding 'em in place." He
gestures roughly to the walls. "All the bells and whistles, as you
see it here, exact. You'd think it was the same room once you're
in it."

Bone, back to examining the girl, pauses, surprise flashing in
his eyes. "Both found dead?"

Stark snorts, says, "How else?"

Bone shrugs, his shoulders tight and awkward in the cold.
"Depending on shock response, physical health, psychological
strength, they could survive for some time before death under
these conditions, beyond the usual span for starvation or dehydra-
tion. The temperature would benefit them by inducing a

hypothermic state, slowing the body's functions. Allowing them to survive longer on less."

Stark scowls. "No such luck. They've all been in abandoned places like this, secretive, close to civilisation, but not close enough by a whisper. A fucking taunt. All three were found by pure chance." A burst of anger tightens his broad face. "It's making us look like idiots. This guy seems to know how long they'll be left unseen, unaided."

"Guy? Are we sure it's a man?"

"I have no idea. But according to all the literature, because fuck knows we have no recent historical reference for this, staging like this generally presents as male psychosis."

"Okay. But this killer can't be working alone. Not even an augment could do all this by themselves." Bone indicates the ropes. "This system could be put up by one, but the balancing of her weight requires two pairs of hands. It's extraordinarily intricate."

Stark's eyes flicker approval. He says, "He's not working alone, no, but this is one man's vision, and considering the mutilation's a reverse of usual physical violence, it's scary shit." He shakes a heavy head and pulls his hand down his face, exhausted. "We're all thumbs here. It's too far outside our remit. If I could, I'd bring in Suge to help us."

"Suge?"

"Been on my team eighteen months or so, replaced a retiree. He's augment. Eyes." Stark heaves a sigh. "He'd be damned useful."

"So why's he not here?"

Stark grunts in disgust. "The Notary's restricted access. It's just me, De Lyon at Lower Mace Mort, and Mitt Faran's Buzz Boy team. The fucking Guards out there don't know shit. They're just here to guard it. I dicked enough procedure calling you in to give the Notary ulcers, but they're throwing bullshit like it's confetti and I haven't the time." Stark returns to his notes. "Bodies have no contusions, no drug traces—lab says possibly a metabolised substance—no sexual assault, prints, fibres … *anything*. Sphinx had a heart attack—De Lyon says an existing problem but I'll go with your evaluation on that when you have it—and Crucifixion died from suffocation." He slams the notepad shut, re-snaps the elastic, and shoves it back in his pocket with undue force.

Bone nods and taps the ripe, purplish blue patches on Ballerina's face with the blunt end of his scalpel. "Acute cyanonsis. Pressure on the lungs. Ballerina suffocated, too. Could've been serene, hallucinogenic, detached."

"So why the face?"

"This is art, pure and simple. She's perfectly suspended, held by the rigging, not her muscles. The discomfort would be from the extreme positioning." Bone indicates the acute curve of her spine. "From that comes intermittent muscle spasms, the slow build of cramping to seizure-like levels. It would've been excruciating. Everyone reacts differently to pain. She either couldn't handle it, or wouldn't accept it, fought it." Bone touches a gentle finger to the puffed pouches of flesh beneath her clouded blue eyes. "Fighting makes it worse. In effect, by fighting, she slowly suffocated herself."

Stark considers this for a moment, his eye twitching a little, then points at the balletic corpse and declares, "You've already noticed the only harm, apart from rope marks, is the removal of mods and the addition of the tattooed tag. She'll be clean, not a fucking whisper, not even genetics. It was all gone from the others. Cleared out."

"Yeah, I caught all that."

With the end of his scalpel Bone traces the patterns of tiny scars that should contain hard nubs of bolts or ball bearings beneath, they're smooth, empty, unnatural to everyone but him. It feels personal, unnerving, especially in the context of this carefully staged diorama. He's inclined to agree with Stark. This killer, whoever he might be, wants him to see these bodies. To figure them out. Perhaps wants to show off to him. The thought makes him want to puke.

"He's fastidious as all hell," Stark says.

Bone nods. "He is, so let me ask you a question. These lights, were they on or off?"

Starting, Stark gives Bone a curious look. "Off. Why do you ask?"

"I wanted to know their purpose. If they were on when she was found, then they're part of the framing, they're significant."

"And what do you make of them being off?"

"That they're for us. For me. So I can see clearly, appreciate his artistry. He left her nothing but darkness and cold. Whatever the reason, it has meaning to him."

"Agreed. You're picking up everything I did."

Stark's impressed, but Bone can only think of how she must have felt and the unease from earlier rises upwards in spasms through his gut. He looks again at Ballerina, into her eyes. Is there despair in that milky blue gaze? Behind his eyes, there's a sensation akin to the soft scrabble of spider legs. The nausea intensifies at the sensation and he swallows. Convulsively. No way he's about to throw up like that Guard out there.

"Anyway," Stark says. "De Lyon checked Notary records with facial recognition, came up blank. These Does are untraceable. He checked his contacts in the Zone for the tatt, and found zip."

Bone laughs. "Unsurprising." He touches her scars again. "I can't even inspect these for familiar cutting techniques; they've healed almost invisible. Same on the others?"

"Yeah. The same. We thought he might be holding them somewhere, but tests showed the only deprivations occurred during their time suspended. If our killer is holding them before he ropes them up to die, then he's treating them damned well, which fits none of the corresponding psych profiles in the books I've had to read to try and get a handle on this." Stark sighs.

"I don't like it."

Stark rubs at his shoulders and Bone sees the outlines of heavy steel implants. How appropriate. This man reminds him forcibly of the tanks lined up outside. "No," Stark says, heartfelt. "Your specialty's Zone tracing; you're the best there is. Is there anything you can do to find our guy fast, before he does this again?"

"I'd have to take the victim's pictures to every single surgeon in the Zone with a psi-augment by my side, to see if one gives off a suspect psych wobble, and you know that's not happening. The Establishment would never allow that shit." Bone shrugs as Stark lets out a huff of irritation. "Stark, even if our killer isn't a surgeon—which is doubtful—I can't even try for simple ID. No surgeon is going to facially recall these patients from the thousands they mod every year. There are no eidets and no memory upgrades amongst surgeons. You know as well as I do how illegal that is. It's a client confidentiality compromise. What the hell can I do for you?"

"I'm running on empty," Stark tells him, sober. "I need someone who looks deeper. You're already seeing what De Lyon, the Notary, even fucking Faran, refuse to see. This is no act of gang propaganda; it's very carefully orchestrated and far too opposite to their philosophy. I'd bet a year of paychecks that it's the virtuoso performance of some evangelical mods extremist, and if anyone can cut clues out of this poor bitch and prove me right or wrong, or point me in a better direction, you can."

"And if I can't?"

"I have my own line of inquiry to follow alongside your efforts."

Bone cocks a curious brow. "Which would be …?"

Stark grimaces and spits out, "Burneo."

"Burneo?" Bone laughs. "You're kidding me. You actually believe some lunatic man-machine who's never once left the sewer is behind this shit?"

"These bodies, they're statements," says Stark, a dark edge to his voice. "If they became public, all hell would break loose. Anarchy. Burneo is all about anarchy, all about forcing ordinary folk to take on change they're just not ready for, despite the Spires more exuberant approach to modification. Couple that with how difficult these bodies are to find, and yet how disturbingly close they are to secure or secret sewer outlets and I've a compelling reason to investigate him. Abandoning these people to die in the middle of nowhere may seem to be a form of sadism ..."

"But that would be contraindicative to what we're seeing. The staging, the deliberation, the care in the process. They're meant to be seen, to be found," Bone interrupts thoughtfully.

"Precisely," agrees Stark. "It suggests our killer is operating under constraint, or to a very precise agenda."

"You're suggesting Burneo is helping to make the vision reality?"

"That's exactly what I'm suggesting." Stark rises from his stone seat. "He's a symbol to any half-baked whack job who wants shit like Transmog, the Monk psi-gen, irreversible animalistic gen-mutations, and meldings made freely available in the Zone."

"How in hell would they meet?"

"By my reckoning, if I'm right and he is involved, then our killer would have had to go looking for him and found him way before the killing started, because this likely took one hell of a planning period," Stark says. "However unlikely it might be, my gut's telling me he's in this, and I intend to find out how. My boss won't like it any more than the Notary will like you knee-deep in this, but her ..." He stabs his pen towards Ballerina sharply, a movement of rage and impatience. "She's my tipping point. I'm done with the books. Time to step off the beaten path."

"So you'll be knee-deep in sewers whilst I'm elbow deep in flesh?"

"Once I get the green light. Lucky for me, my boss trusts my gut, even when he doesn't like where it's taking me."

Bone shudders. "Rather you than me."

"There's nothing I like more than wading knee-deep into the shit," Stark says cheerfully, grinning. The expression transforms his face, animates it, and Bone realises how lifeless it was before. No, not lifeless. Closed. Completely locked down.

"You're a strange man," he says, shaking his head.

Stark comes back at him, sharpish, "So the fuck are you."

CHAPTER 4

*I*n the mucid depths of the sewers, where rusted pipes form elaborate, interlocking puzzles, plumes of steam disperse into shadow, like machine breath. In the mouth of the machine—a vast cavern—drips of water slip to the tips of stalactites before free-falling to join the great, sulphurous body of liquid beneath. Their endless splashing creates a ripple of music upon the giant bowl of urine-coloured waters.

Sedate as an alligator, Burneo floats at the surface, his arms splayed in repose. Around him, the water barely moves, disturbed only by sulphurous bubbles rising to the surface to pop, spewing puffs of invidious yellow vapour. His chest barely rises. He could be dead but for the endless hissing of the pistons at the junctures of his shoulders.

Somewhere far up in the jagged roof, great lights switch on, one after the other. The hollow clack and hum of their activation spreads in ever-decreasing repetitions about the glistening walls. Something flickers in their illumination, a mirage. Cave walls to concrete smooth as marble and then back again. Burneo rolls a mercury eye, blinks its tawny counterpart. Dips his great skull back into the waters and gulps sulphurous brine, sighing deep relief as it travels his parched throat and cascades into the great steel box of his belly.

He expels a rush of yellow gasses, watches the lights as they begin their ponderous revolutions and send searching beams to sweep across the cavern.

"Time to leave," he says, his voice echoing from the cavern walls.

The pistons in the junctures of his shoulders and elbows spit and sigh as he raises his arms to an arc, thrusts backwards, and dives, out of sight in seconds.

He surfaces in a square, shoulder-deep pool under the vaulted ceiling of an overflow chamber. The single exit, a humid, lightless void of a tunnel, rises in the wall ahead. Still as a stalagmite, thick tangle of black hair sodden, he peruses a congregation of massive rats ranged on the ledge, their eyes sparking red in the dull light. He evaluates them as they evaluate him.

Stand off.

Then he wades forwards and grasps the edge of the pool with huge hands, their fingers awkwardly jointed in gleaming steel. There's a rush of stinking water and he stands on the edge, naked, a giant of tormented flesh corroded with metals. He rolls one leg, a shrug of movement. From within, deep metallic pops resound. Eyes quivering shut, he groans at the sensation, pain followed by pain. This is what he lives for.

Pistons fire. Liquid bubbles in clear plastic tubes. Blood, piss, shit. Inner workings exposed. His eyes snap open. He walks forwards, a shuddering lurch of unusual grace.

And the rats part before him.

CHAPTER 5

*F*orlorn grey sky provides a backdrop for the Avenue's procession of black spires; frozen gyres punctuating haphazard, ivy-wound rooftops. In the rest of the Spires, these omnipresent helixes are kept to one aesthetic per district, affording each a different visual key. Here in the Zone, their architects were allowed free expression, and as a result, the spires are often eccentric, eclectic, or bizarre.

Twelve of the seventeen on the Avenue are slender as needles, tightly wound as DNA, bristling ominously between the tiled roofs like porcupine spikes. Of the remaining five, three are bestial, rising to three hundred feet and formed to resemble armies of gargoyles, dragons, and horned serpents crawling to the heavens, their mouths belching lightning. Intricate and grotesque, these guard the two ends and the centre of the street, a dismal sentinel trio.

The last two are gargantuan, so immense they make the eye baulk to look at them. Rising to pierce the Zone's dense cloud cover, they break through at their pinnacles into bright sunshine that spills down their innards and transforms their stark, black solemnity into something altogether more ethereal. One of these giants rises from the courtyard of the Doghouse, an old-timer biker bar painted with fading murals of motorbikes and dusty sunsets.

Perched high in the innards of that Gordian monstrosity, drenched in sunlight that ignites his liquid tattoos to blinding rivers of white fire, sits Spaz, leader of the Establishment. Still and alert as a crow on a distant rooftop, his second in command, Dash, grins, relieved to finally spot him, and sets off across snow-bound rooftops, his feet light and sure, building up speed despite the ice skinning the tiles somewhere beneath that layer of snow.

He hits the Doghouse roof and knocks up a gear. The spire's dead centre in the courtyard, some thirty feet from the edge of the roof, and if he's not going fast enough, he'll plunge to his death. As he hits the apex, he leaps, aiming for the curved edge of the spire. His hand wraps the black steel sure as a whip and he scales the spire in swift movements, with all the skill and assurance of a born runner.

He was a runner when he was younger, as was Spaz. It's one of the accepted ways to rise through gang ranks, though many runners choose to stay on the pulpits and rooftops, considering it their personal territory. They wonder why anyone would reduce themselves to ground level and say that anything beneath the crow's eye is beneath their notice. He and Spaz chose to move on, understanding that it's not always necessary to climb to stand taller than everyone else. But no runner ever forgets how to run, nor ever quite gets the urge to do so out of their system.

Reaching the level beneath Spaz, Dash bunches his muscles and swings around, throwing his body upwards and over in a tight somersault to land beside his boss. He wobbles just a touch and splays his weight out to catch his balance.

Spaz raises a brow. "Nice one. Bit close for comfort, though."

"Fuck off, that was damn near perfect."

"If you say so."

Dash takes a seat. "I've been looking for you. Got word Bone's on it now."

Spaz nods, his gaze distant. "Make sure the runners don't lose him."

"Lace said she's got teams to back her up everywhere, even the

Spine Freaks. Have to say, I'm impressed. Girl's got considerable diplomatic skills."

Spaz allows a smile. "She's also got a directive from me recorded into her chip to play to any fucker who wants to ask stupid questions."

"Ah. Nice one."

"Her idea. And it was."

Dash clears his throat. "This is necessary, right? Those bodies … It's fucking wrong."

Spaz reaches over and clasps Dash's shoulder, his steel-tipped nails pressing into flesh, not aggressive but certainly not agreeable. "I wish it weren't, but you know Yar won't hesitate to use his position as Notary Chair against us."

Dash drops his head. "No. But letting this happen. In *our* fucking city."

Spaz chuckles, a dark, bitter sound. "Yeah. I know." He releases Dash's shoulder and gives it a friendly whack. "I need a drink. Sitting up here like a miserable cunt only makes me feel worse."

Spaz jumps to his feet and leaps down, disappearing from view. Leaning over to look, Dash finds himself unsurprised to see his boss descending in huge, crazy jumps, feet sliding on the curved edge of the spire. He chuckles.

"Mad bastard."

Following his boss's lead, he hits the ground a few seconds later and catches Spaz as he strolls out of the courtyard onto the beaten steel cobbles of the Avenue. Spaz's bar, Snatch, is the craziest, loudest joint on the Ave. Inside, they bypass the noise by heading for the private rooms in back, Spaz's home away from home. To his office, where he pours two generous glasses of whisky. Taking up a seat on the window, Spaz stares out at the unimpeded view across the Zone, his drink forgotten almost immediately. He sighs, and it's a sound of immeasurable exhaustion.

"This shit is a blight on my conscience, Dash. Don't mind using the gang initiates the way we have because that yielded the results we needed and most of those fuckers die every year, anyway. But when it comes to *Bone,* I find myself questioning everything."

"What?" Dash doesn't know what to think. He's never heard doubt in Spaz before. Spaz does not experience doubt. He can't afford to.

"It's a long shot," Spaz says, toying with his glass. "A chance we were forced to take. I don't like that our future rests on it. It's too flimsy, too uncertain."

"But ... I didn't realize," Dash stutters. "I thought we *knew.*"

"We don't know *anything.* Tides did the best he could, but it might not have been enough," Spaz tells him, matter-of-fact. He swallows his drink in one, and sets the glass down on the window ledge with an angry clack. "I tell you, I'm just glad that supercilious fuck Leif's heart packed out on him. Saved me pulling his plug."

Dash is too stunned to answer. He swallows a generous slug of whisky and changes the subject. "I've no word from Lever. Shouldn't she have reported in by now?"

Spaz barks out a laugh. "She won't bother until she's got something concrete to share, or she's in a whole world of trouble. Ages me a decade every fucking time without fail. But she always delivers."

"Is she safe?"

"She never is, Dash."

"But this is different danger than her usual brand, surely?"

"Yeah," Spaz agrees softly, then aims a significant look at Dash. "Now how about you tell me why you came to hunt me down? As edifying as this little chat has been, nothing we've discussed required a face to face."

Dash hauls in a deep breath. "Fine. Fuck it. Your favourite Monk, Creek, finally got through to Burneo, okay? Looks like switching to someone a little stronger did the trick."

The use of Monks, and of Burneo, bothers Dash. Their Monks are no longer loyal to the Notary, nor connected to the Chain, but they're still Monks. Monks are odd creatures; all male because the gen is Y-connected, they're distant, as though the world goes on outside of them and never quite touches them, and far too powerful. Even Spaz, whose gen is only partial, leaving room for human warmth, often looks as if he's stepped too far outside of the world to ever come back, and it's that distance Dash worries about the most, it doesn't feel safe to him. Especially not with Burneo, who is definitely not sane.

"Wade's strong enough, Dash," Spaz corrects him calmly. "He's just too impatient. Burneo's a huge, uncontrolled receiver, meaning he's open to *everything*, all the fucking time. You have to interpret him. To learn to listen for what matters. Honestly, I don't know how the hell he manages to stay as lucid as he does. I get rushes of information sometimes and it gives me a goddamn migraine. His head must feel like fallout."

"Well, Creek didn't exactly pull a rabbit out of the hat, more like roadkill. Some shit about Reinhart in his playground and this bit of nonsense," Dash pulls out his cell, tapping the slender glass with his thumb and reads it out, rapid and derisory, "'He is waiting in the dark and the glass.'" He thumbs the cell to sleep mode and shoves it back in his pocket.

Spaz leans back, shaking his head. "No, no. That's not nonsense at all."

"Really? You trust his visions? You trust him?" Dash finishes his whisky and scoffs, "I find it a little ridiculous to be even marginally reliant on anything so disconnected, so insane, as Burneo."

Spaz's gaze flattens, flashes cold, and Dash winces, wishing he hadn't spoken. He's not like Spaz, can't see what he can. "You're very much mistaken," Spaz says, soft but definite. "I trust him as much as I trust you. Don't ever forget it."

Dash holds up his hands, surrendering the argument. "Just airing my thoughts."

Spaz makes a scoffing sound. "Sure you are. So whilst you're here, aggravating my eardrums, what happened with our canal refuse? I presume it was delivered in time. I wouldn't want to have to send it to that prick De Lyon's lab. Too risky by half."

"Nia sent in a report, discreet as ever."

It's only when Spaz's shoulders relax that Dash realises how much tension they were holding. "Good. Then we can leave that to develop as it will. You spread the word now, no more requests to be honoured. Shouldn't be any legitimate initiates with it anymore but if anyone's found with it who isn't, you know what to do."

"Dispose."

"That's the one." Spaz rises from the ledge and stretches, groaning as his tendons pop back into place. "I've got to strap my arse into a suit. Got some investors to sweet talk up at GyreTech HQ in an hour."

"I thought you'd forgotten."

"Not likely," Spaz snaps. "Your fucking reminders have been sending shocks through my leg every ten goddamn minutes." He yanks out his cell and chucks it at Dash's head as he strides out of the office. "You can stop it now."

Dash catches the cell midair and tosses it between his hands like it's a hot coal. "Not likely," he murmurs.

Spaz loathes these responsibilities as CEO and Chair of Gyre-Tech and Dash dislikes having to push reminders, but Spaz expects him to, despite the frequent snarling. Spaz is all about duty. His people—the gang folk—their welfare is more important to him than his own comfort. And maintaining GyreTech is vital to that end; it's a corporate armour Spaz has used to protect them all for the past twenty years.

CHAPTER 6

*D*awn. A slow break of light seeping through the clouds like water through cloth. On the Southern bank of the Spine, Lower Mace is a schizophrenic frenzy of noise and claustrophobia. Trapped in a car in the midst of the tumult, Stark stares out the window and fumes, fit to explode. The metal barks of growling cars at war fill the air. Horns and sirens blare over the rumble boom of traffic. Crossings bleep; hysterical, as if no one's listening, and tangles of pedestrians, clothed in dispassion, choke the pavements, oblivious to anything but their individual destinations. Indifference, that's the heart of this nightmare.

Stark leans forwards to tap the sheet of black glass between him and Tal. It slides down and Tal looks in the mirror. "Boss?"

Stark jerks a thumb at the door. "I'm out. Only three more blocks to City, and I'm fucked if I'll wait the seventy-five minutes it'll take to reach it on wheels."

"Right you are, boss."

Stark's reply to Tal is a slamming door. Bull-like, he forges through a disgruntled crowd of office workers on lunch break towards City Central, a monument to authority built in bronze and slick-faced granite. Like an ancient temple erected to invoke imaginary gods, it fits awkward as a fake limb into the expansive tower blocks, the slightly grotesque Gothic-style spires of Lower Mace.

As if only invoking chaos, its sides burgeon with childishly depicted visuals, deriding the City Force and mocking the Notary. Even across the dull face of the entrance they exude, a riotous array painted over and over until even the highest echelon is resigned to their presence.

Pushing through into the cavernous foyer, Stark traipses up the wide grin of the staircase, relaxing as the roar of outside fades to a murmur behind thick walls and soundproof glazing. In its stead comes the low hum of networked computers, the subterranean burr of a thousand voices talking at once. The Notary replaced the old City Bureau with this monstrous pile the same year they abolished departmental units. Without those units for order, all floors spew in a free-flow of desks in semicircular arrays. It doesn't work, but neither did the units, and no one's ever bothered to protest, choosing instead to wedge shoulders against an ever-growing tide of anarchy.

Stark weaves through the muddle, squeezing between chair backs. It's hot. The smell of tired bodies overwhelms, yet none of the tall, vaulted windows are thrown open to allow the air to clear. Accustomed to the stench, Stark hollers a few dozen hellos as he works his way to the rear of the room, where a seamless wall of darkened glass punctuated by tall, silver doors demarcates open floor from office space. He shrugs off his jacket and strides towards the middle and largest. Inscribed across its surface in blocky capitals: BURTON. Stark taps twice and pushes in without being called.

Burton's on the phone. His eyes bug, apoplectic, as Stark saunters in and throws himself like a heap of dirty laundry onto the chair opposite. Smile wide as a hyena's, Stark helps himself to a cigar, Burton's lighter, and a shot of pricey malt and drops his booted feet onto the corner of the desk. The only sound in the room is Burton's voice, gathering ice, and then the short, sharp clap of a phone none too gently replaced. Burton watches Stark for a moment, jaw working, then he scoots his chair over, lifts a foot shod in a classy blue brogue, and kicks Stark's legs off the corner of his desk. Stark blows a long plume of smoke, shrugs, and crosses one leg over the top of the opposite thigh.

"You yelled?" he says, voice rolling heavy as a freighter through the silence.

Burton folds his arms. "Damn straight, I did."

"I'm in trouble?"

The look he gets is almost amused. "You're always in some kind of fucking trouble."

Stark's face hardens a touch. "Don't tell me," he says, having played out every last move of the Notary in his head on the way here. "They think it wasn't advisable to pull Bone in on this. They think we should've stuck with De Lyon, despite fuck all results." Burton sniffs. Stark huffs out a sardonic laugh and continues, "What about Burneo? Did they lose their damn minds when you told them I want permission to go after him? Am I to be hung up in red tape to my eyeballs?"

There's another long moment of silence, as they wage eyeball war, then Burton chuckles, relaxes back into his chair, and slowly pours himself a malt. He leans to top up Stark's, and drawls, "Something like that. Officially."

"Balls to officially. What's your poison, brother? How hard can I push?"

"Considering we're dealing with something unprecedented?"

Stark raises his glass in acknowledgement. "Amen to that."

Swallowing his slug of malt in one gulp, Burton says, "Bone isn't a problem, but his profile's too high. This is a restricted case. They're anxious no one gets wind of his involvement, especially not the gangs, so they want you to be *discreet*." Burton rolls his eyes at Stark's sharp burst of laughter. "As for Burneo, hell, that one's always going to be contentious." He gives Stark a pointed look. "Be careful. I trust your instincts, but I've read the files. All of them. He may not be merely accessory to this and you know it. He may well be our killer."

Stark shifts, unsettled. The files they have on Burneo concern his possible involvement in terrorist action against the Notary, and even the occasional attack on the Zone. Then there are the bodies, all found in or near the sewers. Hundreds of people a year enter the sewers, most are never seen again, but some are occasionally found … altered. The City Office and the Notary know it's Burneo, but there's no way of proving it. He's a ghost in the sewers, in the departmental records. An elephant in the files no one's too happy discussing.

With all the certainty he can muster, he says, "I stand by my instincts."

Burton nods. "Fair enough. I'll back you up in this, but only so fucking far, and I need hard evidence soon. *Very* soon. The fact these are all nameless means the Notary aren't particularly buzzed about us making an effort. You make too much noise, and they'll choke off your air supply, and I'm telling you, as a friend, you're already louder than is safe."

Stark's jaw muscles leap. "I'm supposed to make no waves, make no noise in hunting this fucker down? How? Three in less than two weeks, Burton. They'd been there a while, so there's bound to be more, has to be. Did you actually read those fucking books I streamed you after we found Crucifixion?" Stark snorts as Burton shakes his head. "Well, I'm telling you, according to those, he has the hallmarks of an escalating psychopath on a rampage, and the second you separate importance by whether the victim has verifiable ID or not, you're heading for troubled waters."

"Ah, my friend, you know this place as well as I do." Burton raps knuckles on the desk for emphasis, his features pale with stress. "We're pissing daily on the fires of hell and you expect the Notary to get excited about a few Does?"

"We've not seen anything like this guy in decades," Stark says, stubborn. "Much as we dislike their activities, the gangs have at least been useful for curtailing non-casual violence, *and yet they are ignoring this killer*. Why? Why is this guy being left alone to kill when others haven't? It is making me all kinds of nervous."

"I concur," Burton replies, his voice strained. "But it makes no difference to the Notary. Their orders stand."

Stark's face sets like stone. "Nothing to say this killer won't start picking off people we can ID by face alone. It's not happened yet, sure, but the Notary won't be pleased if it does. They'll blame us, despite their reticence being the thing holding the investigation back. You know it, I know it."

"I do. But *you* know it's asking too much to expect the suits to care until it gets personal."

"I care and I'm a fucking suit. You care and you're a suit. Fuck's sake. We've not been blue collar for years, Burton. We're both on higher recom than we ever dreamed and we still fucking care!" Stark jerks a finger at the ceiling, even though the Notary would never deign to park their HQ on City premises. "What makes those fuckers different?"

"Distance. Lack of culpability."

Burton's quiet tone cuts the fury from Stark in one clean sweep. He collapses back, shoulders slumping inward. "Yeah," he says, listless.

Rising up to reach over and clap Stark beneath his shoulder implants, Burton says, "Square up. We've ploughed the shit all this time without benefit of their approval. You thinking of quitting on me now? Over this?" He raises his brows in disbelief.

Stark sucks in a lengthy drag on his cigar. It's almost gone out, the end giving off a fine wisp of dying smoke. He gives it a hostile stare. "Nah," he drawls, bathing the end of the cigar in the flame of Burton's chunky gold lighter and pulling in a long, lung-suffocating blast. "I'm not." Chucking the lighter on the table, he rises to his feet and strolls to the office door. "Not yet. Just keep my arse covered."

"Size of your arse, that's asking the impossible," comes the reply, bullwhip fast.

Stark's still laughing as he exits into the tightly-pressed swell of bodies outside City's vast doors. He heads for his base of operations, wishing he could bring his right and left hands, Tress and Suge, onboard the investigation, but until the Notary have reason to begin caring, he's stuck on his lonesome. If fury were productive, he'd expend energy on a truckload, instead he begins to worry about the ramifications of his chat with Burton. This case will get ugly. He knows this instinctively. Just as he knows it's likely to end in catastrophe. It's an outcome he's too familiar with, one he fights against every day and rarely wins.

He thinks about Ballerina Girl, the rictus of her face, the hopelessness in her eyes, how helpless he feels in this hunt for the man who put it there. Another face rises in front of hers. Teya's. Bright blue eyes, staring out from a devastation of bone and flesh that left cramps in his belly hard as food poisoning. He was Reinhart Strake then, wharf rat, poor boy, seventh son to Calise Strake. A collateral damage kid, fatherless, just like a thousand others, except for one difference: a determination to change what he was.

When he turned seventeen, he became the only locally-born member of the Wharf Guard, the military force created to keep old Wharf gang troubles from exploding out across the Spires, setting him at odds with his closest friend, Aron. And like him, Aron has changed beyond recognition, become a dark legend. A child's nightmare. A bogeyman. Burneo.

Aron was never *normal*, and it never mattered. Stark grew up with him, close as a brother, ended up falling in love with his sister, Teya, only a year younger than him, whereas Aron was four years older. They'd planned to marry, he and Teya, have a family of their own, but after he joined the guard and lost Aron's friendship, Teya abandoned him. She followed Aron's lead, joining the harder, more dangerous gangs who held fort deep in the sewer. Whilst there, she caught a disease common amongst low-gang dwellers: G-Warp, disfiguring and incurable.

When he found out, Stark took his squad in to rescue her against express orders, but it was too late and he was forced to take her life to spare her the horror of its full manifestation. He blames Aron for that. If he'd told her to stay away from the gangs in the sewer, she might have listened, but he didn't. Nor did he help her when she was suffering. Instead, he tried to carry her deeper into the sewers, away from help, and Stark's never been able to understand why.

In the wake of the incident, the slaughter that followed, he had to run, to shuck off his old life and hide in a new one, under a new name. He became Stark. Just Stark. Paring everything down to the sort of focus that's seen him rise through City's ranks, from Buzz Boy to City Officer, a respected troublemaker with more commendations than disciplinaries, despite his habit of going against procedure. But he can't forget Teya's face. That mess of blood and bone spoke into him, a language of ruin. He died with her that day, left Reinhart Strake crumpled in the black sewer mud beside her broken body, and he's never forgiven Aron for her loss. He can't.

Skin tight and hot beneath his cheap suit, Stark wonders what might've happened if he'd stayed a wharf rat, fallen into the mould, rather than tried to break it. But the past remains defiantly unchangeable, even to his imagination, and Stark pushes on ruthlessly through tight-packed bodies, anger his only defence against intolerable pain.

CHAPTER 7

*A*lone in the lab, Nia walks a wide arc about Ballerina Girl's corpse. Dazzling yellow bulbs winnow fleshy surfaces into pools of shadow and light, delineating her frozen, unnatural lines. The angle of her exaggerated arabesque is so precarious, she's strapped down. Coils of rope encircle her limbs, their ragged ends dangling, foul with dirt. They repel Nia, but not near as much as the enforced blankness of her flesh, devoid of modification and therefore expression.

Arriving at De Lyon's lab in the cavernous Lower Mace mortuary early this morning, on Bone's mailed request, she was horrified to discover what awaited her. These denuded remains are worse than lifeless, they're self-less. It's close on 8:00 a.m. At 8:30, Bone will slam through the thick glass doors, hopefully in a better state than yesterday, considering he's so abruptly back on shift. He'll expect to start immediately, as usual, but Nia can't even bring herself to touch these bodies. They don't look human. Especially Ballerina Girl. Her being a woman makes Nia doubly uneasy. It's too close for comfort, to see the damage done, the enforced wiping of personality from her flesh. Those dirty coils of rope are particularly unnerving; they bring to Nia's mind images of cephalopods, pulsing spasmodically on the ocean floor, their movements jerky and powerful as those of the clinically insane. Nia swallows at the thick, metallic tinge this image brings to her throat, strives for rational thought.

"They're just corpses. You've dealt with hundreds. Thousands. Quit being so fucking squeamish."

But she stands rooted in the line of sight of that thrown-back head. Trapped in the gaze of staring eyes, blue diffusing into white, glassy but somehow imploring. That pleading is what breaks her inertia. This woman suffered enough before she died, she's earned the right to some dignity. Gathering her will, Nia walks forwards, only to be arrested by the sight of that outlandish tag, perceptible even in the slipping of skin, as putrefaction gathers in the cells. The tattoo is not unusual in and of itself. It's only a mod, and it's as normal to have mods as it is to wear clothes, to breathe. Nia's had full body silver scrolling implanted since she was a teen and several gens, some gang, some personal. Everyone Nia knows has a mod of some kind, apart, of course, from Bone.

When she joined Gyre West as his assistant, she had major reservations about working with him, until she realised he had no say in the matter. His empty skin, his job, his daily routine and more were Leif's decisions. Bone accepted them only because he wanted Leif to approve of him, but Nia could see what Bone could not, or would not see, that Leif denied Bone even the semblance of a normal life out of nothing but sheer spite. When he died, Nia hoped Bone might be free to find himself, to seek normality of some kind at last. Instead he's unravelling, becoming less every day.

She's left feeling helpless, furious, just as she does now. She wants to restore Ballerina Girl as much as she wants to make things right for Bone. Gift him with normality. Neither is possible, and both impossibilities render her equally distraught. What's so awful here is that, from Ballerina Girl's faint scars, it's obvious how normal she once was. Now all she has to identify her is this ugly tag. It's an insult of sorts. A script tattoo usually only used by gangs, re-imagined as a label. In lieu of any other ID, it makes Ballerina Girl more thing than being.

Nia wonders what that makes Bone, bereft of even an identifying label such as this. Is he real at all? How on earth will these bodies make *him* feel? Nia trembles, her skin clammy, and a strange compulsion sends her hand flying towards the unnerving tag. It looks so foreign, as if it doesn't belong there on the slowly rotting innocence of the girl's calf. Perhaps she'll be able to wipe it away, the black writing reduced to charcoal smears on her finger pads.

Fingertips a hair's breadth away Nia becomes conscious of her action and snatches her hand back, cradling it to her chest.

"Fuck," she whispers to herself, breathing hard.

She's standing there, hugging her hand and sucking air like an asthmatic, when anger at her own culpability crashes down.

"*Fuck!*"

Nia throws the cradled hand from her chest. Squaring her shoulders she strides to the table to begin the preliminary task of scrapes, samples, and combs. She struggles to disregard the leg, suspended above her head, the unsettling label, and Ballerina Girl's hands, reaching backwards towards her in a distressing manner akin to the supplicant.

CHAPTER 8

On cue at 8:30 a.m. sharp, Bone reels in, crazy tired. After five long hours stuck in that awful, claustrophobic cell of a room, examining Ballerina Girl and the mechanics of her suspension, he'd signed her off to the Buzz Boys, supervising the cutting of ropes himself to make sure it was done right. Though desperate to leave, he remained on with Stark until late, sweating in the beams of those spotlights, scrutinising the room for clues. They found none and removed to a bar on the Wharf, a filthy sailor pit, to drink into the early hours, mired in joint melancholy. Slamming back shot after shot to a flat dirge of mindless electro, the same beats over and over till their heads thudded pain in syncopation.

That pain is still present, made pin-sharp by two hours' restless, ugly sleep in the car here. He's a walking bombsite, and Nia's furious silence is eloquent. He'd try to appease her, but he's too aggravated, too raw. The chill of unfamiliar white walls pebbles horripilation along the skin of his arms. He wants to scratch it until skin pebbles blood. Drink-thinking, he knows, but the urge is insufferable. The lights are jaundice yellow, glaring. Make his eyes sting on top of hangover sensitivity. The urge to scratch skin sits uneasily alongside the compulsion to pull his eyeballs from their sockets, dunk them in freezing water, and pop them back in. He can already feel the relief the icy globes would bleed through his hot, stuffed forehead, his roaring brain. Irresistible.

Bone's fingers twitch inside sweaty polymer as he wields a blunt hammer, cracking joints to set Ballerina's limbs straight. He watches from a numb distance as his hands tighten about the mallet's handle, his knuckles flashing white as SOS flares; the compulsion to smash the world alongside the desire to stop. *Stop.* This is what's been happening too much lately, why he's had to have Canard's help. He's losing control of himself to a frightening degree. He tries to unfurl his grip, but frozen digits refuse his control. His knees melt to water and his bowel curdles. He tries to force his mind elsewhere, but it's painful, like scraping melted plastic off of skin. Desperate, he glances up at Nia, who's watching him, her fury replaced by unwelcome concern.

Frantic to erase that pitying look in her eyes, he tries for a smile, and clearly surprised, she attempts one back. He imagines two skulls leering at one other, exposed, surrounded by raw edges of flesh and lank, bloody hair. The thought makes his vision swim and his gut heave, not in queasiness, but in something like excitement. An alarming, spidery sensation skitters inside his head, and the room snaps into focus. His fingers loosen from the hammer. It falls with a heavy thunk. Nia takes it from the table, watching him carefully.

"What's up?" she asks, handing him a scalpel.

He's relieved, but he'll never admit it. He can't tell her what's wrong because he doesn't understand it enough to put it into words. So he tells her a white lie instead, whilst taking care to cut Ballerina Girl's incision perfectly. "I'm thinking that even no heating is better than this shit hole."

Nia raises a brow, wiser to him than he is to himself, but she goes along with it because she's Nia. "It's weird here, and it's not just these bodies you've lumbered us with."

"Oh?"

"It's the co-op thing. All these other labs operating around us.

All these windows." She grimaces. "Creepy. I can't wait to get back to our lab."

"Agreed."

Like a series of fish tanks for corpses, Lower Mace Mort stretches off in a clinical block of identical windowed rooms, like mirrors reflecting one room into infinity. At the windows to this lab, much to his dismay, a throng of staff have gathered to observe, no doubt curious about his skin. He's a freak on display, alluring as the just-straightened limbs of Ballerina Girl. No doubt he could charge them a thousand each and still they'd come, this murder of crows feasting on his exposure like carrion. He has an urge to start eviscerating lumps of intestine and chuck them at the glass. He curls his hands into fists over the incision he's carved between breasts like inverted bowls of lemon jelly, slowly collapsing in the warmth of the lab. It's hard to resist these odd compulsions, to lash out against the preconceptions, the pressures around him, and it gets harder all the time. They've converged into one thing, the longing for an end to it all. He sucks in a long, steadying rush of air and nods at the bodies on the other tables, the edges of their incisions puckered and discoloured and bristling with black catgut.

"Not looking forwards to getting to those two either." Nia perks a neat, black brow. Bone shrugs. "From the looks of those half-arsed stitches, I'd say their insides are a godawful mess. It's going to be impossible to make any sense of them."

"Of what?"

The unfamiliar voice makes them jump. In the doorway, taking up as much space as a lower case I, he's all bland charm on the surface, but underneath there's a slow wave of rising temper. It's in the red tinge on his pale, pointed cheekbones, the slight flare of that long nose, and the disappearing act of already thin lips.

"You'd be Bone," he says, stepping forwards in a precise, snappy motion and sticking out a small, white hand, gloved according to procedure. "JayCe De Lyon. I had five minutes to spare and thought I'd pop by to welcome you."

Bone shakes the proffered hand for maybe a fraction of a second before dropping it, and a silence stretches out. Awkward. Hostile. Then Nia steps in, a mother hen puffed up ready to peck.

"Nia Lark. We won't be under your feet for long."

De Lyon dismisses her. "You'll be under my feet until it's over. I'm off the case, you're on it. This is your lab until further notice."

Nia looks at Bone and her gaze cuts, drawing guilt like blood. He shrugs, helpless. "He asked, I agreed."

"Who asked?" she snaps.

"Stark."

Nia sighs. "Fine." She wrinkles her nose. "But I don't like the thought of Canard running the lab."

Bone gives her a look of rueful agreement. "Lab's gonna look like a glass factory in a hurricane by the time we get back to it. Shame we can't work in our own space."

A malicious sort of smile blooms on De Lyon's thin face. "Isn't it just," he says. "But we're all most excited to have you here, especially me. I knew your father, Bone. He was a great man. It will be fascinating to see whether this reputation of yours is earned or borrowed." He's still smiling, all teeth and insincerity.

"My father's dead," Bone says, soft and cutting, though his insides churn a greasy mixture of nausea, nerves, and adrenalin. "I'm here for one reason, to do a job, and I'm fucking good at what I do." He returns the smile, his face aching, and adds with brutal exactitude, "Which is why I was asked to take over."

De Lyon flushes bright red. He turns on a heel and leaves, pausing briefly at the door without turning to say bitterly, "Matters not one bit how good you are; I'll place bets on you finding nothing in this pile of dead Does because there's nothing to find."

The door slams shut behind him. Nia and Bone watch his small, rigid frame as he disappears down the corridor, shouldering Bone's onlookers aside with little regard for propriety. The two of them exchange glances.

"Professional jealousy," Nia says, her voice thick with distaste.

Insides still churning, Bone considers her words. They ring

unpleasantly familiar. Leif Adams died jealous of Bone's professional accomplishments. It was the worst sort of irony. If Bone had
achieved nothing, if he'd failed, then Leif would have died
despising him for his failures. There was no way of winning with
Leif, and whilst Bone was aware of this fact, he continued to try.
He dearly regrets it. If he'd been able to fail, he'd have gifted
himself with the armour of anonymity he craves more every day.
Would certainly have saved himself from this disturbing case, the
accompanying professional indignities. He looks for De Lyon
again, but his small figure is long since gone from view, and it
occurs to Bone that compared to Leif's, De Lyon's disapprobation
is trivial. He might not like it, but he can choose to dismiss it.

"Very likely," he replies to Nia. "I don't give a shit how much
this upsets his professional pride so long as he doesn't interfere."

Nia dips her head, approving. "We'd better get on with Ballerina, then. We don't want to give that prick anything else to make a
meal of."

She bites her lip after that, but he sees it there, unspoken, a
whole bucket of opinions about the state he's making of himself.
He sees the worry, too, and wishes he had some way to alleviate it,
no matter how much it grates. But he has no answers, no logical
reasons, for his dependences, only the fact of their existence. He's
been told he's drinking to numb the pain, but he has none. Inside
him, where he presumes others might feel the solid certainty of a
self, there lies nothing but a hole so deep, his only presumption is
that, at some point, he must have fallen down it and disappeared.

A surge of need rises up his throat, thick and burning as vomit.
The edges of his vision dim, shutter, and he hears a high whining
like pressure escaping a valve. Goddammit, he needs a fucking
drink. Trembling inside, he watches his hands as they reach out.
This time, they don't let him down. Faint with relief, he takes the
saw from Nia and begins to sever the ribs one by one, wishing it
were as easy to sever this gnawing need from his mind, to sever
the ties that bind him to Leif, even in death.

Two hours later, with only minutes to go till the end of the final autopsy, the phone in their mortuary fish tank begins to ring loudly, making them both jump. Stripping his gloves and dropping them into the bin, Bone lifts the thin sliver of polished metal to his ear, glaring at yet another bystander, who smiles nervously and hurries away.

"What now?" Bone demands.

"More bodies found," comes Stark's steady voice, scything through Bone's anger neat as a scalpel. Bone's roused so quickly, he sways a little, steadying himself with one long-fingered hand on the window.

"Where?"

"I've sent a driver for you, I'll meet you there."

Bone hangs up and pushes back from the glass. Stares at the ghost-like imprint of his hand, slowly fading to oily remnants. It's as unsubstantial as he feels, nothing more than a vague impression. He lifts his elbow and smears it into oblivion.

CHAPTER 9

A scarecrow of angles and tension, Bone leans against the entrance of an empty warehouse on the East Side of the Rat Gulley. It's a half-burnt-out wreck, wide windows a hoard of hungry mouths armed with jagged glass teeth. He's chain-smoking to calm his frazzled nerves, despite the cramp it'll put in his cred chip, the tightness and protestation of his chest, and the cough he can feel winding like a spring beneath his diaphragm. Security Force personnel wielding automatic weapons are all around, their guns pointed upwards with sweating fingers flexing over triggers. There are no tanks to support them here; they're all alone.

Black Frank rules the Gulley, and he doesn't stand for tanks on his territory. He's sent out over two hundred of his boys to encircle them on the rooftops, to make sure the SF don't try and contravene his laws. Known as the Filth, Frank's boys have a hexagonal bolt pattern punctured through exposed scapulas, edged in dirty steel. They're as nasty a bunch of miscreants as you can get in a city of downright scoundrels, and they've driven the population of the Rat Gulley underground. People here populate a vast network of sewers, their ragtag townships built over the waters like something medieval. People and rats, scratching out an existence side by side right under Bone's feet, down there in shadows and shitty water. And Frank's their Liege Lord, protecting them from his own tyranny for a percentage of their food that leaves them nigh on starving.

The aggression of the Filth surrounding Bone and the SF is horrifyingly casual. They stand there, smiling, holding vicious, homemade scythes and heavy, modified firearms. Their attention should be focused on the trigger-happy SF, but some thirty of their number are watching Bone. Why the hell would they do that? To these outlier gangs, he should just be another cunt on their territory, unarmed and therefore uninteresting, but of course he's not. He's the unmodified Mort, and he fascinates them. Their regard gives him hives.

He's anxious to escape their perusal and get to the bodies, to the bit that's familiar, safe, but he's been told to wait for Stark. It's not usual procedure. As a Mortician, he can go in first; it's his right, his privilege, and in a system under perpetual strain, the demarcation of privilege has even greater importance. City Officers uphold the law, such as it is, quash all inner city, non-Zone gang violence, and try to keep the peace. It's not a small task they're set, by any means, not with the current unravelling of always tenuous order in the Spires, but it's nothing compared to what's expected of a Mort.

A Mort is an identifier of corpses, a coroner, a forensic anthropologist, a scene of crime forensics specialist prior to Buzz Boy collation, and a classic mortician to boot. Bone's task when called to a scene is to unravel immediate clues to cause of death, not just on the victim but also in the surrounds. This scene, like all others, has already been trampled by, in this case, the Security Force, a military branch of the CO. The sooner Bone gets to these bodies, the greater his chance of finding something vital, and likewise, the longer it takes to get there, the less he has to go on. In this shit hole, these circumstances, he can guarantee his scene is now thoroughly contaminated.

He's steaming with temper at the delay, but the weapon casually aimed at his balls when he argued the point encouraged his silence. These Security types are numbskulls, have the rules screwed into their heads on a sheet of steel. They'd sooner kill than argue the finer points of procedure, and no one would question their actions. Round these parts, in this sort of standoff situation, the SF has final say, just like the Guard at the Wharf. Bone sucks hard on his cigarette and chokes on the chemical taste of burning filter. He drops it to the floor in disgust. Grabs the packet from his pocket and knocks out another, lighting it up to pull filthy, delicious fumes right down to his belly. His lungs shriek under the blast and he closes his eyes. Pain lets him know he's still here, something he has reason to doubt far too much these days.

A faint sound of disturbance at the cordon the SF has placed around the whole building captures his attention. He cranes his head and grins relief at the sight of that slab of squat muscularity bulling through the line of SF grunts.

Stark calls out as he approaches, "Did I miss much?"

Bone tosses his cigarette aside. "Nope. They kept the scene clear for us, even of me."

Stark scoffs disgust and points. "In there?"

"Nowhere else."

In tandem, they step into a large theatre of soot-smeared rubble and rampant, snow bound weed growth. Negotiate the half-demolished corridors of what might have been a collection of admin offices, skirting the remains of dented filing cabinets devoid of contents, desk fragments, and twisted chairs.

"Sorry they made you wait," Stark says. "Those dumb fucks wouldn't know how to piss straight if they didn't have a diagram. I did call ahead and tell them to shove a pole up the arse of procedure, but my guess is they're a little arse-shy."

Bone laughs despite himself. "They actually held a fucking gun at my balls."

Stark shakes his head. "I'd pay to see that."

"I'd pay to see them try it with you."

Stark's laugh rolls out, echoing through the cracks in the walls, the holes in the ceiling, and Bone finally relaxes. He likes this man, likes his humour, the way he works. At some point the Notary will shut the file on this case and that will be the end of his work with Stark. He can admit to being disappointed with that. No small thing. Stuck by choice in his constituency, Bone generally prefers his lab and Nia, who puts up with him even on the days he can't bear himself, and cares about him enough to chew him out when he fucks up. Without her, he'd disappear with no trace into the minutiae of his work, into the crack between his sanity and what lies beyond it. He doesn't know what to think about that. He prefers not to think on it at all. Just as he doesn't think about how he'll cope when she does what she should and takes on a mortuary of her own.

At a central hub, the building opens out into a vast storage area, reduced to nubs of brickwork, piles of cement and heat-warped jags of steel. A dry rain of dust showers down in intermittent bursts from the shadowed recesses of the roof. It's just the sort of place their killer considers the perfect stage for his works: an amphitheatre of neglect. In the centre of the ruin, poised magnificently within a cage of structural struts and straining rope suspended a few feet above red-daubed concrete, are two corpses. The shape they form is one both classic and mocking. Their toes touch and their bodies curl inward to a gentle arc, arms pointed downwards and joined in a vee shape. Their faces are raised and they gaze sightlessly into one another's eyes, a parody of affection.

They're overtly miss-matched; a bald-headed, well-built male and a willowy, brunette female. She appears too delicate, too refined, for his muscular bulk, his brutal, blunt features. From the pattern and proliferation of his tattoo- and mod-removal scars, it's obvious he was gang. From her lack, it's evident she wasn't. Neither seems to have attempted a struggle, but the ropes are so strong, their grip so profound, that they might have fought like wildcats and still not created the smallest increment of movement. In amongst the straining lines of rope, they hover, serene, only their faces telling the story of how they've suffered.

Bone falters. Like Ballerina, their loss of self reminds him of his. If these two were alive, would they feel the same as he does? It's a dizzying thought; makes it hard for him to find his professional distance. He's overwhelmed with outrage for them. For himself.

"Let's see what Rope's left us this time," he says, unable to keep the edge from his voice.

Stark comes to an abrupt halt. "Rope?"

Bone throws him a rueful look. "Faran's Buzz Boys, they've called our killer Rope. I like it. It fits."

Stark growls a little, swipes a hand over his face. "Fuck. Wish someone'd clue me in on this shit."

"Consider yourself clued in," Bone says.

Stark snorts. "Let's get looking at Rope's handiwork, then, shall we?"

Bone nods and the two men stoop to duck under the ropes, work their way to the apex. Bone snaps on his gloves. He starts with the girl, her fixed eyes pale blue and beseeching. Tear tracks stand out in bold, white relief against the thick dust griming her cheeks, and for a moment, jaw tight and working, he simply stands, fingers cradling her cheek. Stark clears his throat and Bone starts, grimacing embarrassment as he begins a thorough, hurried trail along her limbs, stopping when he finds her tag.

"Here. Under her buttocks. She's Love, I'll bet you my entire year's wages our muscle-bound lover boy opposite has Heart tagged on him somewhere."

Stark makes a sound almost like amusement but closer to despair. "And as usual, we have zero ID. I mean, what the fuck is this? What is it? Why take the ID from folk no one likely gives a shit about? What's the deeper picture we're missing here? Gotta be something."

Bone hums agreement. "I have something niggling at me. Damned if I know what it is though."

"That's unusual for you, isn't it?" Stark asks, momentarily distracted from the corpses.

"Yes." Bone shines a light into Love's eyes, pulling at the lids. Presses the flesh around her chin, concentration etched into his brow.

"They've not been dead long," Stark blurts out, seeming surprised by the volume of his voice.

Bone shakes his head. "Heart there's been dead longer, I'd say twelve hours or more judging by lividity, but perhaps not yet a day." He turns round and stretches up to inspect the staring green eyes, employing an unusual pen he takes from his shirt pocket. "Intra-ocular tension suggests between twelve and twenty hours at most." He turns his attention back to the slack-faced brunette. "Love here," he pauses, grinds his teeth, grates out, "an hour dead, probably less. Probably died after they found her and they never even knew. If they'd let me in sooner ..."

Stark closes his eyes. "You're sure?"

"Till I get them on the table, I can't state it for the record but ... yeah, I'm sure." He swipes a finger beneath her chin and comes away holding a drop of blackish fluid. "Not even dry yet. She was crying. Hoping someone would notice. But they just set up guard outside."

Bent down inspecting the floor beneath their feet, Stark slams a fist into the dust, "Fuck!"

Bone's surprised the concrete doesn't crack. "Stark, odds are we'd have lost her anyway. She's oxygen starved. In extreme ketosis. If she didn't die of mass organ failure, she'd have died from shock." At Stark's reluctant acknowledgement, he adds, "How many do you think there might be? Have you any clue what our killer's going to do next?"

Stark rocks back on his haunches. "Nope, less than fucking useless to try and predict the arc of development. Fuck knows how many he might kill, how many he's already killed. We haven't even got the first clue as to why he's doing it, why he's choosing this method, these places, these particular people. I told Faran to get out as many Buzz Boys as he can, search everywhere, anything old or abandoned, anywhere people rarely go, just to see what we can find."

"Jesus, Stark, that's half the fucking city."

Stark sniffs. "And the rest." He looks up at the carefully posed corpses. "This find has all the markers of extreme fortune, more Buzz Boys free to search in this area, more obvious placement, a happy circumstance of concentrated endeavour we're unlikely to recreate in other areas, other districts. I suspect we'll be a long time finding any others, and there *are* others. I know it. Rope is in for the long haul. He's invested."

"So, what do we do in the meantime, apart from autopsy these two?"

Stark stands and looks Bone square in the eye. There's something dogged about his gaze, something deep down in those implacable black pools glints, like the first flames of an inferno. "I'm heading to the sewers," he says.

"Burneo," Bone says. "You're green lit for that?"

"Not exactly. Not officially, at least. But I can go after him now, if I'm quiet about it. If he's connected, there's more likelihood finding him than there is chasing the ghost of this Rope when we've fuck all to go on."

"Those sewers are endless, Stark, and you're chasing a rumour, a ghost."

"If you have anything better, you let me know."

"Burneo, though?" Bone mutters. "Surely if he were real, and that dangerous to the Notary, he'd have been hunted down by now?"

"They don't consider him a danger. They're too arrogant for that. There's as little justification for the cost of chasing Burneo in their eyes as there is in lending actual CO manpower to the hunting of a killer whose only victims are doubtless nigh on invisible, even before he erases their identity. But I'm doing this for free, and I'll be damned if I'll sit around waiting for evidence to satisfy a bunch of tight-fisted corporate cretins."

Bone blinks at the force behind his words. "Do you know where to look?" he asks.

"Yep. Got a file I've been working on. Years' worth of statements, reports, and collated sightings. He's out beyond the cavern, the lake. I can't pinpoint the location, but I'm confident I can hunt him down by a process of elimination."

"That deep?" Bone's appalled. "It's dangerous down there. Condemned ruins."

"I won't be going that far," Stark says, equally horrified. "The cavern and lake aren't that deep. Spiral City's way below that, and it's sealed off." He grins, humourless and cynical. "Nothing like burying history we find unpleasant, is there?"

That hits tender flesh. Bone winces, but he's still doubtful. There's something about Stark he recognises only too well, a volatility bubbling in the veins, barely contained. Bone corrals his with alcohol, Stark doubtless with the job. It's not enough, nothing ever is—it's like every compulsion, unstoppable, and he knows Stark's not thought this through, knows he's bulling ahead because compulsion says go and he's got no option but to listen.

"What if you find Burneo and he refuses to come quietly? You'll be in his territory. He'll have the advantage."

Stark chuckles, as if the very idea is ridiculous. "He won't come quietly, but I can get his attention all right."

"How so?"

The look in Stark's eyes becomes distant, pained. "Because I know him. That is to say, I knew who he *was*."

Surprise lurches through Bone. "Pardon?"

Stark swipes a hand through the air, a tinge of red colouring his cheekbones. "You heard."

"I know I heard," Bone says, a caustic edge to his voice, "I just want to know what the hell it means."

Stark's face closes down. "We'll leave it there," he says, and he ducks the ropes and strides away from the bodies, a Minotaur of the City Force disappearing into a maze of broken corridors.

"Like hell we will," Bone mutters. He strips off his gloves, shoving them in his pocket and racing after Stark, his long feet kicking up puffs of greyish dust.

By the time he reaches the warehouse entrance, Stark's long, black shark of a car is slicing away through the snow. So, he just stands there, watching it disappear, impotent and furious. After a moment, he lights up another cigarette and wanders slowly back towards the only thing that makes sense to him. Corpses. Though these corpses are fast unravelling any notion of sense, or the making of it.

CHAPTER 10

*I*t's late and Bone's desperate for sleep, but every attempt is thwarted by the niggling concern he's missed something vital about these bodies he's inherited from De Lyon. He's spent hours at Lower Mace, examining skin, flesh, and muscle in minute detail and scrutinising genetic data for alterations until his eyes ached and his brain pulsed with the beginnings of a migraine. Hours trying to justify Stark's faith in him. He's having to admit he can't. The best damned Mort in the business can't figure out who the victims are, or even how the hell their bodies got to where they did, or why.

Worse yet, he indentifies too closely with Rope's nameless corpses. They represent him in some way, their blank skin an unsettling emulation of his, their lack of identity a mirror to his own, their helpless entrapment too familiar to bear. The personal interferes with the professional, can't be tolerated, and yet he's unable to fight it, it ripples through everything, holding him back, clogging his thought processes. It's unprofessional. Unavoidable. Untenable.

He lights a cigarette, stomach constricting with either hunger or hurt, he can't tell which. Extends his arms to stare at the blank stretches of flesh. He despises that he never once found the courage to assert his natural desire to experiment. But what do you do when you long for approval and only one thing seems to bring so much as a glimmer? He bore the humiliation of abnormality for that glimmer, allowing his father to control not only his life, but his identity, too. In truth, because he allowed it, Bone only really ever existed through Leif's approval, a shadow of sorts. And now that Leif's gone, he's fading away. What shadow can exist without an anchor of flesh blocking the light? It's impossible.

Everything has become impossible. All he knows for certain anymore is what he does, it defines him utterly. The only statement of self he could make at this point would be to unscrew the steel panel bearing his name from the mortuary doors and bolt it to his chest, and that won't give him autonomy. It won't give him back to himself. You can't take back what you've never owned.

In his mind, Rope and Leif are indistinguishable. Thieves of identity. Puppeteers. Finding out who these victims are has gone beyond the need to free them from Rope, to take back what he stole and gift it to them. Bone hopes that by reuniting them with those stolen identities, he might be able to find his own, and disprove the conviction that all he is reflects in his mute acquiescence to the blank state of his skin. But even as he dreams of redemption, rebellious truth flutters through his mind, whispered in Leif's voice, written in ropes and empty skin: he was nothing to begin with and will remain nothing, no matter what comes of these bodies.

He stares out at the night sky, bled to inky grey by a glaring wall of light from the tangled sprawl of Gyre West. His throat is parched. A demand for relief, for that bite and burn, flirts with his every cell, much like the nagging urge that he's missed something vital, that a piece of the puzzle is crying out to be seen. He grinds the heels of his palms into his eyes, forcing back misery and raging thirst, willing the kaleidoscope patterns behind his lids to soothe him. Taking his hands away, the lights of Gyre West's windows haemorrhage into a glistening mass and slowly undulate apart. In response, sickness sweeps up, from gut to throat, in an overwhelming wave. The jabber of thirst becomes a roar. With a snarl of impatience he launches himself off the stool, snatches up his jacket and leaves, the door crashing shut in his wake.

A murky, smoke-filled hole of a club. In airless confines, the potent reek of fresh sweat, dry ice, and thick liquor borders on the insufferable. Heavy thumps of music distort the air, violent as white noise. Lasers rip red cuts in grey smoke, illuminating the tangled contortions of limbs thrown up and waving at the air in helpless abandon. Bone sits, nursing a gas-malt, blank-eyed and ragged, his spider-limbs angled into vees. A collection of greasy shot glasses riddles the steel bar in front of his elbows. Delicately roasted and ripe with fumes he's let his mind wander. After hours of hard drinking his nagging urge has become a spark, the forerunner of realisation. In the back room of memory it sits, tantalisingly close, challenging him to trick it into revealing itself. He rubs a hand through his tangled blond hair, sweaty palm pulling at the roots, and grimaces. Draining his glass to greasy stains, he slaps it down amongst the others. The thick base rings dully against steel.

He lifts a long-fingered hand furnished with a thin cigarette, straggling smoke like an afterthought. "Hit me up," he says.

Bar-boy nods, his black hair flopping over a forehead high and smooth as marble cliffs. He chucks a clean glass on the bar, poking an ugly chin towards the collection scattered around Bone's elbows and grinning. White teeth gleam red in the lights, sending a shudder down Bone's spine.

"You on a bender?" Bar-boy hollers.

Bone shakes his head. "Just thinking."

Bar-boy ducks his head, a sage now despite his tender years. Pours a generous glug of whisky. "You're a deep thinker."

Watching with greedy eyes as bar-boy pours thick petrol into the whisky, Bone chuckles. He feels that flicker of knowledge snare again in the back of his mind, a little pull, and frowns. Closing his eyes, he watches a film-reel memory: mottled, rotten flesh, yellowish-grey through to livid purple-red, each marked by the same spiny writing. He sighs frustration as it plays over and over, revealing nothing, and snatches up his fresh drink, gulping half in one go, hissing at the burn of gasoline, the smooth flush of malt whiskey. He's too furious at his brain to take it easy despite knowing how drunk he's getting. Bar-boy whistles long and low.

"Deep," he mutters and wanders off to serve another punter.

There's a hard pinch on Bone's shoulder. He twists to see De Lyon standing there, smirking. The man looks like his work, today more than ever. Bloodless. Grey. He's still disdainful, a shallow depth of icy water, but he's trying hard to appear friendly. It makes him look like he's in pain. He snags a stool and flicks a finger against Bone's empty glasses.

"That'll shorten your allotted years by half."

Bone lifts his drink in an ironic salute. "Join me?"

De Lyon sniffs. "No. I'll have a Lemon slingshot. Sparkling." He shouts that last to Bar-boy, chatting up a genderneut on the far side of the bar. Bar-boy lifts a languid hand in response and De Lyon shakes his head, resigned to wait. He turns back to Bone, that tight, vicious smile still on his face, still looking like it doesn't quite belong there, like you could peel it off.

"How goes the investigation?"

Having decided to ignore De Lyon's attitude, Bone's brutal in his honesty. "Re-did yours, fucking messy. Did the new ones. Going by those, your mess was just mess and didn't hide anything worth seeing. Lucky that."

De Lyon's head lowers once in a rigid spasm, his lips thinned to slivers. He grasps onto the one thing he clearly liked in that response. "So there was nothing to find?"

Bone shrugs. "Not inside. But there's something about them. About those tattoos. Couldn't pinpoint it, hence the bar." He takes a long drag from his cigarette, right down to the filter, and slugs back the last of his gas-malt. "I've seen that style before. I'm trying to recall where from, but it won't fucking come clear."

Bone drops his cigarette butt in the glass, the glass to the bar, presses his finger to the bottom, and slides it into the others. The musical chime it makes pleases him, sending shivers over the back of his head.

"Post-capture," De Lyon snaps in his ear, dismissive. "They're just labels. He's playing with us and you've fallen for it. You *are* aware he's done them himself? Script is child's play, which is, no doubt, why gangs find it so appealing." The contempt is needle sharp.

Bone slides his empties around, thick glass singing in delicate, clinking chimes. He takes a long, steadying breath and murmurs, "No. Not playing. There's something I need to remember."

"If you say so," De Lyon says, his derision all too clear. "We agree to differ."

Bone's hand curls to a fist, tendons tight enough to tremble. He tries to play with the glasses, but he wants to hurt this little man too much. Pushing his fist down onto the steel until it hurts he stares at De Lyon, unwavering.

"So we will," he says through his teeth.

De Lyon makes a show of peering down the bar. Bar-boy's draped over the drink spattered width of it, his fingers toying in the genderneut's hair, his eyes hooded and dark. You can almost see the drool running over that ugly chin. De Lyon slaps a hand down.

"Forget this waiting. I'll see you, Mort Adams." He makes the title a low insult. "You keep thinking on those tattoos, knock yourself out." He snorts out a laugh, confident now he's on the retreat, and adds with relish, "That is, if those gas-malts don't knock you out first."

Bone forgets De Lyon the second he's gone, like an itch scratched. The glasses play out xylophonic music under his fingers, distorted to pink splodges through the thick, rippled curves. His internal eye watches those same fingers rub against dark lines of ink set in turning flesh. Something in that peaked, edgy script scratches at another, more pressing itch deep in the molten pit of his drink-addled brain. The clink of glass becomes a sudden click in his head, painful in its intensity. He knows that hand, that style, why didn't he realise it before?

He's been fixated on those damned tags, checked every scratch he knows, even artists for the Illustrated Movement, on the minute off-chance of recognition, and missed something vital, obvious: scratches who tried and failed. Whose work is, at best, second-rate. This hand is amongst them. His conversation with Stark at Ballerina Girl's stage flits into his head and his stomach spasms with guilt. Now he knows the hand, he knows the name, and this guy, this failed scratch, he's been a surgeon now for four years. He could actually be Rope, or working with him. And even if he's not, he'll have the IDs of their corpses, all of them.

Throwing a wad of cash down amongst dirty glasses, he starts up, ignoring the heavy throb movement awakes in his forehead, and heads for the exit. Halfway through, jammed in on all sides by the raucous crowd, sudden claustrophobia hits him. He throws a wide-eyed glare back to the bar; sees nothing but darkness. It looms behind him cut in smoke and red lasers. He's disorientated for a second, and then the door hits him in the face. He blinks, rears back, rubbing at his forehead, and shoves at the handles, bursting out of the club into sunlight so bright, his eyes contract to pinpoints. He's been drinking all night.

He laughs, sucks painfully fresh air and looks behind again. Just bare doors, peeling flakes of paint onto the white cushion of snow beneath. Glancing up and down the road, Bone starts towards the far-off blot of teeming cloud corking the basin, within which the Zone's sprawling insanity resides. He's tired, in pain, his gut churning over too much alcohol on too little food, his body in revolt against too much work on too little sleep, but he has a lead at last, a chance to make good on his current failures, and there is nothing on this earth that will stop him from chasing it.

CHAPTER 11

*I*n moist, echoing gloom, the splash of gumboots resounds loud as shouting. Knee-deep in effluent waters, Stark kicks aside a tangle of rats, and squeals join the splashes for a moment, careening off dripping walls. Stark wields a torch as long and thick as his forearm, the beam a wide, angry glare of white. It sweeps to and fro, shines rat eyes to luminous demonic orbs and picks up in bold relief the chunks of waste bobbing along the surface. Stark sneers his disgust and wades through it, bow-legged.

He's waited till dawn to come, somewhat reluctant to search this rotten network at night. It's illogical. He can't see without his blessed torch, so it might as well be midnight, but knowing there's daylight somewhere out there eases the heavy thud of his heart. Stark's not one to question that sort of illogic, he's been at the job too long to gainsay its worth, especially when he's only here on sufferance and without access to backup. If he's going to follow this lead, he's going to be as careful as is necessary to survive making it to the end. The tunnel he's splashing along narrows into a doorway of sorts, closing around him like a blocked artery and impacting his whole outer body-line. It doesn't hurt, considering his implants are in the way, but it gives him a shock.

"Ah, fuck!"

Turning in slow steps to the side, he ducks in and through, wincing as sharp brick catches and rips the back of his suit. His torch sputters, threatening to go out.

"Oh no you don't, you cheap piece of shit." He whacks it with a hefty hand, relaxing as the beam springs back full on. He swiped one of the regulation torches, but there's no budget for anything worth having, meaning it's a pile of shit, barely worth the credit wasted on it.

He raises the beam and tries to see ahead. This tunnel is lower, narrower, the yellow brick pocked and crumbling, eaten away by water and time. He grins. It's a remnant of an ancient sewer network, built for cities that existed long before the city the Spires replaced. That city, New Detroit, was destroyed over six hundred years ago, during what history calls the World's End War. It's a misnomer. Though the world warred, all that ended was what *had* been, lost beneath a blanket of bombs. The new world that arose, Stark's world, took generations to build. The Spires, as it is now, has only been around for a mere two hundred years, one of the youngest cities in the City States Union, and having grown almost out of control over successive decades, one of the largest. Too large to manage itself, in fact, and deeply, catastrophically flawed. Stark wonders whether New Detroit was any wiser. The world in which it existed certainly wasn't.

New Detroit, being part of the problem, was particularly badly hit. The city centre was cratered, the suburbs flattened. New Detroit's inhabitants fled down here, taking refuge in vast caverns way beneath his feet. Their refuge eventually became a city, the Spiral City. That city has been buried, in truth and in history books, the story of its lifetime and destruction all but erased, and only those who care to know are aware that the Spires was named in its honour. That the thousands of spiral towers framing the skyline, to whose existence the city's name is now attributed, were, in fact, a memorial to those who sacrificed sunlight to survive long enough to rebuild above ground.

Stark's always wondered about the hidden history of his home city, and he's tempted by the proximity of answers laid beneath his feet, but that's not what he's here to dig up. He's here to dig up his *own* past, a far more dangerous and foolhardy act. The water of the tunnel, hemmed in by close walls, has risen to roughly two feet deep, and the rats, without shelves to run, swim alongside his calves in the water. Refusing to feel claustrophobic, he edges forwards, hoping this is the right path to take. The sewer blueprints for a network stretching almost to the remains of the Spiral City exist, but they're old, rare, and the ladies at the records office are rightfully protective of them.

He was allowed but a glimpse of a few of them, no photos please, and on sufferance at that. Had to try and memorise a route down to the rough area his file on Burneo suggests the lake and cavern might be found. Stark's no eidet, nor a mnemonic aug, but he has a reliable enough memory, and this tunnel, old as it is, feels right. He's taking that as a good sign. He has to because if he's not on the right track he'll have some difficult explaining to do. The Notary has been especially malicious, overruling Burton to veto much of his intended outcomes. They've allowed for further investigation if hard evidence is found, but have refused outright to even consider the possibility of releasing further resources, making Stark's job nigh on impossible. Catch 22. But Stark's got an itch.

His history with Burneo can't be washed clean from his mind. It's like sewer stench, ever clinging and drifting through his subconscious, never allowing him the relief of forgetting, and the instinct drilling a hole in the pit of his belly tells him Burneo's involved in these killings, which means Stark has a chance to make a great deal of wrongs right. It's a chance he'll take, no matter the consequences. More importantly, whilst the Notary and the rest of the CO sit around, twiddling thumbs, people are dying. That's why Stark won't be held back by any lack of resources, why he has to leap in and follow his gut no matter what happens to him. They were out of time even before they found Ballerina Girl.

He marches on, gradually losing confidence in the route he's chosen. This narrow, ancient add-on doesn't feel like it's leading

anywhere. Stinks of dead end. Stark's beginning to wish he were
back at his desk, despite the mounds of paperwork. He growls at
himself. Indecision aggravates him, it muddies clear thinking,
encourages second-guessing, and any good CO knows a second
guess often goes in the wrong direction. He lowers his head and
forges on. If this tunnel has a dead end, he'll turn back and try a
different route. Dogged persistence is his ally here, as it is in all his
work.

With the walls leaning in ever closer, the ceiling shrinking
towards his head, he turns a corner into an even narrower tunnel
and a dense stench of rotten eggs. He slaps a hand over his mouth
and nose, pulls out a full-filter mask pilfered from the Buzz Boys,
considering his department has no such equipment. Faran will
scream bloody murder if he finds out. Snapping it smartly into
place over an exultant grin, he splashes onward, his limbs
cramped into crab silhouette. Too broad to shrug in any further
and armoured by steel implants, his shoulders scrape reams of
damp moss from the sloping sides of the tunnel, wrecking his suit,
but he struggles through, cursing the breadth of his shoulders
more than his own stubborn nature.

Eventually, one cramped step more, and Stark's standing like a
hunchback in a cavern so vast you could build skyscrapers in it. At
the bottom, almost hidden beneath a maze of cancerous looking
pipes, a vast lake forms an offset circle the sickly yellow of pus.
Huge lights, bolted way up, cast bright illumination across walls
pocked with sewerage outlets and collections of stalactites and
stalagmites reaching like arthritic fingers, desperate to clasp
together. Vapourous mist hangs in the air, and from below, under
the network of pipes, the sound of water murmuring against
jagged rocks rises softly upwards. Where the mist hits the walls, it
produces bizarre effects, like visual hallucinations, making
portions of the cavern appear momentarily smooth, like marble,
where moments ago they were jagged and fouled with lichens and
deposits.

Shaken by the sheer size of it all, the strangeness, Stark's unable to remain silent, uttering a short, expulsive, "*Damn!*"

The word echoes round in a circle, multiplying as it goes into a cacophony, rapping back at him from every corner. He bites back on another curse. That echo will have travelled down the tunnels fast as flushed water. He's busted before he's begun. Compounding his exposure, the blaring of his pager echoes into the cavern, makes him jump almost as high as the nearest stalactite. Before leaving, he set it to remote satellite with the help of a sniggering deputy, but he'd forgotten all about the damn thing in the struggle to get here. Scrambling to silence the alert, he glances at the number before stuffing it back into a pocket. Takes out a long-wave comm from another pocket and fiddles with the buttons, ham-handed, his brow furrowed into long lines. The crackles as it's picked up on the other end makes him wince.

"Hello?" he says, too loud. Not like he's still on stealth anyway, may as well be brazen. "Hello, Bone?"

Fuzzy and distant Bone answers, his voice pulsing with excitement, "I have something."

Stark pumps the air with a balled fist large as a cantaloupe. "Spit it out," he all but shouts, grimacing as it bawls back at him twenty-fold.

"It's the tattoos. I know who inked them."

"Is it our man?"

"I wondered that myself, but having done a little digging, I don't think so—not even sure his involvement would go beyond the incidental."

Stark begins to pace. "Details, man, details."

"His name's Satyr," Bone relays, and the urgency still present in his tone works on Stark like adrenalin. "He worked the Aorta four years ago, an apprenticeship. He was a pretty unenthusiastic tattooist, terrible actually, but that crabbed hand is definitely his. He quit after a few months and went into surgical, instead. Underground shit."

"Could he be the surgeon used to remove mods?"

"No, no. I did wonder, but he's a cut-price butcher, not anything like up to the standard used on Rope's victims."

"Dammit. So, where do we find him?"

"He's deep in the Boreholes, getting to him is going to be precarious business."

"How soon can you go?"

"Today, of course," Bone says, and adds darkly, "There's more, Stark."

"Go on."

"I made contact with a girl who assisted Satyr for a while, Regina. She's moved on to legit piercing on Pier Three, but she remembers a little about the tag punters. Says the first came in a month before she quit."

"What time frame are we talking?"

"She quit six months ago."

Stark stops pacing and asks, disbelieving, "You're telling me our victims were tagged seven months ago, in a fucking Borehole surgery?"

"Yup."

"They went of their own accord and paid for that shit?"

"They did."

"What the ...!" shouts Stark, rolling his eyes at the immediate copycat reverberation and beginning to pace once more, furiously, along the narrow outcropping of rock. "What the fuck is going on?" he growls.

"Stark ..." Bone's voice has thickened with unmistakable unease.

Stark braces himself. "What?"

"According to Regina, we might be looking at quite a few more victims."

Stark collapses onto a broad, bulbous stalagmite, his head falling into the fleshy plate of his palm. "No." His voice is flat, toneless. "How many?"

Bone's a long time in replying. When he does, he's so quiet Stark strains to hear him. "She says, close as she can figure it, that over the period of that month she saw as many as thirty-two punters getting those tags."

The cavern is totally still but for the far off lap of water on rock, the slow revolution of the giant lights above, the billow of mist. Sucker-punched, Stark stares down at his feet. "But we only have five bodies," he says.

"But we only have five bodies," Bone returns, an echo of only one voice holding the same pitch of sheer desperation.

"So, why was this so fucking great a find?" Stark asks, heavy with sarcasm. "Apart from knowing these victims apparently paid to tag themselves. How much further in the dark did we need to be? This is ridiculous."

"Well," Bone replies, with grim exactitude, "Regina's going to help us get to Satyr, and chances are he'll know who our corpses are. He should still have his records. Even illegals keep records. We find out who they are, we can look into their lives, see if anything correlates, see how these people connect, *if* they do."

Stark frowns. "The girl doesn't know any IDs?"

"No, the practitioner takes all those details, it's part of the trust."

Stark smiles as it dawns on him. "So, that's how you do what you do?"

"I'm not about to give out trade secrets."

"Well fuck you, too."

Bone's chuckle reverberates down the line, crackled by poor reception, and then he says, all seriousness, "You need to get back here. Little as I like the thought of taking you on official business into the Zone, let alone the Boreholes, you're the head of this case, you need to be present."

"Can you get me in?" Stark's not sure he wants the answer, he knows how hazardous it'll be in the Zone for him, entering as a CO. The Boreholes will be even worse. He likes a challenge, but he's fond of being alive, too, though he knows he often gives entirely the opposite impression.

Bone sniffs. "Of course, I can. But you have to promise you'll stand down from trouble. I can't help you if you do any stupid shit. Now, are you coming back or what? I'm thinking Satyr's a more concrete lead than Burneo."

Stark's not going to question that. It's logic pure and simple. "Sound reasoning. I blew my cover here, anyway. I'll do a touch of recon, so my trip isn't entirely wasted, then I'm on my way. I'll buzz you when I'm close." Bone grunts, then there's a click and silence. Stark replaces the comm in his pocket. He looks down into the depths of the cavern. Breaking his cover wasn't smart, but secretly, he's always wanted Burneo to expect him, to know that judgment is coming. Justice for Teya. That unspoken desire causes him to say aloud; promise, not threat, apparent in his gruff voice: "I'm coming back for you, brother. You can count on it."

CHAPTER 12

*B*ang in the middle of the Spires, the Zone dominates a crater that was once New Detroit city centre. Time and the creep of nature have softened it to resemble a deep geographical basin, but the scorched rock at its edges will never allow it to forget its origin. Thick clouds drift across its breadth, slow moving as vast cattle. Through their white bellies protrudes a disarray of mismatched architecture, sharp as teeth. Amongst unclassifiable composite creations rise spears of plascrete, the bleak stone roofs of ancient-looking terraces, assorted spires, and haughty glass skyscrapers, their surface reflections casting ghosts of light onto the backs of the clouds.

Near the crater's centre, the Zone Lake gleams oily black under mid-morning sun. Huge and lethargic, this blackened slick is fed at its arse end by both the Spine and the Wern. Their brown waters boil over steep cliffs at the Zone's west border and race along to enormous weirs, where they burst through colossal outlet pipes to disappear beneath the lake surface, as if consumed, tamed. Stretched out across that surface are five piers, each crammed along its length with a tangle of spiked and aggressive masonry. Here, amongst bohemian malls and rag markets, between clean, white laboratories and the granite-faced splendour of the genetic industry's corporate buildings, some of the most exclusive and private Zone clinics reside.

In the Zone, modification's the main trade. From surgical enhancement and augmentation to genetic re-coding or patching, whatever's desired, as long as it's legal, someone in the Zone caters to it, whilst the Boreholes beneath provide adequate surgeries and practitioners for an eye-watering range of illegal requirements. Here in the Zone, through delicate relationships with surgeons, modders, artists, and scratches, Morts negotiate for IDs when no other record exists. Imagine very little body left, but attached to the anklebone, a spike like those used in cock fighting. Chances are, it's the work of Tyrone on Bash Street, or perhaps Pedro out on Pier Five, or tiny, shifty Misha at Lock House on Yarrow Square, three of many artists who make such spikes.

If the inquiring Mort has a good relationship with the artist, or asks politely, they'll make an effort to look through their records and provide ID info. In every case, it's not just in who a Mort knows, but how they treat them, their aptitude for diplomacy. The Zone's an independent state, owned, protected, and run by the Establishment, and the ability to maintain often tripwire working relationships is an essential skill. Consequently, Zone etiquette comprises an integral part of a Mort's training. If they fail at any level, they find another profession, which is what makes Bone so unique.

After his difficult start, his inability to gain their trust, he's become revered here for his encyclopaedic knowledge of mods and his deep respect for Zone folk and their way of life. In recent years, their respect has come to encompass the purity of his flesh, the strength of his imagined convictions. They've recreated him as a legend, one the man himself has been caught up within almost as an afterthought. Usually he finds it uncomfortable, has no idea how to take it, but today it's served him well, the guards at the Zone wall allowing Stark in purely on Bone's rep, despite their intended destination.

Now Stark and Bone stand at their next hurdle, the large black iron extrusions of the gates marking the entrance to the Boreholes, the helter-skelter network beneath the Zone. With them is a tall woman who stands mid-way in height between the squat breadth of Stark and the vertiginous gawk of Bone. She sports a blood red Mohican of medusa-like braids caught atop her head in a clasp to expose the stripes of jagged steel puncturing her skull. Rising from behind her ears to the edges of her Mohican, they turn her head into a savage display, a hedgehog ball of razor-sharp defences.

She regards Bone with an amused lapis gaze, the specks of gold glittering. "You sure you want to take City Pork in there with you, Bone-Man?"

Stark snaps his head around to glare at her and Bone chokes off a laugh behind his hand, spewing the lungful of smoke he's just inhaled. "I'm sure."

"Your burden." She sniffs. "I'd as soon leave him here. He's going to shut mouths you might need open." Bone just stares and waits until she carries on with a flippant, "Whatever." She points at the gloom. "You go in and keep going straight, don't deviate, there's tunnels down there even I don't know, you dig? You'll reach a shop called Terrox, belongs to a guy named Striga. You give him my name first, and then ask about Satyr." She jerks her spiny head at Stark. "You tell this tombstone to keep his lips zipped."

"All right, spike," rumbles Stark, "less of that shit!"

She raises a much-pierced brow at him, disdainful. "Whatever, dick. You just do as I said, or Bone-Man here is going to get about as much from these folk as you get blood from a stone."

Stark raises his hands, chuckling. "Okay, sister."

"Don't mind him," Bone says, sharing a grin with Stark. "I'll make sure he behaves. Thanks, Regina, you've been a help."

"I've been a fucking idiot," she replies, scornful. "If you come out of there with all the limbs you went in with, it'll be a holy freaking miracle. I'm out. Try to stay intact." And she strides off without a backwards glance.

Bone drops his cigarette butt and grinds it beneath his toe, nodding to Stark.

"Nice girl," says Stark as they enter the lair of the Zone's more unprincipled practitioners.

"She's not wrong," Bone answers, tone dry. "Getting you into the Zone was one thing, entering the Boreholes could be seen as grounds for insanity. This place is for Skats and gangs, fucking psychos who get distinctly nervous when they smell pork."

Stark pulls at his suit. "You saying I should've come casual? Tried to blend in?"

Bone snorts. "These guys can smell pork at a thousand paces."

"If I'd have known, I'd have worn pink," Stark quips with heavy amusement, then looks Bone up and down. "You look like shit, by the way."

"I feel worse."

"Ever thought of trying a meal you have to chew?"

"Ever thought of minding your own business?"

"Nope."

The tunnel's steep, heading deep into the ground, and they're no more than fifty feet in before the last vestiges of surface light fade away, drawing uneasy darkness around them like bad company. No true breeze makes it this far, and the air's unpleasantly clammy. Around slow vents, the sweating bricks of the tunnel are covered with flyers and vast works of graffiti, all spattered with Rorschach patterns of blood. Doubtless the aftermath of some recent Skat fight. The stench is all grease, steel, and gore, the scent of a massacre in a machine shop. Small red lights overhead illuminate their way, making the blood gleam almost black against the bright chaos of the ornamental array it despoils.

The Boreholes spiral for miles, this entry boulevard merely the tip of an amaranthine tangle, all of it dank, dark, and dangerous. Deeper in, just as the red lights space out to ten metres apart, reducing visibility to almost zero, the first small shops start to appear, casting out bright oases of radiance. These initial dens are all bespoke steel workers, tattoo gun merchants and dealers, who serve the needs of the surgeries, further in. The sound of lathes, polishers, and loud, insane music pours out of them, accompanying a sharp smell of heated metal, burnt plastic, and the underlying tang of sweat. Bone wonders how deep Satyr is, worries how they'll get to him without trouble.

A ragbag of Skats in brothel creepers and drainpipe jeans, their vari-coloured hair schooled to ducktail mohicans, begins to follow them in the gloom, flexing unnatural muscles and displaying spike-knuckle mods and fortified joints. Bone tries not to panic. Spaz knows they're down here; he even sent a tag-team to follow them through the Zone—Bone heard their feet pounding across rooftops, their bird-like cries trailing them until they reached the Boreholes. It's a given word will have spread about these watchers outside the gates and the implied expectation of good behaviour, which means these Skats are all show and no intention, towards him at any rate. Stark's another matter entirely, and he's radiating repressed hostility. Bone can see this going all sorts of pear-shaped.

"How'd your first foray pan out?" he asks as a distraction, and out of genuine curiosity—Stark's connections to Burneo intrigue him, as does his undeniable preoccupation.

Stark breathes out slow. "I found the lake. The cavern."

Bone glances sidelong at the stocky man pacing along at his left side. "Big?"

"You wouldn't believe it unless you saw. It's ridiculous. Weird. Hallucinogenic almost. Makes you see shit you haven't seen." Stark huffs, disgruntled. "I can't fit my head around the size of it even now, and it's only the first one. The caverns where they built the Spiral City are supposed to be even larger."

"Just don't be getting any ideas about looking."

Stark throws Bone a look that just about screams, *shut the fuck up.* "I'm looking for Burneo," he says, "not abandoned cities."

"Okay. Fine. So what about Burneo? Who was he?"

Stark shrugs, clearly uncomfortable. "He used to be a man, just like you and me. An ordinary guy."

Bone chokes a little. "Ordinary?"

Stark gives him a wry half-grin. "Well, maybe not ordinary, but a man, nonetheless, however strange. Whatever he is now, don't forget that he was a man and that he's acting as a man. The whole legend crap is the same as yours. Half based on what he's become, and half based on the way it's seen. It has little to do with the man himself."

Bone's not surprised by Stark's insight, but he's deeply disturbed by the airing of it. He feels pried open, exposed. "You're really not worried about going after him?" he asks. "I don't know about you, but these subterranean places make me distinctly uncomfortable. You get lost and you'll be real far from safety, from any kind of assistance."

Stark utters a dark chuckle. "Sometimes, brother, you've got to get lost to find your way, and when I find my way, when I find him," he says, his voice filled with shadows, "I'll find a way to put an end to all of this."

Something about that tone in Stark's voice disturbs Bone even more deeply than Stark's too perceptive observation. He asks quietly, "What if he's not involved at all?"

Stark stops walking. Several of the Skats shadowing them crowd in, menacing, but Stark doesn't seem to see them; he's focused on Bone. "You ever see any of the people who made it back from Burneo's sewers? People he's *changed*? You see what he does to them?"

Bone glances around at the Skats. They seem confused by Stark's lack of interest. He licks his lips, hoping the confusion keeps them from attacking. "No. But I've read reports; it's an interesting research project."

Stark catches Bone's eyes in a stare that seems to start from miles away. "I've seen some," he tells him, voice weighted with repulsion. "One of them, think it was female, you couldn't really tell. Don't know how the poor thing was alive, the mess he'd made. Just a pair of eyes staring out from a pile of broken up crap that might once have been a body, lumps of steel wound into muscle and bone. I put a bullet through the skull. Felt like I was shooting a fucking puppy. I know they make a choice, I know they don't go into it innocent, but what he does, it's inhuman. And leaving that poor thing suffering, it would've been a cruelty, you understand?"

Bone's chest tightens as though his ribs have become fingers and curled into a fist. He nods. "I understand."

"Before he became what he is," Stark continues, as if he hasn't even heard, his voice low and intense, still miles away, "there was another girl. I had to put a bullet in her, too. Through the chest. The heart. That was just before he disappeared down there for good. Afterwards, like he'd *planned* it, all the unrest in the Wharf, the Gulley, the Outskirts, started to bubble in towards the rest of the Spires. Twenty years of gradual escalations, and now it's like we're trying to contain all of hell in a little paper bag." Stark looks at Bone, who finds it almost impossible to hold a stare so bleak, so very lost. "I wonder at times if this hell we're struggling so hard to contain started with that girl, that bullet. I wonder if, when he ends, it might not end with him."

"That's a hell of a thing to wonder," Bone says.

Stark smiles, it's a thing of pain and horrid tension; makes Bone's jaw ache to look at it. "That it is."

A thought strikes Bone. "Why is he in Rope's game, then? If his thing has been such extremes of modification, why side with a killer who strips mods? It's a huge degree of change."

Stark considers that for a moment. "It's not his vision, but it is his cause. Message has got to be to the Notary, to the Zone. Something about mod restrictions, about taking down those last few barriers to modification chaos." He laughs, a grim, dreadful sound. "As if that wouldn't go wrong here just as much as trying to restrict mods has. Fucking madness."

Stark sets off again down the long, red-tinged subway. The Skats look at Bone, who shrugs and follows Stark, hoping the psycho-billy crazies will keep their distance. Stark's unintended display of superior cool might just have been enough to make them decide to content themselves with keeping an eye on the intruders into a place they consider their responsibility, but with Skats, you never really know what might hold them back or set them off, they are not much beholden to convention.

As he catches up with Stark, Bone has to ask, "Is Burneo sane enough, clever enough, to be aiding Rope? He's supposed to be a raving lunatic. Supposed to be trying to make himself immortal by transforming into a machine."

Stark cocks a brow. "Dunno about immortal. But he was always smart as hell. Look at how he operates. Half Spires folk think he's a fucking myth, wouldn't believe such a creature could be real, despite the shit they see day in, day out, right on their doorstep. But every year, dozens of believers go down to the sewers to find him, and do we ever hear of them again? Like hell we do. He spirits them away into oblivion, and of those that resurface, they're either too damn far gone to speak of what they saw, what happened to them, or dead. No witnesses. No proof. Nothing. Clever."

Bone recalls what he's heard of Burneo, the man-machine whose whole body is a modification in progress. Those who seek him are deviants for whom even the most extreme modifications in the Boreholes aren't enough, the type of folk who campaign endlessly for gut-churning perversions of the body to be passed for new clinical trials by the Notary. If the woman Stark shot in the head sought Burneo in the sewers, chose her fate, what is it Stark wants to believe here? Why does he really want Burneo? The anger's real enough, but there's something darker, much too personal, behind it.

Stark's got a reputation for digging his way through to the truth, but he's making his own truth here, or hiding truth he doesn't want to share. Bone thinks Stark has the capacity to be a very dangerous man. When he sets his mind to believing something, he goes for it at full speed, ploughing through any obstacle in his way, including, it would seem, his own logic. He's not just a bull in a china shop, he's a hammer in a world of glass people, bound to leave debris.

CHAPTER 13

$\mathcal{H}$alf an hour later, their Skat escort still in tow, Stark and Bone pass the first murky hollows, marking the entrance to offshoots from the boulevard. There in the heat, the dank air, the clamour and bustle, they finally find Terrox. It's a ragged hole chopped out in a roughly semi-circular shape, selling bright ripples of metal and fierce spikes. At a worktable, curved around one edge of the hollow, a tangled-haired man in goggles and a leather apron stands polishing a riddle of metal on the whirring brush of a lathe.

Beside him, through a grime-streaked cloth and down a dingy passage, is a surgery where you can get your ribs bifurcated, half pulled outside your body and encased, or spiked, in steel: Striga's specialty. It's not illegal to bifurcate ribs, but the dangers of pulling one half outside the body and adding foreign objects without the aid of expensive immunogen mods places his business just outside of what's legal, forcing him to work down here.

Though the Zone holds itself outside the Notary's full control, it's still subject to law everywhere but in this looping maze of a loophole, engineered to keep the Notary at bay. The loophole constitutes a major headache for the Notary, but they've no recourse to counter it as long as it hovers this close to legal and keeps its records clean. As Bone and Stark enter Terrox, the muffled resound of distant screams ricochets into the room from somewhere down that corridor. Stark tenses and reaches towards his holster, but Bone stops him with a cat-fast hand clamped around the forearm, praying the Skats outside haven't seen. When Stark relaxes, he eases away and approaches the tangle-haired man at the lathe. The man knocks off the power switch, leaving the distant screams, the burr of noise from the tunnels, to fill the void.

"Yes?" he asks, terse, slightly rude. He doesn't remove his goggles, but it's obvious he's spied Stark and isn't impressed.

"I'm B—"

"Bone-Man, I know, you're welcome here. But why," the man snaps, still fixed on Stark, "do you bring pork into my shop?"

Bone waits until the man's gaze returns to his face. "Regina sent me," he tells him. "You're Striga, yeah? Regina says you know where Satyr is. That's all we want, just directions to his place."

The goggles are pushed upwards, revealing orange eyes with vertical slits of pupils like a snake. "I'm Striga, all right. Regina send him, too?"

Bone smiles. "Not really. She said best to leave him tied up outside."

Striga cracks a grin, and sharpened teeth flash in the dim lighting by virtue of the metals encasing them. "You should've listened to her," he says. "Down where Satyr is, they eat live pork."

A LONG TRUDGE into hell later, they head into yet another side-tunnel off-shoot, following a simple scrawl of a map doodled in haste on a scrap of ill-cured leather Bone suspects is human skin. They're both exhausted. Streaks of grime riddle their faces, their arms. They've abandoned the idea of jackets, leaving them in a heap somewhere far behind, and wander along in shirtsleeves, see-through with sweat. Their heads wring with it, too, hair plastered flat to boiling foreheads. It's small relief that none of the punters or their considerable Skat escort are any better off.

Satyr's place is deep in what's known as the Apex, a collection of natural tunnels found whilst digging the Boreholes eastwards. It's become the place where only the most illicit of the surgeries available can be found. Satyr's shop is a small, womb-like obtrusion within the rock, dripping milky water from various tiny stalactites on its roof. A sputtering neon sign is welded over the opening. If it worked, the shop would be called Scourge, but half the letters are out and instead it reads "sore." Stark chokes with laughter as Bone drags him inside.

Satyr's in his surgery, and Bone and Stark are forced to stand watching his arm-deep intrusion into the tender-looking cavity he's sliced into a man's gut. It makes Bone, accustomed to the view under skin and past muscle, a little queasy. He's used to seeing this sort of handling on a dead body, not on a soul who expects to wake up from anaesthesia in a few hours, and he realises this is why Striga's shop runs to a soundtrack of screams.

After a moment, Satyr pulls his mask down under his chin and grins at them, busying his hands once again in the viscera of the man on the table.

"Well, well," he says, "The Bone-Man and a genuine side of pork. To what do I owe this insalubrious trespass?"

Bone nods. "We want to talk about some tattoos you scratched a few months back."

Satyr raises a brow, expressing surprise. "Months?" he says. "Make it last week and you'd be right."

Stark and Bone exchange stunned glances and Stark exclaims, "A week?"

Satyr nods, he's found what he was looking for, a vaguely healthy looking section of lower intestine, and is preparing his needles, a 3.5 mm and a 4 mm. "That's right," he tells Stark, then volunteers, "They started coming about seven months back. A whole flock of them at first." He chuckles and leans in to concentrate on his piercing. "I was a bit taken aback, you understand. My tattooing skills were always a little … deficient."

"No shit," mumbles Bone.

Satyr glances up, his eyes dark with humour. "As I said, deficient, but they came and they paid and who the hell am I to question what these idiots will pay good money for?" He pokes the man he's working on. "Take this moron here. This is the third time this month he's been in. I've had to remove two lengths of necrotising intestine, but he still wants more of it pierced. Fucker'll be shitting out of a nostril if we remove much more. He's got a colon like a little finger." He blows snot out of one nostril onto the floor of the surgery, leaving a smear of dark blood on the side of his nose. "They're dumb, but I don't ask questions. That's the beauty of this little world down here. No fucking questions. You do what you're paid to, and if they die, it's their fault, their choice."

"Right," says Stark, his voice hard, angry, "and you have no responsibility whatsoever."

Satyr stops for a moment, his largest needle stuck, a spit of silver, amongst purplish coils. "No," he says, betraying only light amusement. "I'm a mod-surgeon. I work the Apex. You come to me, you know what you're coming for. I'm not here to act as anyone's conscience. I'm not their fucking nursemaid. I'm here to cut, to pierce, scarify, and otherwise mangle organs. If you don't want that, then don't come. And if you do, don't ask me to feel any kind of guilt for your choices or their consequences."

Bone's impatient to get back to the point. He gives Stark a fierce look to silence further argument. "The tattoos," he asks. "You said you had one a week ago?"

Satyr nods. "End of last week. So a few days ago. They used to come regular, almost in packs. One after the other, like there was a damned line. Now I'll get maybe one every week or so." He sighs. "That was some good money for almost nothing."

Bone's feeling dangerously off-centre, as if the ground beneath his feet has shifted, become fluid. He doesn't know what to say, to ask. He glances at Stark and sees the same look of bewilderment in his eyes, an identical air of loss. He raises his brows at Stark in a silent plea. Stark clears his throat.

"Packs?" he asks Satyr, his voice cracking on the word.

"That's right." The energetic movement of Satyr's hands never ceases as he replies. "Three or four tags a day, every week they'd come, two or three days of it without fail. Then the numbers started tailing off, and now, like I said, I'll see one at a time. Still fairly regular, but not like it was."

Stark swallows. "They, er … tell you what it was for?"

Satyr frowns. "No," he says, as if the very idea is ludicrous. "No one's required to explain anything down here. They pay, I do."

Bone finds his voice at last. "Do they seem at all reluctant?"

Satyr flips a loop of metal through a series of pierced holes, winding it around the loop of small intestine and shrugs. "Not really. They look like everyone I get down here, determined and brainless."

"Do you have their details?"

At this, Satyr stops entirely. He seems reluctant to answer, but Bone lets the silence draw out, as does Stark, and eventually, defensive, Satyr tells them, "No."

Bone lets out a furious deluge of the most repellent curses he can draw upon. "Even you fucks are required to get their details!" he yells, advancing upon the table. "What the fuck were you thinking? If you're found out, the Establishment will rip your fucking face off and shove it up your arse."

Until Bone mentions the Establishment, Satyr's all fixed up to fight, scalpel raised, teeth bared, but at their name, he pales, drops the scalpel, and steps back, raising his hands in placation.

"Look," he says, his voice shaking now. "I usually push, but these people paid triple." His face begs them to understand. "They wouldn't put down their names, only the tattoo tags they wanted. All their records, all I have, are the tags. I can give you those and I can give you whoever comes here next. Just don't grass me in."

Bone's still standing over the table, belligerent, as Stark explodes. "You really think they're blind to this? Are you *that* insane?"

Satyr shoves the intestines back into the cavity, hard. "They don't hold us to much scrutiny. We're all of us just struggling to get by. I took a chance I was given. I won't regret it, and I won't justify my actions to fucking *pork*."

Bone leans further forwards, every line of his body an implied threat. "If you don't want to regret this, Satyr, you give those records and hold that next tattoo job. Hold them till we get here. I don't care how you do it. Anaesthetise them, if you have to. You do that, and I won't accidentally let anything slip next time I see Spaz, understand?"

Satyr's mouth whitens. "You have my word." He jerks his head to a metal drawer unit in the corner of the surgery, crammed into a slight depression in the rock. There's a slender, rather outmoded alu-glass monitor on top of it, jacked into a huge battery. "Tag records are in the top drawer, in a red folder. You take them and leave me your cell number in their place and go. Please. I have work to do, and the longer you two stay here, the more curious people who I don't want even *thinking* about me are going to get."

As they exit Scourge to begin the long trek to the surface, their Skat patrol in tow, Stark keeps looking sidelong at Bone, his face full of questions, and when they reach their jackets, still in a heap by the filthy wall, Bone finally cracks.

"What the fuck're you staring for?"

Stark screws his jacket to a ball rather than putting it back on. It's soaked with sweat and foul with dirt. "Way you spoke about Spaz," he says. "Got me to thinking is all."

"Care to share?"

"I'm not judging," he says as they resume their exit, "because I know you have to do your job. It's just … look … the Establishment machinates a great deal of the shit we at City deal with."

"And you wonder if I'm not in bed with the devil?"

"I do."

Bone doesn't reply at first. When he does, it's thoughtful, considered. "Spaz offered the hand of friendship after I was made Head Mort at Gyre West. I got the feeling that it would be impolite to reject it, and so I didn't." Bone looks at Stark. "Maybe that's not very commendable, but the alternative is to say no to the Establishment, and the fact is that saying yes means I get to give some extra families their loved ones to bury. That's a lot. It's worth the price I'm paying. I'm not much good for anything else."

"You ever thought to question why he's made a point of befriending you when it doesn't benefit him?"

"Of course I have," Bone says, "but never to his face. Questioning the Establishment is about as unwise as it gets, and Spaz *is* the fucking Establishment." He gives Stark a frank, meaningful grin. "He has a pretty harsh policy concerning people who ask the wrong sort of questions."

"Extermination?"

Bone shakes his head. "The last person who asked too hard about the Establishment had his mouth removed. Nothing left of any of it. Lips, teeth, tongue, vocal chords, all gone. Just a hole in their place."

"He die?"

"No. He isn't dead. He just can't ask stupid questions anymore." Bone shudders and strides on, too fast, saying over his shoulder, "Let's get the fuck out of here and read those records. I can't breathe in this fucking place."

OUT OF THE APEX, the Boreholes, sitting in light refracted by mounded banks of snow, Stark and Bone neck bottles of water. The cold is fierce and they're both shivering, but they're swathed in shock and silence and barely notice it. Stark's reading the records for the third time in a row. Bone's read them more than once himself, and still can't digest the contents; they won't filter through. Stark lowers the papers to his lap. He's drenched in sweat and grime and his fingers leave smears on the documents.

"There's too many," he says, his voice laden with defeat.

Bone breathes out, trying to hunt for reason. "They can't all be waiting somewhere, already bound, hoping we find them. It's not possible."

"But we have to assume they might be," Stark says heavily.

"So, what do we do?"

Stark sighs. "I've got every man I can spare out looking with Faran's Buzz Boys. They've found nothing, only LoveHeart, and it takes hours to search even *one* of the deserted tenements on any given street near likely sewer exits. Too dangerous to hurry it. I don't anticipate we'll have anything new any time soon."

"So?"

The silence catches like a chill, stretching out, long and frozen. Bone knows what Stark will say. He wants to prolong the moment, because he knows what his response will be, and it frightens him. He's invested in this case. It's a puzzle directed solely at his particular abilities, and not just his abilities, but *him*. *For* him. *To* him. *About* him. These bodies are his body. Their controller, Rope's, remarkable ability to coerce them into cooperating with the removal of their identity parallels his experience with Leif. Like Rope's victims, Bone chose the label locked into his empty skin. He wants to excise it, wants to excise his father with it, and it's easy to convince himself that helping Rope's victims is the answer. By freeing them, he may free himself. He understands it's illogical, but that's how his end will begin, and you can't have an end without first having a beginning.

At last, Stark speaks. "I'm going back to the cavern tomorrow," he says.

Bone nods. "Okay," he replies. "Okay." He readies himself internally, shoring up his reserves because he left his comfort zone behind what seems like forever ago and all he does these days is wander ever further into territories that make him feel thin, excoriated. "I'm coming with you," he says.

CHAPTER 14

*I*t's about 3:00 a.m. Lower Mace is submerged in a profound hush, but then, this part of Lower Mace is a residential area next to the Zone, with no clubs or bars to speak of. It's the safest route in, but it feels dangerous moving in such silence. Skyscrapers surround her, a modern day henge illuminated by the white glow of solar lamps in lieu of starlight. They loom, almost threatening, making the delineations between light and shadow severe. Leaving no clear line to be taken that will evade unwanted eyes.

Lever glides along at street level, sticking as close to shadow as possible. Tension thrums along taut tendons, vibrates through muscles, and she takes extra care to move unnoticed, alerting none of the runners she knows must be above to her presence. At night, in this preternatural stillness, the streets are their webs, the tiniest movement or sound will alert them to her presence, and it's imperative she reaches Spaz unseen. Lever shivers. She's cold inside. She's never been this frightened, never had the need. It's a new experience to feel openly threatened and out-manoeuvred. She won't run from it, but she has to see Spaz, has to have Spaz see her. Reaching the Zone's edge, beside the twin roar of the Spine and Wern waterfalls, she peers over the edge, and a deep, burning ache blooms in her chest, to see the Zone glistening in the darkness, all those familiar haunts and heights contained within sheer walls, secured from the city. She's not been back in weeks, too damned long, and the loss of it is a hole in her centre, ragged and sore, a sort of homesickness. It surprises her. She's never seen the Zone, or the Spires, as her home. There's no way she can scale those walls, so she'll have to use a loop.

Gang-loyal Monks created the first loops as safety routes, but they seem to spring up by themselves these days, and only gangs know them all and use them. Loops are a network of etheric pathways, strung across the city like a cat's cradle, above and below. They compress time and distance, make the city an easier, safer place to navigate. It's how she's made it here so quickly, how she'll get back before her absence is noted, though she still has to hurry and it won't be easy, not here. Most of the loops around the Zone are as heavily guarded as the gates, but Lever knows one beside the Spine she can use to sneak in. It'll take her near to Pillion, near enough to Spaz's home that she won't have to worry about evading the Establishment runners.

She slides down the cliff, under cover of the roaring of the waterfalls and their clouds of vapour, on a steep path a long way away from the conventional lift platforms and travel-pods. It's scary steep and slippery, and her feet slither down the precipitous stone barely under her control. Her heart pounds so loudly she's worried some random gate guard might pick it up even under her watery camouflage. Half of them were once runners, making them perfectly suited to a life as a gate sentry, always on the alert. Rising to a half-crouch, she runs the last fifty yards, not as steep, though just as wet. The waterfalls are almost equidistant between the west and south west gates, and directly ahead of her, through a thick stand of trees, beyond a natural rock formation, are the gated semicircles through which the Spine and the Wern enter the Zone. She flits amongst the trees to the rock, towering in craggy leaps over twenty feet above her head. This outcropping ranges between the banks of the Wern and the West Gate, a forbidding wall on its own merits, but still easier to scale than the Zone's precipitous defences.

The Spine's drilled a channel through these rocks, a too-narrow tunnel, widening further along to become an open passageway. That's where the loop is, and Lever scrambles up and over, the solid gold fingertips of her left hand clicking on the stone. She lowers herself in cautious increments to a narrow shelf just above the water. This route is perilous, dipping in and out of the rock and often disappearing for several feet at a time, requiring leaps only a runner could make. Even the most experienced runners have come a cropper here, but Lever's got a psi-gen implant to help steady and guide her leaps. Still, she holds her breath as she makes her way towards the faint purple shimmer of the loop entry, far too aware of the rushing power of the Spine mere inches away. It's about twelve feet deep here, savage with riptides and forced by the compression of the rock to terrifying speeds. She wouldn't even want to go down it in a white water raft, safety-jacketed to the gills, let alone fall in and have to attempt a swim. These rocks would mangle her.

As her fingers dip into the loop she exhales a sigh of relief, but moves no faster, the smallest mistake will cost too much. She edges in, slithering the last few inches, and then she's off, running, ignoring the mild headache these things always give her. She pops out behind an empty marketplace and, in her element, fleets through the narrow streets to Spaz's home, scaling the walls swift as a shadow across street lamps, her hands and feet sure on the brick even under cover of darkness. She slips in through the window, and as her feet soundlessly touch the floor, a small bedside light pops on. His eyes reflect in the glow like a wolf's.

"About time you checked in."

She shrugs. "What can I say? It's been difficult."

Spaz slides up, resting on his pillows. His sinewy torso and arms crawl with the same liquid tattoos that cover his face and neck. Even here, in the quiet comfort of his room, he looks danger-ous. It makes her feel a little safer. "How've you been?"

She folds to crossed legs on the polished real-wood floor; Spaz does enjoy his little luxuries. So does she. It's just a side effect of where they've come from. "Honestly?"

"As always."

She shrugs, now that she's here, she can let go just a little, just enough to clue him in. "Not good."

The air in the room draws in. "You've not been harmed?"

"No. Not yet."

"Yet," he repeats flatly. "You're my best freelancer. We're going to need you. I can't countenance the proximity of threat to your person."

"And I can't just throw a job because I might get hurt. I'd have quit a fuck ton of jobs by now, if I thought like that." Lever raises her left hand. "You remember why I got these?"

Spaz nods, murky anger flickering across his eyes. "I do."

She nods back, determined, and holds his gaze as she says, "If you see these on a corpse, you know not to fucking mourn me because I'm aware of what I'm risking, and I accept the risk. You know I won't go down lightly, I won't make it *easy*, and I'll take action to channel any danger that comes for me, make sure it's of use to you."

"What manner of action would that be in this case, Lever?" he asks, almost through his teeth. "It's not a game."

She conceals the clench of her gut, the rise of nausea. "I'm not sure yet."

Spaz frowns. "You're not usually so vague."

"No, but I'm not usually involved in something so bloody well complicated." She raises her chin. "Bone's in a lot more danger than you thought, and I know you anticipated a shit ton. This is no lunatic we've unleashed, for all it does a good impression. A number of our actions have been clocked. We're lagging these days, by one or two paces."

Spaz rubs his face. He looks exhausted. "I was worried about that."

Reining in hard on any worry for him, because he wouldn't welcome it, Lever presses her wrist and glances at the fading glow of numerals on her sub-dermal clock. "Time's up." She rises from the floor and says mulishly, "I won't pull out."

"I'm not asking you to." He leans forwards. The wolfish glow of his eyes disappears as he moves into the light proper. "You get word to me if you need me. I don't care how. Don't take him on single-handed. And run, if you have to. No one is *asking* you to risk as much as your life. Not yet."

"Okay."

It's not a promise, not even close. She and Spaz are alike. They take chances fearlessly and generally succeed. That's why he hired her, and why he gives her the toughest jobs to run in spite of her age, her history. But he worries about her like a father. It irritates and comforts in equal measure. She doesn't need a father, doesn't even remember the one she must've had, but it's nice to know someone gives a shit. She needed to know that tonight. She takes one last look at him, sitting there in the warm, the closest thing to family she has. He smiles at her and the light blinks out. She climbs out the window and begins to scale the wall. As she does, she hears his soft reply. It makes her grin because he knows her so well.

"Fucking liar."

CHAPTER 15

*B*one's curled over, groaning. His entire body's a welter of grievances, having spent the last hour or so bent into the sort of shape it's not attempted since leaving the womb. He thinks he might just be crippled for life. Stark's not suffering at all, he's one of those incredibly annoying people who seem to take discomfort in their stride and shake it off without effort. There's something indomitable about him, something dependable, despite the unsettling edge of unpredictability.

When the pain in his limbs and spine begins to settle down, Bone stands slowly and says without enthusiasm, "Let's do this."

Stark gestures downwards with his torch, switched off in deference to the illumination of the lights above. "There's some old maintenance stairs down there. They're a touch rusty, so don't fucking attack them. I doubt anything in this atmosphere stays stable long." He re-adjusts the mask to ensure none of the sulphuric reek can insinuate past, leaps off his makeshift seat and sets off boldly down the side of the cavern, stepping fast from rock to rock, ungainly but limber.

Bone bends to rub his joints for a stubborn moment longer, checks his own mask and follows, moving with a great deal more circumspection. The way down is steep and crusted with stalagmites both small and monstrous in size. Their sides gleam sickly in the dim light, as if rotting, an oily mixture of limes and quartz riddled with mineral deposits. Between them, huge spiders wearing carapaces tough as crab shells scuttle in close packs, leviathans built of limbs. The articulated click of their passing plays savage music on mottled stone and Bone rears away at his first sight of them, panting hard.

Their path down becomes a sheer track on slippery rock, and Bone keeps seeing things out of the corners of his eyes. Not spiders, or apparitions: it's the walls themselves. Sometimes, in the periphery of vision, they're smooth as glass, free of entrance or egress, but when he looks again, they're cragged steeps covered in lichens, minerals, and punctured with outlets. Stark said something about that in the Boreholes. It could be anything, from hallucinations caused by the gasses rising from the lake to fear working on his senses, but it feels real. Inarguable. Leaves him steeped in anxiety.

He can't help but think of the city that lies way below them, what it would've been like to live that deep down, lightless and trapped. He can't imagine. He's already longing for sunlight. Bone looks down the incline and, seeing Stark much further ahead than he thought, hurries to catch up as they enter the first wisps of mist. It's cold, clinging like dusty spider webs, curling reluctantly off them to trail behind, turning their progress into a dance of the veils.

"You call this a minor recce?" Bone whispers, trying to keep his voice from echoing.

Stark cocks a shoulder and replies softly, "I like to know where I am." He halts then, holding out an arm. "Careful here, there's a drop. I almost tumbled in head first. Damn thing's easier to climb up than get down. We gotta jump."

"My knees'll never forgive me for this," Bone grumbles, hopping down after Stark, his legs all but collapsing out from under him as he lands. "Why didn't you bring climbing gear?"

Stark stares, bemused. "What climbing gear? I have none, and there's none to find in the whole of City. I could try and steal from the Buzz Boys, but Faran would haul me up on a complaint. They have the same budget issues we have." He rolls his shoulders and stretches. "Your knees'll forgive you. Besides," he grins, wolfish, too many teeth showing against stubbled cheeks, "you chose to come, so quit bitching."

Bone makes a strangled noise, throws Stark a look of pure disgust, and scrabbles down the slope, steeper now and even more slippery. The sound of spider limbs clicking in the shadows drives him to move too fast, and his feet skid and slide on the rock, fumbling for purchase. At this speed, it doesn't take long to reach the place where the stairs rise out of the mist, slick with dew. Bone slows his descent on a small outcrop and slithers to a halt, raising both brows at the skeletal collection of metal attached to the cavern wall.

"A touch rusty?"

Confidently skiing down on boot soles behind, Stark stops at the same outcrop and replies with dispassion, "Give or take a tonne."

Bone makes his way to the frankly dangerous looking platform, stepping on with exaggerated care and heading for the stippled brown rail that might once have been clean steel to peer over the side, careful to withhold his body weight. Down through the mist, clinging by some precarious will to the sides of the cavern, the stairs wind away, swallowed at the bottom by layered pipes and thick vapour.

He throws Stark a disbelieving stare. "Down there? All the way down there?"

"All the way down," Stark confirms, his face set. "That's his territory. That's where we have to go."

Bone raises his eyes to the cavern roof in disbelief and says, "I am losing it. Entirely."

Stark steps onto the platform, his footing steady and assured, and gestures for Bone to continue ahead. He does so in tentative steps that, for some reason, amuse Stark to no end. Bone peers with narrowed eyes at the moist black bolts holding rusted steel to rotten stone.

"You can pray, if you like," Stark reassures from behind him.

"You can fuck yourself, if you like," Bone mutters by way of response, and doesn't imagine the soft snort he earns in reply.

After the network of boiling pipes whose sulphur stench makes them wheeze despite their masks, the stairs end abruptly. In front of them lies the lake, vast and shadowed under the roiling curtain of a yellowish vapour, thicker and more tenacious than the mists above. Close up, the waters are remarkably clear, rendering the ripe, loathsome bubbles rising to the surface even more sinister. A thin lip of metal runs around the edge, barely twelve inches wide, and they shuffle along warily, backs welded to the cavern wall. At the opposite side, dozens of tunnels are sunk into submerged outlets, going off in three directions.

Bone stares at the array. "Please tell me you have some idea of which one of those to take."

Stark points to a small selection of tunnels rearing off to the left. "His territory lies in that direction. We go that way. I say one of the middle tunnels, just for symmetry's sake."

Bone lets Stark lead. Inside the tunnel they encounter a twisting spaghetti of offshoots disguised by profound darkness, the overhead lights having long since been nibbled useless by rats the size of small dogs. These ugly rodents shadow them, too close, their paws thumping rather than scuttling in the gullies to the side and below. Bone begins trembling at the sight of them and can't stop, nerves sparking like faulty wires, and when they start attacking, flying at them with wild leaps, needle teeth on display, he loses it, unable to do anything more than throw his arms over his head and hunker down. Stark keeps most away with vicious swings of the fist or torch, but neither man spots the rats climbing above. One of these, a sack of heavy fur with malicious eyes and teeth, drops onto Stark's forearm, claws deep in cheap fabric. Stark lets out a primal yell and smashes his fist on the rat's whip-strong body, dropping the torch into the stinking waters. The rat drops after it like a sodden stone, shakes itself just under the surface and swims away.

Stark watches it go, breathing hard. "Fuck me, that's a goddamned monster. Don't think I even stunned it." He bends to retrieve the torch, guttering now like a burnt out candle. "Shit."

Panic bubbles up from Bone's toes to the itching top of his scalp. He grabs the torch and wipes it on the soft material of his shirt, gagging a little as the scent sneaks in under his mask. "Goddamn, it stinks."

He manages to dry it almost completely, but his efforts are for nothing. The torch sputters and dies, plunging them into blinding darkness.

"Well that's torn it," Stark says in a resigned voice. "What do you want to do?"

Too busy trying to remember how to breathe, Bone can't find a coherent thought to answer with. The darkness asphyxiates him, too much like the dreams he suffers every night. Something is after him in the dark. He wants to run, but his limbs are frozen, feet heavy as lead under the water, and he can't remember which way is back. Can't even see where he is to know where to run.

"Bone?" Stark's voice in the darkness comes like a guiding rope, just as it did at Ballerina Girl's scene, and Bone hangs on to it for dear life.

"I … I'm here … can we go back?"

Stark rumbles an embarrassed cough. "I'm not sure I could find the way we came in without the torch, but there's hundreds of exits throughout the whole network. It may be a safer bet to go forwards and feel out one of those, and continue our search whilst we're at it."

A scream rises in Bone's throat, but the rage beats it. "What the fuck, Stark? What the *fuck*? We're just going to skip along in the goddamn dark until we happen upon a fucking exit? Is *that* what you think? Fucking marvellous!"

"Relax. I'll get us out of here. I've seen the plans, there *are* exits." Stark's voice is filled with unshakeable calm. He's not afraid. He knows what he's capable of. Bone envies him that. The only two places Bone is anywhere near competent are in a mortuary and in a bar. Fortunate, then, that he's not alone down here.

"Fine. Fine. You do that. You get us out. And when we come back to this shit hole, we bring guns, flamethrowers, fucking grenades."

Stark snorts out a laugh. "I might stretch the budget to at least one of those things, and a couple of torches, though I suspect I'll have to swipe them."

"You fucking better."

They move on cautiously, Bone trailing the splash of Stark's gumboots in the disorienting pitch. The sound of distant water raging through pipes is his undoing. Beginning a soft rushing in the background, it gradually rises to a gutsy roar, blocking all other noise. It takes him a while, but soon he realises that what he imagined to be Stark's footsteps splashing before him are in fact an aural hallucination.

Bone calls Stark's name. At first quiet, in respect of how they've tried to steer clear of announcing their presence to Burneo, and then with all the strength in his body, half-hysterical. He strains his ears for any responding cry as the echo dies in the throatier roar of rushing waters. No response. Frightened to be alone, too scared to move, Bone stands there in lightless, dripping entombment, hoping Stark will magically reappear. Then it occurs to him, Stark isn't coming. He probably doesn't even know Bone's lost him. He's up ahead somewhere, still moving, and if Bone doesn't move, he'll be trapped in this dark forever. The thought catalyses action and Bone lurches into a run, fast as he can against the drag of water.

CHAPTER 16

*R*educed by sheer exhaustion to a haphazard, plunging walk, Bone stumbles on. Rank water sloshes in the bottoms of his boots, his legs are soaked through and freezing, his teeth chatter incessantly, and his mind races in a nightmarish loop through black tunnels to the moment he realised he was alone in the dark. The only thing keeping him from total meltdown is that loop, his absolute terror of being alone. If he keeps moving, he might find Stark, or light, or a way out. He has to keep moving. He *has* to get *out*.

The long wave comm Stark provided slaps against his breast bone. It hurts like hell, but he leaves it there; pain helps him retain the tiniest glimmer of rationality. He has no intention of taking the comm out, anyway. Not yet. Stark explained how to operate it before they came down here. Patiently. Thoroughly. It's all gone. If Bone could think, he might be able to recall enough to try and call Stark, but he can't think at all, not here. Not yet. When he finds light, then he'll stop, then he'll think. For now, he has to keep moving.

The tunnel flares to a wide passageway. There's still no light, but the close grip of walls disappears and the muscles of his back ease a little in response. He forges ahead, one hand caressing the edges of his mask, checking the fit remains seamless, and the other hand curled about the slender comm, counting off buttons over and over. It's reached the point where he can't feel his fingers anymore, he can only sense, deep within, sensations of bones articulating. The notion scuttles across his mind that his hand, denuded of flesh, has escaped his control and transformed into a spider made of bones.

Yanking his hand from his pocket, Bone slams it against his face, hard enough to hurt. It's a hand. Just a hand. He's going crazy. He jams it back in his pocket, raises his eyes, and comes to an abrupt halt, breath freezing in his throat. A huge shadow dominates the tunnel ahead, a colossal man-shaped void of nullity within the gloom. It can't be real, he can't even see his hand down here. How could he being seeing *that*? Has to be his imagination on overdrive. First ghostly marble walls in the cavern, then a bone hand-spider, and now a giant man-shaped black hole. Next, he'll see the rats tapping veins in the shade, shooting up needles full of toxic water.

Bone giggles, he can't seem to contain it, until the enormous shade takes a step forwards, sending a wave rolling into his knees. He yells alarm then and stumbles backwards, reeling, nearly losing his footing on the slick bottom of the tunnel.

"Be still, Bone-Man," says a voice, rumbling with the thunder of water through pipes.

An urge to dart screaming in the opposite direction hits Bone, so intense he can taste its sour flavour in his mouth. The skin on his face pulls tight, as if his skull has risen to hackles, bristling hair. He knows who this is, who it must be. It can't be anyone else. This is no faceless monster. It's Burneo, the creature he and Stark have been hunting, and Burneo *knows his name*.

Heart beating in huge, deep cadences, Bone asks, "You know me?"

Burneo moves again, great rolling paces, hissing a symphony of strange sounds, bringing him to within mere inches of Bone. In the murk, all Bone sees are outcroppings of muscles worked to peaked perfection and unnerving shapes jutting at angles from long limbs. The gleam of a single eye.

"I know you." That voice again, so deep it resounds in his ribcage, thrumming like bass guitar amped to the max.

And Bone knows how those small animals, enraptured by the blinding glare of headlights, feel before the awful weight of tyres at speed grinds them to paste. He still wants to run, but he's transfixed.

"Come," says Burneo, and walks away.

This is Bone's only chance. He could run now. He could escape. But where? Back through the darkness, becoming ever more lost? What kind of option is that? His only choice is to follow, find out what Burneo wants of him. Hope it's not his life. Or his flesh. Resigned, Bone wades after the man-machine, who flows like water despite his bulk. He leads Bone to a thick steel door in the side of the tunnel he'd never have seen, and Bone guesses, with a sinking stomach, that he may have passed many the same. The door opens onto an immense canal of seething yellow water, the source of the roar that engulfed the sound of Stark's progress. The light is sudden, too bright, and Bone cries out, raising a hand to protect his eyes. When they adjust, he takes his first proper look at the other living legend of the Spires.

Nude and gigantic, Burneo towers above Bone's lanky frame, his ivory flesh corroded with thick ropings of scars. Where his genitals should be, there's a blank wall of flesh framed in steel, spouting tubes filled with a sluggish flow of bodily fluids. Plates of polished and rusted steel coat him like buried scales, like armour, merging seamlessly into the ravage. The shapes Bone saw in the dark are pistons. Slicked with thick brown grease, they hiss and blow flumes of hot steam, spit and shudder, oozing a clear straw-coloured fluid. Where's the engine that drives this beast? Bone can't see it. It must be contained within the ruined vault of Burneo's chest. He raises his eyes to Burneo's face. Finds one amber eye regarding him with serene detachment. The other eye rolls in the skull, a lustrous ball of mercury, fluid yet contained. Bone swallows, fighting for air, for lucidity.

"Stark ..." is all he manages before Burneo raises one enormous hand, fingers clicking with inset metals and sighing with miniature pistons.

"I have words for you."

"Words?" Bone has no clue how to respond. This is not what he expected. For a start, he's still alive.

"The words are a message. Messages must be spoken." Burneo's head lolls backwards, that single amber eye clouded with dreaming. *"Find him and the ropes will guide you. Follow the coils."* Burneo's immense chest rises and falls, a bellows built from flesh. *"He is waiting in the dark and the glass."*

Bone's breath deserts him. The edges of his vision blur and blacken. Extreme vertigo hits in a wave, his gut rising in instinctive response. The darkness around his vision contracts, pupil-like, thrusting him into darkness more complete than the tunnels he's just left. In that obscurity he feels naked. Exposed. Impossibly high whining explodes into his skull, heard as if from far away, and he begins to tremble violently. Another sound breaks across the first, like glass shattering in the distance, and the ground rushes up towards him. Panicking, he thrusts his arms out to catch himself, but they slam into thin air, and partial reason, comprehension, slams back into his awareness.

He comes out of it blinking madly, not falling after all. Too shaken to be embarrassed, Bone snaps his arms back to his sides. His head rings with the echo of that endless whining, and there's a faint, greasy residue in his mind, the glutinous slew of his dream world invading the daytime. He wants to reach in there and scrub it out. Feels tainted, insecure, and rendered too vulnerable. It's enough that these dreams have stolen his sleep; if they begin to attack during his waking hours, he'll go mad. He thinks he might puke, but the sensation goes swift as it came, replaced by the jabbering demand for gas-malt.

"What the fuck?" he yells at Burneo, terror making him angry beyond all reason.

Burneo says nothing. Stands there staring into the middle distance, the fractured mask of his face complete only in its emptiness. Bone has no idea what to make of it. He was certain this might be a set-up, a trap of some kind, but there's no Rope here, no trap, only this poor, insane creature. He begins to wonder if Stark's right at all. How on earth can this unbalanced Goliath be part of anything as complex as the game Rope's playing?

"What the hell is going on?"

Burneo raises one hulking arm and points across the waters, criss-crossed by long bridges wrought in blackened metal. On the other side there's a steel door, adorned with bands of yellow and black. "There is something for you. A gift."

"For me?" Bone asks, but Burneo only continues pointing. "What about Stark?" Bone murmurs.

The great blunt mass of Burneo's head falls backwards, damp black hair trailing in tangles down to sculpted buttocks, and he responds in a voice that shakes Bone to his marrow, "I will see Reinhart. He is in my playground."

"What? Reinhart? Are you going to bring Stark here?"

"He answers a greater call." Burneo fixes Bone with that single amber eye, as piercing as it is laced with distance and dreams. "As do you."

"Why can't you talk *sense*?" Bone spits, threadbare.

He has a growing feeling that all this madness is just mad, no meaning to be found in any of it. A cruel joke some maniac, perhaps this one right in front of him, has chosen to play. Striving for calm, he grinds the palms of his hands into tired eyes, wringing away frustration and the sensation of Burneo's unsettling gaze. Looks up to find Burneo's no longer there, his huge body moving away at shocking speed down the side ramp.

Bone slams his fist against the wall and yells, "Bring Stark! Don't hurt him."

Burneo pauses, vapourous piston steam rendering him an

apparition. He laughs, the sound too human, before diving down into the roiling waters and disappearing beneath the surface. Bone fights back the urge to continue screaming.

"Fucking *hell*."

With no more time to waste, Bone races across to the door Burneo indicated. Straining its massive weight open, he slips into the brightly lit viaduct beyond. Spider-long limbs propel him down the passage. Smoke trashed lungs gasp deep, rasping gusts of oxygen. His mangled liver sends jolts all the way down to his toes. He grits his teeth, his face a mask as savage as Ballerina Girl's death rictus, and scrabbles for the comm. Clumsy fingers struggle away at buttons, reaching after some response—anything. At the first inkling, he'll use it to call Stark, lost in the dark water and the rats, and warn him that Burneo is coming.

CHAPTER 17

*P*roximity to his old friend creates anticipation painful as the cut of glass to flesh in Stark's belly. Somewhere in these dark, endless coils, Burneo—once Aron—has made his home. How far Aron has fallen that he would consider this place his home? The sewer townships under parts of Mace and Helix, with their modern conveniences, are parlous traps of privation compared to the living found above, but this hellhole's worse by far. Worse than the Rat Gulley. No better than a lightless dungeon, discombobulating to the eyes, the senses.

Ghost walls leap out in the corner of his vision. Viaducts that, at first glance, seem blocked, drop away to form endless, echoing portals when seen at periphery. On second glance, the portals are gone, but Stark's convinced they're there, that he has spectators he can't see. It's honing his nerves to a fine point, sharp enough to cut his confidence. Above his head, the tunnels creak and groan, their spines seeming to protest the weight of the city above, the unerring burden of the past. These tunnels carry the burden of Stark's past —the mountainous man-machine Burneo, a walking testament to extremes of modification, if the sightings can be believed.

He remembers Aron as a giant, even then, and heavily modified, the kind of black-market, backstreet chop-jobs they'd all been forced to in their poverty; his own shoulder implants are a testament to that, bulky and somewhat ill-fitting; their scrollwork bold, rather than fine. He's never changed them because he wants to remember what it was to have nothing. But it wasn't how Aron looked that marked him as distinct and unusual, it was how he *was*, detached by some fundamental difference to those around him.

Stark is certain that difference was behind his choice to run with the gangs, that it influenced his unfathomable decision to take his sister further from help. Very likely, it's also the driving factor behind his cooperation with Rope and the activities he's engaged in down here in the sewer. The brutalisation of willing fools. He's afraid he'll have to kill his old friend to make him stop, and despite what he said to Bone in the Boreholes, Stark has little desire to end Aron.

He wants to catch him, though, and make him answer for the damage he's done to those pilgrims of modification. For the troubles he's supported in the Spires and the Zone. For collaborating with a killer whose actions horrify Stark, who imagined he'd seen everything humans could do to one another. But above all that, personal and unprofessional as it is, he wants to ask him why. Why Teya? There were hundreds of Wharf kids he could've taken with him to the gangs, plenty more capable and less precious to them both than her. So why did it have to be her? Why did they have to lose her? It wasn't worth her life. None of it was worth that.

Up ahead, a watery slew of light appears, highlighting the bend of the tunnel.

Hope rising like flood water, Stark turns to say to Bone, "I think we're onto something. Do you see that light?"

There's no reply.

"Bone?"

Stark waits a moment before he allows panic to make him shout, "Hey!"

Nothing.

He splashes back through the tunnel, passing some of those freakish goddamn viaducts, but Bone's nowhere to be found. Stark slams a fist into the water, frustration riding him too hard for self-control. Bone probably got his fool self lost somewhere back there after the stupid torch failed. Hell alone knows how far back he lost his way; they've been down here a good two hours.

"Fuck!"

What should he do? Bone's an adult, and he has a comm. Stark gave clear instructions on how to use it. If Bone finds trouble, he's fully capable of using the damn thing to call for help. Once activated, the comm's signal will pinpoint Bone's position and lead Stark directly to him, wherever he might be. Will he think to, though? The panic he heard in the Mort's voice when the torch went out, that was no simple fear of the dark. That was trauma of some kind. If Bone's alone, he's probably not thinking coherently enough to activate the comm.

Going back for one last look at that elusive light, Stark finds it gone. Winked out of existence in the few minutes since his realisation and partial backtrack. He curses out loud, scaring rats into the water around him, their wet bodies pressing against his thighs. He knocks them away with balled fists.

"Oh, fuck it," he says through his teeth. "Mort-sitting it is, then."

Before he turns to leave, though, he looks once more down the stretch of tunnel. If that light was real, if it wasn't his mind at play, where might it have come from? And, more to the point, just where the hell did it go?

CHAPTER 18

*a*t the end of the viaduct, there's another door. Bone's still on the comm. The screen's lit, but he can't make it work. Every last muscle aches, his lungs are in tatters, and he'd skin a limb for a gas-malt to make his liver quit bitching. Slamming full force into the new door, he opens it to a reluctant shriek of rusted hinges and stumbles forwards into yet more darkness.

"Shit!"

On the last ragged edges of patience, Bone steps in and feels his way along the wall to the right, stumbling over unseen objects. He moves his hands over the wall until he snags on the edge of a square of steel. Shoving the comm into a pocket, he feels for the switch, using both thumbs to drive it upwards. The lights snap on. He turns to face the room and falls to his knees, retching, not feeling the unforgiving impact of stone. He's not eaten in hours and nothing but elastic spools of spit come up. They cling, astringent, to his bottom lip, trailing in slimy ropes to the floor as he retches until his ribs ache, his stomach spews bitter acids.

He's afraid to look again, but he wipes the spit away and raises his eyes in a painstaking arc. It's another victim of Rope, standing at the centre of the room. It must be Rope's work because ropes hold it static, despite the almost casual positioning. He realises, now, it was ropes catching his feet in the darkness, pulled so taut they're like steel cables. The switch he pressed doesn't work the usual spotlights, but the lighting down here may be too fixed to modify, and it's bright enough to suffice. The sweeping coverage of red is also missing. Instead, a blackening circle of drying blood surrounds the corpse, perhaps a substitute made in haste, or an ironic nod to the usual framing. But this sculpture is not like the others. Instead of clean flesh, denuded of all identifying marks or mods, it's been altered, modified almost beyond recognition. He saw the face first, the sight that threw him to the ground, threw his stomach into his throat. The flesh has been removed, exposing the skull beneath, and a series of pistons forced through the cheeks into the jaw. The jaw itself frozen into a scream rictus so wide it's dislocated.

A plating of rusted steels obscures the majority of the bone, framing startling blue eyes, glazed with terror even in death and slowly forming a white film frosted as Bone's breath in the cold of the room. Above those staring eyes, from the brow, a double row of ragged horns trail over the skull and continue down the full length of the back. But that's not the worst of it. The whole body, including every last limb and digit, has been skinned, the muscle woven with a disarray of steel implants. There are black slicks of blood, as if the work were frantic, hurried. Drying gobbets of poorly incised fat and strips of peeled skin spatter the floor. Muscle flaps hang like rags, remnants of the person this machine, this thing, might once have been.

Still kneeling, Bone gapes at the sheer magnitude of invasion, the catastrophic loss of skin. The skin. The fucking *skin*. His face goes numb, then cold, his gut rising as it did with Burneo, in reaction to the same phantom sensation of falling. Petrified that his dreams will attack again, Bone clutches at his skull, fingers digging hard in a futile attempt to contain them but ripples of pain flare behind his eyes instead, intensifying in waves to become a screwdriver of hurt boring right into the centre of his head, causing something in there, something *physical*, to stretch taut and snap.

The pain becomes so raw, so profound, it's as if rough hands have torn one of the pistons out of that poor sculpture and slammed it straight through Bone's skull. He falls forwards, one hand braced on the floor, the other dug into his belly as he heaves and heaves again, thrown back into helpless nausea, only there's nothing left to throw up except stomach lining and blood. He coughs and a few drops burst from his throat to speckle the concrete. Their bright ruby ovals against pale grey grow huge in his vision. Become red circles. Red in the white.

At the sight of them, the high whining he heard before, not a sound from his dreams, but somehow worse, explodes like steam escaping a valve and fills his whole skull. Only it's not whining anymore, it's screaming, reedy and hoarse, as if from a throat torn to shreds and Bone hangs there, paralysed by the sound. Someone's in his head. Someone's in there, screaming at the red circles of blood. And it's not *him*.

A blind urge to escape, to stop the screaming, rips through him. He lurches to his feet. Desperate and disorientated, he goes in the wrong direction. Slams straight into the body at the floor's centre, tangling in the ropes, his shoulder wedged against that dislocated mouth, his face inches from the wicked row of horns. He remains there a split second, blinking in shock, and then he's yelling, pushing away, fighting to untangle himself. His hands are covered in dark, clotting blood, they slip and slide, and his legs won't cooperate, but by dint of sheer panic, he manages to somehow extricate himself and races to the wall, breathing hard.

Weakness shoots through his limbs like sickness. He's fighting back tears, overwhelmed with horror. He needs to find some way to step back from this, gain distance. Reflexive, like a fight response to panic, his inner Mort takes control, covers panic with the need to answer questions, to *know*. Ignoring the pounding in his head, the oily churning of his gut, he pulls gloves from his pocket, forces them onto shaking, gore smeared hands. He's already contaminated the site, the corpse, but the routine and the normality of gloves sharpen his concentration, his resolve. He has work to do here, a gift to unwrap, and time waits for no man to recover from being dumb enough to run when his body's on the verge of perpetual collapse, even if his mind's decided to join the party. He'll deal with this later, when he has the fucking time.

Bone returns to the corpse, relaxing as he steps into the familiar territory of examination, though the body is anything but familiar. Apart from Burneo, whose mods comprise appalling, incomprehensible damage, Bone's never witnessed modification this extreme. Such a vast amount, and so brutally done, should have killed this man straight away, and yet Bone's knowledge of the human body tells him this man lived, at least for a while, and he becomes so angry, he almost loses every last vestige of control. He's forced to stand a moment, sucking in hard breaths through clenched teeth.

When he calms, he looks for the tag, finding it on a strip of flesh below the back of the knee. It's been reattached like a clothes tag—that innocuous—one end tacked to the muscle with black mortuary catgut, the rest dangling down in a long curlicue like a pig's tail. Above it, the whole infrastructure of thigh is exposed and punctured through horizontally, with lengths of metal attached to piston-like apparatus rooted in the knee. Gently, he stretches out the thin piece of skin, somewhat dried and shrunken. Tattooed there, in fading black, the tag: THE GIFT.

There is a gift for you.

Burneo, not Rope. A gift from Burneo. Why? What can it mean? And why for him?

Bone drops the skin, close to tears, close to screaming again. The world has become muffled. He can't begin to understand the low cramp of excitement beneath the waves of sickness contorting his belly, nor the giggles, less nervous than anticipatory, escaping his mouth. To reassure himself, he takes out the comm, covering it in thick, sticky blood from his gloves. If he could work the damned thing, he could have Stark triangulate his position, bring him here fast, bring Buzz Boys just the same. But it's useless; he can't remember anything Stark told him. Bone throws it to the floor, furious. It bounces, unharmed, and he raises a foot to smash it, but some impulse staggers across his brain and makes him hesitate.

"The pager," he mutters between frozen lips. "I beeped Stark when he was in the cavern."

He rifles through pockets, frantic, energised, oblivious to the streaks of grime and the smears of rotting fluids his filthy gloves leave on his clothing. He finds the hard rectangle of the pager in his back pocket and sends a fleeting thanks to whatever quirk of fate prevented his falling backwards into the water before punching in Stark's code.

Minutes later, the comm on the floor bursts into life, jumping up and down on the concrete as it vibrates in frantic response.

CHAPTER 19

Inky red spurt of blood, a watery emulsion. Metal sticks against bone. He angles the rod, thrusts it down between fibula and tibia, his hands sure, keeping pressure constant against the stubborn refusal of the body. Corded arms burst out in sculpted hillocks. Perfect tension. His face is a serene mask. Beauty is agony. Sweat spatters from his brow to mingle with pools of blood, a human ichor. The faintest click and the rod connects. He twists it until it secures deep into the socket embedded at his ankle.

Blood slips in slow rivulets, coiling down the ridge of his foot with each swift movement. His hair falls, lank with heat, over a faraway amber gaze. This is pain and pain is beauty. It is his penance. Burneo flicks the top of the pole, a practiced twitch of the wrist, to settle into the outer casing on his knee. Gives a final twist, hearing with a soft, dreaming smile the deep *thock* that marks the settling of the new joint. Takes thick, black catgut and darns the ripped, bloodied muscle and flesh back around the metal pole, paying no mind to the look of it. Perfection, beauty, lie not in appearance, but in evolution of form.

He is the machine-man. Mix metal with his bone, his blood with oily machine residue. His body, his penance, is a construct, a work in progress. It is his message to her, unspoken, carved into the matter of his substance. He raises his head to the ceiling, the reflective orb of his mercury eye rolling and rolling, the amber glazed, faraway in lucid dreaming. His gift has been delivered. The tide is rolling in, bringing the past back to him like stones from the deep scoured smooth by persistent pressure. Ah, but it hurts worse than the invasion of cold steel into soft tissue.

Dirty sewer waters drip from leaking pipes somewhere in the distant vault, metres above his reformed countenance. He stands. A vision. A terror. A jerking, elegant array of limbs and machinery; mottled, scar-riddled flesh revealed by muggy yellow light.

CHAPTER 20

*C*ast iron chairs throw spiked shadows over the slippery red floor, sending black jagged shapes into a sleazy neon glare, diffused through smoke. Bone's at the corner of the bar, drinking fast, beating alcohol at a brain made frenzied by exhaustion. He sits, leather-backed and vacuous, staring at his reflection in the bar's polished steel surface. The last moan of a dying blues tune rings hollow through the room, laying melancholy waste to his inner ear. He's physically wrecked, managed only an hour of broken, terror-filled sleep before giving it up as a bad idea and opting instead to spend his time actively pursuing alcoholic paralysis. Unfortunately, he's still fucking sober.

It's been almost a day since receiving his gift, deep in the belly of the sewers beyond the lake, and the hours have bundled together in a blur so dense, it sits in his head like a tumour, insidious. He and Stark waited seven long, cold hours for the Buzz Boys to arrive, enduring a skeleton-mangling journey to the morgue to autopsy the Gift's remains in a closed room, under lock and key. He worked without Nia's assistance, couldn't cope with the thought of her perceptive gaze looking at him, through him. The questions that would surely follow. She's the only person who can look at him and see everything he's trying to hide, and he's not willing to discuss what happened in the sewer. Not yet, maybe not ever.

An hour or more in conference followed the autopsy. Bone told Stark a heavily expurgated version of his encounter with Burneo whilst they waited for the Buzz Boys, how the man-machine seemed to have been waiting for him, and his direction to Bone's gift. Bone's autopsy only confirmed what he already knew, that this gift was indeed from Burneo and that such a pointed redesign of Rope's intent, and the determination to lead them to it, can only constitute an about-face in his commitment to the killer's game.

This conclusion has Stark sparking like a cannon about to loose. He plans to convince Burton, his boss, to petition the Notary for authorisation to mobilise whatever resources he can for a return to the sewers. He's almost one hundred percent certain Burneo will be down there, waiting for them. That he'll lead them to Rope. He expects Bone to join him. Thinks it's important that he comes. But Bone's unbearably on edge about everything.

He needs time to come to his own conclusions about what happened between him and Burneo, what happened when he found the Gift. His memories of those moments have taken on the bleary queasiness of a drunken dream, one of his worst. He can still hear the screaming, a sound he'll never forget. It's left him a thinning hollow, filled with static, and after all this drinking and thinking, he's only sure of one thing; Rope's not only the puppeteer behind these bodies, he's also pulling Bone's strings. Bone doesn't yet know what the bodies mean, only that the idea of them being *for* him repulses him and fills him with a slow, curling dread. Who wants to be known, to be seen, to be *sought* after—even intellectually—by a creature like Rope? Thanks to the subconscious parallel between Leif and Rope, he feels more haunted than ever, as though his father stands right behind him, waiting to see him fail.

He's afraid he's failed again already. Thinks there *must* be another important connection he's missed, like the tags, but he can't figure out where it might be, can't see the wrong numbers in the equation. He lifts his glass and drains the contents, one long gulp of fire down his aching throat. He thinks there are tears waiting to come, or laughter. Either way, he's losing it. Lost it. Has no idea how to start finding his way back to whatever sanity he once had. He signals to the bar man, points at his glass and waits, head pounding, stomach floating in the abyss, thoughts diffusing much like the mist of smoke curling sinuous coils through the close-walled claustrophobia of the Wail.

As he sits there, feeling deranged, a woman appears out from a thick eddy of smoke as if materialising. Gleaming in gold and fire orange, glaring as a bar sign, she strolls to the sharp curve of the bar, tips a head haloed in peacock blue to stare at him with laser-bright eyes, and smiles, her teeth white razors in the neon. He feels his balls tighten. Shit.

"You look as though you could do with sleeping," she murmurs and her voice curls between rasp and ripple, husky enough to send tremors through his skin.

He laughs. Coughs. "Sure could."

"What you drinking?"

"Gas-malt."

She chucks her cred chip towards the barman. "Another gas-malt, on me. I'll take a beer. Asian. Nothing lite." She's got long, prehensile fingers just like his, all bones and edges, and on her left hand, they're dipped in gold right down to the first finger-joint. Bone reaches out and strokes one.

"Implanted. Tricky."

Her eyes sparkle. Predatory. Nice. "Real gold, too. Eighteen carat alloy."

Bone's impressed. "Gold's for conducting, not modification. You've got a fortune as your fingertips."

She grins, a vicious spike of humour. "Funny."

He accepts his gas-malt and lifts the glass towards her, his eyebrows raised. "Cheers."

"No sweat."

"So what do I call you?" he asks. "Gold fingers?"

She turns to face him. Her long cheekbones knife down, making her chin appear pointed, a delicate weapon. She has a smile like treacle. It sticks to her face. Looks like it might slide off at any moment. "Lever."

He chokes. "What, like the car?"

"Nope, like that's my name."

"You Mech?"

"Not even a little."

He wipes spilt drink off his chin and chuckles. "I'm Bone."

"No. You're the Bone-Man."

Awareness rips through him, bright and hard as his attraction to her. So, she's Zone folk, or gang—he really can't tell which because there's something slightly off-key about her, as if she's only wearing gang, not living it. But knowing his honorific means she must be one or the other, and this is a play for him. It's happened before and usually irritates, but not this time. As if sensing that, she smiles again, in slow motion, like a crocodile. It takes forever for those sharp teeth to flash between juicy lips, making his head spin and contract beneath that band of throbbing pain. He's finally heading for mildly pissed, definitely completely screwed in the head after yesterday, but he's not imagining the pull he feels towards her. It's viral. She's about ten years too young for him, but he decides that doesn't matter. He's going to let her play this out to wherever she wants it to go.

He touches her on the elbow. "So, exec, or com?"

She grins, slugging a great mouthful of beer. "Neither. Freelance."

"Freelance?"

"I freelance organs."

Bone stares in amazement. "Pardon?"

She touches a gold tip to her juicy bottom lip and rolls expensive eyes. "You know, get organs and sell where I can, mostly to brokers. It pays better than licensed."

He's stunned. "You buy?"

"Course not. I harvest." Lever flicks a stray ice-cube on the bar.

It shatters to pieces on her solid fingertip, the shards sliding off towards the floor.

Bone's blindsided. "Well, fucking hell. Nice to meet a fellow meat."

Her laugh is like cancer. Invasive. "I like that."

The music stops and they sit, drinking in the quiet, keeping each other company. Bone tries to recollect when he's felt comfortable in this situation. Never. But here's this woman with blue hair and a Mech name he feels totally at ease with. He's attracted to her, of course he is, but she feels familiar, too. Feels like he's lost a body part and she's sitting there, wearing it.

"Did you ever," she asks at last, pinning him to the bar with a long look, "feel trapped in your own skin?"

Bone shrugs. "Whatever. Doesn't everyone?"

Lever tips her head, and tendrils of shaggy blue slice across the white slate of her face. Tribal, like woad stripes. He wonders if she's practiced the move in a mirror. "I guess not," she says, her expression cryptic, oddly pleased in a way that makes him a little uncomfortable.

"Why?"

"You're the first person I ever asked who answered yes."

"You ask a lot of people?"

"Everyone I meet. Hundreds, nearly." She smiles cadaverously. "They're all too busy adorning their flesh, making it into an ornament, to understand what I mean."

"So, what about it?"

Lever's eyes devour his face like his thoughts are carrion and she a vulture. "Nothing. Except for all that delicious muscle and tendon. Wrapped in red inside, and no one can see. I look in the mirror and I see my face and I try to imagine it just bone and glorious red muscle. Makes me feel free."

Bone sips his malt. His stomach sways, a boat on the ocean of her words. "Maybe it's because of our work," he murmurs.

"Or maybe it's because we're sick of the skin we're in," she replies.

Bone has no response. Ever since he can remember, there's been that slow burning sensation of skin closing in tight around him. Strangulation in stages. Not the physical organ, as such, more the fact that he can never walk away from the person he is. His skin locks him into this identity, and he'd give anything to be anonymous, unrecognisable. Even his skin. He flexes his fingers through a sticky patch of half-dried beer. Long, bony fingers for a bonecutter. It takes only a second to imagine fine drops of blood curling off the white stretch of a tendon. He thinks of bone-spider fingers. Thinks of the Gift. Skinless. Recalls the rush of unwelcome excitement and is stunned to find that this was the reason. What kind of man envies a corpse the loss of its skin? He's overwhelmed with sadness and self-loathing.

"I'm going to enjoy fucking you," she says out of nowhere, hooking him with a neon green glare, almost angry with delight. She stands and chucks her empty beer bottle at the barman. Holds out her gold-tipped hand. "Come on. I need a fuck. Now. With you. Or I can find someone else."

He takes her hand and catapults off his seat. "Don't do that," he says. "I'm not arguing."

She laughs, pulling him out of the smoke infested club into the thick belching roar of the street and tugs him until they're running. It feels good, a little young and stupid, a touch desperate. He's known the island of Gyre West, isolated in the left aorta of the Spires, his entire life, but he loses track of where they go. Maybe it's her, or the drink, or the promise of sex, maybe just the sluggish indigo of night, but he can't tell, in the end, one black, choked street from another. When they arrive at a skinny mansion house sliced into apartments, somewhere out on the island's edge, he doesn't know where the hell he is anymore, but she's kissing him in the elevator and he doesn't give a fuck.

Lever sheds her top and silver-mesh bra on the elevator floor for some sour-faced old bugger of a guard to find in the morning, and they stumble into the topmost room—a gallery of sorts. End up fucking like animals in the centre of a harsh circular rug covered in shapes like leaves, surrounded by his trousers, jacket, shirt, and boots, her tight leather skirt, heels, and silver-mesh panties. They make a tangle of limbs and gleaming sweat, blue hair and gold, mouths fused as if they're on fire, and their flesh melts together. It's brutal, all teeth and nails and violence, limbs striking the hardwood floor beyond the rug, bruises blooming on pale flesh.

She has a snake tattooed down her back. An incongruous mod. It writhes in copper coils from her neck, across her shoulders and down her spine right to her arse. He's never liked tattoos but he traces this one with his tongue and rakes it with his nails, drawing blood until the copper is tinged with beads of red. It's hypnotic, gorgeous, moving against her movement, writhing of its own accord, and shines under the light like oil on water, a luminous sheen. His attraction to it, to her, is ravenous. He loves the hard rasp of her gold-tipped fingers tearing channels down his rib-defined chest. The scent of her, raw and drugging.

He loses himself in the sleek texture of her flesh, in the sharp sting of nails, the dragging flare of gold fingertips. The heat suffocates him, burns his skin. He's dripping with sweat, with blood, and filled from head to toe with a pain so intense it can't be anything but pleasure. An orgasm of startling intensity builds from his bones, through the strung-out web of his nervous system, and into his muscles, radiating out to his extremities. Lever leans down as his body succumbs, whispers in his ear. He can barely make out the murmur through the clamour of his body, but the effect on him is immediate and powerful. His whole body explodes, lightning sensations bursting through him, agonising in intensity, and in the background of his mind, something fights to be unleashed.

As his orgasm shudders away, Bone's mind relaxes and calms. Body so drained he can feel it only at a remove he opens his eyes to share the moment. Instead, he begins screaming.

The skin of her head has split in a long fissure from forehead to nose, oozing thick, dark blood. It slowly widens, dropping by degrees away from her face, revealing a mask of raw muscle.

Loose skin slips down her neck, gathering to ugly folds, and the split creeps down her torso, peeling away with a noise of paper sliding down metal. Exposing sticky muscle and gelatinous red breasts, fat-less and androgynous. Uncovering a stomach of perfect statue-like composition before splitting her pubic hair to fork down her legs, sending her slithering bloodily into his lap. Cast in crimson she curves over him, her eyes rolled back to sclera, their boiled egg hue shocking pale against the bloodied surround, white in the red, and he's screaming so loud it fills his ears with a deep, buzzing burr. He tries to pull away, scrabbling at her slippery thighs with clawed fingers, only to find he's still inside her, and despite their slickness, her legs won't move from round his waist.

Her skin sags, drops to the floor with a thud that makes him think incongruously of the weight of the integumentary system. How it functions. The impossibility of what he's seeing. Lever's eyes roll back to irises, dazed and aware. She untangles herself and rises above him on exposed kneecaps, a thing of woven bone and coiled tendon. She pushes away to stand, leaving two perfect, red handprints on the scored expanse of his pale chest. Black spots spiral over his pupils, the first signs of too little oxygen. His scream is hoarse, fractured, and refuses to end. Rearing away from her, from *whatever* she is, he curls in on himself, eyes fixed on her and glazing with horror as she follows the impossible with the inconceivable.

She stretches up towards the ceiling, attenuating to unnatural length, disentangles to an amorphous mass of muscle, bone, and tendon, and then, like the copper coiled snake decorating her shed skin, she coils herself around her own bones. Becomes a writhing tangle of innards and draped muscle. A blood-smeared jigsaw with the oval, green-eyed, meat draped skull set atop. Absurdly, Bone notes the glittering gold tips of her fingers sparking diamonds of light from within the ravage. His screaming fractures to a halt as his throat packs up, grinding to uselessness. Lever looks from him to the caul of her skin and explodes upwards, tearing through the ceiling in a sinuous movement of unbelievable power. Drops of blood fall from the jagged spars of roof tiles, landing with soft splats like fat rain on a face, and the light fixture, half-destroyed by her passage, sparks and flickers like a strobe. In the silence and dust swirl of her departure, watching her rise to the starless sky, his reason fogs. An unaccountable itching sensation crawls across his forehead. The meatless flop of skin wavers in his sight, a graphic mirage, and his mind collapses.

Swift as a rising tide, the drone of bees fills his head, morphing to become *the shatter of broken glass … a sharp searing in the skull … distant laughter rising like wind …* Bone jackknifes. *Glass, pain, laughter,* boom loud as thunder, smashing against the insides of his skin. He gasps for air, clawing at a sudden constriction on his chest, and he realises he can't see. No light strobing, no flop of skin, just endless pitch, cold as the depths of the ocean. He tries to tell himself this is not real, it's not real. It's impulses, ghosts in the wires, misfiring signals, nothing but bad dreams, trauma, the aftermath of shock. But they inhabit him like his breath. Like gold fingertips in skin, they bury deep until there is nothing but *glass, cold, dark, pain.* Terror bubbles up, acid sour, carrying with it a scream from the pit of his belly, unstoppable.

The splintering pain in his throat snaps the grip of the nightmare for a second, and realising he has a way to fight, he screams again and again, until darkness leaches from his vision. But seeing is worse than blindness. The sputtering bulb, the ragged hole in the roof, the empty sack of skin laid on the round rug amongst those shapes like leaves, these are his reality and they are a nightmare all of their own. He struggles for air, his throat filled with shards of pain hard as glass. Lever's blood drips from the broken ceiling in slow motion, lights travelling the surface of each droplet. As they hit the carpet, the floor, they spread to form small, perfect circles, like his blood on grey concrete, and in the back vaults of his mind, searing fierce as a brand to flesh, blood becomes … *bright red circles … red in the white …*

He heaves, helpless, choking on a throat full of vomit. Barely manages to lift his head before every last drop of alcohol in his system hits the carpet in one heaving wave. His ribs creak under the pressure of the deluge and he groans, the sound bubbling as vomit pours from his mouth and nose. Hot and cloying, it soaks the carpet, splashing his hands, knees, and arms. He's shaking violently now, a compulsive, full-body shudder worse than tremens. Ingrained knowledge informs him calmly that he's in deep shock, therefore in big trouble. But he can't move, stuck on his knees in a rank pool of vomit, holding onto consciousness by sheer force of will. If he passes out, he won't wake up.

As he kneels, fighting the urge to give in and sleep, the first amber fingers of dawn stretch across the window, edging delicate light into the room. The incongruity of it hits hard, driving him out of his stupor, his shock, and into coherence.

"Daylight?" His voice is a broken husk, crackling with pain. "How?"

He met Lever no later than midnight, and they spent all of two hours together, so where's the night gone? Stolen. The loss of time feels like an act of violation. Kneeling there, naked, makes it worse. Filled with an unbearable need to cover up, he stirs out of the pool of vomit. His whole body below the waist is smeared with congealed blood, hideously uncomfortable, and those two hand-prints stand out in stark relief on the ghastly, half-torn canvas of his chest, smeared a little by his frantic clawing. He uses his shirt to wipe off the worst, and then, hands shaking, he scoops his trousers from the floor and pulls them on unsteadily, sighing with relief. With tentative fingers, he touches the deep grooves Lever left in his chest.

"I'm a fucking mess."

He sways and coughs, unable to breathe for a moment. He's a tripwire, seconds from losing it completely again, so he does the only thing he can to steal distance from unbearable proximity and forces himself to dispassion, to see the scene from the perspective of a Mort. Taking a breath he feels in every inch of his scream-burnt throat, he crosses to the skin, nudging it with his toe because looking at it says nothing about the realness of the thing. To his relief and horror, he feels the weight of it shift against his foot. He steps away, circling it, his limbs slowly gaining strength. The overwhelming shock response reduces to teeth chattering shivers as his mind works the angles, coming to the only logical conclusion.

"Transmog." He whispers it to himself, as though saying it aloud will conjure demons.

It's the forbidden zone of alchemic meddling, painted monstrous by decades of Notary propaganda based on trials in the heady, early days of deep genetic experimentation. Transmogrifications gone hideously awry, the results inhuman and insane. Bone's no fan of the Notary, but he's read the papers backing their campaign written by the late Walken Grey, the century's most eminent geneticist, when he was a mere graduate, no more than nineteen. Lever's nothing like the Transmog case studies Grey recorded. She maintained her shape, spoke and acted with coherence, shed her skin and lived—fucking *flew*. It wouldn't be Grey's mistake, despite his youth when he wrote the papers. His legacy speaks for itself.

So, what exactly is going on? If transmog is illegal, its results so devastating, how was she able to get it? Was she the first successful patient? Somehow he doubts it. Where there's one successful mod, there's always more. So, are the Notary lying, or is this a Zone secret?

"What the hell is Spaz up to?" he wonders because, if it's Zone-based, Spaz knows about it.

A rush of needle-sharp adrenalin pulses through him, the excitement as impossible to ignore as the heavy ache of fear in his gut. He has to know. He has to find out, find *her*. She knew his name, made a definite play for him, and brought him here. He thinks she wanted him to see this; why else talk about skin the way she did? But why him? Why his eyes? It's like Rope, someone or thing reaching out to him for an unknown agenda. It should sicken him, perhaps, what with transmog being what it is, but instead he's excited. This is *important*. Means something to him personally. Here's evidence that nothing is immutable or set in stone; that even the skin you're trapped in need not define you. Reeling, he goes through her skirt pockets, struggling with the fabric and hunting for some clue that might lead him to Lever, to answers. But there's nothing. He throws down the golden scrap in frustration and grabs the sheath of skin instead, before he can stop himself. It drips blood in still-congealing blots onto the weave of the carpet.

"So long to congeal," he rasps, entranced, and touches the thick, wet blood left on his chest. It's the same. "Must be important, some necessary by-product or co-factor. No way to tell without equipment."

He looks at the skin. Between his shaking hands is her tattoo, that gleaming copper snake winding her spine, as though it came from within her body. It's lost the sheen that entranced him when they were fucking—gone dull, lifeless. Something special, then, some kind of specialist ink, most likely intelligent. Probably nanites of some kind. He's struck afresh by the incongruity of the mod. Gang members have tattoos; it's ritualistic, hierarchic. Members of the Illustrated Movement also wear them, but they're an art collective whose skin is tattooed, laser-cleared, then tattooed again, used for everything from advertisement to fashion modelling. Tattoos are not popular as personal mods. Lever's tattoo is definitely personal, and it's better scratchwork than any he's seen on the IM, which is saying something. The work is incredible. Intricate. He's never seen anything like it, yet the fluid congruence of the coils tugs at his mind. He should know this, shouldn't he? His head swims, the impact of the night's events straining to crash in on him. He holds onto the skin for dear life.

"What is it, Lever? What?" he mutters, studying each liquid curve. "I need to keep it," he tells himself, and is surprised by the depth of conviction: a physical need.

Placing the skin on the floor, he rifles in his jacket pocket for a sheathed surgical blade given to him by Leif. It's a relic, more sturdy than the throwaways he uses at the lab. He oils and cleans it often, keeps it to remember that there was at least one thing they understood about each other: the work. Kneeling by the skin, refusing to question his motives, he carves around the copper coiled snake in a neat, wide rectangle from shoulders to buttocks. As he cuts, methodical, barely paying attention to the swift work of hand and blade, he realises he's no longer shaking, but crying. Soundless floods of tears washing her skin clean of blood. He has to get home, get to safety, before he succumbs to shock.

He folds the skin, placing it in his jacket pocket, the sheathed blade beside it, and pulls on his leather jacket, zipping it up over the mess of his chest. The lift is empty, her top and bra gone, but he doesn't stop to wonder about it, just presses the button marked "G." Within minutes, he's strolling down the street, soothed by the pain of freezing air and no longer lost. Unable to fathom how he became lost in the first place, he puts it down to drink. Wanders home in a daze, his hand tucked into the pocket of his jacket, curled around the folded section of her skin. He looks up into the clearing sky. Somewhere out there, skinless Lever coils among the clouds. It makes him dizzy just thinking about it, as though he stands on tiptoes over an abyss of improbable depth, arms outstretched, preparing to leap.

CHAPTER 21

*B*ack in his apartment Bone takes a long, very hot shower, scrubbing hard at the wounds on his chest, buttocks, and thighs. Erasing the remains of those dried hand-prints, the residues covering his lower body. It's only when he's drying that he thinks he should've taken a sample, that perhaps her blood might hold the most important clues. He contents himself with a sample scraped hastily from the back of her skin and tries to sleep, twisted up in blankets too restraining, choking his body. He throws them off but he's still stuck in his skin, sweating, aching, and his dreams are worse than usual, colliding with images of Lever, flashes of those red circles.

He wakes after less than an hour with a shout, sweating hard. Takes another shower and dresses for work, craving routine, normality, a break from the madness of Rope, the desperate longing sparked by Lever. It's nearing on nine in the morning, and he's missed the car they send to chauffeur him to Lower Mace by hours. He can't walk there, it'll take all day, longer, and so he catches the Bullet. Sits screwed up in a corner by a window, trying not to panic, trying not to think, and holding on tight to that skin in his pocket, as though it can keep him safe. Arrives at Lower Mace mortuary full of piss and vinegar. He wants whiskey. Fuck the whiskey, he wants petrol, the pure cold burn of gasoline.

The bitter chill of the morgue does nothing to revive him. Draws his skin tight across his bones, making him think of Lever again, and then again. He wants to go to his jacket, slip a hand inside the pocket and touch the leather of her skin, caress the hardening edges. It's going to need curing soon, if he intends to keep it. He's not sure how rational that would be, but he can't bring himself to throw it in the furnace. The tattoo, the snake, it's too significant to destroy. He's not sure what to do with the sample either. He's fairly expert on DNA mods, but this is transmog, there's no stored gen baseline for him to compare to, and asking at the Zone feels too dangerous.

Nia's too angry at his tardiness to talk to him. They work in thick, uneasy silence on several corpses requiring immediate autopsy. Lower Mace population alone stands at around 18.4 million, and mortuaries drown in bodies, in nameless flesh. Ninety percent of the time, all a Mort can do is cut bodies up to locate and record mods for chasing in the Zone, then dump the bodies, crudely stitched, in the cooler for the Scorch Boys. They'll go to the furnace en masse, the fuel that drives the machine, an endless, churning mill of self-sustaining production. If one of these bodies should gain an ID, and the family can afford an urn, it'll be filled with nothing but nameless ash, the residue of some countless hundreds burnt on the same day, in the same furnace. Today, with untapped energy like nervous agitation in his bones, the memories of last night buzzing his mind, the thought stops Bone in his tracks. Pulls him away from the lab to isolated rooms daubed in blood-red paint. To the empty horror of bodies stripped of all self, too similar to his for comfort. And then to Lever, who chose to lose herself, to let all identity fall away at once.

How casually she discarded her skin.

What was it she'd replied in the Wail? *"Maybe it's because we're sick of the skin we're in."* Bone thinks it over, twisting it this way and that. Every which way he looks at it, translates to the same meaning he felt then. Skin as entrapment, the unrelenting grip of definition. His skin is nothing but a prison, and he no longer knows why he's wearing it, why he's colluding in his own suffering. The feel of the scalpel nicking into bone and jarring awakens him to the fact that he's still working, driving on automatic pilot. He looks closely at the cut. His incision, though a trifle deep, okay, very fucking deep, is still perfect. He finds it amusing, but Nia finally snaps.

"What the fuck is up with you? You come in stupid late, looking ten times worse than normal, which by the way is bad enough, and now you cut a fucking *valley* in this poor bastard? Please tell me you haven't found a new drug of choice."

Respecting her right to be mad, Bone wonders what to say that won't sound insane. There's not much he can take from last night, from yesterday even, that won't sound like he's gone off the deep end of crazy. He drags off a glove and strokes a hand through his hair, unusually sensitive to the harsh pull of follicles under his palm. Hits upon the one part of it he can admit to. He hopes it's enough.

"I got laid last night," he rasps, tugging a clean glove on and wincing at the pain in his throat. He knew it'd hurt to talk, but this is ridiculous, like he's swallowed a handful of scalpel blades.

Nia's surprised laughter rings in his ear sharp as the shatter of glass. "Oh, is that it? Shiiit. And there I was worrying myself into early wrinkles. So, who was it?"

"A woman."

Rolling her eyes, Nia says, "Honey, I kind of guessed that bit. Never had you down for anything other than straight. I meant, what was her *name*."

"Oh." Bone smiles. "Lever."

Nia blinks. "Lever and Bone, Bone and Lever. Sounds like a bar. Probably a good one. I'd go, at any rate." She sluices leaking fluids and adds gently, "You sound horrendous, hon, truly. Shoot me if I'm prying, but what the hell did you and Lever get up to?"

Bone's lost for an answer. If he starts to go over what happened to make his throat hurt like this, his head will start hurting, too, and he'll drop his basket right here in front of Nia. He pulls whatever random bullshit he can out of midair. "Ran out of cigarettes, bought some cheap shit from a vendor. I think they used gun powder."

Nia quits sluicing and fixes him with a leery eye. "Tell me you're kidding. Because they do use shit that's potentially explosive, you know."

"I know. I try not to buy them."

"Yeah, right," Nia scoffs. "Just like you try not to drink liquid suicide. Oh, look." She rears back, aping shock. "Gas-malt and a gunpowder cigarette makes a Bone-bomb." Nia throws him a look of pure disgust. "You utter fucking remedial!"

He bites his lip and watches her sluicing his incision in angry sweeps. The water swirls round and round, becoming copper coils. His thoughts turn to that square of skin in his pocket, the inert shape of the snake, and that rush of familiarity comes again like a compulsion. Thoughts of the snake, of Lever, of transmog, race circles in his head, blurring into one another. Lost in the whirlpools and desperate for stillness, Bone grabs a spreader from the rack and rams it into the twisted torso of the corpse on the trolley, tugging hard against the torque of ribs and rigor mortis. Ribs creak, then crack, and the chest pops wide open, spraying whipped viscera into the room. Bone and Nia leap back.

"Fuck! Frag bullets." Bone's furious. "Sorry, Ni."

"Fine. It's fine," Nia says with the calm of a soul on the verge of homicide as she plucks bits of scrambled intestine off the front of her blue scrubs. "At least it provides an interesting visual of my Bone-bomb allusion."

Bone suppresses the urge to laugh at the comical distaste on her face. She'd probably punch him. She begins a lavish sluice of the floor, nozzle held at an exaggerated distance. Still raging, Bone's thoughts rush down the drain with those scraps of purplish red, lumps of faecal matter, and shards of bone. His stomach drops after them, hard and hurting, and in the new made quiet of his mind, another image unfurls. Lever. The tower of her flesh rising above him, coiled like a snake. Like the tattoo. Cold sweat explodes down his back. The walls of the lab distort, close in, transforming into a glass prison. His body twitches like fingers, like the urge to chase a bad habit. He tries to calm himself. What she did seemed impossible, magical, but it's just a mod, and he's a Mort. Finding mods is his business. He can make cold, hard fact of this. Find the way to her freedom for himself. He needs to start tracing her. Start with the scratch and see where it leads.

Bone yanks at his chest, his gloves, rolling the gored scrubs about the balled up ruin of his gloves and lobbing the resulting wad into the corner bin. "I'm out of here."

Nia pauses her sluicing, her shoulders tense. "Pardon? First you're hours late, then you want to leave after less than ninety minutes of actual work? We've got a cartload coming from the Buzz Boys at Precinct 60 after this lot's done. Zeoger'll want them processed stat."

Bone shrugs, beyond caring. "Zeoger's not my boss. We're doing these as a favour to him, not an obligation. We both know he's taking the piss."

"He's not the only one."

"Huh?"

Nia rushes the remaining gore down the drain with jerky swipes of the sluice. "I saw the records. You had a new Rope victim. Why was I not called in?"

He sighs, wishing she'd picked another moment to broach this. All he wants is to get the hell out, and now he has to add lies to abandonment. If she ever finds out, he'll lose the only person who gives half a damn about him. "Did you look in the drawer?"

"No."

"You do so, then, and let me know if you'd have appreciated being dragged out of bed for that. It gave me fucking nightmares, just wanted to spare you the same."

"Spare me? Oh please, do spare me, Bone. Spare me your bullshit!"

He wants to make it right. Make amends. Wants to tell Nia the truth, all of it, but she's not ready to hear it, and he's not ready to say it, and the need to start hunting the scratch burns a hole in him, the edges smouldering urgency. Bone attempts a smile, trying to make it warm when there's little warmth left in him to work with, to keep from showing how desperate he is to get away.

"I'm sorry, Ni. Really. It was a long fucking day, full of way too much weird to process, and I just wanted to get that body shifted and out of my sight. I should have brought you in. I fucked up."

"Yes, you should. So, why should I let you off those bodies? Give me one good reason."

All his reasons are good, and all of them way too personal to share. All he can do is stand there, staring. But Nia does what she always does and sees it all in him, anyway. He watches as her anger becomes aggravation, then worry, then a weary resignation he wishes he didn't have to put there because she has too much of that shit to deal with, what with who she is and where she came from and what that obligates her to.

"Fine. Go. Technically, you're still off shift, anyway. I'll cover you. I can manage."

"Are you sure?"

She snorts, crossing her arms, then uncrossing them, her face filled with horror at the mess she's smeared on them from her scrubs. "I'm clearly deranged," she tells him, grabbing the sluice again and turning it on herself. "Now fuck off before I come to my senses."

He grins, can't help it, and blows her a kiss that earns him a snort of amused derision. Grabbing his jacket, he races out of the lab, and bypassing the lift, takes the stairs two at a time. His fingers travel to his pocket, dancing over the fold of skin. It's been a long time, if ever, that he felt so full of purpose, so awake. Ironic, considering his mind's more unbalanced now than it's ever been. The dichotomy is laughable, but perhaps this is how he operates best. Who knows? He's never been given the chance to find out.

CHAPTER 22

*P*assing through the iron-bound southeast gate, Bone heads east to where the Zone's edge falls below the River Head, the industrial centre of the Spires. To the Avenue, a wide thoroughfare cobbled in gobbets of battered metals, worn and blackened by countless feet and wheels. On one side, tall buildings stippled with an array of unusual spires rest against each other like old men, exhausted after a hard day's work, grimed by ash drifting down from the River Head. On the other side rises a dizzying breadth of cliffs, made terrifying by the heavy weight of factories perched at the top, their walkways and hubs reaching into the clouded sky, black and distorted.

This avenue of pubs, clubs, and biker bars is where the Zone's most connected and fearsome personages wile the hours away between business deals and appointments. Most Morts don't know this place, and of those who do, few would dare to come. They wouldn't be welcomed. Bone walks to one of the more eccentric edifices, placed centrally along the boulevard and designed to resemble an Elizabethan tavern, whose beams of beaten steel crawl across lurid orange stonework. Snatch is a pounding Speed Punk pit owned by Spaz, leader of the Establishment. Inside, a mindless din from three jukes pumping out meaty down-tuned trash at an exaggerated volume fights with loud conversation, laughter, the chime of glass. Bone strides to the bar, nodding to a few acquaintances on his way. Snags a stool, his head already pounding.

He lights up a cigarette and orders his usual from the bar, from a girl called Caraway, too young for bar work. The daughter of a gang boss, in training for bigger things. His Mort's gaze catches the sprinkling of needle-fine dots in the corners of her eyes. New gen-mods. Bone wonders what she's had done. She takes his order with a nod and a cheeky grin.

"Hey, Bone-Man. How's shit?"

He smiles, "Shit's okay. Where's Spaz?"

"In back. You want he serves you next?"

"I do."

"No sweat." She places his drink down, winks, and scoots away to the side door, off to hunt down Spaz.

Gas-malts vary in quality. Here, the petrol on top is sluggish, slightly foggy, and stinks as though unrefined. It probably isn't as refined as it should be, but somehow eases him better than something the Wail might offer, sparking heat in his belly and easing the fingers of tension gripping his shoulders. He's just started to enjoy his smoke when the side door opens and a large, disreputable-looking rake saunters out, dressed in tatty punker gear. His skin's a riot of exquisite, tangling liquid-metal art, esoteric and obscure. It's expensive work and perilous, but if done correctly, astonishingly beautiful. Spaz. Snatch landlord, Establishment boss, stone cold killer, the gnarliest motherfucker in the whole of the Spires, he reaches Bone and leans on the bar, treating him to a lazy grin of welcome. "Well, well, what brings my good friend the Bone-Man to my humble tavern?"

"I need to know an artist," Bone says without preamble. Spaz likes dealing out small talk, but isn't so fond of it being returned; he's rarely ever encountered a moment he felt inclined to waste.

"Faceless wonder?"

Bone gulps his drink for false courage and shakes his head. "Not this time."

He reaches into his pocket and pulls out the rectangle of

Lever's skin before he can think better of it, straightening it out on the bar with loving fingers. It adheres to the wood just a little, still sticky in places, and Spaz's gaze hits it like frag missiles. He whistles low through his teeth, the sound grating, short and sharp, not a sound of surprise or admiration.

"Thas a piece of work, mate," he says, his face suddenly sharp as his accent, composed of planes and edges. "Where'd you get it?"

"Woman by the name of Lever left it in my care."

"Lever? She Mech?"

"Not even a little," Bone says, unable to hold back the smile.

"Fair enough." Spaz scrutinises Bone's face. "What is it you need?"

"I need to know the scratch."

Bone struggles to hide his elation. Spaz's initial reaction could've been anything, but Bone's sure it's the snake tattoo because he's never seen that demeanour crack before, not even a little. The snake is significant to Spaz, too. A question about transmog hovers on his lips, but he swallows it. Perhaps the tattoo is connected and perhaps it's not, but sharing his knowledge of transmog with Spaz might be hazardous to his health. He's not ready for hazard. Not yet.

Spaz pours Bone another drink, letting the reeking petrol pool, sinuous and thick through the whisky, and agitating the glass as it settles to mix the two just a touch. "Mind if I ...?" he asks, gesturing at the skin.

Bone reluctantly pushes it towards him and loses himself in what happens to be a perfect gas-malt. Spaz lifts the skin in his steel-tipped nails, holding it up to the meagre, reddish light. His teeth chew on a selection of custom lip metal, not available in the Zone for anything less than a small fortune. After a moment, he slides the skin back under Bone's fingers.

"That's Nathaniel's work," he says.

Bone looks up, curious. His fingers begin to stroke the skin, tracing the coils of the snake. "Nathaniel? I've not heard of him."

"You wouldn't have." Spaz leans close, his tattoos shimmering with the movement. Brings with him a smell of musky sweat, the warm citrus of alcohol, and a metallic twang that tickles the nose. "Colour me intrigued, but just how do you end up with this section of skin?"

Spaz can smell a lie from a mile away, but Bone can't possibly share. He'd have to admit to that knowledge of transmog. He licks his lips. "Very unusual circumstances," he offers and begins to feel a little dizzy, sickly heat pooling in his skull.

"Is this Lever still with us, or on your table?" Spaz's stare is unusually intense and Bone sweats under the scrutiny, the insides of his skull molten and liquid.

"She's quite alive," he says, though he can't imagine how life must feel to whatever it is Lever became. "At least, she was when I last saw her."

"So, why do you need to see the scratch?" Spaz asks, watching Bone's fingers ceaselessly tracing the coils of the snake.

Bone blinks sweat from his eyes and tries to force his fingers to leave the skin, to stop tracing those coils round and round. Only he can't. In the end, he has to roughly fold it over so he can't see the design. His head's swimming. Thoughts slipping through his grasp like eels. He racks his brain for an answer to Spaz's question because he hadn't thought of this. Stupidly, he hadn't thought much at all.

"She, uh … she's walking around missing a fair amount of skin. I need to locate her, make sure she's all right."

"Missing skin ain't no big problem round here, mate, and you know it," Spaz says, the ice blue of his eyes too bright in the dim light of the bar. He taps the folded skin with one razor-sharp nail. "Nice design, that."

Bone feels that nail as if it's on his own skin, and shivers. "It's interesting."

On Spaz's metal-laden mouth, a smile grows in slow motion, sinister as a shark's. "You looking to take some ink, my friend?" he asks, his voice so soft Bone's forced to lean in further, bringing them nose to nose. "Looking to mark that skin of yours, now Daddy's gone?"

Bone wants to look away from Spaz's too-direct gaze. It's hurting. Driving holes into the hot, soft tissue of his brain. His head ripples and dislocates. Needles of heat surround his pupils. He wants to blink them away, but he can no more move than he can stop staring. His heart palpates, and prickling sweat breaks out on the back on his neck. Crawls down his spine, snake-like. He shivers as the sensations refuse to dissipate, becoming part of his skin.

"I just want to ID her," he murmurs, but the words don't feel like they belong to him anymore, his intentions become blurry, uncertain.

Spaz leans back, abruptly freeing Bone from his gaze, leaving him rocked and shaken. "Well, if the urge strikes, Nate's your man. You'll need to cure that skin soon, no longer than a day or so."

Caught off guard, Bone says thoughtlessly, "You don't need to tell me."

"No, I don't." Spaz raises a brow one meaningful increment.

"Oh." Bone blinks. His head won't clear. Feels heavy, swollen with hot liquids. "Any suggestions?"

"Take it to Buster. He'll do a decent job." Spaz swipes his cloth across a patch of beer spilt by one of the bikers shoving past and growls at the man responsible, who flushes red, then white, and stammers an apology.

"Will do. And Nathaniel? Where's he?"

"On the edge of Pier Five, in the market beneath Adorn."

"That's not open to outsiders," Bone points out, tucking the skin carefully back into his pocket.

Spaz chuckles, the merry sound at odds with his uncompromising face. "They won't say no to the Bone-Man. Especially not Nate. He's one of ours."

"Ah." Bone nods. "Much obliged."

"No sweat." Spaz offers him a humourless, toothy grin. "You look after that skin."

Bone has no idea which skin Spaz means, but that's his cue to leave and he takes it in a rush, feeling Spaz's eyes on him even as he heads to the Zone Lake. He can't stop thinking about the snake tattoo. Spaz is right; Leif's dead and he no longer has to do as he's told. That thought in the lab about colluding with his suffering reoccurs. He wonders what the snake would look like on his back, what the needle would feel like, the prickles still tingling on his spine, almost a presentiment of the sensation. Curiosity about mods is something he's experienced before and dismissed as pointless. Now he's finding himself drawn to the idea, a heady sense of rebellion swirling in the pit of his belly. It would be so simple to ask Nathaniel to put the snake on his back. Bone laughs aloud, drawing more stares than usual.

"This shit's getting to me," he mutters to himself, willing the stares away. Wishes he could will himself invisible. "I'm not myself."

The thought stops him in his tracks because it's ridiculous. He's never known *himself* outside of Leif's expectations and Leif's not here anymore. He's reduced to a shadow, a ghost haunting Bone's head. Why should he listen to a ghost? What can a ghost do? There's no point being afraid. Fear is a box, and he's tired of living in boxes. Look where it's got him. Inexpressible rage fills him, pushing at the inside of his skin. He's fed up of every choice being made for him without his permission. He wants some fucking autonomy. Wants what Lever had, the power to leave who he is behind completely. But whilst he's still himself, whilst this skin is still attached, why not alter it? If he's going to get rid of it, surely he can do whatever he likes?

CHAPTER 23

*P*ier Five's a ramshackle jumble of concrete and steel, laced into a whole by time and invention. Bone threads his way through stifling streets, lit even at midday by guttering holo-torches, breathing in the sharp scent of burning metals and the rank odour of scorched flesh. The first sight of Adorn, above the cramped patchwork of shops, is always outlandish. A vast genetics lab still gleaming with new-build sheen, it sprawls with unconscious superiority across the final third of the pier.

Wandering into the open-plan yawn of the spartan reception area, Bone feels like a ghost himself. It's the aura of stillness, the anaemic palate of whites, creams, and beiges. He makes his way to the desk, accompanied by the rude clack of his shoes on polished plas-crete. There's just one girl manning reception, lost behind a mile of featureless cream plas-wood. She's new, but Adorn has a high staff turnover, so it's no surprise. Her face is more metal than flesh and reflects pale colours, rendering her a human puzzle of disparate pieces.

"I'm looking for Nathaniel," he says.

"At the end of the Arcade, through the tunnel." She points to a square portal, disguised by the bland colours of the wall. "Follow the signs to Mare's place, if you can." Dazzling violet-tinted eyes flash laughter. "She'll show you to Nathaniel's."

He peers at her name tag and stifles a grin. "Thanks, Violet."

She smiles, flirtatious. "You're welcome, Bone-Man."

Bone sets off down the cool, glass tunnel, wincing at the raucous advertisements scrolling its surfaces. Beyond the tunnel, the Arcade is unmistakably gang. A schizophrenic maze of workshops built from oddments of other buildings, totally out of place between the smooth underbelly of Adorn and the wood of the pier. There's a circus atmosphere of friendly chaos, and he finds Mare's place in the madness not by following signs, which are frankly confusing, but by asking. Mare's place is a hovel of a shop, colourful and brash, somewhere near the heart of the market. She's a blowsy, friendly sort, quite happy to drop everything to take him to Nate's place, despite the market being full of eager punters. Being a legend has its perks.

Nathaniel holds court in a clear glass box, jutting out over the water; a precarious, almost invisible studio. The thickness of the glass mutes the buzz of a scratch at work, but it invades Bone right to the marrow, vibrating there like an impact, and he has to drag his feet the remaining metres to the door. He's heard this sound a million times, but he's never felt the pull of it before. He didn't realise how much gravity there was in it. He stops for a moment to give the feeling his full attention. It's incredible. Through the floor, the water of the Zone Lake undulates, lazy as petrol on a gas-malt, throwing reflections of black light onto Nathaniel's face. Small, dark, and dressed like a pimp, his sleeves rolled up to expose sinewy forearms, he sits deep in concentration over the shoulder of a Skat three times his size. The Skat, a crew boss by the looks of the spike-pattern across his back, has his face all screwed up like he's shitting backwards, and Nathaniel looks up to Bone from his work, scornful amusement written over neat features.

"Mummy's boys and piss-ants," he says, as if to an old friend. "Mummy's boys and piss-ants, the lot of them." He holds up his free hand and beckons, a collection of silver rings flashing. "Come on in. I'm finished here before this weasel drops his bowel-load."

Bone longs to do as requested but his feet are welded to the floor. He continues watching, feeling almost supplicant, supple with longing, as Nathaniel finishes a deep well of black with two decisive passes, throwing a glare of disgust at the relief on the Skat's flattened red face.

"You sicken me," he snarls. "Get fucking lost."

The Skat nods politely, gathering up his jacket from the floor. "Same time next week?"

"Eleven sharp, leave your cowardice at the bar this time." Nathaniel dismisses him with a sneer and turns to Bone. "Well, what brings the Bone-Man to the Scratch?"

Bone loiters, teasing the threshold. "Business of an unusual kind. Spaz gave your name in connection to a piece of scratchwork."

"Really now? You got a corpse wearing my work?"

Bone finally manages to enter the parlour. "No." He hesitates for a second, but there's no point being coy so he just says it outright, "I met someone wearing it. A woman called Lever."

Several expressions fleet across Nathaniel's face, too fast to be interpreted, and the level of tension in the parlour cranks towards the oppressive. "Lever," he says quietly. "I've tattooed her only the once. She had the snake."

"That's right." Bone draws the skin out of his pocket and passes it to the spry scratch.

Nathaniel spends a long time looking at it. "Hell of a waste, this," he says, without looking up. "What would you like to know?"

"Everything. I want all her ID info."

Nathaniel sighs and raises his eyes to Bone's. "Sorry to disappoint, but there's nothing. She's a top tier Establishment freelancer and comes with the security allocation to prove it. SA means no fucking information."

Bone's stunned to silence. Spaz knows every freelancer his gang employs. The sly bastard didn't need to send Bone here; he could've told Bone everything there is to know about Lever himself. He doesn't know whether to laugh or lose his temper, and somewhere beneath, he worries that he misinterpreted Spaz's reaction to the snake. Perhaps it was only recognition. He looks at those copper coils between Nathaniel's palms and that irrepressible tug of knowledge hits hard, eliminating his fears. The snake is important. He feels it. Knows it. He's known it since he first touched it when he was fucking her.

Nathaniel lays the skin flat on his knees. "How did you get this if she's not dead?"

Bone leans forwards, touching his fingers to the snake's coils because he can't help himself. Nathaniel watches Bone's fingers move just as Spaz did, but his dark eyes are shuttered and inscrutable.

"She left it for me," Bone says, not really thinking about what he's saying and not really caring anymore.

"I see." Nathaniel treats Bone to a very straightforward look. "So, is that all you needed? I can't help you, and I have an appointment coming."

Bone sits back, his mind in a kind of turmoil, swirling round and round and encased in heat. He could go. But that's not what he wants. Not really. What he really wants is to leap into the unknown, into the abyss. He wants to choose, for once, what scares him instead of having fear forced upon him, and if he's honest with himself, he can't leave this parlour without doing that. He takes a deep breath.

"No," he says, "I'm not done. I wanted to ask if you'd scratch me. With that snake. Just as it was."

"As it was." It's no question. It's a statement groaning with meaning Bone is desperate to comprehend, but doesn't dare query in case he breaks the moment, breaks his resolve. Nathaniel places the skin on his workbench, a phantasm of glass etched with writhing, ghoul-like figures, and reaches out, not for his usual guns, but for one resting in its own exquisitely rendered glass rack. "Take off your shirt," he says.

"What about your appointment?" Bone asks.

"Fuck it," Nathaniel says. "I get to be the lucky bastard who pops the Bone-Man's mod cherry. Under these circumstances, I'd tell even Spaz to go fuck himself."

The prickles on Bone's spine sharpen and dig deep. His organs turn slow, aching somersaults as his body acknowledges the sudden loss of solid ground. He can almost smell the ozone scent of clouds brushing the undersides of his feet and adrenalin scours through him, making him light-headed. He shrugs off his jacket, and barely able to feel his fingers, pops his shirt buttons one by one.

Nathaniel spots the sore, puckering wounds caused by Lever's gold fingertips and chuckles. "Yeah," he says, almost to himself, "you met Lever all right." Then he frowns. "Did she wound your back?"

Bone shakes his head. "No," he replies. "I wounded hers."

Nathaniel looks at the long square of skin on his workbench. "Doesn't look wounded to me," he says. "Looks like it's been well cared for." He points at the roll bar behind Bone. "Turn round and lean over that."

He waits till Bone's in position, then sets his needle to Bone's back and begins, freehand, to mark the outline. The pain of the needle is a revelation. It hurts worse than Bone expected, but it's good pain. With every fresh pass, he can feel himself solidifying. This tattoo will not only change who he is, the way he's seen, it'll change the way he sees himself. Every time he looks at his face, he'll *know* who he is. He's the Bone who chose. It's such a huge difference, it feels almost unreal.

Nathaniel's breath cool on his burning skin, Bone asks, "What's she like?"

"You don't know?"

"I only knew her for a few hours," he says, smiling.

Nathaniel draws more ink into his needle and settles back over the blood-smeared symbol tangling over the skin of Bone's back. "I've met her maybe three times, myself, all told."

"What do you remember?"

"That she's trouble. I heard of her before I met her. She's young, reckless, takes too many chances. That, and her tenacity, is what secured her the position with the Establishment." The drone of the needle accompanies his voice like a counterpoint in a symphony, uplifting and strangely moving. "She took the pain like you are. Without fear. That Skat you saw with me earlier. Medlock, his name is. Wants to be scratched for the notoriety. Can't handle the pain because of it. Your reasons have to be solid. He'll find out the hard way. They always do."

Bone squints as spectres of light like handfuls of gold dust dance off the water, lancing into his eyes. He can't think of anything to say, and so remains silent. Nathaniel stops only once to tell his appointment, a skinny-looking freak with a wasp-thin waist and black eyes, to come back tomorrow at the same time. Otherwise, he remains bent over Bone's back, deep in concentration. Hours pass, and the pain of the needle flows over Bone, building him bit by bit as it forms the snake on his skin. His chin digs hard into his forearms, and his legs start to cramp, but he's never felt so content.

"Going to add a haze of red melting into the copper here, to soften it," Nathaniel says, finally snapping the silence. "Lever's had no such haze, but I want this to be the best work I ever do. Your skin's the perfect canvas, like a sheet of ice. I can live for free till I rot on the type of renown this'll bring me."

Bone thinks of the blood his nails drew up into Lever's snake as they fucked, and watches Nathaniel fit a new needle into his gun, filling it with a colour somewhere between dried blood and deepest poppy. He drifts off as the drilling heat begins again, and his gaze is drawn up to the sky, sucked higher and higher, until he's sure he can see beyond the farthest atmosphere. Dragging his eyes away with an effort, he focusses on Nathaniel's profile, reflected in the glass, intense with concentration. He's not really in the mood for talking, anymore, but there's something else he needs to ask before they're done here.

"What is this snake, this tattoo? I know it's nano, intelligent. But in what way? Like IM shit, or something more?"

Nathaniel stops again for a moment, considering. He starts back in with the needle and says, as if picking his words with great care, "It's deep wet-tech. Not remotely like usual nano-ink, more intelligent. It'll link to your neural networks, sync with your brain-waves. React to your moods, your thoughts, but not in a static way, not like feedback. It thinks, not like we do, but as near as damn it in a basic sense, improvising movement and response based on your rhythms and emotions. Perhaps even more. It's deeper tech than I can understand, in truth. I'm just a scratch."

"So, it's alive?"

"In so far as nanotech *can* be alive, yes, it is."

"What will it feel like?"

Bone senses Nathaniel's shrug through the needle. "I don't know. I don't have one, and I've never asked. But it won't start interacting with you until you're healed. It has to build connections first, make contact as it were."

"Fuck," Bone says, light-headed, "I picked a hell of a thing for my first mod."

Nathaniel lets out a short bark of amusement. "No shit. Just this red, then we're finished. Sorry it's a bit of a marathon session, but you have to do it in one sitting or it won't activate, the nanites'll fail to synchronise with each other and die off. Not much'll kill them once they're all set, but until they are, they're vulnerable. How's your pain level?"

Bone shrugs. "It hurts." He doesn't care. It doesn't matter.

Night draws in over the lake, and heat begins to morph to pain that fills Bone hard as a skeleton, binding him deep into his own flesh and then catapulting him outside of himself. He concentrates on the clouds dissolving through the dark grey of the sky, hypno-tised by the rhythmic movements as they billow and fade, thinning to a haze and dissipating like smoke. By slow degrees, his mind revolves around what's happening here. He can't begin to regret it. It feels right. Nathaniel continues for another forty minutes, making the session nine hours in total, before replacing the needle with his spray gun, suffusing the sore skin with a fine wash of cool antiseptic solution. Chuckling at Bone's moan of relief, he swipes away with a clean cloth, his hands gentle, clearing the blood so he can view his work.

"My finest work yet," he says proudly. "Better than Lever's by a clear mile, and I actually took greater care with her at times. Thin skin she had, delicate. You could see the veins beneath, see the blood pumping."

Bone peers round at Nathaniel. "She looked like she had no skin."

"So do you," Nathaniel says as he adds a layer of protectant from a different spray gun. He begins to dismantle the needle gun. "You can shower as normal, but don't over clean this or it won't heal. You can spread salve or antiseptic cream if you need to, thin and even, just once every twenty-four hours. It'll scab over in a couple of days. Don't pick it, or you'll disrupt the process, not to mention destroying my finer work. At which point I'd hunt you down and ram this here needle up a choice orifice."

Bone chuckles. "You got it."

"How you feeling?" Nathaniel asks with a sudden grin. "Different?"

Bone cranes to see his back reflected in the glass. Seeing it there, etched permanently on his skin, makes him want to burst out laughing. It's amazing. Beautiful. The snake looks real, just as it did on Lever, but on his skin it looks like it's waiting in the cool shadow of a rock, coiled to strike at unsuspecting prey.

"Different? Oh, yeah. To say the least."

Nodding understanding, Nathaniel says in a gentle tone unlike his usual, "It's customary to get your permanent mods at puberty, you're, what … mid-thirties?"

Bone dips his head. "Thirty-five."

A disbelieving snort escapes Nathaniel. "That's a long time naked, man. A long time. Might be wise to cut yourself a little time to get accustomed to it." Nathaniel hands Bone his shirt back and says, "You can stay in the Zone a while. There's places open all night serve good drinks, good food."

"Don't be fooled by my honorific; I'm not Zone folk, I still can't hang around," Bone replies, fumbling with buttons. "I'll be thrown out *over* a fucking gate rather than through it." His hands are shaking. It's not that nagging urge for alcoholic ease, though he certainly could use a drink; he's actually feeling rather hungry.

"I'm sure Spaz has told you this already, but you're different. That's why you have an honorific. You'll be okay here for a night, no problem." Nathaniel strips his gloves off and washes his hands with brisk motions under the antiseptic spray gun. "You go back out through Adorn, stick to the left, along the eastward edge of the Pier, and find a place called Neophyte. It's a Skat bar, rough and noisy as hell, but the barmaid's a good lady, good as they come. She'll look after you, and she's a friend of Lever's. Knows her far better than I. You can pick her brains and satisfy that burning curiosity I'm sensing I did nothing to get rid of. But I wouldn't mention this business with Lever's skin."

"Hah, no, not a good idea." Bone pulls his jacket on, wincing as the heavy weight of it awakens a chorus of pain. "Thank you. For everything. What do I owe?"

Nathaniel holds his hands up, white teeth gleaming like stars. "No, Bone-Man, this was my pleasure. Like I said, I can mooch forever off this job. You just wear it with pride."

Bone thinks of Leif's face, and he's amazed by how little he cares what his father would say about this. "Oh, I am. You have no idea."

He shakes Nate's hand warmly and leaves his parlour, gentle ripples of pain swelling and ebbing beneath the harsh weight of his jacket and shirt. Wrapped in serene excitement so intense it consumes him whole, he trails the streets of the Arcade, still heaving with vibrant life. Strolls through the tunnel, back into the manic overload of Pier Five proper, and for the first time, he's not merely an observer, or seeker of information; he's an interlocking piece of the construction. The sudden collapse of his isolating bubble shouldn't feel this good. But it does. Some small, essential part has begun to wriggle its way loose, pulling towards the icy sky, straining to join with the black of night.

Bone wanders along the east side of the Pier to the club called Neophyte. It's tiny, a rusted shed of corrugated iron and old cement formed into chaotic bubbles. Inside, a live band stands cramped on a stage of upturned steel crates, tearing at their instruments in violent, eye-clenched rage, the singer roaring with incoherent anguish at nothing but the smoke. The room is filled with Skats, piped up, bonged up, and toking on massive reefers. He squeezes through cramped tables to the bar. To the barmaid Nathaniel said would be his caretaker tonight. She doesn't look caring, her face unbending as iron under a rioting mess of red and purple dreads.

"You want a drink?" she shouts over the racket.

"Gas-malt," Bone says, wondering if this is the right woman. Perhaps her shift has been and gone. But then, a smile of pure silver glimmers through the iron and he sees what Nathaniel meant. She slaps a hand on the bar, as though tickled by some mad joke.

"Comin' up, sugar."

The malt, when set before him, makes him groan with profound satisfaction. It's perfect. The whisky a syrupy brown so rich it looks like poured caramel and the petrol a soft olive, slightly smoky and reeking of engine metals. He downs it in one, feeling it ignite in his belly, and orders another. She sets two more down before him and grins widely, silver all through.

"I like a man who can drink."

"I like to drink." He shifts his stance at the bar, closing his eyes and smiling at the scrape of material against his sore skin.

The woman leans across the bar, her arms folded before cleavage as luxurious as the falls in her hair. "You don't come to the Zone to change, do you, Bone-Man?" she says, her eyes curious and sharp with interest. "But today you seem different. Today I feel change took you by surprise."

Bone shakes his head and says with no small pride, "Today, I took change by surprise."

"That's the best way to take it." She reaches a slender, ring-laden hand over the bar to him. "Ebony. Ebony Waits. You'll get to know me."

He shakes the proffered paw. "A pleasure."

"You look like a man with a hankering for a good, solid meal," she says, soft and warm and entirely silver.

"I could eat a fucking herd of cows," he tells her.

Ebony busts out a laugh, explosive and luminous as a bomb blast. "Lucky for you, the lout who passes for a chef in this dump used approximately an entire herd in tonight's attempt at stew. One hot bowlful of cow coming up."

They exchange a moment of absolute cool before she rushes off to serve another punter yelling for *"more beers now, Ebony babe"* over the din. Content to wait and knowing she won't forget him, Bone turns to view the stage, his gas-malt cradled in loving fingers. He tunes into the noise. It's not discord or aggression, but harmonious melding of bloody fury and pounding rhythms, a heavy reservoir of human gasoline. Fuel for the soul. He falls forwards into it, letting it ride over him.

Several hours later, when Ebony's shift is ending, his phone vibrates. Bone wrestles the phone from his pocket, yelping as it pulls his jacket too hard against sore skin. Ebony's promised to escort him to the Bullet, so he can get home; maybe grab some sleep, so he can turn up at work later somewhere near to functional. He's been hoping to finally find the time to ask her about Lever, the bar being too full to grab more than a few minutes banter here and there. He checks the screen and groans.

"What the fuck, Stark, it's a bit bloody early."

"Early?"

"As in, it's already tomorrow."

"Well, go and get some fucking sleep then," comes the brusque reply. "Miracle of fucking miracles, I finally got green lit for going

after Burneo. We hit the sewer at first light. I'll stream you the location and the exact time. Don't be late."

Several hours of drinking wipe out in one fell swoop, leaving
Bone way too sober. This business with Lever has offered a temporary, much needed diversion from the unpleasant realities of the
Rope case. His failings. Those expectant, nameless corpses. He's
terrified of going back to the sewer, but his new understanding of
the nature of choice has strengthened his connection to those
corpses. Their choice was stolen, too. That they chose to get their
tags is incidental, they didn't choose what came afterwards. The
look on their faces is eloquent proof of that. He has no choice but
to help them.

"I'll be there," he says, and hangs up, watching as the flickering
lights of his cell announce the arrival of Stark's stream. He glances
at the location and groans yet again, even more profoundly.
There'll be no time for talking; he needs to sleep, and soon. Dawn
comes in three hours. Ebony strolls around from the bar, winding a
scarf about her neck. "Ebony?"

"What's the matter, hon?"

"Change of plan," he says with a rueful smile. "Can I possibly
surf your sofa for the night?"

Ebony puts her arm through his and gives it a little squeeze.
"Of course, you can," she says, and as they walk out into the brisk
cold of early morning, she adds playfully, "Just lucky my girl-
friend's not over. A pretty boy like you on my sofa would take one
hell of an explanation."

CHAPTER 24

*B*one hurries along scrubby pathways, wound between mountainous factories, worried he might be late. Last night, contorted onto Ebony's tiny sofa, he did the unexpected: slept. Deep, dreamless sleep. He feels so awake now, it's like light pours through his skull, illuminating every last corner. He reaches a row of massive silos and squeezes through the gap. Just ahead, over a wasteland of gravel and brush, the ground falls away to a steep bank. At the bottom, on the opposite side, sewer hub portals yawn in the base of a concrete wall, covered in Establishment graffiti. Bone squints hard, but he can't see anyone there, meaning he's not the one who's late. Grinning, Bone runs across the wasteland and over the edge of the bank, his feet sliding on loose gravel.

He settles against the wall to wait, his body balanced as usual on the angular jut of a shoulder. The steady ripples of soreness on his back make him grin again, he feels so different already. He pulls a hot sandwich from his pocket, bought from some diseased-looking grill shop beside the River Head Zone gates. The greasy stench of bacon makes him feel a little sick, but one mouthful in, he's overwhelmed with the flavours and begins to devour it, just like last night's cow stew and the cinnamon roll Ebony sleepily shoved into his hand as he left her apartment. He's not used to hunger taking him like this, whole and sensual, a derangement of the senses. He finishes the sandwich in four bites, balling up the greasy papers and tossing them aside. He's usually way more mindful, but this place is all desolation and belching toxins; a little rubbish won't make any difference.

It's too early for the factories to be active, and the air is still. Into the silence chirrup the low, fluting calls of Establishment runners. Bone resists the urge to yell at them. There's no guarantee they're here because he is. The River Head has long since been Establishment territory, and the runners use it as a training ground. The dangerous heights and funnels of factories, the perilous walkways and bridges between, make it the perfect place to drill green runners, especially at this time of day. He pulls out his cell instead. There's something he should do but he can't for the life of him think what it might be. It's driving him a little crazy now. He's still striving to figure out what it is when Stark's car skids down the bank and slides to a halt some twenty feet away. Bone lays his thumb over his cell's activation pad, the light blinking out as Stark exits the car and makes his way over.

Two of his team are with him. A man built like a tank, the same width as Stark but almost as tall as Bone, with a rough-and-ready sort of face the colour of polished teak. He's ex-military by the looks. Probably Suge. The other team member is a small, slender woman who barely reaches even Stark's shoulder. She's got the same demeanour as Spaz, and he knows she must have been raised gang without even asking. She's got ruby red hair and direct brown eyes that hit harder than a bullet train. Behind her shoulder pokes the thick stock of an immense gun.

"This is Suge," Stark announces as they reach Bone. "And this here is my right hand, Tress."

"Hi."

Suge nods his head and Tress says, "He's prettier than I thought he'd be. Are you sure we want to get him all filthy?"

Bone snorts. "I could give a shit about keeping clean, I'm aiming for leaving alive."

"Then you'll fit in just fine," Suge informs with a big, toothy grin. His teeth are like plasterboards, flat, white, and even, probably mods. Bone wouldn't want to end up being bitten by this man. Fuck knows what those teeth are hiding.

Stark chuckles. "Tal, boot," he yells and it pops out. He hands them each a long, thick torch and a pair of black rubber waders. "This is all we've got," he says. "So don't fucking wreck it."

Bone hefts his torch. "This is it?"

"And that's luckier than you know. I'm here on sufferance and so are you. We could've been told to bring our own torches and strap plastic around our legs. I'm the Notary's least favourite person right about now—next to you, of course."

"Me? What the hell did I ever do to them?"

Stark raises both brows. "Not a clue. But I tell you what, I got the distinct feeling in my oh-so-delightfully brief meeting with the Notary Board that if you weren't who you are, you'd be in some hole somewhere, bound up in a strait jacket and summarily dismissed from their concern."

"Interesting," Bone says, for lack of anything else to say.

"Isn't it?"

Stark taps the window. The boot snaps shut, disappearing seamlessly into the body of the car, and Tal drives off up the incline, spattering them with loose gravel. They pull the waders on over trousers and boots, and follow Stark into the outlet, setting a swift pace through the confusing muddle of the sewer. Moving in a tight knot, their torches on full beam. At this pace, it takes an hour and a half to reach the first wafts of sulphur. They pause to snap on their masks and continue at the same speed. Bone reckons that if Suge and Tress would countenance it, Stark would have them all sprinting.

Fifteen minutes or so later, Suge moves closer to Stark.

"Movement. Up ahead."

"Rats?"

"No. Too big. Someone's walking in the tunnels."

"Sewer folk?"

Suge shrugs. "Maybe. Not big enough to be Burneo, if reports hold true."

"Okay, keep track. Let's see what they do."

From that point, it gets very weird, very fast. Every tunnel Stark leads them into, the figure is already there, in the distance, either waiting or already moving, as they're being encouraged. Shown they're on the right path so far. The pattern continues for almost an hour until their distant companion disappears down an unknown offshoot, reappearing a moment later only to stand, as if waiting. Expectant. As soon as Suge reports the change of tack, Stark calls a halt.

"Are we gonna follow?" Tress says, getting straight to business.

Stark nods slowly. "Wary as we go. Reckon Burneo's expecting us. What say you?"

"Don't disagree," Tress replies. "I second on the wariness, though."

"Agreed," Suge says. "I don't much like the way this character's managed to stay at the edge of my range."

Bone's not really part of the team, but Stark looks at him next. Bone shrugs. "I guess we follow with caution," he says.

"Suge, take point."

They trail their enigmatic guide deep into parts of the sewer Stark says he's never seen on the maps he's had access to, ending up in tall, narrow tunnels that look far too old to be meant for the Spires' use.

"These must be for the cities before New Detroit," Stark says, awed, flitting his torch over the vaulted ceilings, riddled with mineral deposits building into thousands of tiny, sharp stalactites. "We've got to be close to the cavern again. Burneo's close."

"You sure?" Bone asks, through teeth beginning to chatter a little. He's not fond of all this unrelenting dark and cold, even surrounded by Stark's team, with their easy comraderie and confidence.

"Positive. Come on, we need to speed up."

They move faster, into the necrotic shadows of an even

narrower tunnel, startling a huge colony of rats gathered on the hissing length of a pipe. As the torchlight hits their eyes, the rats scream. They boil off the pipe in a panic, frantic to escape, straight over the small group in their way. Claws tangle in hair. Tails leave stinging red marks on skin as they scramble for freedom. Trapped in the narrow confine of constricting walls, the team form a tight scrum to protect each other from the worst, but Bone freezes in place, paralysed with shock. Seeing his distress, Suge grabs his jacket, yanking him to safety.

"Protect your eyes, dammit!" Stark yells through his mask. "These things'll eat their way through, if they have to."

"That's about the last thing I ever wanted to hear," Suge yells.

Stark laughs. "You'll be all right, your eyes aren't exactly edible."

"And that's supposed to make me feel better how exactly? I got plenty organic bits to chew through, thank you."

"And here I was, counting on you chewing them first. Tell me, Suge, what the fuck use are those teeth if you don't utilise them in these situations?"

"On *rats*?" Suge gives his boss the middle finger. "You want them chewed, you fucking chew them."

"Without salt? Philistine."

When the last rats have scrambled past, the four of them separate out, soaked and filthy, and check each other over for scratches that could putrefy in mere hours down here.

Stark whacks his hands swiftly through the mess of his hair. "Fuck knows what they've had their paws in," he mutters.

"Next time you tell me you need me on a special case, I'm telling you to go fuck yourself," snaps Tress. She glares at him from under her fall of red hair, scrabbled to knotty tangles and larded with dirt.

"Ah, come on, you love this shit."

Tress kicks water at his legs, chuckling as he leaps away. "He do this to you, too?" she asks Bone.

Bone's shivering openly now, clutching his jacket closed with both hands, convinced a rat might appear and try to wriggle inside. "Last time I followed him down here," he tells her, "I ended up face to face with Burneo, and then fell on a corpse."

"Sounds about right," she says dryly, making him laugh.

Suge briefly flicks his torch at Stark's face to catch his attention. Stark squints and rumbles, "Put it down, Suge. Fuck's sake, before I go blind."

"I saw our guide before those rats swarmed."

Back in business mode, Stark splashes over to his side. "Show me where."

Suge leads them ten metres down the tunnel to a deep indent where a maintenance box could've been at some point, but now it lies empty and Suge flares his torch from the top to the bottom.

"He was here," he says. He swings the torch around, hunting for exits of any kind in the slick walls in the immediate vicinity. There are none. "Must've gone ahead when the rats swarmed."

Stark huffs, clearly annoyed to have lost time, and Tress pipes up, "So let's hustle before we lose the fucker."

"Right on, sister."

Bone envies their insouciance. His heart is still hammering away, aching in his chest. One more thing goes wrong and he'll lose it like he did before Burneo found him last time. Burneo. It's only now, when he's already down here, looking, that he truly understands that he doesn't want to find Burneo again, or be found by him. He does want answers, and he believes Burneo may know enough to give them a lead, if he can find enough sanity to convey it. But how can they trust him? The Gift was horribly mutilated, and Burneo did that just to get his attention. To get Stark's. Whatever he might have to show them, whatever side he might think himself on now, he's no less deranged, no less dangerous. They shouldn't forget that. Bone won't. But he's not sure about Stark. He's not sure Stark sees anything but what he wants to see. And that's dangerous, too.

CHAPTER 25

As they set off again, nervous tension flares beneath Stark's skin, a subcutaneous net of fire. He's worried about leading his team into danger, as always. Determined that if anyone is to be lost or hurt, it'll be him. That's what he took from his experiences at the Wharf, the losses he caused going after Teya—better him in the line of fire than anyone else. He's thrown himself into danger a hundred times and more, to save his team, and there isn't a bone in his body that doesn't hate him for it. How he's alive is a mystery to him, but he keeps demanding it of himself because apathy is intolerable, it costs too much. Trudging on through freezing, calf-deep water and musty darkness, they come swiftly to a bolted steel door.

"Is this where he wants us to go? Through a locked door?" Stark's thoroughly pissed off.

Suge looks worried. "Hope I wasn't following an implant glitch this whole fucking time."

Stark dismisses the notion with a snort. "Your eyes have never failed me yet." He turns to Bone and Tress. "You two wait here. Stay vigilant. Suge and I will run a double-back and sweep."

They take the tunnel two feet at a time, examining every last inch of the walls. On the right, multitudes of pipes, barely an arm's thickness, cling flush to the slimy brick, no doors or exits to be seen, and on the left, the side of the indent, sheer walls drip with unnatural-looking, yellowish-white growths of sewer moss. Stark touches one and rears away, grimacing. The tunnel floor is smooth, slippery under foot and it's unlikely anyone would happily submerge beneath the water, there's no telling what chemicals might lurk in the yellow slew's composition. So, where did their guide go? Reaching the section where the rats waylaid them, they peer at the pipes, but there's no way out big enough for a human. Disappointed, they turn back, pointing their torches at the roof despite its height. Too high to be a likely escape route, even for an augment. About thirty paces on from the wall indentation, Stark spies something.

"Move your beam over to mine."

In the roof of the tunnel, almost disguised by darkness, there's an opening. A round portal, similar to those used to exit to the street, but there are no streets at this depth and no ladder or inset rungs, either up to or within the hole itself. If it's a route to anything, it would be for maintenance, only there are no rungs up the brick, no way to reach it.

"How the hell does anyone climb that without a rope?" Suge says, frowning. "And where's the rope, if they did?"

Shining the powerful beam of his torch right up into it, Stark shrugs. "Beats me."

"I can't see an end, even at full range," Suge says. "If we're being led somewhere, I'm pretty sure it's not there."

"I fucking hope not. Do me a favour," Stark demands of his team member. "Access your recorder. Describe what you saw in the indent."

Suge takes a deep breath. "I hate this; it hurts."

Closing his eyes, he's silent for a moment, his face contorted with discomfort and then he begins to speak, voice sing-song as memory reels out the imagery, seared in by his augments. "It was a snapshot. A glimpse. Light reflected on eyeballs. Wide eyes. The light reflected off a good portion. Too much sclera, very white, very clean. But he or she must have been wounded. I saw denuded flesh, bloodied muscle, a lot of it with no yellow of fat. So, a deep wound, catastrophic. Recent, too. No chance to heal as yet, or no money to buy medicare." His eyes open, the glow of his augments flicking out a second or so later. "That's it."

"Sounds like one of Burneo's people to me," says Stark. "So, we're definitely on the right track. Reckon we're supposed go through that door, then, so let's get on with it."

Back at the bolted door, her facial expression a textbook for anyone seeking to convey disgust, Tress is tapping a foot. Quite a feat, considering she's submerged to the calves. "I think you need to take a close look at our exit, here."

Stark steps up to examine it. A quick check of the bolt, almost as thick as Stark's thumb and fully the length of his forearm, finds it choked with rust and sulphurous deposits.

Bone, standing beside Stark as he surveys the blockage, raises a brow. "So? We didn't bring equipment for this kind of shit."

Stark makes a face. "Like I said, my permission to come down here was on sufferance. I'm lucky I was given leave to sign out torches and waders. Had to pay for ration bars out of my own fucking pocket." He blows out, frustrated, and taps at the rust with the butt end of his torch. "If I'm willing to break one of these fucking lights, we could bash the stuff off. It's rotten."

"So, what's stopping you?" Tress inquires from behind.

Stark turns to look at her, hefting his torch at the door. "We have no map for what's behind there, and our guide's gone AWOL. Losing a torch would be a bad idea. I've been down here with a broken torch already. Not fun."

"Hell no," agrees Bone wholeheartedly, shivering in his jacket. He worries Stark. He's too vulnerable, too fragile. If he had any option to leave him behind, Stark would have, but time is not their ally. Whilst they stumble about, more victims are dying, he's sure of it. There's no *time* to be careful.

"Gun?" Tress asks, reaching back to clasp the butt of the massive firearm at her shoulder. It's an antique, found down here in the sewers generations back and passed to Tress from her father.

A Smith and Wesson magnum, reworked to take the type of bullets that reduce human bodies to pasta sauce.

"Leave that relic be, you fuckwit," Stark snaps, too irritated by this setback, the Notary's parsimony, and just about every damn thing else in his way to keep his temper. "Add explosions to this sulphur, and we're looking at third degree burns." He stares at the door furiously, until something occurs. "You didn't happen to bring *all* your ancient shit with you, did you, Tress? That old cosh maybe?"

Tress takes a step back. "Oh, no you don't," she says to him. "You're not wrecking my cosh."

Stark holds out his hand. "C'mon, one for the team."

Grumbling, she wrestles it out of her pocket and shoves it into his hand. "Don't you dare destroy it," she snaps, as he slaps his torch into her hand in exchange.

"Of course not, sister, it's the bolt I'm going to destroy," he says, hoping that's true, because she'll have his hide if not. "Now give me some light on this bastard."

Wielding the cosh in a way that makes Tress wince, Stark pounds the bolt until his hands are covered with a fine dusting of damp, brownish muck that seeps into his sleeves, staining his shirt cuffs. When clean steel finally begins to gleam through the murk, he stops and wraps the meaty strength of his hand about the whole protruding end, pulling with all his strength. There's a deep, squealing grind of noise and the bolt moves back a clear inch. Stark hands Tress the cosh, snorting at her immediate scrutiny of its surface, and takes the bolt again, this time with both hands.

"Brace me up, Suge."

Suge stands behind Stark and wraps his arms about his chest, his torch held across like a bar. "Go."

Stark bares his teeth, bunches his muscles, and yanks. The bolt makes a loud skree of metal on metal as it shoots backwards, sending Stark's arms flying. Suge stumbles, struggling to keep himself and Stark upright as the squeal of the bolt echoes back through the tunnel into silence, eerie as a rat's scream. The two men wobble for a moment before finding their feet.

"Get those torches up," Stark says, and holds out a hand to Tress for his. Shoving it into the crook of his shoulder, he faces the door. "I want all those beams in there the second it opens, understood?"

Grabbing the handle, Stark turns it and pushes with all his might, crying out as it slams open and dazzling lights sear his eyes. Shadowing dazed eyes, blotched with after-images like half-exposed photographs, Stark walks in to the glare, narrowing his gaze to slits. The long throat of a steep, narrow stairwell spirals on and on into liquid shadow. Its rail and risers aren't quite as rotten as those on the cavern stairs, steel still visible through portions of rust, but the distance is twice as deep. The light flicks off, a shuttered eye.

Bone elbows in beside him, triggering the light to flash back on and illuminate the abyss. "Fuck!" he snaps, blinking and gritting his teeth. Points with a shaking finger. "Down there?"

Stark grins at his tone. It's the twin of his horrified reluctance in the cavern. "You got a problem with heights or something?"

"I fucking hate them."

"I can only apologise, brother. We do indeed go down there, but gently does it." He turns to take in the whole team. "Well-spaced and soft-footed. Be on your guard, all of you. You can turn your torches off. If we keep moving, that light will stay on."

The reverberation of feet on steel follows them loud as an avalanche as they make their way down under the brash yellow light. Fine, reddish dust billows up around them, falling in a continuous stream through the risers. By the time they reach the bottom, they're smeared head to toe, dust transformed to thick paint by sweat, despite the chill in the dank air. They're in a cramped stairwell, lit by muddy green light, and face a single emergency exit door emblazoned with the GyreTech logo, faded to a cracked blur.

"GyreTech?" Suge frowns.

"Probably their portion of the sewer," Stark says. "Fucking mega-corps have to scribble over everything they own."

A smaller logo sits beneath GyreTech's, reduced to a few hints of circular reddish-brown lines against the dirty blue of the door. Bone rubs a finger over it, frowning. "Wonder what this was?"

"Allocation number? All these corridors will be numbered if they're owned."

Stark's not interested because it doesn't matter. Not now. They've come in the right direction, he's sure of it, and impatient as he is with all these fucking obstacles, he's determined to keep pushing on. There's little time to waste. He assesses the door. It's sealed from the outside with large metal straps, so corroded their edges crumble in Stark's hands.

"Let's get these off."

It takes them long minutes, using the long, reinforced butts of their torches as levers, to pull the metal bands off rusted bolts, working them to and fro till they snap or fall loose. The only obstacle after that is the fact that the door's locked from the inside.

"Someone really doesn't want us down here," Bone says quietly, sounding as if he'd like to oblige them.

"Screw what they want," Stark says. "I want in. I want *answers*. I think they're through here." He bangs the door with a fist.

Tress coughs, trying to wipe her face. It looks like a mask of blood. "My cosh won't work on that son of a bitch. What do you suggest, boss?"

He considers only a moment before saying, "You may use your gun."

Tress's eyes flash surprise. "But, the sulphur."

Stark shrugs. "It's either we shoot this fucker out, or we go back." He pulls his mask down briefly to sniff the air. "Sulphur's not so bad down here. Just traces. Don't know about you, sister, but I want to carry on forwards."

Tress nods agreement. "Sure," she says. "But you're telling me you're not the slightest bit concerned about going through a door someone felt needed barring on the outside when it's locked from the fucking *inside*?"

"I didn't come all this way to quit at the first hurdle," he tells her dryly.

She raises a brow. "Strictly speaking, this is the second hurdle."

"I love it when you're strict," he says, and points at the lock. "Now, blow a hole through that fucker for me."

Tress salutes with her middle finger. "We'd best move back up the stairs a bit," she says. "This is likely to get messy."

From the top of the first rise, Tress takes aim and blows half the door off. The team ducks, yelling, as a hot blast of fragments and ignited sulphur gas flies backwards, debris raining across the stairs in a deafening crescendo, bouncing off skin, hair, and clothes; singeing where it lands. Stinking smoke fills the air, stinging dust-reddened eyes to tears. Stark glares at Tress.

"I said blow a hole through the lock, not blow half the fucking door off."

"Well, at least we're in," she replies lightly.

The ringing song of steel fades as smoke thins to an opaque whisper upon the air. Striding out of cover, Stark pushes the remains of the door. It teeters, creaks open a few inches, and crashes down as the top hinges give way, making another cloud of choking dust. There's a moment where, despite an urge to cough debris from aching lungs, they all cease to breathe, waiting for something to happen, but it passes, leaving them edgy, over-ener-gised, and then Stark leaps across the threshold, with Bone and Suge following. At the rear, Tress moves on swift feet to the wall, locating a switch. With a low-level hum and buzz, the line of bulbous, caged lights above their heads attempt a flicker into life. Only a few make it, casting out soft, greenish radiance identical to the lights outside, illuminating a long corridor.

Bone frowns. "This is not a fucking sewer."

"No shit," says Stark, as bewildered as Bone sounds.

At the end of the corridor, Stark's heavily strapped shoulders break through another locked door into a long, fairly wide room.

Down the central line of the room, computer equipment, large screens, and strange, tall, black objects lean against one another in a mess of smashed glass and dented metals. Ranks of suspension-unit tubes line the walls. Long since empty, they're blighted with wide blooms of thick, mottled mould pushing through a crazy paving of cracks. The team edge inside on uneasy feet. There's a faint, putrid scent. They've all seen things that'd make less-exposed humans never want to see again, but something here, some taint or vapourous memory on the air, primes the nerves to full alert.

"I don't like the look of this," Stark mutters. "Spread out. Let's scout fast." He moves his mask, sniffing the air. "The extraction units are still working. Remove your masks, but keep 'em close. We can't rely on tech this old."

"What were they *doing* down here?" asks Suge, fiddling with the black units in the room's centre.

"I don't know," Stark says. "Whatever it was, it either went very wrong or got shut down with extreme prejudice. Can't have been above-board, that's for sure."

Checking out the suspension units on the wall with Bone, and holding a low, intense conversation, Tress speaks up, "Bone says it's transmog."

Stark looks at Bone. "Seriously?"

Bone nods, his eyes on the units. There's something in his gaze that makes Stark uncomfortable. "No doubt in my mind," Bone confirms quietly, trailing his hand along the tubes, his face rapt. "Mod history is my thing; I know it back to fucking front. These suspension units were developed for transmog research, to stabilise subjects during testing. They worked, but transmog didn't, and the only place you find these now is on a tiny number of critical care wards."

"This is no care ward."

"No. It's a gen-lab."

"Doesn't look old enough for transmog trials. Are you sure?"

Bone laughs softly. "These are second-generation sus units.

Trials went on far longer than any publicly available reports might document. There was a fuckload of private money behind it. Someone very rich wanted transmog to work."

Stark stares, disbelieving. "Fucking hell."

"Yeah."

Cracking tension from his neck, Stark says, "Burneo wanted us to see this. It's obviously relevant to him in some way. I hope it's nothing to do with the goddamn Rope case. I can't see the Notary allowing *any* level of investigation to continue, if so."

"No," Bone replies, looking at the units again, as if he can't stop. "I imagine they wouldn't."

His disquiet and anger growing by the second, Stark peers closely at Bone, frowning. His face is emotionless, but there's a fathomless look in his eyes Stark doesn't much care for. He wonders what talk of transmog does to the mind of a man who's never once taken a mod.

"Let's go," he says. "The sooner we get out of here, the happier I'll be."

Beyond the lab, the rest of the complex is equally disassembled. Filled with loaded silence. It makes Stark all the more determined to get to Burneo, hunt down Rope, and find the remaining victims. Because he can't do it again. He can't walk in on another room moments too late to change an outcome. He hasn't got the strength. Chewing on meaty ration bars without enthusiasm, they search for a way out to the sewers on the other side, but every likely door they find is sealed and can't be forced, not even with Tress's gun. Her bullets ricocheting around over their heads to blow huge craters in the walls.

They're beginning to give up hope and consider a backtrack when Bone finds the elevator to the holding cells. Small and damp, these chambers emanate pathetic horror. In one or two, instead of the basic toilet and shelf to sleep on, there are sus units, empty again and clogged with decay. And the corridor goes on and on, cell after cell, each as small and hopeless as the last.

"There must be well over two hundred of them," Tress whispers.

"Of course," Bone answers. "This kind of lab runs high on test-subject mortality."

Stark exhales hard, uncomfortable with too much talk. The place makes him feel filthy. "Just keep moving."

Tress opens her mouth to respond, her eyes bright with outrage, but Suge, up ahead and scouting in the cells, calls out, "There's something here."

They follow his voice to a cell containing a large suspension chamber, heavily fortified with steel bands, the top secured with a thick, lockable seal. Its glass tube is perhaps the only one in the whole facility still filled with fluid, whey-coloured in the torch light, and cloudy, floating with scraps of white material fine as lace. Suge points behind the chamber itself.

"There's a door behind this thing. It's almost invisible."

Stark runs his torch over the tube. "Looks like they had a little security issue with whatever they kept here," he says. "Let's see if we can move this beast."

Suge grasps the unit's base. It moves easily, sliding outward with barely a squeak and revealing a heavy door built flush to the wall. Suge turns a large, inset handle to send four rods sliding backwards, one after the other, with dull, clanking thuds. Behind the unit door lies a narrow corridor with a steep downwards gradient. A rank sweat of moisture leaches from the walls, collecting in shallow puddles on the ground beneath their feet. The smell of sulphur, long since lost to them in the lab, begins to drift back in. Stark pulls his mask back into place, nods at his team to follow suit, and sets off down the endless incline, his feet splashing up foul waters. Walking blind, they exit without realising. One moment walls, the next, an echoing void of black. Torch-light illuminates in flaring bands a room identical to the first room they found, furnished with banks of mobile computers, black units, and screens, undamaged here, but long since useless—clogged with sulphur residue and grime. Tress peels off to look for lights, but the switch she finds produces nothing, so instead, they spread out to sweep with torchlight. Bone takes the near side, his light raking over and up the first of the suspension unit tubes. When he catches sight of what's inside, he makes a low, helpless sound of distress.

"What?" Stark says, coming over and playing his torch where Bone did. He nearly falls on his arse, too, when he sees what it illuminates.

In the tube, staring out through ragged holes that were once eyes is the rotting remnant of a corpse, lying slumped against the side of the tube on a slick of blackened matter, thick and dark as an old scab. Despite the wasting and warping of time, the brown relic of its skull is intact, the jaw gaping as if to loose a scream. What lies beneath can't be classified. Nothing but a twisted maze of broken, yellowing bones and scraps of leathery muscle and skin, bound mummy-like about a network of warped metals. The broken residue of what might be a hand is splayed flat against the glass before that mass of curdled flesh and rusted steel. It doesn't look like an attempt to escape. It looks like a plea, a mute appeal for mercy.

Stark steps to one side and moves his torch along. "There's more," he says, and his jaw trembles with rage. Shock. Disgust.

Similar remains are dotted about the sixteen or so suspension units down the room's length. Nine corpses in all. Only remnants remain comprehensible within the whole, a limb here, a hand there, a section of torso. The rest is almost whimsically altered, twisted and malformed. Remade so far from human that Stark and his hardened team struggle to control the workings of throat and stomach.

"Any ideas for time of death?" Stark says to Bone.

Bone shakes his head. "These tubes are full of hairline cracks. Damp and toxic air leaking in at differing rates make it impossible to pinpoint ratios without proper tests. Even *with* the tests, I couldn't give you anything like accuracy."

Suge, gone to scout along the recesses at the far side after staring in mute horror at the remains in the tubes, yells out hoarsely, "Boss!"

"What?" Stark calls, dreading the answer.

"More here, boss. At least, I think so."

In three tubes tucked at the end of the room are conundrums of flesh. Puzzles. Too many limbs and too many heads oddly combined, as if several subjects had been forced together and interwoven with no regard for form or function. Nothing but an amorphous meshing of parts. Nightmares made real and frozen into positions of awful contortion, as if trying to tear their separate parts asunder, fully aware of their predicament.

"Who the fuck does this?" Tress snarls out, clutching her torch, her eyes blinking and blinking, wet with tears. Rage more than distress, but both keenly felt. Her heart has always been tender, it's why they get along. So is his.

"Mother fucking GyreTech Military Branch," Bone says, radiating fury like heat. "This is an adjunct lab for Notary-funded military contracts. You wouldn't believe the shit they fund. I could've been Mort at one of these. Got a request from GyreTech based on my first year Science results. Luckily, my dad was Chief-Mort and he wanted me elsewhere. It's the only time I've ever been glad of his meddling. All Morts do in these hellholes is autopsy ruined bodies trying to work out where the science went wrong." He shakes his head hard. "Not my fucking bag at all."

"Think Burneo knew we'd end up here?" Tress asks Stark.

"I reckon so," he answers, feeling sick. "Though how it connects is beyond me at the moment, *if* it does."

Bone slams a fist into his thigh. "Fuck! I should've *realised*."

"What?"

"Some labs remove mods to have a clear baseline for testing," Bone says. "Not all of them, it's not always required. But it looks like they were trying to meld transmog with implant-tech here …"

"So, they would've had to," finishes Stark. "Meaning Rope is likely to be directly commenting on this shit, meaning he *is* connected to this lab, which is a pain in the goddamned arse." He pinches the bridge of his nose, almost too tired to bear it. "Well, I sure as shit can't tell the Notary about this. We all know what'll happen, then. They'll shut us down and have their Monks deal with Rope. Let every one of his victims die just to keep it under wraps."

He looks at his team and sees a growing sense of yearning to be back in sunlight that matches his own. The horror in this room is sticky, fetid, and clinging as old sweat. They need to refocus, to be reminded why they're here. "Whatever he was: lab assistant, surgeon, or subject, it doesn't matter. It *can't* matter. We still need to stop the cunt. There are people counting on us to save them."

"Then lead us the hell out of here," Tress snaps, brittle as sulphur.

The way out is an incoherent tangle of false ends, loops, and curlicues designed to fool the wanderer. It makes them anxious, disorientated. Provokes swells of nausea and the nascent throbs of impending headaches. Even following the unmistakable scent of sulphur, and with Suge's expert eyes to lead them, it takes over two hours to find the way back into the sewers, lightless and drained of all but the merest slick of water. Stark and Suge take point, then, Bone behind them, with little Tress, huge gun held ready to fire beneath her torch, taking the rear. The sulphur's too strong to fire it, but no one's going to tell her to put it away. Not now. They're all on edge, all need something to cling to, to make them feel secure.

This part of the sewer is a back route of intersection points with multiple outlets, some small, others positively massive, ranging overhead and to the left of the team. It's featureless but for these exit holes, and seems to continue on forever, the echo of waters filling it with murmurings like far away voices, the resemblance perfect and disconcerting. Above that, only the splash of feet can be heard, the occasional sharp intake of Bone's breath as his torch-light illuminates rat eyes.

"We're getting nowhere," Suge exclaims, frustration colouring his every word.

Stark claps a hand on his shoulder. "I can smell the sulphur clean through my mask. We're close."

They follow the tunnel farther for an hour or so, until it turns an abrupt right corner into a vast, echoing chamber, filled with watery music. Up ahead, there's a line of huge, circular outlets. As they approach these outlets, the reek of sulphur blows with such strength, they begin coughing. Stark holds out a hand to halt the team. He chooses the middle outlet, suspecting they all lead to the same place, and walks in alone, the sound of his feet echoing loud in his ears. He only goes far enough to see the yawning breadth of the cavern beyond the outlet's exit, and then turns back, his face flushed with triumph.

"The cavern's through there," he yells as he approaches his waiting team.

Suge punches the air and shouts, "Hell yeah!" as Bone lets out a whoop that betrays more than a hint of exhausted relief.

Stark's beaming behind his mask. Then he stops, swings his torch to and fro, and says in a tight voice, "Where the fuck is Tress?"

CHAPTER 26

*S*hades of light drift across the surface of a tawny iris.
Flutter the pupil wide. Shrink it to a pinpoint. A full stop.
The end. The eye jumps, showing a sliver of white as Burneo
watches himself. Serene. Detached. Aware. He stands waist-deep,
hands splayed flat on the surface. Head lowered, his features
reflect in the yellowish mirror between thumbs. He pays no mind
to the rats gathered on the rim of the outlet pool. They are mute
witnesses. Nothing more.

Echoing from in the distance, amplified by the throats of the
tunnels, comes the sound of footfalls in his playground, just as he
knew there would be. In precisely the place he expected. This is
what he's been waiting for. Ripples undulate the surface, agitating
mirror smoothness to liquid coils as his great bulk wades through
and rises up onto the edge, scattering the rats. Bare legs lurch
along in that half graceful, half awkward glide as he follows the
sounds.

Closer now, Burneo perceives the distant flicker of lights and
picks up the tatters of conversation, broken and faint, fluttering
under the splashing of boots in water. But that's not all there is. He
stills for a moment, scenting the air. They have followed the path
he scattered for them just as he willed it. But there is danger
awaiting them, danger he has led here. And they have brought

with them the one to whom he gave his gift, the Bone-Man. Fool-
ishness. That one has danger all around him.

Burneo shadows them, huge and silent as the lightless void.
Watches them from the recesses, from behind the curving edge of
outlets, observing the rise and fall of beams as they progress
towards the entrance to his cavern. The small one at the back
falters and stops. She, too, senses danger. Her head swings to and
fro, constantly scanning. His nostrils flare. She's afraid, he can
smell the tang on her breath, but she does not falter. Strong, then.
This is good. Better her than the Bone-Man. There are sights left to
share that the Bone-Man needs to see. He will fetch her and they
will lead him together.

He stands and waits as she retraces her steps, her image
growing ever larger in the shrunken black lens of his eye.

A full stop.

CHAPTER 27

*S*tark runs full tilt, back around the corner, hollering for Tress, a raw scrape of panic in his chest. Stands, eyes closed, to listen for a response. The sound of rushing waters in the depths of the outlets grows loud in his ears like the roar of an approaching mob baying and howling, but there's no distant cry for help. Not even the ragged tail end of a scream. Tress has vanished.

"I want an inch-by-inch sweep, every fucking corner," he rasps. "We scour this place, you understand? We *find* her."

And he's off down the tunnel, the light of his torch frantically sweeping the walls and the floor. He ends up side-by-side with Suge, who, by the brightness of the glow at the back of his pupils, has switched his augments to full power, recording and analysing everything. It hurts to use it at that level, even for a few minutes, and he experiences an overwhelming rush of affection for Suge's dedication. They survey every inch of ground they've covered, throwing light down the outlets as they pass them. Farther back than they expect by a good long way, the light of beams pick up the bulk of Tress's gun and torch. They're about twelve feet into one of the outlets, a forlorn heap of discarded metals in a pool of blood. Stark slams his fist into the wall, splitting his knuckle and leaving a smear of blood behind.

"*No!*" He shoves his torch into his pocket and grits out, "Give me some fucking light." Holds out a hand to Bone. "Glove."

Bone reaches into his jacket and pulls out a glove for Stark, who fumbles it on, ripping through the palm in his haste.

"Fuck!" He shoves the remains at Bone and snaps, "Another." It takes him a further two tries, swearing and graceless, to fit a glove onto his shaking fingers, then he scoops the gun from the floor, cradling it in his hands. "Do you have an evidence bag big enough?" he asks Bone, his voice a rigid dam against a tidal wave of boiling emotions. Bone nods, going through his pockets again, his face pale and set, and Stark says to Suge, "Check the walls, the floor. You're looking for more blood. If you find it, see where it leads. We're relying on your eyes, now."

Suge walks slowly ahead, his eyes throwing light on the wall to illuminate small spatters of blood that appear black as tar in shadow.

"Is it Burneo?" Bone asks.

Stark breathes out through his nose and calms, trying to listen to his gut, the instinct he's spent his career relying on. "No. This is not his work. It feels like punishment."

"Rope," says Bone.

"Guarantee it." Stark fights the sinking of his gut, the grip of his heart, clenching in his chest. This is his worst nightmare. It's everything he worked to prevent. "I should have taken into account that Rope might be down here as well, *especially* after finding that fucking lab! Just didn't think. Too fucking set on Burneo." He's so *fucking* stupid. It was supposed to be him facing any possible danger, not one of them. This should be his blood, not Tress's. "Let's get after Suge. We're not going to let Tress go without a fight."

They move off down the outlet, into the dark heart of the sewers, travelling in the grip of darkness, in the chorus of the rushing waters beyond the outlet. They pass knots of pipes, choked ventilation grills, rungs leading to exit ducts; long narrow holes webbed with fine veins of moss, slick and black from the constant drip of moisture as Suge's eyes continue to illuminate the pathway of blood spatters. Until it stops. For a moment, they're all caught in a mutual flare of panic—this was their only link to Tress—then Stark snaps out of it and issues a command to backtrack.

"There's got to be something."

"How could I have lost it?" Suge sweeps around, the glow in the back of his gaze lending him a demented air.

Stark grabs his arm. "It's okay," he says. "It's okay, Suge. You just lost focus for a minute. We're all struggling for focus. Find yours and get back to where you last saw the blood. See it for me," he demands. "Right now."

Suge closes his eyes, wincing only the tiniest fraction as he begins to intone in that singsong manner: "Ten metres back. Last splash of blood. Diffuse. Angled. Means she was moved. He's done that a few times. She's likely slipping. Patterns suggests he's holding one limb, has her body draped like a coat thrown over his shoulder." His head twitches. "Four metres back. A drip. Small. Like an inverted triangle. Pointed at the bottom. Angled left."

His eyes flare open, filled with surprise. He steps back four long strides and stares at the wall. In the light, they see the droplet, a thin, ragged smear, triangular, the point facing down and to the left as he'd described it. Suge flicks his torch on and raises it. Above them, in the centre of the outlet roof, is another of those ducts, this one large and gaping as an outlet tunnel. The rungs to it climb the opposite side of the tunnel.

Bone crosses to the rungs and scrambles up to the lip of the duct. Calls out, rough relief mixing with the anxiety in his voice, "There's more inside here, a big smear, he must have hefted her in hard."

Suge points his torch into the hole. "How far does it go?"

"It doesn't matter," Stark says, making his way to the rungs. "If Tress has been taken that way, that's the way we go."

The exit duct climbs a long way, changing direction to horizontal and veering to left or right with no warning. Though spacious, it leaves them disorientated, fighting off tension headaches like screws wound into their temples. It leads to another tunnel—daylight revealing filthy walls and a rubble-logged stretch of brown ice. They run towards the light, slipping and sliding, to find their way blocked by a heavy steel grille, hinged to rise upwards. Working together, Stark's shoulders and Suge's height, they force it open by reluctant degrees. Then Suge holds it in place as Stark and Bone trudge out, covered head to toe in black filth. They're on a concrete platform, ranged along the edge of a canal, surrounded by a thick growth of lank, slimy reeds, like a tatty fringe. Further on, where the water's clear, ice covers the surface, choked with rubbish. There's a low bridge to their left, and where the water disappears beneath, it's swallowed by deep shadow.

Suge lowers the grille, letting it drop the last few inches to clang in the silence. The sound startles a flock of pigeons roosting beneath the bridge. They swell out in a blurred cloud of blue and grey, the loud shuttering of hundreds of pairs of wings lifting them into cool, slate sky. Stark yanks off his mask and watches them go.

"Where are we?" Suge asks, coming to stand by his side.

"I haven't a clue, and I don't really care, as long as we're still following Tress," Stark says. "We need to scout for blood traces."

"On it." Suge moves off down the platform.

Stark turns to look for Bone. "What the hell are you doing? Fancy going for a fucking swim or something?"

Bone's at the edge of the platform, his toes sticking out over the water. He's staring at the opposite bank, at the crowded maze of high rises blocking the sky above, his jaw sagging. "Stark, how the fuck did we get here?" he asks, his voice high with shock.

"We walked."

Bone swivels round to face him. "No. You don't understand. Those buildings. I know where we are. This is precinct 17 in *Gyre West*. This is *miles* from where we were. There's no way we ever just walked from the River Head to here. No way at all."

Stark blinks, convinced he heard wrong. "Precinct 17? Are you sure?"

"Yes."

"But that's over six *hundred* miles," Stark says faintly.

Bone steps away from the edge, both brows raised high. "No shit."

Stark looses a low growl. "What in the fuck is going on?"

"I do not know," Bone responds, his voice filled with disquiet.

"Got blood here," Suge yells, beckoning them over.

Stark and Bone run to join Suge at a short flight of half-cracked concrete stairs leading up from the platform. There are fresh streaks of blood, small but distinct on the broken crusts of snow piled on the risers. Those smears look too real, too red, in the bright light of day, and Stark fights to contain a wave of anger and misery, of terrible guilt.

Bone places a hand on his shoulder. "There wasn't enough blood around her gear or in the tunnels for her to have bled out. You have time."

Stark grabs the hand Bone's rested on his shoulder in gratitude for a second and they follow Suge as he tracks the trail to a thin spit of derelict land just above the canal, fronting a muddle of what was once workshops for the boat trade. Whilst Suge does a swift search of the area, Stark and Bone stop behind the edge of the first buildings. Bone's back scrapes the corner as he scoots to the shadows. He sucks in hard and flips to his side, resting on his shoulder.

Stark raises a brow. "You okay?"

"I got a tattoo," he says quietly, as if still getting used to the idea but absolutely loving it, nonetheless. Stark always assumed his clear skin was voluntary, but something about that note of pride, almost shy, in Bone's voice, makes him rethink.

"Well, well," he says. "Welcome to the human race."

"I was never outside of it," Bone replies softly. "Not voluntarily."

Stark nods. "I'm beginning to see that, brother." Sensing this topic is not an easy one for Bone, he catches Suge's eye and signals him over. "Anything?"

Suge points. "There's an open workshop. Snow's been disturbed in the last hour. Reckon they went through it."

"Well, okay. Weapons drawn, ready to fire." Stark takes out the evidence bag and pulls Tress's still-bloody gun from it. He hands it to Bone, who takes it between his fingers, screwing up his face. "Quit being squeamish," Stark snaps.

Bone shows his teeth. "It's not the blood, it's the gun," he snaps. "I like weapons with edges, not bullets. I have too much experience in dealing with the results of projectiles."

"Ah, well, unless you fancy fighting in close quarters with Burneo, you'd best put any reservations aside for the next few hours."

Bone winces. "Got it," he says, but he holds the outsized gun away from his body as they move in a small group towards the building.

It's not far, the whole spit of land being only thirty metres wide. The door is, as Suge said, flung open with a heap of snow built up behind it. Stark moves to the fore.

"Let's see what's in here."

Behind the door lies an echoing barge workshop. Gaping holes in the roof let in pale beams of light and gusts of freezing air. The drip of melting snow plays a soft rhythm on damp wood. A large, unfinished barge takes up the majority of space, and they split to move around it towards the shuttered sliding doors at the workshop's end. Bone and Suge take a handle each, and at Stark's signal, pull them open. As one, the group lurches backwards, coughing. Sweet and cloying and with an undertone so sour, it tightens the throat, the stench rolls around them, tangible, like a shimmer of heat from tarmac.

"He didn't take Tress through there," says Bone, staring into the darkness, pressing Tress's gun back into Stark's hand and reaching into his pocket for gloves. "Those doors haven't been opened for a while."

Stark nods. "We'll check outside again. You deal with … that."

CHAPTER 28

*A*s Suge and Stark head back outside, Bone snaps on his gloves, walking into the room beyond the sliding doors. He flicks the switch, shading his eyes as four spotlights spring to life. Not a gift from Burneo, this time, then. This is Rope. Why would Rope lead them to his own work? Is it a warning? Is this what he'll do to Tress, if they don't stop chasing him? Knowing Stark, that will do nothing to deter him, it will only cement his desire to bring an end to this killer. It'll make it personal. The room Rope's used for this diorama is an old equipment shed, narrow and long since empty of its contents. Taking up the slender space is that all-too-familiar webbing of taut ropes, and suspended in their centre, framed by walls slicked in red paint, awaits a tableau of exquisite grotesquery.

Two women face one another. They're both small and brunette and greenish-black with decay. Swollen and oddly blurred, their skin slips downwards in folds like ill-fitting clothes. Molten whites droop from under half-closed lids, their faces distorted, as if a series of strokes had rendered their muscles useless before they died. Twin streaks of thick, clotted fluid stream from their noses, down necks, and onto breasts sagging and misshapen from putrefaction. But Bone's eyes are drawn, as though magnetised, to what lies between them, a part of the sculpture that separates it from all

others. Their arms are raised, as if to clasp hands, but instead Rope
has scrambled them together from elbow to fingertip, creating a
single frozen limb between the two bodies. The end result is both
harmonious and terrible.

Tendons weave around interlocked bones, and the small shapes
of finger bones lace delicate patterns at the humerus through the
intersections between radius and ulna. Muscles and thick arterial
veins droop like forlorn decorations, stippled with black stalactites
of dried, coagulated blood. There's no skin encompassing this
ruined mass of forearms and hands, it's been left exposed, as if to
allow an audience to witness the perfection achieved in the fusion.
Drawn close, too close, to that sticky paradox of parts, Bone feels a
liquid shifting within his head. The ground spins away from his
feet and a wave of vertiginous sickness sweeps up his throat.

He moans. "Oh, fuck, no. Go *away*."

Darkness seeps into his mind on icy waters, and the hallucinogenic whirl of red circles on white rises behind his eyes. Inexpressible agony clamps his ribs, and then his limbs. Bone grits his teeth
so hard, small flecks of enamel break off, rolling gritty and harsh
against gum and cheek. His mind threatening to slip away, he
hangs on by will alone, reminding himself over and over that he
has a job to do; he can't fall apart here. At first, the words are
empty repetitions, collections of letters that mean less than nothing, but gradually, inch by inch, they gain strength, conviction,
cohesion and, as sudden as they arrived, the red circles vanish,
leaving Bone hanging on to his ribcage and breathing hard against
the abrupt cessation of pain. Footsteps echo into the silence. They
move behind him and stop.

"What the *fuck*?" Stark wheezes out, as if air has deserted him.

Bone sucks in too much air, almost in compensation for Stark's
lack. It makes him lightheaded. Fills his mouth, nose, and throat
with the thick stench of the women's putrefaction, strong enough
to root him back to reality.

Shaking, though he tries not to show it, he says, "Transmog."

And saying it catapults his thoughts to Lever, to her jaw-dropping, mind-bending display. It was meant for his eyes, but maybe he was mistaken in thinking it was a message *for* him. Perhaps instead it was a message *to* him, about what they've seen today. It's all connected to the lab. To transmog. To the brutal enforcement of change upon the helpless. Perhaps Lever was once in cells like those. Perhaps she knows who Rope is. She could be in danger. In need of his help. But he hasn't a clue how to help her, how to stop this. He swallows against a vast knot in his throat. It's becoming too much to cope with. There's nothing special about him, despite the reputation he's achieved. All he knows, his entire knowledge of mods, of Zone practitioners, is the result of years of hard work. That's the sum of his skill: dedication.

Stark's voice rumbles into his ear, making him jump. "So he's not a subject, then, our killer, nor a lab assistant."

"No. Only a gen-surgeon could do this."

"So, why have we not found more bodies like this?"

Bone glances at him sidelong. "What do you know about transmog?"

"Scientifically? Fuck all."

"It requires a specific combination of frankly anomalous proteins to adhere to," Bone tells him. "They're highly complex. We can make them, we have the tech, but they're fragile and degrade swiftly. Most people haven't got them, and transmog will kill them outright. For those very few who do have them, it's an unpredictable gen, and horribly violent." Bone indicates the girls' arms. "This is targeted. I've not heard of transmog working properly, let alone used so specifically." A spurt of acidic self-reproach paints his tongue sour because he should explain Lever to Stark, but he just can't. She feels too personal. Too much *his*. "I think they made transmog work in that lab. Enough to think they could do more with it. Enough to try."

Stark closes his eyes. "Oh, fuck *me*." His eyes open, revealing helpless rage. "I'll call Faran, we need to keep continuity. I don't want Gyre West Buzz Boys on this. And I have to speak to Burton; not only does he have to know about this, and about Tress, but I want to see if I can get a personnel list for that lab. Two leads are better than one, and I've got Tress relying on me to save her." He cracks his jaw and points at the brunettes. "What's the deal here?"

"Well, they're identical twins," Bone says. "Meaning they'll both have the same anomalies. That's very likely the reason they were chosen for this particular display."

"I *wish* we knew how he's choosing these victims, how he's targeting them. It seems so fucking random, but it can't be. When the fuck is that Satyr going to call?"

Bone shrugs, equally frustrated, but he knows the Zone works by its own rules. "Fucked if I know. I'm betting none of our victims, thus far, have been missed yet, either. Who the hell cares about the lost in this fucking city?"

"Ain't that the truth. Labels?" Stark's staring, again, at the raddled link between the women, that woven umbilical, as if he'll never cleanse it from his mind.

"Slipping and putrefaction levels make it difficult," Bone replies, but he's on the hunt, using a small glass from his scalpel pocket to magnify the flesh. He alights on one section of skin, just above the buttocks, and leans in close, squinting. Is unable to prevent himself from making a tiny sound, distress and incredulity combined.

"What?" Stark's voice is tight, too strained.

Clearing his throat, Bone replies, "It's pretty badly blurred, but this lady is 'Share,' and." He straightens. "I think you can guess her twin's tag."

"Share and Share Alike." Stark's hands curl to fists. "Is that supposed to be *funny*?"

"Fuck knows."

They're quiet for a moment, trying to come to terms with what Rope might consider to be humour, and then Stark says suddenly, "They're too rotten." He looks like a ridgeback ready to leap.

"That's right. Well over a week older than any we've found so far."

A muscle leaps in Stark's jaw. "So, where's the flies?"

Bone breathes out and points at the faint gust of frozen breath. "Weather. They probably have larvae in the deep tissue, but they'll be dormant. They've no rodent damage, either. I guess the rats gave up looking for scraps here years ago, and the doors held the smell in."

Stark slams a fist into his palm. "Dammit, I thought he was escalating! He's not. Fucker's probably got most of these up exactly where he wants them." Despair creeps into Stark's voice. "Just how many of these have we lost before we even knew he was killing?"

Bone takes off his gloves. "I daren't think about it. Feels useless. Even knowing what we know after today, it feels useless. *I* feel useless."

"Get in line, brother. Way ahead of you there," replies Stark, and he stalks from the shed.

Bone strides at his heels, happy to leave the contents of the shed behind him. When they reach the warehouse door, he grabs it and tries to wrestle it shut, wanting to give those girls back some semblance of privacy and dignity, at least for now. But with the door only halfway shut, he stops, staring at the wood. Glistening at the centre of the door, in what can only be Tress's blood, fresh as it is, is daubed a large, double-looped spiral.

"Now, what the hell is that?" Stark says, catching sight of it.

"It's a tag," Bone replies, thoroughly blindsided to see this here of all places. "A gang tag. Or at least that's what we thought, Nia and I." He turns to look at the canal and another wave of dizziness flashes through him. No, it can't be. But this *is* the same canal, and there's a clear line between where the warehouse stands and that length of water just beside the platform, the water choked with reeds. "A Canted was found in this canal, in the reeds. I'm willing to bet it was those," he says. "He was executed, had a spiral tattooed on his shoulder, the same as this, and he's not the first execution I've seen with this spiral. Spaz has had me dealing exclusively with a raft of initiate deaths just the same, off record to boot."

Stark frowns. "Off record? What the hell? First the gangs let Rope kill all over their territory and do nothing, and now Spaz is … what? Actively killing off gang initiates, thinking the marker means more than it does? Does *he* think they're gang?"

"I'm not sure," Bone replies, his mind working overtime, seeing those remnants of circles on the door of the GyreTech lab and making connections he does not want to make. There are things about Spaz that he cannot share with Stark. Gang secrets. Secrets he's sworn, on pain of death, to keep. Secrets that render any connection between GyreTech and these spiral deaths and Rope look more than a little suspect. He picks his words very carefully, wanting to lead Stark to an answer that might give him a way to move forwards without giving anything of those connections away because Spaz would kill both of them if he found out Stark knew anything he shouldn't. Bone traces his finger above the spiral on the door. "Remember the door of the lab?" he asks. "The first one?"

"Sure."

"Those red marks I asked you about."

"I recall 'em. Didn't think much of them at the time. I was too busy wanting to get on, get to Burneo." Stark's annoyance has turned inward by the looks.

"I'm thinking that if you joined them together," Bone says quietly. "They'd very likely look like this."

Understanding dawns on Stark's face. "It all leads right back to the fucking labs. Would the gangs know that?"

"Perhaps. The Notary takes gang folk above all else for that sort of experimentation," Bone says quietly. That's a fact he can share, a kernel of truth to convince Stark of the veracity of a lie.

Stark nods slowly. "His reaction makes a rather unpleasant kind of sense then. Not helpful to us, though. I need to get the Buzz Boys looking for these spirals," he says. "But Faran won't buy it without proof. He's fed up with this shit. Thinks it's a waste of his resources."

"I'll have a look at the Rope photos when we get back," Bone says, feeling a rush of something like hope. "If we can prove a correlation, then we have something concrete to search for. We might even find some of these poor fuckers alive."

"Rope led us here," Stark says suddenly, and he sounds certain. "I'm willing to bet he led us to the lab, too. What if we've been wrong all along? What if *I've* been wrong?" He looks up at Bone, his black eyes blank with panic. "I assumed Burneo left us the Gift as a sign he was willing to trade Rope in. But it could have been a lure, a false message from Rope himself. I didn't even consider the possibility," he spits out. "This is all my fucking fault."

Burneo's words, *"There is a gift for you,"* those deep, compelling tones, reel out in the distant hall of Bone's memory. He shakes his head. "Burneo said the Gift was for me. He staged it with his own particular brand of violence on purpose, to demarcate which body belonged to whom. The Gift was Burneo's message, not Rope's. No question." Thinking of his time in the sewer, of how frighteningly abnormal Burneo was, Bone recalls his response when he begged him to leave Stark alone. "Who's Reinhart?" he asks.

Stark grabs Bone's arm, his grip tight enough to hurt. "What?"

"Reinhart. Down in the sewer, before the Gift, Burneo told me that Reinhart was in his playground, that he would see him." Bone looks at Stark. "Are you Reinhart?"

Stark's chest rises and falls hard. "That's who I was," he murmurs. "And he said he would see me?"

Bone nods. "I'm sure you're right about who took Tress," he says. "But you were right about Burneo, too. He wants to help, and we did as we were supposed to do, but somehow we found our way to the wrong man, or perhaps the wrong man found us. Rope's been ahead of us the whole way. Perhaps he's ahead of Burneo, too. Think about it. It fits the ton of shitty luck this case has laboured under thus far. Fits how easily he's played us."

Stark releases Bone's arm and sweeps both hands backwards across his cheeks and his head, his hair pulled taut under the pressure. He sighs out, too much fury and unsteady emotion in it. "You know what we say up at Central when shit like this happens?" His voice an attempt at jocularity that falls too horribly far of the mark. Coloured by unbearable strain.

"What?"

Eyes empty as the starless sky, Stark replies, "Luck's one *hell* of a bitch."

CHAPTER 29

*P*assing from Key Square into the Hub, Spaz checks the time, the numbers of his sub-dermal clock flashing red, and growls irritation. Time's racing. He doesn't buy subjectivity bullshit. Time can leave you flat in the dust just for shits and giggles. Fact is, it's got a bad sense of humour. *"Time's a bastard and life's a bitch,"* his father, Kane, used to say. *"It likes to poke at raw wounds."* The last twenty years have been a testament to that, especially this past year. The raw wounds of his people have been poked half to death. Spaz sees only one response to that: insurrection. Defiant refusal to submit.

It's not merely a punk ethic, it's gang code, and as the leader of the Establishment, it's up to him to be the first to raise that middle finger, to refuse to be moved. But, sometimes, it feels like he's the only one doing it. The only one who cares enough to stand in the way of the wave that threatens to obliterate gang folks' rights, their hard-won independence. He hangs a left, heading into an alley hidden between a tower of fluted green plascrete, delicate as glass, and a shop built of reclaimed monitor screens, all colours and sizes, held together by a filigree of metal, reworked to resemble sentient vines, coiled and malevolent. Beyond these two creations, the violet haze of a loop entry shimmers between the bulbous glass windows, bulging like eyes from a cydraulics surgery. He flutes out a whistle to the runners guarding the loop on the opposite roof and passes through to a constricted space between buildings so tall they induce vertigo. Slender windows punctuate the walls, and soft light pours through painted glass, creating rainbows. This constricted causeway leads to the Parade, part of the Zone that can't be seen on the skyline. One of several locations built within loop pockets.

The Parade is a procession of baroque, cathedral-like buttresses, rising to an archway so high, clouds drift through them like ghosts. Squatted between the buttresses are huge stone edifices, sinister-looking, with leaded windows and unfriendly brassbound doors. Down the centre of the Parade marches a line of impossibly tall trees, their leaves a riot of red, orange, and yellow detaching from delicate boughs and floating down to create fires of colour in the snow. Spaz turns right, towards the head of the Parade, a dead end. There, beneath a gothic-esque six-storey house hides Pillion, the centre of gang business in the Zone, its massive oak door manned by two slender individuals. These two are no lightweight security solution. Restrained power surrounds them in a tight aura and their incurious eyes form black holes in impassive faces. These are Monks, some of a small number loyal to the Establishment, to Spaz. They stand aside, motioning the door open as he approaches.

"Thanks, boys," he says with a swift grin, and takes the steep staircase down to the bar three risers at a time.

In direct contrast to the splendour above, Pillion's a cave; damp, unfriendly, and lit by muted bulbs that spark as if in prelude to explosion. Carved out of bedrock, its corners are tight, shadowed, and the thick coldness of stone is too close for comfort. Clusters of old, worn tables and stools scatter the floor, some of them shoved, haphazard, into misshapen holes cut for booths. Nathaniel's leant back against the bar on his elbows, a tall, frosted glass of pale beer perched beside him, probably some piss-ant lager knowing Nate's tastes.

"Nate, good to see you."

They hug briefly, a warm greeting between old friends.

"I'm glad you could get away. I'd rather speak in person."

A beer lands in front of Spaz on the bar. He nods thanks to the barman and says to Nate, "You always were old school."

"Ain't much of old anywhere, anymore. I like to keep the side up." Nate takes a swig of his drink and offers Spaz an enigmatic look. "So. You sent Bone Adams to me to be scratched with that snake. Dare I ask if we are entering into perilous times?"

"Times were always perilous for us," Spaz responds. "But I'd say the level of immediate peril does look markedly higher. Certainly lending quite the frisson to my nervous system."

Nate leans back on the bar again. "It'll take a good few days to heal," he says frankly. "Might not be of any use to him when it comes to the crunch."

"Don't you worry about that," Spaz says. "I'm all for giving him a remote nudge if need be. I'm not taking any chances."

"You found Lever yet? That was one hell of a brave move."

Spaz's shoulders tighten. "No. She's not reported in."

"Ah, fuck." Nate shakes his head. "She doesn't deserve that."

"No, she doesn't. But he's protected, that's what I have to take from this."

"Quick thinking under the circumstances."

"Yeah, but it's far from ideal."

"Really, now? Alive is the optimal end here. Without the protection, under these circumstances, the opposite would have been pretty much a guarantee."

Spaz pinches the bridge of his nose and drops a sigh like a cannon ball. "Yeah, but I wanted to avoid unnecessary suffering, Nate. It's disrespectful."

Nate clamps a hand onto Spaz's shoulder. "You have done your level best."

Spaz nods, but his shoulders remain tense. He sips at his beer, introspective. Then he looks up at Nate and says with heavy irony, "Kane used to say you roll with the punches, but he never faced times like these. I'm a bare-knuckle scrapper, Nate, and I'm bloodied to fuck. Sometimes I wish I'd left it to Jell to deal with, no matter how incompetent he was."

Nate makes a sound of inestimable scorn. "Jell was worse than incompetent, and you know it," he says. "He favoured limp-wristed diplomacy, kow-towing to those Notary bastards. As if that'd ever stop them. They've never had any interest in negotiation, especially not since that Connaught Yar fucker took the Chair. We need you, Spaz, bloodied or not. We need you to have the courage to do what we can't, what Jell *wouldn't*."

"Need my conscience, is it?" Spaz asks drily, but with a faint smile.

Nate laughs. "Exactly."

"Well, I'll tell you," Spaz says, turning his beer on the bar. "It's taking a beating."

"Then perhaps we should be drinking something a little stronger than this piss."

Spaz grins. "Now you're talking." He beckons the barman over. "Two gas-malts." When they're placed down on the bar, Spaz takes one and hands the other to Nate. "To Bone," he says. "To survival."

Nate raises his glass. "To survival."

CHAPTER 30

*N*ia's stood clutching the edge of the table, breathing in calm and breathing out every shitty emotion today has piled onto her plate. She cannot *believe* Bone right now. She's so angry with him, she's beginning to wonder if her patience with him is running out altogether. That's not the kind of person she wants to be, but he's taking the fucking piss. It's not that she can't handle stress, she can, it's this poxy lab and the arsehole in charge of it she's finding impossible to handle without resorting to violence, and she loathes that. Nia came from violence, from a culture that solves the vast majority of its problems with reckless, bloody conflict. That's not who *she* is, it's not who she wants to be. That this situation, the unbearable impertinence she's forced to endure, is making her think this way, *feel* this way, is intolerable.

The elevator pings, and she looks up in time to see Bone and Stark, both in the most repulsive mess imaginable, pushing a trolley with the biggest body bag she's ever seen balanced on top. Her first reaction is relief, that he's okay, that he's alive, and then, directly on its heels, red rage blooms right up from her toes, suffusing her entire body. She's moving before she realises, taking three running steps to the door as the trolley squeaks up, and punching Bone hard on the arm.

"You fucking bastard!"

Bone rears back, rubbing his arm. "What the hell was that for?"

She slams her fists onto her hips. "I had no idea where you were, dickhead! I was happy to cover for you *yesterday*. Bit surprised when you didn't turn up for work *this morning*. Do you have any idea how many excuses I've had to make for you today? The trouble you've caused me?"

Bone covers his face with his hands. "Ah, *shit*. I'm sorry, Ni. I knew I'd forgotten something this morning."

Of all the things he could say after an apology, that may have been the most stupid, giving her a head's up on being the thing he *forgot* to do. Rage sets into an ugly lump of hurt, because, much as they both know she's ready for her own lab and able to handle this situation and all the bodies it can throw at her with her hands tied behind her bloody back, no *professional* Mort would have left even the most competent and seasoned assistant to handle this crap alone. Not for *days*. Not without sending word.

"You really think that, at this point, I'm going to be appeased by an apology?" She's livid, has no idea what to do with this anger, this hurt, but throw it at him with all her might. "That De Lyon *bastard* has been blaming me for your absence. He's been tap dancing on my nerves all damned day with his ever-loving sniping, and I'm about ready to commit violence, Bone. Violence. Me!"

He pales. "Oh, fuck, Ni. Fuck. No, I don't think an apology is enough," he says. "It's inadequate and it's cowardly, and I owe you way more. I want to make it up to you, I do. I want to let you chew me out as hard as I deserve, but—" He touches the bag, and his fingers are trembling. Not alcohol this time, he's scary sober. Something else. "We have to do this. Stark needs to witness it, and he needs to be at his office. Someone is missing. With Rope."

"Missing?" She spits the word out, still unable to hold her fury.

"One of his team. Taken whilst we were looking in the sewers."

Now she understands the stench. The state of them. "You went into the *sewer*? Are you nuts!"

"We had reason."

She regards him with vicious intensity for a moment. This is not a Bone she knows, this reckless, sober creature who goes running after danger. Her Bone only ever leaves the lab to drink or sleep or work. What the hell is going on with him? Whatever it is, someone is missing, and they have a body to autopsy.

She points to the door. "Go scrub up, you're fucking filthy."

And without a word, he does as she says. She points to the middle of the room, then.

"Stark, push the gurney to the table, there. Let's set up, shall we?" Her tone brooks no argument and offers no welcome.

"You don't much like me, sister," Stark notes as, between them, they lift the heavy weight of the body bag onto the autopsy table.

"Perceptive," she says, barely containing her scorn. Pulling the table of equipment to the proper position, Nia chucks a mask and some gloves at Stark. "This is the first time he's ever forgotten to call in and let me know he's out on a scene or a case," she snaps. "It's out of character. I blame this case, and I blame you for getting him involved in it."

To her surprise, he inclines his head. "Sounds fair enough."

"No, it's not," she replies, flaring up again, her eyes flashing. "It's not fair at all." She struggles for calm, and says to him candidly, "I can handle that twat De Lyon just fine. It's Bone being gone without a word of explanation I find hard to deal with. He's a mess lately, okay? I've been worried sick all day because I thought the stupid fucker might have finally drank himself to death."

Stark pulls on his gloves and hangs the mask loosely about his neck. "Not much I can do about his current state," he says, clearly choosing his words. "But if he's out with me, I'll make damn sure that he calls in from now on."

"I'll hold you to that."

"To what?" asks Bone as he comes in, snapping on his gloves.

"Never mind. Let's get this over and done with." Nia grasps the zip on the bag, but Bone's hand falls on her wrist. Her gaze flies to his. Encounters a look of pity, apprehension, and more than that, an unmistakeable border of distress. Anxiety curls hard into her belly.

"Brace yourself," he says, and the curl tightens to a knot.

As the zip peels open, the stench hits. Between them, they part the edges, pulling them open until the bag lies flat, its sides dangling off the table, the bodies fully exposed. Two women. So young. By the looks of it, younger even than Ballerina Girl was, barely into their early twenties. At this stage of their decay, they're beginning to resemble crones. Faces shrunken to skulls, teeth bared in lipless mouths, stained brown with a slime of purge fluid. The skin of their torsos is no longer taut and trim; it sags, gaping in places, beaten by its own weight. It's just the outcome of death, but it's cruel, too cruel to ones as young as this. Nia's stomach squeezes in sympathy. Then she sees the arms and rears back, colliding with the equipment trolley hard enough to hurt. She barely notices the pain.

"What is that?" she asks them, unable to control the pitch of her voice, unable to quit staring. "What the hell is that!"

Bone clears his throat. "It's transmog, Ni."

Nia clutches the equipment table at her back, the steel edge digging into her palms. "No. It's not." She stares and stares at the arms, battling nausea, hysteria, gut-deep distress. "That's not possible."

"Turns out, Rope was a transmog gen-surgeon," Stark says, and that voice of his weighs her down, holds her steady. She feels like she could hang onto it and it would be more real, more solid, than the steel beneath her palms.

"The Notary would not let this happen," she says to him, sure of it. Absolutely convinced.

"We found a GyreTech lab today, hidden in the sewers," Bone tells her. "There was a military adjunct, a *Notary* adjunct, and there were corpses. Transmogged corpses. It wasn't an old lab, Ni, not much more than a decade, maybe. There's little doubt Rope was involved with it."

"Oh my fucking ..." Finally letting go of the equipment table, Nia folds her arms tight across her chest. "I don't want to know this. I do not *need* to know this. I've just about had *enough* of this *fucking* case." Leaving them no time to argue, she steps forwards. Snaps, "Session, on," at the recording equipment in the lights, and goes to wait by her trolley, feeling small, vulnerable, too edgy by half.

To her relief, Bone keeps the autopsy brief. A sample run followed by close examination of the transmog. The whole process takes place in awful silence, and when the body bag is zipped up, the scrubs chucked away, Nia's left fighting a riot of ugly emotion. During the course of this case, Rope's taken an unquestionable part of who she is and turned it upside down, making her think about mods in a way she hasn't before. Forcing her to encounter her dependence upon them, her distress at their loss. But this new sculpture is far worse, exposing a dark side to modification Nia doesn't want to think about, doesn't want to know. She's left wondering if they've lost any humanity they held claim to. Wondering if it's too late to turn back the tide Rope came in on, too late to salvage anything worth keeping.

"What do we do?" she murmurs, more to herself than the two men in the room, and jumps when Stark's voice, low and deep as the grumble of an earthquake, breaks the impasse with a response.

"I'm off to report to Burton," he says, touching his wrist and wincing as he sees the time.

"I'll get on those scene photos," Bone says briskly. "The transmog samples have gone to a trusted contact in the Zone for a little secretive gen deconstruction. That's all I've asked for, because we know what it is. If we can unravel it, we may have a way of helping any victims found alive in this state, and I'm willing to bet there's more."

A low snort of disbelief comes from Stark. "No need to bet, reckon it's a given. Good call there. Let's hope we can use it." He makes his way around the table, towards the exit, towards Bone, placing a wide hand on Bone's arm as he reaches him. "Call me if those scene photos prove useful. I'll answer even if I'm in with Burton. Tress is a priority, but the case comes first. She'll tear me a new arsehole, if I put her before pre-existing victims."

The door swings shut after him without a sound, as if consuming him, and the room shrinks in his absence. Bone looks across at Nia, his eyes wary.

"Tress?" she asks, curious.

"Stark's right hand officer. She's the one Rope has."

She looks to the door again, though Stark is long gone, and feels an ache for this Tress, whoever she is. An ache for Stark that's quite unexpected, considering how much she blames him for Bone's current lack of professionalism. "What the hell will he do?"

"Whatever needs doing."

"This must be killing him. I mean, I'm not fond of him, but he clearly cares way too hard for his health. He looked awful."

"Yeah, and he's the most stubborn fucker I've ever met. If there's any way at all to save her, he'll find it. You want that explanation now? You can help me check the scene photos as I attempt to ingratiate my way back into your good books."

"That," she tells him as they carefully transfer the body bag back to the gurney, "is going to be tough."

Bone's mouth curls into a wry grin. "I wouldn't expect it to be anything else," he replies, as they set off for their first port of call.

WITH SHARE and Share Alike secured in the freezer, Bone and Nia grab coffee and head to the records department, stealing two of the fastest machines from a severely disgruntled techie. It's an archaic system, here in De Lyon's Mort, and Nia's the expert. As she makes her way into the system, and through the pointlessly labyrinthine files for the photos they need, Bone talks, and as he does, her fingers slow and then stop. By the time he's finished, she's sitting there with her mouth hanging open, her coffee cold and long since forgotten, thinking that her friend, her colleague, must have tipped over the edge into raving madness. Because there's no way any of that is real. No way he didn't dream, or hallucinate, or imagine it all somehow. But then, the curdled connection between Share and Share Alike is real. Unquestionably so. And if *that* is real, who knows what else might fit into reality?

Beside her, Bone stabs at the flat keypad, trying to bull his way into the system. He's really bad with tech. With an exasperated sigh, she shoves his hands aside, and in three pointed taps, brings up the streams he needs. He flashes her a grateful smile and starts with the Canted corpse, discarding most of the picture files, keeping only two close shots and one taken at a distance. Then he scours the other scene streams, zooming in and out, dismissing those he doesn't need, until he's left with a handful of photos centre screen. Sipping at his coffee, he muddles about with enlarging until he can make the pictures the size he needs.

"I don't trust it," Nia says suddenly, fiercely, finally finding words for the horror and disbelief and plain old terror boiling about inside her. "This whole fucking case is twisted. I looked at those girls today and I wondered why the fuck I have mods. I've *never* wondered about that, never *questioned* it before. I don't like what this Rope bastard is doing. To them, to you, to me." She stops for a moment, breathing hard, close to tears, and then she says, "I want it to stop. I want you to catch him."

"Stark and I won't stop until we've caught him. We can't."

"You better not. But you'd better be careful." She raises a hand as he goes to speak. "No, no more. I said it earlier and I meant it, I've heard more than I can stand today, seen *way* more. Let's just get this crap over and done with so I can go home and get stupid drunk." Nia turns her attention to the screen. "So, what is it I'm looking for?"

"Tell me what you see," he asks her simply.

Nia looks over the photos. "It's the spiral."

"It's at every scene."

"But how?" She blinks, bemused. "We thought this was a new gang. Are you telling me it's Rope?"

"I'm certain of it. They're markers. That exact spiral was drawn in Tress's blood, on the door of the warehouse where we found Share And Share Alike," he tells her. "It was placed there because the Canted corpse was removed. That corpse was Rope's initial marker. Look at the photo. See how he's tilted towards the warehouses? That tattoo's pointing right at that door, you could draw a straight line directly between the two. It's so subtle, it's impossible to see unless you know to look, and it's the same at every scene. Hell, if he hadn't left the spiral in Tress's blood, I wouldn't have thought twice about there being any connection at all."

Nia sits back, her brow crumpled with confusion. "But why a spiral?"

"There was a remnant of a spiral on the door of the sewer lab. Could be a project logo, maybe the lab's designated symbol. Who knows? All I know is that he's messing with us. This is a game, remember?"

Nia points at the photos. "These were all in different locations across the Spires," she says and then slaps her hand on the desk, suddenly furious all over again. "My fucking uncle. That's *his* lab. GyreTech's lab. He must have known what was going on. Must see the connections now. What the *fuck* is he doing, hiding these bodies, preventing us from finding Rope's victims?" Why is it she forgets what Spaz is? It always happens. He'd do anything to protect gang folk, including letting a bunch of nobodies die, even if one or two of them were gang. That's how it's always been with him. Gang above everything. The many over the one.

"I suspect," Bone says softly, "that he's trying to duck the Notary's attention. Because they'll know this spiral, too. They'll know what it means. And it will bring nothing but trouble. They'll blame the gangs, or rather, Yar will, and he'll go after them like he never has before. And the Notary will let him. There'll be no argument, if it gets out that a surgeon from those labs is the killer."

They're both quiet for a moment, struck by the sheer level of chaos one man may have managed to unleash. Current levels of tension in the Spires wouldn't take much to ignite, and if the Notary finally acquiesce to the demands of Connaught Yar and allow him to try and take down the gangs, the wave of violence they'd unleash would be unspeakable. Once begun, such a war would bring to the inner city all the devastation wrought upon the Wharf, the Gulley, and the Outskirts and worse because populations towards the middle of the Spires are exponentially larger. The body count would be breathtakingly high.

"You need to call Stark right now," Nia says, reaching over to snag the nearest phone. "I'll work up a stream so these can be easily distributed amongst the search teams. So they know what to look for. The sort of places to look."

"Thanks, Ni." He offers her a grateful smile and asks, "So, am I forgiven?"

She takes a deep breath. "Maybe. But don't you ever, *ever* fuck me about like that again. I cannot and will not spend another day working myself into a panic, wondering if the next body they bring in is going to be yours."

CHAPTER 31

There's blood. Too much blood. So much. It's dried down the length of her body in blackening slicks, making her skin unbearably itchy. The biting reek of her sweat engulfs her. Beneath it, above it, and around it, the too-sweet stench of the urine that's soaked the seat of her pants cloaks her in a sickening cloud. She can feel it drying stiff against her aching flesh.

If she had energy for shame, it would overwhelm her, but she's convulsive with the tremors of hunger and exhaustion racking her body. They trap her in the weight of tiring flesh as she waits in the blurred light of a single, dim bulb, blinking away grit and sweat and sinking humiliation, bearing the sharp pull and muscle deep ache of wounds cobbled together with thick black catgut, the type used in mortuaries.

Those thick threads make her feel dead already, but she's not. Thanks to Burneo, his rescue and his skill with her wounds, she's still alive. And Stark's never let her down. He'll come for her; even if he waits until after he's caught Rope, he'll come. The thought keeps her going.

The air's dry, but filled with the sound of rushing water. Torture. She swallows, the walls of her throat grinding together and peeling apart. How does thirst become like this? So powerful, it's a thing within itself, within her. She'd kill for a drink, right now. Can see the glass to her left, a small, clear cup-full. It taunts her. So close, but she hasn't strength to reach it. Doesn't know where Burneo's gone, either, which worries her. He's badly injured, too, from blows he took that were meant for her body.

Her thoughts veer dangerously close to thinking about what happened in the hub, in the tunnel. About what attacked her. Mouth trembling, she resolutely blocks the memory and wills Burneo to be okay. She hopes he's not lying unconscious, somewhere, because then she'd be entirely alone, and that's more than she can stand right at this moment.

She flutters out a long breath, tries to concentrate on saving whatever reserves she has for when she needs them, but she can't control the swell of tears in her throat and lets out a little moan of frustration. She wants to be angry. Anger is good, anger will hold her when she's nothing left to hold onto, but pain rips through her body again in unforgiving swells.

Nerves shrieking, muscles bunched into knots, her jaw hangs wide, a scream wheezing out. The pain reaches unbearable proportions, and just as suddenly, begins to ebb away. A helpless sob breaks from her throat. She's so weak, so cold and tired. She just wants to go home.

CHAPTER 32

*B*one waits outside Lower Mace lab in thick snow, struggling to keep warm in leather and thin cotton. He's smoking a slender, black cigarette swiped from one of the receptionists. It tastes faintly of aniseed, making his head spin and whirl. He likes the acidic bite of flavour on his tongue, it suits the equally acid pain in his stomach. Takes his mind off the irritating soreness across his back. He showed the tattoo to Nia. She thinks it beautiful, but she's worried that he's got wetware. Perhaps she thinks it's too much for his first mod? He can't really disagree, not when it's literally his job to know mods and what they entail, but he doesn't care. He loves it.

Way above his head, amongst the pinnacles of Lower Mace Mort's tower blocks, he hears the discordant caws of a team of runners. Their rooftop world must be unbearable this morning, icy and even colder than down here, but they sound cheerful—playful even. Mace is Spine Freak territory. Spine Freaks are extreme, closer, perhaps, to Burneo in terms of mods than any other single group or gang. They're so altered, he wonders how they recognise themselves anymore. Perhaps they don't. He envies that. Their calls are distant and sound almost like real crows, laughing at some helpless chick about to be devoured. He hopes they're not communicating anything about him. The fact so many disparate runners seem to be following him around is bad enough without them gossiping about his movements.

Spying Stark's long black car nosing through the traffic, he tosses his cigarette into the snow and dodges between cars to knock on the window, desperate to be in the warm. The door swings open, and Bone jumps in sideways to keep from putting pressure on the tattoo.

"So," he says. "Where're we going?"

Stark presses a button and shouts to Tal, "Get us out of this godawful jam." Then he turns to Bone, his face about as thunderous as Bone's ever seen it. "Your call came during my meeting," he says.

"Yeah? You said it was okay."

A jolt of annoyance crosses Stark's thunderous face like a lightning bolt. "I know, and it was. That's not the fucking problem."

"So, what's the problem?"

"Burton refused my request to hit GyreTech for a list of personnel."

Bone's jaw drops open. "What?"

"Yep. Point blank."

"You argue?"

"Of course, I argued! We got into a bit of a shouting match, truth be told."

"Don't tell me you got fired?" Bone's aghast.

"Worse. I got given the reason for his refusal."

"Oh?"

They're both pressed back into the soft leather upholstery as Tal spots his opening and shoots off down through an underpass. Stark shifts to peer out the window as they emerge from the underpass onto a five-lane freeway rising upwards through Lower Mace's densely packed skyline, the car reflecting in mirrored glass. He nods satisfaction and turns back to Bone.

"It's about GyreTech," he says, and his gaze becomes solemn. "If I find you knew this, I'm going to be pissed."

"Well, I don't know if I know unless you tell me."

Stark nods, accepting that as a given. "GyreTech's not what it seems," he says heavily. "I thought the same as everyone else, that it was a private corporation owned by some Spires business cartel because that's how it publicises itself. It's not. It's fucking *gang* owned. The Establishment owns it." He's watching Bone closely for his response, but Bone keeps his face carefully blank. "Gyre-Tech owns the mortuary network, the research lab networks. Hell, it owns almost all healthcare practices, hospitals, and clinics in the Spires, too.

"If it's just a front for the Establishment, that means it also owns the fucking Zone. So, the Establishment not only *controls* modification, they have a fuckload of political sway over anything to do with mods. According to Burton, they've used it to tie up the Notary, the CO, and the military in a series of highly unattractive knots over the past twenty or so years, since Spaz took over, and apparently this means that Burton hasn't the authority to demand *jack shit* from them. Hence my request being bombed to oblivion." Stark's black eyes bore into Bone's. "Did you know any of this?"

Bone licks his lips. "Okay," he says. "I know who my bosses are. Of course, I do."

"Of course," Stark replies, and his voice is hard. Unforgiving.

"But," says Bone, holding up a hand, "I'm like every other employee, Stark. I signed a non-disclosure, and it being *gang*, the terms are my silence or my life. Understand?"

Stark considers this a moment and then inclines his head. "Can't judge you for that. But you could've mentioned it when I said I wanted to get the personnel list."

Bone shakes his head. "No, I couldn't. That would be exposing privileged information, and that would constitute a breaking of my silence. But honestly, I assumed the CO could get a court order, circumstances being what they are."

"Nope."

"So, what do you plan to do?"

Stark offers Bone an unpleasant grin. "Shortly after Burton finished dragging me over the coals, I recalled you telling me about the spirals. About Spaz having you deal with them exclusively?" He stops there and looks expectant.

Bone lets out an incredulous shout of laughter and exclaims, "Oh, fucking hell, no! You cannot roll on in there and ask Spaz about his business."

Stark's face twitches. "Oh, really?" He leans right in towards Bone, implacable. "Way I see it is this, Spaz was in charge of Gyre-Tech when that lab was operational, and some serious shit went off there. It was trashed. I'm betting Rope was involved, and Spaz would've had reports detailing the incident." Fury flashes in Stark's black eyes. "Now since these killings began, the gangs've let Rope run loose all over the fucking city, when usually they'd mop that shit up straight off. And don't feed me any bullshit about avoiding the Notary, because he has them over a fucking barrel. I'm thinking more in terms of them not-so-subtly nudging us in Rope's direction, when he's one hundred percent *their* problem. I mean, *come on*, all that tagging shit went on right under Spaz's nose in the Boreholes. You know he'd have known about that."

"I do."

"He's had you dealing personally with these spirals, which he *must* know connect to the lab. Keeping those off record reports bare bones, too, I presume?" Bone nods and Stark continues, his voice almost a growl, "Your good friend knows who our killer is, but he's chosen to play ignorant. Left us to clean up his mess. He knows information that could help us, too, I guarantee it, and he's kept it to himself. That does not fly with me. Not at all. So, whether it gets me gutted and hung up by my toes or not, I'm going to get some answers from him."

The beginnings of one hell of a tension headache swell behind Bone's forehead. He wants to tell Tal to stop the car right there, so he can get out, walk away, and never look back. Trouble is, the gangs distancing themselves from this killer's activities is something they've wondered about from the start, and now the situation is even more confusing because this is GyreTech business, therefore very clearly Establishment business. Spaz makes a point of dealing with Establishment business with brutal exactitude, so why is he choosing to allow this killer free rein until the CO can catch him? It's so far from usual gang policy, from Spaz's personal code, that it borders on the unbelievable. Rope should be long since dead. Executed. Buried somewhere he can never be found. So, he's still alive for a reason, and Bone has to know it. Moreover, now that they know to look for spirals, the Buzz Boys may find survivors. Both those victims and the ones they've been too late to save deserve justice.

"I have no desire to witness your hideous demise," Bone says. "But I agree. He has to be asked, even if he chooses to continue to hold out on us. And he probably will."

"You think?"

Bone nods. "I don't think we'll get jack shit." He smiles thinly. "But do me a favour, anyway."

"What's that?"

"Try and keep it level, Stark. Don't aim to provoke."

"I'll do my best," Stark says with a twisted grin.

Bone's headache ramps up by several degrees. He groans, dropping his head into his palms. "This is not," he says with dark presentiment, "going to end prettily."

Stark barks out a laugh and claps a meaty hand onto Bone's back, making him yelp as it catches the tattoo square on. "So let's go face certain evisceration with smiles on our faces."

"If I were you," Bone responds drily, knowing he won't face Spaz's wrath in the same way as Stark and not liking it at all, "I'd go with hysterical hand wringing and frantic clenching of the anus." He doesn't share Stark's amusement. He knows Spaz too well. But he settles back and tries not to panic as Stark confidently outlines their strategy.

At the Zone, they drive through the gate with little delay, thanks to Bone's presence, arriving at Snatch far too soon for his comfort. Spaz doesn't take kindly to the law in his territory, or to awkward questions, and both together are likely to provoke one hell of an unpleasant response. Fighting intense reluctance, Bone leads Stark into the mindless roar of a live band. From the frenzied pulse of drum and guitar and the underlying stridence of synths, it's some form of Black Metal. Sounds like the sort of noise some of his more deconstructed corpses might make in the moments between whole alive and ripped to fuck dead. He wonders if he'll see Stark making the same noise and sincerely hopes not.

Spaz is at the bar, serving. He does no more than raise a brow at Stark, and then gifts Bone a large, toothy grin. "Pork roast? How thoughtful."

Bone chuckles. "My apologies, Spaz, but we need to talk. Out the range of ear holes not our own."

Spaz treats them to the kind of stare that's made gang bosses almost as large as Burneo run off whimpering into the night. The two meet it, unflinching. Bone's got his own steel, he knows how to conduct himself here, and Stark just doesn't give a shit. A long, slow smile takes over Spaz's face, his liquid tattoos glistening and seeming to writhe with a life of their own. He jerks his head towards a small door at the end of the bar, black and unassuming.

"Come with me."

He leads them to a conference room full of sleek woods and luxurious fabrics. Only the brushed steel and glass screens on the walls suggest the doubtless vast array of cutting edge tech hidden in the luxury. It's so at odds to Snatch, it borders on the ridiculous, and yet seems to fit, as though it makes perfect sense to have all this opulence hidden behind a façade of visceral metal savagery.

Bone lets out a low whistle. "You hide this in here?"

"No need to hide anything," Spaz answers, a thread of humour in his voice. "Take a seat." He fetches a decanter of whisky and three chunky quartz glasses, pouring with his usual panache. "You'll have to go bareback on this malt, Bone-Man. There's no force on earth that could make me destroy it by slugging in gas."

Taking an almost reverent sip, Stark cracks out, "He's an alcoholic, not a philistine."

Bone raises his glass. "Fuckin A," he says, and slugs back a good mouthful.

Spaz throws himself into a chair, long legs thumping up on the table. Metal chimes through the room as his boot buckles jangle together. "So," he says. "Bone, my friend. Talk."

Bone sends a warning to rebellious guts and gets down to business. "I need to know why it is I've been asked to deal with those spiral corpses off record."

"Now there's a question," Spaz murmurs. His face is expressionless, but Bone gets the distinct feeling he's suddenly listening very hard. "Might you perhaps elaborate?"

Bone swallows another fortifying shot of whisky. "You may recall my asking what the tag meant once or twice. Whether or not it might be a new gang."

"I do."

"You're probably aware of this case I'm working on, too."

"The Rope killer," comes the terse reply.

"Exactly. Now, I know you keep a track of official streams, so you probably already know we discovered the killer's been using those spirals to mark the locations of victims."

Spaz's eyes are hooded, swallowing secrets. "Ah," he says with dark, heavy amusement. "You think my reason for insisting the spiral corpses are dealt with privately is because I know who your killer is? You think I'm letting him run loose in my city?"

"We think it's a distinct possibility, yes," says Bone, choosing his words with care. "Although that would be contrary to gang policy maintained over the past few decades, and to your personal code as I've come to understand it."

Spaz's aura thickens with menace. "That's quite the assumption."

"It is," Bone acknowledges. "Thing is, we're up against something truly fucking terrible here, and time's running out for the people he's targeted. His victims. We haven't time to tread carefully. These conclusions couldn't be left unexplored."

Spaz regards Bone, almost as if trying to read beneath his surface. Then he nods. "Fair enough. I'm aware the spirals aren't connected to the formation of a new gang, but I've had to act as if they are." He gives an elegant shrug. "I'm sure you gentlemen are aware of the current, delicate balance in the Spires. Maintaining that balance is my foremost concern, above and beyond *any* other." Spaz drains his glass and places it down on the table. "Is that all?"

"Is that why this killer's been left to act without challenge?"

Bone watches Spaz roll the question through his mind because it's illogical. Purposefully so. Gangs don't challenge. They don't need to. They merely remove that which needs removing. The real question here is, "Why do they think Rope doesn't need removing?" and Spaz would expect to be asked that, but something's off in his responses and Bone needs to figure out why. He's been nowhere near as aggressive as Bone expected, not to mention, he actually gave an answer, however misleading. Bone's got the feeling Spaz is humouring them in some way, hoping to be rid of them. That doesn't mean he won't resort to violence. He appears entirely relaxed, at ease, but Bone isn't fooled, he can feel the levels of threat in the room rising by the second.

"You're still assuming I'm aware of this killer's identity and therefore able to order an elimination." Spaz's reply is softly spoken, but there's zero elastic in it.

"Are you?"

"No. Was that all you needed?"

Bone grits his teeth. Spaz is lying. He's not even trying to hide it. Something's definitely off. It's not just annoyance that they're here asking questions they shouldn't be either. Spaz is playing dumb on purpose, meaning there's a subtext he and Stark are unaware of. This case may be more complicated, more dangerous, than he or Stark realised. Bone wonders if Stark's clocked to that yet. Knowing him, he has and doesn't give a shit. He watches uneasily as Stark leans forward towards Spaz, who flashes a needling sort of smile at him. Sharp, vicious, and filled with poison.

"Careful, pork," Spaz says gently. "You're on borrowed rep here."

"I'm aware of that," Stark replies. "But I'm way beyond the

valley of give a shit, brother."

Something a little like respect flickers so briefly in Spaz's stare, it could be mistaken for just about anything else. "Then speak," he says.

Stark's gaze hardens to obsidian black, calculating and precise. "Took my team hunting down the sewers recently," he says, his casual tone at odds with those stony eyes. "Bone here came with us. Imagine our surprise when we come across a sealed lab owned by your good selves here at GyreTech." He says the name pointedly, letting Spaz know he knows, and Bone nearly dies right there. "That lab had the mark of a spiral on the door, the spiral used by our killer to mark his scenes. The killer whose identity you claim to be unaware of."

The air in the room becomes thick enough to suffocate. Spaz's face slips from genial but guarded to something lethal. Foreign. There's a flatness to it, indicating a dearth of anything merciful. This is who Spaz is behind the amiable face he presents as camouflage. Bone's seen it before. Those few times he has, someone has died, often quite horrifically, and so swiftly he's barely had time to flinch. With great deliberation, Spaz places his feet back squarely on the floor and regards Stark silently for a long, drawn-out moment. His eyes are drills, burrowing through lens and optic nerve, into soft brain tissue, the meat of Stark. He looks hungry.

"And have you shared this extraordinary discovery with anyone up at Central?" Spaz's voice is too soft, devoid of inflection or emotion, and Stark shifts, going into flight mode, his eyes wary. Bone almost feels sorry for him.

"Only my boss," Stark says, refusing to break Spaz's stare, although he's sweating. Bone can see it on his brow. "One of my team, someone I hold very dear, whose loss I will not countenance, was taken by this killer you're choosing to ignore. Following her trail led us to something unexpected, and so I was forced to tell my boss about what we'd seen. Otherwise I'd have likely kept it to myself."

Spaz's piercings and tattoos glint under the lights. They make him appear demonic, composed of steel, but some of the danger recedes and Bone understands that this was a good answer. "Fortunately for you, I trust Burton," Spaz tells Stark lightly. "He knows how to behave. Now, what's your interest in this lab you came across? Because I'm certain you're not here to make any further unfounded accusations." Despite the polite, measured tones, the threat is clearly a promise.

"I wanted a personnel list," Stark says carefully, finally putting his anger behind him and showing proper respect. "I made the request to my boss, but he made it clear he's not permitted access to GyreTech files. Thing is, we know the killer used to work at that lab. All the evidence points to that conclusion. But without any idea who worked there, that knowledge is useless."

Easing back into his chair and stretching long legs encased in ragged grey to their full length, Spaz says, "I'm curious. Why not simply continue to pursue Aron? I can assure you, he'll be of more use than any list of personnel from GyreTech's lab."

Stark jumps at the use of that name, and Bone understands that this is who Burneo must have been. Why on earth is Spaz letting Stark see how much he knows of his real history? Because that's what Burneo is, history Stark has buried and left far behind come back to haunt him, and now here's Spaz using it to pry under Stark's skin. What the *hell* is going on here?

"I'm not ruling anything out, but we have reason to believe our killer is onto Aro ..." Stark catches himself and starts again. "We believe he's onto Burneo's willingness to cooperate. I don't like being at a disadvantage, and at the moment, that is precisely what I am, in every way."

Spaz grins. There's no humour in it, just teeth and intent. "Is that so?"

"Absolutely."

Resting his elbows on the table, Spaz says deliberately, "The personnel list from that lab would not provide the advantage you are looking for, even if I were willing to share it. And I'm not. Not yet."

"What the fuck does that mean?" Stark snaps.

"It means that question time is over," Spaz says, standing. "A pleasure talking to you both."

"But ..." Stark begins and snaps his mouth shut as Spaz holds up a large, tattooed hand.

"I'll have one of my people see you out," he says, and leaves the room.

Stark collapses against the back of his chair, wiping his brow. "Fucking hell."

"Well, you're still alive," Bone says, as caustic as he feels.

Stark blows out. "Yeah. No better off, though." He slams a fist into his thigh. "Dammit, why is he refusing to help? He *knows*."

Before Bone can answer, the door whispers open and a large, burly Establishment guard crooks a finger at them. He leads them through numerous winding corridors to a back exit.

As he opens the door for them, the walking slab of muscle says to Bone in an unexpectedly refined voice, "Spaz says to tell you that you missed a call this afternoon. He says it was important."

He throws a small salute to Bone and slams the door shut in their faces. Bone drags out his cell and works it with an impatient thumb, waiting to see what call he's missed and hoping it's not the one he's most needed to catch.

"Who was it?" Stark cranes to look.

Bone tuts. "Don't know yet. Gimmie a sec. It takes time to activate."

"You had it deactivated?" Stark asks, appalled.

Bone grimaces and snaps in defence, "It's no fucking use in the sewers, is it?" The screen on his thin, translucent cell lights up, and he scrunches his brow as he reads the number on the screen. Then he yells, "Fucking mother *cunt*!"

"Who in hell is it?" Stark demands.

"Satyr," Bone says.

Stark slaps a hand to his forehead. "How long ago?"

"Coupla hours."

"Ah shit. At least we're in the Zone already. Let's hightail it."

CHAPTER 33

*D*eep in the sweating entrails of the Boreholes, Stark and Bone enter the Apex. This time, they've no Skat escort, but they've been watched closely every step of the way nonetheless. Stark lifts his shirt away with a grimace and tries to tuck it down behind the top of his jacket. Perspiration has seeped in a slow, unstoppable waves from the bottom of his shirt, darkening the fabric of his jacket from collar to shoulder seam. He swears at the sopping stains.

"Thank fuck we don't do this much; that's two jackets destroyed."

"Mine was fine." Bone checks the leather wrangled about his hips. "Fine now, too. Didn't you get that other jacket cleaned?"

"Yeah, I got it cleaned."

"And?"

Stark sniffs. "Seems Boreholes air is full of corrosives that don't mix well with the kind of fabrics I have my suits run up in, especially when combined with sweat and humidity."

Bone apes surprise. "You mean your fake, cheapo polyfibre didn't survive a little Boreholes action?"

Stark grits out, "Who'd have thought?"

"You might want to shell out for something a little more robust in the future," Bone suggests.

"Fuck off! I'm a cheap bastard."

"It's good to know yourself."

They find Satyr waiting by his operating table, tense as a caged lion. Strapped to the table, motionless and breathing in long, shallow draws, is a male no older than eighteen. Slim and pale, he's wearing clothes that place him in a sphere of the population for whom a trip down the Boreholes would be an anomaly, to say the least. He has a light sheen of sweat on his forehead, and Bone, ignoring Satyr at first, holds the back of his hand to the glistening expanse.

Bone sighs. "How much have you given him?"

Satyr shrugs, unrepentant. "You missed my call. Couldn't let him wake too soon." He holds up a small syringe. "Got something here to pull him out."

"You sure that much won't harm him?"

"Won't be fun," Satyr admits with a smirk. "But he's young, fit, in good health. He'll be all right."

Stark, who's pacing fit to dig a grave, stops and snaps, "Let's just tank him up and get him awake, shall we!"

Satyr cocks a brow at Bone, who moves aside. "Be my guest."

For two minutes after Satyr shoves that needle into his vein, the boy's body thrashes and Bone and Satyr press down hard on his limbs and chest to make sure he doesn't damage himself on the leather straps. When the thrashing ceases, his eyes whip open, dazed but far too aware. Bone leans over and flashes his penlight in and out of each eye.

"Wakey, wakey," he says.

Breathing in short, frantic puffs, the boy begins to struggle against the straps. "Wha ... wha happn'd, why c'n I mov, lemme go." Despite the lax quality of his face, he's able to talk almost clearly. Bone takes that as a positive sign.

"Easy there, kid. Our subterranean friend here prevented you from doing something monumentally dumb," he says.

"I jus' want'd a tattoo, f'fugg's sake."

"Boy," Stark says, his gruff voice holding all sorts of censure, "that was no simple tattoo."

"Don' unnerstand what th'fuck y'r on 'bout," the boy says and then his face grows mulish. "My paren's send you? I c'n pay double." The blurring in his speech is clearing rapidly, a testament to his youth, rather than the quality of whatever was in Satyr's needle.

Stark leans over the boy. "No, not your *parents*. This is far more serious than that, boy. He's Mort, I'm City, and that tattoo was a toe-tag on your skin. We saved your life. Show some fucking gratitude."

"Gratitude?" The boy's face flushes red as he struggles against his bonds and indignation wipes the last of the slur from his voice. "If this is what you call saving someone, I'd like to see how you leave them to fucking die."

Stark's face shuts down and Bone quickly steps in front of him. "You're probably best minding your manners with him, he's had a tough week and it's only getting tougher. Now, who are you? And I don't want your tag, I want your name."

The boy gets a smug little grin on his face, and sneers out, "Harris. Harris Kermody."

Bone stares in horror and Stark boots the wall of the lab, almost breaking his foot. "A Kermody?" he yells, scowling at Harris, as if he's being purposefully inconvenient.

"That's right," Harris says. "Now let me go."

Stark closes his eyes for a moment. He looks in pain. "This was a lucky save," he growls to Bone. "We better keep it that way. Burton couldn't stop the Kermody's from starting a very loud and public hunt for our killer if this little nugget of information became public."

Harris's grin wipes from his face. "Killer?"

Bone ignores him. "Your tattoo was going to be script. A tag, right?"

"Uh-huh. You said, killer?"

"He was Martyr," offers Satyr, the amusement level in his voice too high to be accidental.

"Are you shitting me?" Stark spits out. "He was going to be a fucking publicity stunt?"

"Definitely a lucky save," Bone says, fighting panic because this is not a good development. It feels like Rope breathing down the back of their necks. Up until now, the game's been played to Burneo's limitations, but Rope knows Burneo's not on his team anymore and he's stepping up the game, seeing how far he can push this before it explodes, taking the Spires with it.

"*What about a fucking killer?*" Harris shouts the question as a demand.

With no time for charm or diplomacy, Stark answers, "You were one dumb move away from dead. I've got a list of victims so long, it gives me vertigo to look at it, and you almost ended up another nameless wonder, rotting in some out of the way hidey-hole we couldn't find in fucking time."

The hectic colour in Harris's cheeks disappears like it's on a dial spun to zero. His bravado goes with it. He looks exactly what he is, a very scared little boy.

Bone leans in to catch his eye, "Stark here's going to ask you questions, and you need to answer them honestly. This killer doesn't give a shit who you are, he just wants you to fucking die, so if you know anything about him, you need to tell us."

Harris frowns bewilderment, and then laughs, some of his colour, his bravado, returning. "You're wrong."

Stark snorts. "We're not wrong, boy. Our man intends to kill you, no doubt in my mind. If we hadn't had Satyr hold you here, you'd be halfway dead already and not even realise it. You're still not one hundred percent safe, not by a long shot."

Harris looks impatient, surprising them both. "No, it wasn't a *guy* who sent me to get this tattoo," he says to them, scornful. "It was a woman called Lever."

Bone opens his mouth, but there's nothing there to speak with.

He's almost thankful when Stark makes a noise of excessive exasperation and demands, "So, give me a description then, boy!"

"Well," Harris says, pursing his lips. "She was exotic looking, from an Asia-side CSU, but maybe part Euro. She had pale skin, like a Ghoul or a Goth, but natural. She was tall as that fucking pole." He nods his head at Bone. "Had sexy blue hair and dressed all kinds of bright, like a neon bar sign. And she had these cool surgical fingertips. Gold. She told me they were real. Fucking insane to have real gold on your fingertips."

Bone's still speechless. Sucker punched. Lever and Rope, working together? It couldn't get any worse. Lever said she was freelance, though, and Nathaniel confirmed it. Could a paycheck have pulled her into Rope's game? If so, then logic dictates he was part of that paycheck. He was aware her finding him in the Wail and the display of transmog were calculated acts, but he hadn't seen them as entrapment. In fact, after seeing Share and Share Alike, he thought Lever might need his help, but he's clearly wrong. She was a messenger, and the message was from Rope. Messages in ropes, messages in spirals, messages in shed skin. After the lab and the twins, Bone's sure the message regards transmog. But sending Lever to him seems overmuch. Flagrant, in fact. What's Rope trying to say?

He examines his memories of that night from a distance, but looking too close calls shadows of red circles behind his eyes. He can feel his sanity threatening to go reeling after them, and that's when the pieces click together and make a whole. He came so close to losing his grip. Too close. He's been walking around, wary of his own mind because he's still in real danger of losing it. Could Lever have been sent solely to unhinge him? Terror flares through his veins, quicksilver and chill, because it almost worked. But for what reason? He's no threat to anyone, and he has no idea who Rope might be, yet this whole thing seems to have been about him, designed *for* him. Why? What in the hell does Rope want with him? He realises he needs to do what he couldn't after getting his tattoo. He needs to talk to Ebony about Lever. Needs to find a way to track her down. The answers, all of them, lie with Lever.

There's a tap on his arm and Bone realises Stark's been talking to him. "Huh?"

Stark narrows his eyes. "Where were you?"

"Wondering how this fits in," he says quickly.

Stark nods. "Yup. Me, too. Got to be an accomplice. We did wonder how he was recruiting all these victims. Makes sense he'd have someone do it for him. Someone personable." He turns to Harris. "When did you meet her?"

"A month ago," he says, his bravado dulling back to fear as he realises it's misplaced. "I was at a party in the Lakes. She wasn't the usual sort you find there. It's an exclusive crowd. She bought me a beer."

"She hit on you?" Stark demands and there's a look on his face suggesting he knows she did, and why.

"Hey," Harris says, unsettled, "I'm a Kermody, man. It happens. But we ended up talking, instead."

"And that's when she told you about the tag?" Stark asks.

"Yeah, that's right. She was a Zone activist. Gang. She was talking about the Notary introducing enforcement laws: genetic barcoding, military checkpoints and scans, that sort of shit. Like you get in other cities. The kind of shit we've always avoided here. The kind we don't want. Her group are gathering people from across the Spires, people willing to remove all identifying mods as a form of mass protest."

Stark snorts. "And you bought that?"

Harris frowns. "New legislation is supposed to be in response to gang troubles moving into more heavily populated areas, yeah? But if they only need to keep track of gang movements, why punish the rest of us? What we choose to do with our bodies is not the Notary's business. This isn't any old fucking city in the CSU, it's the *Spires*."

"So, you joined because you're morally opposed to enforcement, right?" Stark sounds as if he thinks it's more to do with rebellion against the his parents than any conviction. Bone's inclined to agree.

"Yeah, that's right." Said with too much defensiveness, all but shouting an affirmative to the suspicion of rebellion.

"Why come to have your tag now, then?" Stark asks. "Why not go straight away?"

Harris is pale again, beginning to shake. "She said if the Notary found out, we'd be shut down. So, she took my stream info and said someone would contact me when it was my turn to go in."

"So, when exactly did that happen?" Stark asks, and there's poison in it, as he's guessed none of this is going to help them. Rope's outsmarted them yet again.

"I got my notification yesterday," Harris answers. "I was given a time to come for my tag, what the tag would be, and told where to pick up my cash to pay for it."

Stark looks at Satyr. "They were booked in?"

"Yeah."

"And you chose to hold this back from us?" Stark takes a step towards him, bunching his fists.

"They were booked in on my online system," Satyr says, as if he's speaking to an idiot. "It doesn't tell me names unless they type one in. It doesn't usually matter. I fill out a form when they get here. But this time, with these tattoos, it was all cash and tags, and like I said before, I *don't* question cold, hard cash in large amounts."

Stark's muscles bunch and flex under his damp shirt. "Fine," he says through his teeth. Then to Harris, "Pick up cash, you said?"

"Yeah, from a PO Box in Lower Mace, by Cary and Fifth. I can show you, if you need it."

Stark swears again. "No, I know it. And then?"

"I had to come get the tag done. Then there's an appointment in two days with an Apex surgeon called Trax to have my surgical and gen mods removed." Harris looks unsure even saying that bit. It's clear his rebellion might not have been enough to cover that step, but it wouldn't be enough to save him. The clue is in the tag.

Rope means for Harris to be the victim to break the Notary's impasse. "That bit's kinda fucked up. My mods—they're *me*, but if we left any mods in, then we'd still have ID, which kinda misses the point." He tries to make it sound offhand, but the fear is too strong to be hidden. "After that, Lever'll deal with the records wipe, and I'm gone."

Stark lets out a furious shout. He leans in close to Harris and grates out. "Trax?"

"Leave the kid be, Stark," Bone says. He raises his brows at Satyr. "Trax?"

Satyr shrugs. "Good surgeon. Too good for the Apex, but he came here nonetheless. Arrived under a cloud a few years back."

"A cloud? We need a little more than that, Satyr."

"Might have been struck off from the Piers for a bit of malpractice," Satyr says smoothly. "You'll want to investigate a little scandal involving anaesthetised rape."

Stark growls. "I know the son of a bitch. But he wasn't Trax, then; he went by the name of Carmichael. Got a friend from High Court worked that case for a while. The good doc took advantage of some Spires elite offspring, some of 'em only pre-teens. Families in question threw the book at the cunt, but he managed to slither away." He grins, feral, adding with relish, "I'll be having a word with this Trax."

"No, you won't," Satyr says without any doubt whatsoever. "He's protected. Got himself a contract for doing Establishment surgicals. Private consultations. He was always connected. A little scandal can't dent that sort of clout, and you know he won't be doing that sort of shit again, not if he doesn't want to die imaginatively. Pretty sure his contract demanded he submit to as many types of castration as Spaz saw fit, even before he began practising. Gang don't mess about."

Stark grinds his teeth. "What the fuck *can* we do, then?" he snarls, a wealth of pain behind the fury. "This cunt's got one of my team and a whole ream of victims, some of whom may still be alive and in desperate need of being found. I need to catch him, but there's fuck all I can do because everywhere we turn, we come up against brick walls. My nose is beginning to feel like a fucking pancake."

Bone grips Stark's arm. "You'll find Tress; you'll be in time."

"I don't know it, not any more. I'm lost, Bone. I'm losing. Bastard's got me beat again."

A savage mix of emotion curls from Stark. It's alarming to watch, even more alarming to be in proximity. Too much relies on Stark remaining in control.

"Tress knows the score," Bone tells him. "She's City, just like you. You've got to stay focused. If you lose it, then she's definitely lost, and you will *never* get a second chance to make that right."

Stark holds Bone's gaze for a long moment, secrets whispering at the back of those black eyes of his like flickering apparitions. But there's also steel, and Bone sees that he's touched some unknowable core in Stark, drawn something from that deep well to the surface.

"I appreciate that, brother," Stark says, the intensity still present, but subdued, reined in. "It was required."

Bone nods. "I'm betting Trax has no more record of these sorry bastards than Satyr has, so he's a lost cause, anyway."

Satyr nods at that. "You're better off getting *Martyr* here—" he points a finger at Harris, his smile mocking "—to safety, if he's got some fucker after killing him."

"Yeah," Stark admits, gravel voice filled with irritation, and says to Bone, "We can check Harris's stream at my HQ and track the message from Lever to a source. It'll probably be a dummy account, but it's a start. I also need to catch up with Suge and touch base with Faran's Buzz Boys, see what those spirals have given us in the way of body count." He looks miserable again for a moment. "I told him to call if we found one still alive."

"So, was this a help?" Satyr asks with a rude grin.

Bone grabs Stark before he can launch at the man. "Fuck off, Satyr," he snaps. "This isn't a joke. People are dying."

Satyr shrugs, careless. "And? People die every day. They die under my hands all the fucking time because they're too damned stupid to know when to stop, and you expect me to care about some guy killing randoms? Good luck with that." He flicks a finger at Harris again, his disdain all too apparent. "Get that kid off my table. I've wasted enough time and lost enough money, on your behalf and his. I'm done."

And with that, he stalks from the surgery.

CHAPTER 34

*N*ot long after 8 p.m., Bone makes his way back through the Zone, to the area nearest the Boreholes. There's been fresh snowfall, and the sun's simmering bright as a coin on the horizon as it begins to set, stinging the eyes even as the frigid air stings the flesh. He sucks in a freezing lungful, his nose burning, his torso filling with acrid cold. He follows it up with a searing blast of smoke, provoking a coughing fit of throat-scouring proportions. With Stark distracted by the Buzz Boys, come to transport Harris to Central, he's off to find Ebony. Stark won't be pleased, and neither will Nia when she receives his mail about not coming in until tomorrow, despite his obligation to start on the new bodies being found by spirals, but he'll handle them later. He has to talk to Ebony about Lever. He'd planned to go and speak to her again after the Rope case ended, but it turns out Lever's an integral part of the Rope case, and he needs to have that conversation now.

He needs to figure out why he was targeted, why he probably wasn't intended to come out mentally intact. What benefit would Rope have gained from his mental ruin? He's no threat to Rope and never was. Stark's the threat. And there's the undeniable fact that it was Tress taken in the sewers, not him. Surely, if Rope intended him harm, that was the perfect opportunity? These questions boil inside of him, leaving no room for anything else. So, here he is, wandering further out of Stark and Nia's good graces to go and hopefully catch Ebony in her shop before she closes, because he has no idea if tonight is a Neophyte shift and couldn't find her apartment again if he tried. It's hidden deep in the turbulent labyrinth of the Zone's Hub, a resident-only area he'd never been in before that night. Tucked away in a quaint line of shops off one of the Zone's main squares, Ebony's shop, Natty Dreads, stands out in bright purple, exactly as she'd described. There's light beaming from the porthole windows. He breaks into a run.

"Hey, Ebony babe," he calls as he enters the shop, setting off a ripple of entrance chimes.

Ebony raises her arms in delight. "Bone, well, what a pleasure!" She comes out from behind her console to envelope him in a generous hug. Holds him at arm's length, looking him up and down with a searching eye. "And what brings you to my humble store this fine but rather chill evening? Come to liven up your mop to match that new ink of yours?"

"Hell, no," he says with a smile. "I came to pick your mind."

Ebony shimmies back behind her console as her screen pings and takes a brisk second to deal with whatever's required before shoring her elbows up on the shiny purple surface. "Pick away."

Bone leans on the other side of the console. "I wanted to ask you about a woman called Lever. Nathaniel said you know her."

Ebony frowns. That worries Bone because she's not the frowning sort, not once you get to know her a bit. "Dresses like a bar sign? Blue hair? Gold fingertips?"

"That's her."

"She's been missing for a while. What do you want with her?" There's a buried lilt in her tone that's far from friendly—it may be accusation, or suspicion, he can't tell. Whatever it is abruptly switches to sharp concern, edging into anxiety. "You haven't got her corpse? Tell me you haven't, Bone."

And just like that, Bone's scared for Lever all over again. He recalls the strange things she said about skin. In light of her shedding hers, they took on new meaning. He thought that meaning was transformation, but perhaps it wasn't that at all, perhaps it *was* her cry for help. If she's in with Rope, she could be in the same position as Burneo, at odds with Rope's agenda and trying to find someone to help her put him down. Should that be true, he's failed her just as much as he's failed Rope's nameless corpses. Bone feels as if he's blurring. Why are all these messages and gifts for him when he so blatantly has no idea what the hell to do?

Ebony grabs his arm. "Bone! Do you have her corpse?"

He pats her hand absent-mindedly, barely feeling the pressure of her fingers. "Don't worry, I don't have her corpse," he murmurs. "And as far as I know, from when I met her, she's still very much alive."

Ebony lets go of his arm. "When did you meet her?"

"Two days ago, I think. Time's got a little out of my control of late. No longer than a few days, though." And remembering the first part of it, before it all went severely fucked up, he can't help but grin. "Well, I say *met*. To be honest, she picked me up in a bar, fucked my brains out, then kinda left me in the lurch." He's telling most of the truth, so it's easy to look sincere. "I wanted to speak to her. Just make contact. See if she's all right. She seemed like she might need help, and it's been bugging me that I didn't ask."

Ebony looks worried again. "If she's still alive, which is not what I was expecting to hear at all at this point, then I'm pretty sure she could do with a friendly helping hand. I'm also pretty sure she'd never ask for one."

"What do you think's happened?"

"You're aware she's Establishment freelance?"

"I am."

"The mortality rate's incredibly high. Usually, the Establishment would help her deal with any trouble she couldn't handle alone ..." Ebony falters, her face pinched.

"Unless?"

"Unless she was doing a job that wasn't for them. That'd be her own mess to sort."

"Is she dumb enough to try that?"

"Reckless enough. Lever is about as reckless as you can get. It's why she's a top freelancer."

"I guess they aren't much use if they're sensible."

"No." She sighs, offering him a candid look. "*Can* you find her? I mean, it's what you Morts do."

"Maybe. With your help."

"Mine? How?"

"Do you know where she lives?" It's a long shot, and unlikely, but if you don't ask, you don't know. Morts *always* ask.

Ebony tips her head to one side in a move that reminds him bizarrely of Lever. "Why go to the cost of getting someone an SA, if they tell everyone they know their contact info? If she was in the habit of sharing that shit around, you'd never have had the chance to fuck her."

"Long shot. Were all her mods done at Establishment surgeries?"

"No. Why?"

"I'm not without resources. There's a chance she hit a surgery where I know someone who can crack SA coding."

Ebony's mouth drops open. "Are you *kidding*? Have you any idea how dumb that is?"

"Dumb, but occasionally necessary. Do you think it's necessary we find her?"

"Fuck. Fuck you, yes, I do. But you be careful, and this does not come back on me."

"Oh come on, Eb. I'm an outsider, but I'm not an arsehole. Spaz would have no time for me at all if I were."

That mollifies her because it's truth. "Okay. Non-Establishment surgeries, yes?"

"Yes."

"Right. Most of her surgical work was genetic. Her hair, for a start. Chameleon gen. Expensive like most of her shit. She had all the enhancements: muscular, vascular, respiratory, ocular, aural, and psi." She pings the rim of a glass jar full of beads with a finger and says, "I saw her blow up a glass once. *Kapow*. Glass mist. It was epic."

"Wouldn't that all be Establishment, though?"

"Yeah, I have a point here."

"So, get to it."

"All Establishment freelancers get those gens as standard, but a few top of the pile freelancers, the ones most in Spaz's trust, get a little more."

"Really? Like what?" Bone wants to ask about transmog. Has to practically gnaw his tongue off to stop himself. Dropping transmog into this conversation would obliterate her trust, whether the Establishment has kept up those secret labs or not. There are some things he hasn't the right to discuss. He's not gang, not family.

"I don't know the whole list, but I know it includes that blastema-acceleration thing from Edgeway, and ..."

"Edgeway aren't Establishment," Bone interrupts, feeling the first tendrils of real excitement.

Having the blastema mod means that, with the help of a few other accelerants and gen-patches, Lever could re-grow her skin, should it be lost. It also explains the slow coagulation of blood. It doesn't explain the impossible, horrific poetry of muscular-skeletal re-design that comprises transmog, as Lever has it, but it throws a layer of logic over some portions of the encounter. Like the psi, which would perhaps explain the flight, and might also explain how strange he felt when talking to Spaz. He hopes his tattoo *was* his decision. He'd be pretty much devastated if he ever discovered he'd been manipulated into having it. Right now, he has to focus on Edgeway. It's exactly what he was hoping for. He's got a solid contact there, in the records dept, someone who finds it child's play to crack an SA. Light glimmers at the tunnel's end, a way through to answers.

"You know anyone there who can help?" Ebony asks, trying not to sound anxious and failing miserably.

"Indeed I do." Bone stands up, wanting to leave, now he knows where he's going.

Ebony grabs his arm again. "If you find her, Bone, be careful. Whatever trouble she's in might find you."

He offers her a smile. "I'm not sure it hasn't already," he says, and leaves before she can ask. There's nothing she can do to help him or Rope's victims. Only Lever can do that.

Darkness saturates the sky, stealthy as ink, and the larger solar lamps come on one by one. Being in these areas of the Zone this late is pretty much illegal, but it's a chance he has to take. He slips fast as he can through narrow streets filled with sloping terraces; temples to modification in glass and steel; blocky, minimalist squats holding surgeries in their dimly lit bellies, and places that seem to have been built from whatever's at hand. Reflections of sunset glint off the tops of glass spires like eyes in the gathering dark, watching him, warning him. Too aware of the time, he cuts through the organically sprawled innards of a small central Zone residential area, its buildings a haphazard rainbow of reclaimed wreckage ingeniously re-imagined. Urban gardens grow in the courtyards and across rooftops, lush and richly scented in the evening air. The silhouetted forms of Establishment runners appear in his peripheral vision, flashing silently across the jumbled rooftops.

At first, he's worried they'll catch him, perhaps take him to the gates, or maybe chop something off as a warning, but they seem content to follow. Bone relaxes. He zips up his jacket, disregarding the clammy cling of wet cotton beneath. His back stings a little, the salt in his sweat niggling at the scabs. He grits his teeth against the urge to scratch and continues on to Edgeway, its oblong mass a monolith on the horizon. When he exits twenty minutes later, it's night proper and the snow has begun to fall again, a slow drift of tiny flakes tumbling from the darkness. He lifts his face, smiling, the small points of icy wet tickling his skin. He reaches into his back pocket and touches the square of paper covered in his own chaotic handwriting.

Lever's address, in Gyre Central of all places. In the end, it was so easy to get, it was almost anticlimactic. His contact, the bio-drive Caden, was happy to break security to hunt her address, as if it were no more trouble than fetching an unsecured client listing. Bone's fixed the words on that paper into his memory much as he's had the snake etched into his flesh: 328 Willough Block, The Rise, Kirk Falls. Rising and falling. That's where she is. That's where he is. Aware that he's now well past his welcome, Bone takes a cab to the Zone gates and hitches a ride on the open platform up the steep sides to the city proper. The snow becomes heavier as he ascends, falling in thick bunches of messy white that soak him in seconds, and at the top he half runs, half stumbles to the nearest Bullet station. Takes a seat on the next train to Kirk Falls without any glimmer of his usual phobia—it's just so good to be warm.

At this time of night, the Bullet goes at half speed and he dozes fitfully as it cruises along, almost missing his station. He exits on feet still numb with cold, his teeth beginning to chatter. Gyre's Canted Cross runners call above him, their cries snatched by wind and snow. He should probably be on his guard, especially this late, but he's beyond caring. He stops only to check on the station map for where he has to go and then he's off, running in the mix of black ice, slush, and soft, new snow. The storm gathers pace, as if mirroring his urgency, a screen of white static, obscuring vision. It forms like a skin on the ground, on his shoes, his shoulders, stippling in his hair and making the mess underfoot more treacherous than ever. But he doesn't stop until he reaches Willough Block, where he slithers to a halt, transfixed, gazing up into the boil of dark grey in black, the insane swirl of descending white.

Is she home? Or is she up there somewhere? A bird made of viscera in a sky full of paradoxes, playing with the bundles of flakes as they tumble down helter-skelter. He wonders if she misses her tattoo like he'll miss his, even though he's had it less than two days. He's so close to asking her. He steps to the entry-way, his mouth dry. If this door is locked, he'll have to wait and hope someone comes home late, but in this weather, he'd be signing his own death warrant. Bone licks his lip, shuddering at the frozen numb of them, and pushes. The door swings open. Heart contracting in his chest, sharp as hope, he steps in, taking the stairs at a pace his legs and lungs fiercely protest. Outside 328, he hesitates again, trying to gain control over the sudden and over-whelming urge to smash the fucking door in and be done with it. He doesn't know if he'll find empty, abandoned rooms, or Lever's dead, skinless body, he just knows he can't walk away without entering. Bone taps softly at the door. Waits, and then taps again, louder this time. There's no response.

"Okay," he says. "Okay. One more try."

He bangs at the door with a fist and puts his ear close, listening. Muted sounds from elsewhere in the building float to him in inco-herent scraps, jumbled snatches, but from behind this door, there's only silence. He sets his shoulder to the door, clutches the handle tight, and shoves with all his strength. There's a low cracking noise, a little give. Reaffirming his grasp, he slams hard again. Twice more. The final time, the door gives under his shoulder, pulling away at his fingers and stretching his knuckles to burning point. He steps back and pushes the door inward, following it as it swings towards the wall, his feet sinking into the pillowed comfort of soft carpet.

He stops, astounded. Carpets are a ridiculous extravagance. Lever's clearly wealthy. The building is old, the area poor, but her flat is filled with luxuries beyond his paycheck. Beyond the paycheck of most everyone he knows. He gapes around at every-thing, disbelieving, clocking bespoke furniture, real wood blinds, and silk drapes, before realising how exposed he is with the door open. He turns to wedge it carefully shut. If Lever comes back, she'll discover the door is broken, but no one else will, not just by looking. He's safe for a while. Pacing around her living room, he peers through open doors to the empty rooms beyond, the rest of the apartment, marvelling at the size, the contents. There's so much on blatant display. Three thin tablets and two glass desktops sit on her desk, sucking power. Several tiny, slender drives ranged beside them mean there must be exabytes of information stored here. On the wall, the small glass screen of a digital sound system that would've cost thousands blinks patterns of lights next to a plasma screen thin as a poster.

He catches a man's reflection in it and walks up to the screen, realising as he does that it's him. It's got to be. There's no real shock in the lack of recognition, he's used to moments like this. The disconnect, the struggle to catch up with reality as it races away from him. Like when he's stupid drunk and stands at his own door for excruciatingly long minutes, staring at the number and wondering why he's there, sure he's not in the right place. Impatient with himself, unable to spare the time to catch up with whatever hiccup of the brain this might be, he resumes his sweep of the room. All Lever's hardware is integral, controlled by a panel on the wall next to the sound system panel. He can't see a security system, but it must be here, so why are no runners smashing into the apartment to protect her? A sharp stab of uncertainty hits below his diaphragm. This is too easy. Too damned convenient. Bone's not crazy, not yet.

Common sense dictates he should collect Stark from his office and show him all of this because Lever may not come back and there are people waiting to be saved, Tress amongst them, and it's not for Bone to decide whether they live or die. He's not a good man by any means, but he's not Rope. Common sense, however, is not in control of his mind. Nor is his better self. Whatever is in control is hungry for answers and says with infallible logic: *one look can't hurt*. He approaches the computers, peering at the symbols on the screens, gently spinning data nodes in the glass for anyone to access. Why is it not protected? Surely she'd be more careful? His gut screams at him again to call Stark, and he promises himself that he will just as soon as he finds what he needs. Definite proof that Lever needs his help. Some scrap of information about Rope's plans for him.

He peers at the screen, his fingers tapping the desk. A node formed of a gently spinning stylised A catches his eye. It's the self-same symbol he sees when he logs into any mortuary system or his home tablet, the symbol created for his personal file stream when he gained certification. He's not really surprised that she has it, not with how he's been so deftly targeteted, but from the translucent blue hue about the edges, someone, perhaps Lever or Rope, has woven new data streams into its weft on this system, and that *does* surprise him. His finger hovers over the screen, ready to access it, but he's too terrified to look, his belly churning sick circles.

"I'll come back to it," he tells himself and hates the uncertainty in his voice, his lack of courage.

Another node captures his attention, a red spiral dancing through its own coils in hypnotic continuation. Jackpot. Inside, he finds a number of streams, one marked with a cartographic motif. Heart sinking, Bone accesses the map. Unsurprisingly, it's a map of the Spires, showing the location of every spiral in the city. But here's what he didn't expect: most of the spirals are dated.

"Fucking hell."

Bone feels dizzy, looking at them all. So many victims, and almost the entire list has been taken by the looks. If the dates are accurate, they're likely all dead by now. Rope's much further ahead of them than he imagined possible. And his victims? They were always meant to be left to die alone. This was never a chase, or a game, but a carefully crafted exhibition. All they were ever intended to witness was the aftermath. Closing the map with a rigid finger, he scans the rest of the node contents, stopping when he sees the revolving glyph shaped like a paradoxical teardrop. Saved mail streams, a whole nexus by the looks. Tiny snippets float across the glyph like shadows across the moon. Mini hieroglyphs. Bone touches a shaking finger to the teardrop. He doesn't want to read these, but he has to, and not just because he failed to look into his own stream. He has to know for sure how entangled she is. Whether their encounter was a cry for help or not. From the sheer amount of information here, he fears the worst.

The emails are all brief, too difficult to interpret. Sets of instructions for making and placing the spiral around the sites chosen. Orders to continue searching for suitable additions. He's left with no real information about *her* intentions, only the intent of the thing she's working for. He steps back from the computer, pulling his cell from his pocket. Now is the time to call Stark and tell him everything. Even if he were capable of helping her, he wouldn't feel right about it now, not after seeing how far she's gone to aid Rope. Rope's victims are the ones to whom Bone is obligated, and it's time he did right by them. Using his thumb to swipe up contacts, he feels a succession of swift pin pricks on the back of his neck, like goosebumps, or raised hairs. He whirls about, but he's alone in the room, the door still rammed tight in the frame. He stands like a statue, his ears straining. There's no sound. No whispers of movement.

He rubs his face, tired to the very ends of his being, and so very cold. Not the cold left from being out in the snow, nor in this heatless flat. It's an absence of internal warmth, as if his organs are bathed in ice. Prickles crawl across his neck again, insectile and disturbing and he scratches them, his fingers thick and clumsy. They scratch too hard, causing a bite of pain as nails scrape into flesh. He sucks air through his teeth, wincing as they freeze and shocking needles of hurt shoot through his jaw. There's something wrong with his vision that he can't pinpoint. He peers around the room, his breathing becoming shallow, a touch wheezy. He feels weakened, deeply nauseous, lightheaded. He needs to sit down. Registers a small swell of surprise as his legs obey instinctively, folding him to the carpet: a heap of Bone. As he hits the floor, the edges of his mind peel apart, a sensation much like an old wound reopening in flesh. From that wound, like thick blood, oozes darkness, pain, and red circles. Red in the white. The room tilts about him and his eyelids sag, so heavy. His body breaks out in a freezing sweat, and through his mind, pulsing like radar, come flashes of dreaming trauma ... *cold, dark, alone, pain* ... a neverending cycle. Alongside them, slow and deep, his stomach begins to clench in a physical counter-beat.

Sour liquid bursts from his throat. He chokes on it. Chokes on his inability to scream as the nightmares lap against the insides of his eyes. His last lucid thought is that it must be raining, because he feels wet drops on his face, warm and heavy. Can see them landing on the pale weft of the carpet in slow motion. Then darkness and night terrors swallow him whole.

CHAPTER 35

*S*tark sneers at the bright wash of light cutting into his skull like a serrated edge, sawing and rending. He's running on maybe ninety minutes of sleep, dream curdled and too shallow, and utterly savage with it. Strung like a victim of Rope in his own exhaustion and too pissed off to even begin to express it. His team is avoiding him, giving his desk a wide berth.

"Someone dial up the fucking filter," he snarls, failing to relax even as shadow snaps over his eyes and removes that knife of sunlight.

He shouldn't take this aggravation out on them, but it can't be contained. Freaked about the GyreTech link and the narrow rescue of Harris Kermody, Burton's put a block on any kind of action until he's spoken with the Notary. He won't share information about GyreTech—that would be insane—but the involvement of the Kermody lad is enough to cripple the investigation. The Notary are very likely going to shut it down and deal with it themselves—send their Monks in to bury it by killing everyone, Rope *and* his victims. And Tress, because he won't be allowed to save her. She'll be yet more collateral damage, and there'll be no justice, not for anyone, not even Rope. Stark wants him to pay by trial. To suffer. Not to die in obscurity under the mental reach of Notary

Monks. With no choice but to sit and wait until that happens, Stark's anger is consuming him whole, demanding action. He needs to finish this. Needs to save Tress before it's too late. He slams his fist on the desk, wincing at the amount of people who jump and cry out. He's reached a limit of endurance, and Bone, who he was relying on to help him, pissed off yesterday and never returned. He doesn't care what's up with the man, there's no excuse for his neglect of the case. They're so close to a break-through, he can smell it. Feels it sit in his gut, so deep it's part of him. Rope is near, and yet he can't move to find him. Unacceptable.

A throat clears softly and Stark raises his head. Standing in front of his table, poised for flight at the slightest hint of agitation, is Carl, one of the youngest of his team. The boy's pale green eyes sidle everywhere around Stark's face, avoiding contact. Carl thrusts out his hand.

"This came for you."

It's a thick, white plastic envelope. Courier mail. Stark unclenches his fist and takes it. "Thank you, Carl."

Carl drops a hasty nod and runs from the room. Stark watches him go, bewildered.

"Am I that bad?" he asks no one and everyone at once, and the room clears in a swift flurry of feet, the door slamming behind them like a full stop. "I'll take that as a yes," he says to himself.

He turns his attention to the envelope. Along with the two locking print pads, there's an indented red print pad near the corner, indicating an audio message. He rolls his thumb across and listens to the recording.

"Stark." Stark tenses as Spaz's low, cold drawl echoes into the room. "I thought about your interest in our laboratory and I've sent you a little gift that may provide you with answers." His eyes flare wide. It was clear Spaz had closed this door, and yet now it swings wide for some reason. Why? "It comes with a warning." Spaz's voice hardens to lethal frigidity, and Stark's diaphragm constricts to knots. "This will bring up questions. You may want to ask me these questions, but that would not be advisable. I suggest you concentrate on acting on this information with all expedience."

Those last words cut to Stark's core, leaving trails of tension in their wake, fine and dangerous as striations of mental fatigue. He presses both thumbs into the release pads: black, for top-level restricted communication. Only the print information of the person sending and the person receiving will work. It's not a perfect system, not in these modified times, not even before, but who would tamper with Establishment mail? Only a fool. He doesn't question how Spaz has his thumbprints. As GyreTech's CEO, he'd find it a negligible task to obtain them. GyreTech runs the force's healthcare, and Stark's used it many times. He finds he's holding his breath as the sides pop open. Inside sits a slender plastic folder, beige and unassuming. His heart begins to pound. It's a confidential report file, one of the few things still produced only on paper, for the sake of swift disposal. He sets the plastic envelope aside and runs his fingers over the cover, snagging it open to reveal crisp white pages covered in cramped typeface and begins to read, a groan of despair and fury escaping before he's even finished the first page.

"Bone," he snarls, "what in the hell have you done?"

He breathes deeply for a moment, reaching for calm, and then reads on. As the pages on the left begin to pile up, so his shoulders rise higher and wind tighter until the pain is almost intolerable. At the back of the file sit two holos in a small, clear sheath, their images wavering. At the sight of them, a weary sort of desolation, akin to grief, mingles with the anger lining his bones, and he seals the file back into the plastic envelope, feeling *old* for the first time in his life. Stark reaches for the phone. Neither of Bone's numbers elicits any kind of response, so he leaves an alert for Bone's pager and lowers the phone back to the cradle, his head working fast. After a few seconds, he leaps to his feet, jamming the envelope under his jacket to keep it from prying eyes, and leaves the room. Racing down the stairs to avoid waiting for the lift, he calls Tal. Tells him to bring the car around. He has somewhere he needs to go. Right now.

CHAPTER 36

*M*ia stands in the aisle, rubbing her arms. De Lyon's moved her from his lab to this basement room, not wanting her visible in the windowed levels above, and this featureless white cavern does what she presumes it's meant to: it makes her feel small and useless, her years of experience meaningless. It's too open and too empty, despite the long double line of corpses. Their only effect is to transform the spartan breadth into a gallery of contortionist statues, their waxy, yellow skin tinged with green and soaked in putrid, drying waterfalls of purge fluids. A gallery of horrors, some so rigid, she'll have to practically pulverise their joints to straighten them. Yesterday's experience of that particular necessity makes her ill even now. But it's not the smell, the required methodology, nor the poignant spectacle of twisted limbs that disturbs her most. It's the faces. Howls of misery frozen to rictus, they make her flesh crawl across the tense framework of her skeleton. Leave her sickened to the pit of her belly.

She wishes and wishes that Bone were here, working beside her, but he hasn't turned up this morning like he said he would in the mail she received last night. There's been no sign of him at all, no rush of anxious feet slamming through the door, only the anxious slamming of her heart. Nia pushes down the nausea and allows her fury to rise. How dare he desert her again? In all the years she's known him, he's never been so unreliable. She knows he has reason for it, or at least he thinks he does, but this case is shredding her patience. And the Buzz Boys keep finding bodies, now they know how to look for them. Old, rotten corpses, flesh slipping heavily from the relentless pull of gravity, and some so new, they're still too human to look at. It aches within her, how close some of these discoveries have been, how fresh. Twelve new victims await her attention now, five of which have been transmogrified in some way, making seven bodies thus brutalised, if she includes the Share and Share Alike twins.

She's taken samples from both types of corpse. Not that it'll help. Bone's contact, a woman named Yanna Freyn, is resistant to handling any further specimens. Her results from Share and Share Alike generated nothing but confusion and anxiety, and she's worried about being asked questions she can't answer. Nia doesn't hold it against the woman; she's done all she can. They're all doing whatever they can, and it won't be enough. Rope's meticulous cruelty has ensured that many more victims will be lost. It makes every effort seem utterly futile. Makes Nia want to sit down and give in to tears. Taking a deep breath, ignoring the smell of decomposing fluids that refuses to dissipate, she struggles to find her professional face. Find her centre and focus on what needs to be done. But it's so hard, her resolve far away and receding further by the second. Behind her, the door squeaks as it swings open. She turns, ready to let loose at the idiot they gave her when she requested an assistant—as much of a fucking insult as hiding her away down here so no one can see that a woman's working on such an important case—and ends up merely flapping her mouth in surprise.

"Stark?"

"Tell me Bone's here."

She frowns. "What do you want with him?"

He strides up to her, his body filling the aisle, solid, reliable, overwhelming. He irritates and frustrates her in equal measures, and she still doesn't like him much. This too-focused man is bad for Bone. He's tenacious in a way that isn't quite healthy, and Nia sees all too clearly how that tenacity is leaking into Bone's habitual work-obsessiveness.

"I can't get hold of Bone and I need to have a word. Several fucking words."

"What's he done?" she asks, seeing it written too clear.

There's a long, long silence. Stark stares at her with those eyes of his, black holes filled with far too much debris, and her stomach begins to sink. "Is he here?" he asks, pointedly ignoring her question.

"No," she says. "He didn't turn up this morning. And he's not answering his cell, or responding to his beeper. Stark, what's he done?"

Again, he doesn't answer immediately; he merely stares at her. Then he says, "We'd best sit down. I need to ask you a few things."

His voice holds many layers; rage, disappointment, and an underlying reproof that makes Nia's stomach go into freefall, just like that. One second sinking, the next in her shoes as she realises that whatever Bone's done, it's something dreadful. Stark walks past her and pulls her with him to the back room, placing her without ceremony into the single good office chair. He takes a small plastic thing for himself and it creaks a protest under the weight of his muscled bulk as he leans towards her, not exactly menacing but filled with determination. Whatever he has to say, he's not going to take any nonsense. Nia folds her arms and leans away, not about to let him steamroll her.

"Has he told you anything about what he might have been doing lately? Do you know of anywhere he might want to go that he'd not want me to know about?" he asks in a voice that brooks no refusal.

Nia bites her lip. Since Bone shared the details of his encounter with Lever, her mind has been a muddle of worry and half-expressed fears for him. It's obvious he still hasn't shared that encounter with Stark, but she's not about to drop him in it until she knows what's going on, no matter what he's done. Two stupid, thoughtless absences won't wipe out eight years of a solid working relationship, and over seven years of good friendship.

"All I know is that he's not here," she says, shrugging. "What in hell has he done, Stark? Come on, talk to me. I know he's done something."

"You won't like it."

Nia snorts. "Stark," she says, "I haven't liked *anything* that's happened over the last week. What's a little more going to hurt?"

"You have no idea."

"You're right, and that's the problem!"

"Okay. Fair warning, this is one hell of a burden. You might not want to carry it."

She watches his hand clench and unclench. He's not exaggerating. Not that this man could, or would, but even so, fingers of worry become knives as he pulls an envelope out from his jacket and thumbs black seals. Top level security. After the tiniest hesitation, he removes a file and hands it to her. The thin file contains a typewritten incident report from a GyreTech lab, countersigned by her Uncle Spaz, and by Leif Adams, who was Spires Chief Mort before his death. Most peculiarly, two prominent members of the Notary, Treasurer Daved Faulk and the Chair Connaught Yar, countersigned the report, too. She looks a question at Stark.

"Read it," he says. "We'll talk afterwards."

Disquieted, she reads on. It's a report from the lab Stark and his team found in the sewer. When it was still operational, less than fourteen years ago, the chief geneticist was none other than Walken Grey. She's read some of his papers, including his work on transmog, written well before the lab's creation. He was fiercely opposed to such experimentation. She wonders what changed his mind. Whatever it was, his work was brought to an abrupt end on an evening in late September. Needle points of fear invade her chest because she's seen what Stark was talking about and he's right, she doesn't want to carry this, but it's too late. Bone Adams. Her Bone. Assistant geneticist. Guilty of atrocities in the field of genetics. She covers her mouth, holding in too much. He can't have been more than twenty; he's been hiding this for so long.

On that evening in September, something escaped, the subject of an experiment no one in the main lab was aware of. By the time Walken managed to raise the alarm, half the complex was in ruins and several people were dead. The subject was cornered, tranqed, and taken to an unused secure sus unit in the cellblock, and that's when Bone's lab was found: a military adjunct built behind a door, camouflaged by the unit itself. Inside, they discovered twelve dead bodies, horribly warped, and worse; a small number of units containing creatures unrecognisable as human, but living still, like the one who'd escaped. For almost a year, Bone had been experimenting. At least ninety-seven subjects. Ninety-seven victims. He'd found a way to grow proteins directly within the body—a breakthrough—creating living specimens and subjecting them to horrific tests.

Nia wipes away furious tears with a forearm, hurting her face, and continues devouring the words on the page. Looking for answers. Unable to process what she's reading. After the discovery was made, the team members remaining realised Walken was not present. A search of the lab was undertaken, but it was too late. Walken was found unresponsive in the comm suite, having succumbed to a massive myocardial infarction. Bone was hunted down, arrested for murder, malpractice, and fraud over accounts he'd falsified to cover his endeavours. For Walken's untimely demise, GyreTech wanted to add manslaughter to the list, but when Leif Adams arrived at City, everything changed. Concerned about his reputation, he was unwilling to see Bone prosecuted. He contacted several connections in the Notary and had them speak with key members of GyreTech. Nia's not surprised to see her uncle's involved. What's unbelievable is that an agreement was reached that he and City both consented to. Unheard of.

Bone's choice was made simple, disappear to a penal colony, wiped from record, or take a job as a Mort, just like his father— except Bone would be under constant scrutiny from GyreTech, the Notary, and even City. Perhaps frightened, now he was caught, under pressure by his father, or simply uncaring, Bone agreed, and the past was wiped clean, in truth and from his own recollection. The file doesn't state by which method, memory patching or wiping, but it doesn't matter, really. The deceit is the issue. Then the lab's records, the research, the bodies, were made to disappear, too. Even Walken's death was altered to the history she knows, sudden death in his sleep of unknown causes at twenty-five, a shocking loss to genetic research.

This report is the only remaining evidence of actual events, and reading the final words, Nia's barely able to breathe anymore, crippled by grief, by unimaginable rage. This explains so much of how Leif was with Bone. He was terrified the wipe would fail, terrified his son would relapse and be put to death. As she folds the file shut, the last page slips aside to reveal a clear sheath at the back, holding two holos. Incongruously, they're black and white, likely built from laser-copies of lab IDs, but there he is, staring up at her: Bone. And she doesn't know him. This younger version of Bone is a stranger. He might be wearing a familiar face, but the man behind it is not the man she knows. Her knuckles blanch white as she grips the file, her tears spattering the plastic, but she no longer notices them.

She looks at Stark, helpless. "Tell me this isn't true. Please."

Stark thumbs the recording and Spaz's voice fills the room. Though he can't know her connection to Spaz, it's the final nail in the coffin of her disbelief. Nia's pole-axed, too much to even continue crying. How's she never seen this in Bone? She's got gang instincts, sees far deeper than other folk, and there's no clinical method guaranteed to override criminal impulses. Wipes are barbaric, often clumsy, and memory patches can be time bombs in the brain. Neither has any impact on behaviour. Reprogramming can change behaviours, but he couldn't have been a Mort after that level of rehabilitation. The only possible conclusion, is that the patch he was given, was created to become part of him, overriding his previous personality, and that's not good at all. Because if it fails, he could disappear. Disgust and anger mingle within her like gasoline, ready to implode.

"So, what does it mean, Stark? Are you trying to suggest Bone is Rope? Or that Rope is someone from the lab, intent on exposing Bone and making him pay for his past?"

"I know Bone's not Rope," Stark says to her, his hand tugging through his hair, making a mess. "I investigated him before pulling him on the case. He's predictable, fixed in his routines. He works, he drinks, he sleeps. There's nothing else in his life, and no way he could have masterminded this level of gameplay. He expends all his energy just surviving a day."

"So, you think exposure is the end game?"

Stark acknowledges that with a sober nod. "Yes, and the intricacy of the game suggests significant premeditation."

"Fuck. You don't fix an atrocity by creating one." She shakes her head, way beyond disbelief or disgust. "We have to stop Rope. Are you any closer to finding him?"

"Even if I were, I couldn't. I've been ordered to stand down. The Notary are likely to take over, deal with it themselves. All searches for victims will be suspended, then. They'll let them rot."

Nia's horrified. "We can't let that happen. And what about Bone? He's unravelling, could be on the way to a patch rupture. Hell alone knows what might happen then, or who might end up hurt."

"Agreed, hence my earlier question. Do you think you might care to answer with the truth now?"

Of course, she will. This changes everything. "He met a woman. Said she did something incredible, impossible—shed her skin and flew off through a fucking roof into the night. He said it was transmog." She rubs her forehead, inexpressibly weary. "I thought he was a bit delusional, to be honest, but I didn't tell him

so. Even Share and Share Alike's mutilation can't convince me that
transmog could ever work the way he described it."

"What was her name, Nia? Can you remember?"

"Yes," she says softly. "He said her name was Lever."

Stark rears back. "Lever?" he asks, and she can see the shock in
him. It's rid his face of expression, whitened his cheeks. "Is that
where he is now? With Lever?"

"No. He can't find her. He's been trying to. That's what the
tattoo's about. She had it, and now he has it, too. He mailed me
yesterday evening and said he was going to talk to a woman
called Ebony about Lever. He told me he'd be back this morning." And her temper rises again into sharp peaks. "He
promised."

"Nia," Stark says with dangerous calm, "we need to contact
Ebony. Do you have any idea who she is?"

Nia sniffs. "Not a clue, but he said she's Zone gang, so I know
someone who will." She pulls out her cell, activates a quickdial.
"Hey, Unc, I need a number."

"Nia! What number's that, little hen?" Spaz shouts over the
noise.

"A woman called Ebony, she works at a place called
Neophyte."

"Should I be asking why?"

"No. Probably not."

"Fair enough. Two shakes and it'll be on your cell." There's a
soft click as the phone hangs up.

A moment later, Nia's cell pings softly. She thumbs the number
on the display and waits till the other end picks up. "Hi, is this
Ebony?"

"Sure. Who's this?"

"Nia Lark. I'm a friend of Bone's."

"Nia Lark. Spaz's niece?"

"Yeah."

"What do you need to know?"

"If you have any idea where Bone is. He's not answering calls."

"Oh no," Ebony says, her voice full of dismay. "I told him to be careful."

"Ebony, please, if you know where he is …"

"I don't know where he is," Ebony interrupts. "But I know where he was going."

"Where?"

"Edgeway. Records department. He was looking for an ID. An address."

"Lever's?" Nia asks, careful to give Ebony an easy way to acknowledge.

"Yes."

"Thanks, Ebony." She ends the call and says to Stark, "Edgeway."

Stark gives her a sharp nod. "Let's go."

He's got that long, black car of his waiting outside, and it amuses her how the engine purrs to life as soon as he exits the Mortuary doors. His driver clearly knows him well. He pushes her without ceremony into the back seat, leans forwards to the driver, and snaps, "Edgeway, Tal. Fucking tank it. Use those security pass codes you ripped from Bone at the Zone gates; we'll deal with the fallout later."

Tal grins, touching a finger to his forehead. "Right you are, boss."

Nia squeals a little as the car shoots off, wheels ploughing through the snow as if superheated, as if there's actually some road surface there to grip. Even the SF's tanks slide, if they take off anything like this fast.

"What the hell kind of tyres do you have?"

"Damned good ones. It's necessary. I sink a good deal of my crappy budget into this. I make sure I can get where I'm needed."

Tal speeds them to the Zone, subsonic sirens blaring to unlock the lights and open restricted routes built for a city force stretched beyond endurance. The guards at the Zone gates are suspicious, but they don't argue the use of Bone's codes, and Tal's in, booking it to the Lake, to Edgeway. Rearing up into the clouds, bold and imposing, Edgeway's one of the oldest, most prestigious genetic surgeries in the whole of the Zone. In this building, specialists can make anyone pretty much anything, within the realms of legality. For a price. Nia's presence gives them leave to go direct to the records dept. Printed copies and computer back-ups of patient files are in a bunker, miles away in Mace, but the computer files, filled by each surgeon in the building, are collated in a huge lab on the twelfth floor. She knows the Records Master well, having come here in her capacity as Bone's assistant. No corpses on Gyre West tables have expensive gens from here, but quite a few have surgeries from theatres on the seventh and eighth floors—complex implants and bodily alterations less pricey than delicate gen manipulation.

In the records room, all is silent. Sat in his enclave, far away from light or people, is Caden. Facing the thin glass of his screen, he says without turning to look, "Nia Lark."

"Caden."

Stark leans in, frowning, but before Nia can warn him to keep his counsel, Caden speaks again, "A City Detective. Stark, no less. Interesting. Would you both perhaps be after the same information as Bone Adams?"

"We are," says Nia.

Caden swivels to face them, but he has no face, only a smooth glass surface running with data streams like illuminated tears within the glass. His body, too, is stripped to bare essentials, wired into his chair, a mobile station hovering above the floor, with a haze of heat beneath. Caden's a bio-drive, rewired and genned to become a living network interface, safer and less unstable than AI. Somewhere under that shining facade is what's left of this man's face, the skull and his network of facial and cranial nerves wired to circuitry. He's hanging on to human by a bare thread of body parts, but almost all machine in the mind.

"It is an unusual request, most hazardous to obtain," Caden says. His voice is disembodied, floating on the air. "You being here so soon after Bone Adams, and with a City Officer, too, would suggest either Bone Adams, or myself, or the both of us, are in trouble."

"You can't calculate that?" Stark asks, only a dab of sarcasm wafting through genuine interest. Bio-drives are uncommon and too costly. City budgets don't stretch to such extravagances. Nia stifles a smile, her first encounter with Caden was equally confounding.

"I am a glorified computer-mind, capable of making many seemingly instantaneous conclusions resulting from calculations so fast, they would burn out your neurones, but I am not a medium," Caden replies without inflection, though the humour is blatant.

"You're in no trouble, Caden," Nia says politely, shooting a warning glance at Stark. "I'm sorry to ask you to crack SA files again, but it's important."

"I am certain it is, Nia Lark, and do not fear, I am working the encryptions already," replies Caden. "It won't take me as long as it took for Bone Adams. I know where I am going this time." There's a pause in which a soft humming can be heard, the sound of a multitude of programs running to crack Establishment encryptions. "If this address is the crux of the problem, then you may wish to hurry," Caden says to Nia. Though there's no inflection in his voice, she doesn't imagine the increased hum of the room's computers, almost anxious in tone.

"Why?" Stark demands.

Caden's bland voice informs him serenely, "I provided said address to Bone Adams yesterday evening. I might deduct from your being here, and requiring this information from me, that he is not able to give it to you himself. By which fact, I take it that he is missing. If so, then it must be concluded that he has been missing since going to this address, and he will have gone there last night. His agitation and excitement were palpable."

Nia throws a worried glance at Stark. He smiles reassurance, but the depth of worry in his eyes sets her stomach to boil. "I understand," she says.

"Information received," Caden says. "Sending to your personal account, Nia Lark. Bone Adams insisted I dictate. I assumed it was paranoia, but perhaps he had reason. I have disguised and erased my tracks and this transferral well, as I did with Bone, and I will now erase both visits, but I advise great care nonetheless. Breaking into Establishment files twice in so short a span is perilous. They may catch the breach and trace it. Once they trail it back to me, they will be within sniffing distance of you, despite my camouflage work. No matter your connections, I am very much afraid you would bear the brunt of their disapproval."

Nia nods. "Understood. Thank you, Caden."

"A pleasure. Now, if you will excuse me, I have new files coming in."

Back down in the forecourt, beside the open door of Stark's car, Stark takes Nia's arm. "You don't have to come; you know that."

Nia inclines her head just a touch. "But I want to," she says, "and you know there's no way of stopping me."

"Unless I'm underhand," Stark tells her.

Nia runs her tongue beneath her top lip, over her teeth. "There'd be consequences," she says, soft and definite, so he hears the threat.

Stark releases her arm and leans over the edge of the door. "*Spaz* is Unc?" He's resigned, a little pissed off.

"My dad's younger brother," she says. "He took over from Uncle Jell, who was the eldest."

"Inherited?"

"No, he killed him. It was necessary."

Stark huffs out. "That's some family."

Nia gets into the car. "That's right," she tells him, her voice cat-satisfied. "And I'm not afraid to use them."

Stark barks a laugh. "I admire that," he says, surprising her. "But you may not like what you see," he warns, taking the address from her cell and sending it to Tal's console. The car purrs forwards.

"I work in a mortuary, Stark. Even if we find Bone in pieces, I'll stay professional until I have the privacy to fall apart, myself."

Stark raises a brow. He doesn't need to express what he's thinking, she sees it all too clear. He doubts her mettle. He saw her reaction to Share and Share Alike, and probably caught her this morning, too, being all unprofessional and fucked up, surrounded by those awful, twisted corpses. Nia turns to stare fixedly out the window, her heart rattling in her chest like machine gun fire.

CHAPTER 37

arkness ... cold ... such pain ... such fear ...

Foul tasting vomit floods Bone's mouth, runs over his chin, and drips to the floor, muffled and distant. The sound is frightening, holds the immediate resonance of memory, but these are just his dreams invading during waking hours. They have to be. His body shakes with fine, sweated shivers, like when it's so very bad, he could drown in that amber, olive swirl, corrosive and sublime. He coughs to clear rank vomit aftertaste and ropes around his ribs sear deep into his skin, biting and constricting. So familiar. Dreams become reality. The Mort becomes the victim.

No reason to doubt it. Rope has him.

Another mouthful of puke rises, thick and caustic. He retches, his head drooping, his hair sticking to his face in sodden strings. Vomit bubbles from his nose, acidic and burning. Bone closes his eyes against the sting of it and tries not to hear the rush of liquid hitting the floor, the rhythmic drips that follow. Aching in waves, he heaves and heaves again. There's nothing left to come up, but still he heaves, the thick taste in his throat making it impossible to stop. He gasps at the pain, ribs creaking and straining with each contraction until he's able to stop.

Darkness surrounds him like water, closing in around him, hard as the ropes that bind him, and panic unravels his breathing to sharp pants. Scraps of dreams rise from the darkness, both inside and out, assaulting him hard as physical blows.

The shatter of glass ... Soft laughter ...

They're vivid. Too real. He wants to run from them, but there's nowhere to go. He tries to cry out for help, but all that comes is a husky wisp of noise that hurts worse than the pain rimming his rib cage, and panic takes over. He starts thrashing against his bonds, his whole body twisting hard. The pain is immediate and catastrophic, a thunderstorm of shrieking nerves. It halts the breath in his chest, suspends the beat of his heart, and brings more of those dreams crashing through his mind.

Migraine sharp pain ... red circles ... red circles in the white ... screaming ... screaming ...

And he's screaming, too, harsh bursts of high-pitched air he's unable to stop. He struggles for air. Bright snatches of light pop, snap, and sparkle across his vision until the darkness around him looms and snatches him back into itself.

CHAPTER 38

*T*al's driving so fast, the scenery's blurred to a featureless smear, but it takes him over an hour and a half, weaving and playing through insane traffic and using the side ways and passes, to drive from the Zone's south gate to the address in Gyre Central. This area is far enough in to avoid actual violence, but there are still the quietly tense figures of City Officers and local gang members—Spine Freaks—posted on the rooftops, standing sentry, keeping the uneasy peace. Tal pulls up outside the tall, grizzled aspect of a building, which looks to have been unchanged for decades, the warped windowframes of dirty plastic speckled with pigeon shit, the plascrete slab-work faded and crumbling. The street is quiet of traffic, like most residential back roads, and the car engine cuts off to unearthly silence.

Pressing the button, Stark says to Tal, "We don't know what we're walking into here. If anything happens, call out for local backup and then get the hell away to a good distance until it arrives."

"Got it, boss."

Stark leads the way into Willough Block, pushing Nia behind him as they reach the stairs. Gun raised, he sticks close to the wall, stopping briefly at each level to scout for trouble. The building looks too thin to have so many apartments crammed into it, but

Nia knows how deep these buildings go, and even the smallest holes in a place like this cost a bomb to rent. It's Gyre Central. If you want cheap living in the Spires, there's only two options: the Outskirts, where war between the gangs and the City rages at full fury, or the Wharf, where you may as well just paint a target on your arse and be done with it, if you're not gang. There's the Rat Gulley, too, under Black Frank's rule, but it's no place to live if you're not fond of rats or gang law. Everywhere else, everyone just makes ends meet as best as possible. Near the third landing, Stark slows, tensed for action, freezing as soon as he sees the door.

Nia peers out from behind his arm. "What is it?"

He looks down at her and murmurs, "Door's broken." He turns a bit and pushes her against the wall. "Stay." She opens her mouth to protest, but he puts a hand up, his gaze forbidding. "I'll call you in when I know it's safe. Far be it for me to protect you from a trauma, if you're determined to have one."

Light on his feet, despite all that brawny mass, Stark moves swiftly across the landing. Tense and enervated, she watches him as he flattens himself to one side and disappears into the room in a movement so soundless and fast, it startles her. She breathes out slowly, trying to calm the pounding of her heart. Time thins and stretches, seconds taking as long as hours to her as she waits in the corridor, her eyes glued to the doorway. Then Stark peers out. His face is a dour mask.

"Come on," he says.

Nia hurries over, struggling to summon her detachment. She needs to concentrate on helping him figure out what's happened, if anything. Hysteria won't aid that. Besides which, she doesn't think Bone's dead body is in there, Stark would probably give fair warning. She steps into the room and cries out softly in surprise as her feet sink into carpet. Her eyes fly to Stark's face. He shrugs, raising a hand to sweep at the room in general.

"Lever's not lacking," he says with a rueful grin. "She's left all this shit unprotected, too. I've already sent a map of the Spiral victims to Suge."

He's over at a table filled with an astonishing array of computer equipment, busy on the screen and his phone, transferring streams, but his body is oddly cramped to the side. Nia frowns as she sees why. A long patch of carpet just before the computer has been flattened, the indentation too unusual to be natural. Something very bad happened here. To Bone. Her gut cramping, she moves closer, needing to know what it was he endured and whether he could have survived it. Several droplets of crusted blood surround the flattened patch, and a thin, sticky area darkens the edge nearest the computer. Vomit. Drying now, but soaked right into the carpet. She sees straight away that he threw up whilst on his side, and feels dizzy with relief. That probably saved him from drowning in it. She refuses to believe otherwise. She looks back towards the door. Their boots carried snow in from outside, just as Bone's will have done. Some was lost on the stairs, but the remaining traces dampen the carpet, flattening it where they both stood the longest, by the threshold. Any further traces beyond are slowly leaching from the pile.

She turns back to the patch of flattened carpet and says, "His body was soaking."

Stark raises a brow. "That's relevant?"

"Very much so."

"Explain."

Nia nods over at the carpet by the door. "Our shoes lost most of their snowmelt on the stairs. Just there, by the door, is a flatter patch where we first entered the room. The last of the damp from our shoes has compacted the pile just there. Bone's shoes dried as he moved into the room, just as ours have, but his body was wet and hadn't dried by the time he fell, and then got significantly wetter, drenching the carpet pile through." She kneels down, touching her fingers to the edge of the indent for a split second. "Still damp, you see, and we haven't just missed him. It's been evaporating for a while, even in these temperatures. The top fibres are reconstituting. Something brought him out in a perpetuating sweat. A drug of some kind."

"Explains a bit about our other victims." Stark nods sharply. "Good. Now, explain these blood droplets. I'm coming up blank. After what you said about drugs, I'm thinking he maybe got spiked and pitched a fit because there's so little of it. But there's no sign of a struggle. It's plain weird."

Nia lowers her head to examine the droplets more closely. There's no pattern to them, they're random drips, but so thick, the blood must have been like syrup. It's unusual, to say the least. Like nothing she's ever seen. She looks around the carpet, trying to identify a splatter pattern, and her eyes flare wide. The drops aren't confined to that flat patch of carpet. They're everywhere, small enough to miss, but obvious now she's looking for them, and the answer flashes into her mind.

"It's not his blood."

Stark stops what he's doing. "What?"

Nia indicates the drops around the room. "They're all around. Something was dripping very thick blood from a height."

They hold each other's eyes and say at the same time, *"Lever."*

Stark slaps a hand to his forehead. "Of *course*. We had it all wrong. It's not fucking exposure Rope's after. Bone's a fucking target; he's *the* target."

"He wants to kill him. Of course." Nia's overwhelmed, but something in her thinks that if she'd witnessed what he'd done in those labs, she'd want him to pay, too, though not like this, not with this wanton, mindless loss of life. Then she feels guilty for thinking that way about him at all. He's been her friend for so long, such thoughts are a kind of betrayal.

"I thought the sculptures were out of the way because Burneo was involved," Stark says. "He was, that's for certain, but I think the real reason they were hidden is because they were just for *Bone*. Not to solve, not as a sign of Rope's superiority, but as some sort of progressive attack." He snaps his fingers. "And Harris. Harris was a fucking lure, pulling him back to Lever. His fucking *face*, when Harris mentioned her ..." He directs that black gaze at Nia and asks, though by his tone, he's already got some idea, "What might Rope have been doing with such an attack?"

"Memory patch degradation," Nia says, immediately grasping the direction of his thoughts. "There's a well known shortcut to breaking patches."

"Trauma," Stark says.

Nia nods. "Severe trauma."

Stark rubs his cheek, deeply troubled. "But doesn't it have to be *direct* trauma? Our victims are one hell of a sucker punch, but they're not *personal*."

"They are," Nia says. "I've watched this case gradually compromise his confidence in his competence, in his skill. You know that's all he's got. He's already coming apart. You've seen it. I have. One sharp shock to Bone's mind and the whole thing will collapse."

"So, he'll remember. You think he'll remember all of it?"

Nia shakes her head. "I think Bone's patching was designed to *become* him. There's no other way to explain how he hasn't reverted in all this time, how he's been stable enough to work, to gain his rep. In that case, if his patch ruptures, there'll be one or two bright, almost abstract memories, but the rest will be fucking insanity. He'll be gone."

"Shit."

Nia finds she's fighting back tears. Her Bone, the Bone built over the patch, has been through enough. Leif was a vicious little man. He would have worried about Bone only in connection to his own reputation. The damage it might do to his public image. In private, he was incredibly cruel. Enjoyed humiliating others. Enjoyed control, especially of his son. Though it's no excuse for what Bone did, Leif's manipulation was likely the reason he transgressed in the first place. To the man Bone's become with the patching in place—and she believes it has worked on him, that he *is* a better man—Leif's cruelty was a form of mental torture resulting in immense psychological damage. She finds that she can't help but feel angry for him. Devastated and angry.

"What can we do?" she demands. "I know he's done wrong, Stark, but we have to help him."

Tension spirals from Stark. "Of course we do, and we have to get Tress back from Rope before …" He stops, staring at the floor for a moment, his shoulders too tense. When he looks up, his eyes are absolutely clear, the resolve in them frightening. He thumbs a glyph on his cell.

"Suge. You got a copy of that map I sent out to the Buzz Boys?"

"Of course." Suge's voice comes clear over the mic, as if he's in the room, making Nia jump.

"I want you to program it into a flexscreen with those sewer maps you sourced, and meet me at the River Head."

"What are we doing?"

"Situation's picked up a few notches. I'm about to go rogue."

"How rogue?"

"Rogue as it fucking gets. Badge-loss rogue. The Notary is about to shut us down."

"Tress?"

"They'll abandon her."

"Not on my watch."

"Nor mine. And now we have another victim: Bone. The accomplice we learned about yesterday, that Lever woman, she got him. She'll have taken him to Rope, which means his life is in the balance, too. I'm going in after Burneo, to get that help he was trying to offer."

"What the hell does Rope want with Bone? I thought he wanted Bone to solve these bodies, not become one."

"Nope. Turns out the whole damn thing is about him, and I'm not about to let him die when he's got one hell of a lot to answer for. I'm done with pussyfooting this shit. I aim to end it."

Suge laughs. "Then there's no way you're going without me."

Stark grins. "Good man. Meet me in two hours. I've got Tal, we should be able to get there that fast. Bring torches and a spare gun. We're taking Nia with us."

Nia gapes at him. "Me? I'm not equipped to go hunting killers, Stark."

He gives her the benefit of a deeply serious look. "No, but we may need someone who knows their way around bodies. I presume you have med training, too, yes?"

Nia swallows, realising what he means. "Yes," she says. "I can do that, but I'll need a med kit."

Stark nods. "Suge, bring the best med kit you can source. I'd say swipe it from the bay."

"Done. See you in two hours."

Back in Stark's car, speeding towards the River Head, Nia clasps her hands in her lap, her nails scoring bloody crescents in her palms as she fights to stay connected to the here and now. She feels sick and can't stop it. Within her chest, a terrified heart contracts in rapid-fire bursts, leaving her breathless and ragged. She's so frightened, she feels sensitised. But she's empty, too. She's lost her centre and doesn't know how to go on. Everything she thought she knew, every certainty she had, lies in ruins, and she hasn't a clue how to put them back together, or even if it's possible.

CHAPTER 39

Spaz runs his hands over his hair. It's usually in a fairly messy Mohican, but he's tamed it and tied it back, as he always does on these occasions. He's suited up, throttled by a silk tie and wearing fucking wingtips. It's not anything he enjoys doing. This complete subsuming of his style has always felt like too much of a concession because the members of the Notary don't respect him, they fear him. Moreover, they fear what he's capable of. They should. Even though their understanding of the lengths he'll go to is incomplete. He's not a man of many principles, and they've pushed him until he's prepared to break the few he has remaining.

He shoves a sleek frag-pistol into his shoulder holster. It's plas, bullets and all, and doesn't show up on scans, and he knows he'll be scanned. He's no intention of using this today, but he'd never be fool enough to appear at a meeting with the Notary board unarmed. He buttons his jacket, checking the fabric flows over the gun, concealing it properly, and makes his way out to the waiting car. Dash is already inside, his fingers speeding over the flat pad of a tablet as he liaises in a simultaneous face-call through a screen attached to his right ear with the runners who'll shadow them all the way to the meeting and back. Spaz doesn't ask for this courtesy and protection, nor does he particularly require it, being more than capable of committing violence on his own behalf, but he receives it, nonetheless. He raises a brow at Dash as he settles into his seat. Dash stops talking for a moment and looks him up and down.

"You look normal," he notes.

Spaz tugs at his collar. "It's fucking throttling me."

Dash shrugs. "Par for the course." He indicates the driver to move off and finishes his call.

When he's done, Spaz replies, "Makes not a damn difference what I look like. They all treat me like an unexploded bomb when they've never seen one, and wouldn't know what to do if it made to blow up in their faces."

"You'd think they didn't live in gang territories, the way they act," Dash agrees scornfully.

"They don't, Dash. Eyes closed, fingers in their ears, humming up a storm to cover the sound of runners above them. Using the Zone like a fucking mod supermarket. They've blanked out the uncomfortable bits. They think the Spires belongs to them. Think we'll go nice and quiet when we're told."

"Rude shock awaits."

Spaz leans his head back against the seat. "Not half as rude as the one they'll get if we pull this off."

"You still think we will? After all that's happened?" Dash is unconvinced. "We lost him. Best runner teams available shadowing his arse twenty-four seven, and we lost him. We're being outsmarted in our own game."

"Maybe," Spaz replies quietly. "But I've responded."

"Really?"

"Of course. We can't lose Bone. That's a solid, inescapable fact, a boulder blocking my path. So, I've offered Stark the extra nudge he needed to put an end to this."

Dash puts his tablet to one side. "How's that?"

"I've given him the file we cobbled together after that little incident at the lab."

"Holy fuck! He could make one hell of a mess with that."

"Not really. Any damage to us, the Notary, or Central will be minor in the scheme of things. Thing is, Stark's only been stalling because he knew the Notary would order him to stand down, and he's been warned it'll be his badge if he disobeys orders again. I needed to provide him with sufficient impetus to disregard that."

"But he's a fucking human tank. The Notary'll clock what's going on in a flat second with him barrelling about."

Spaz lifts his hands, a helpless gesture. "We can't keep this from them forever, that's another inescapable fact. All we can do is try and get Bone safe under the radar. Get him to where we can protect him. That's it. You know war's coming. Connaught's determined to find a way to provoke it, and that man is not somebody I would *ever* underestimate. He's got gang levels of cunning in him. He's dangerous, does what's necessary. I respect that, even though I can't allow it."

Dash acknowledges that with a nod, but he says nothing more. He knows the score. At the face of it, they're fighting a civil battle of words over tables like the one they're headed to now, but beneath the surface, the talons are out, tearing at the structures put in place to protect gang folk. Spaz slips down within himself, where scraps of things he's seen mingle and merge, building an incomplete picture. He knows nothing of the future, he doesn't even know for sure if he's making the right moves. There are only possibilities, and many possibilites will always lead to failure. That's just how it is.

The Notary building is a monolithic structure at the heart of Mace Central, featureless, seamless, and haughty as a spire. The black glass at the bottom is not one-way, it doesn't need to be, and the entrance lobby is larger than Central's, with no stairs, only secure lift pods. The Notary are paranoid, and rightfully so. This building was designed to repel runners, a smooth plain of polished concrete, impossible to leap to from nearby buildings. The levels above the lobby are all one-way glass and shielded from both Xray and psi-gens. It's a fortress. As expected, both Spaz and Dash are scanned as they enter. Spaz feels the buzz on his body, the prying in his mind and holds it out effortlessly. Once cleared, a small guard of four Monks escort them to a pod, their faces blank as usual. But they're on edge, they don't like dealing with Spaz because they can't read him. They struggle with Dash, too, who possesses natural protections against invasion. It's the only reason Spaz allows him to accompany him to these sorts of meetings.

At the fifth floor, Dash leaves the pod with one Monk at his side to join the Notary PA's, whilst Spaz continues onward to the tenth floor, where his Monk guard ushers him out. He knows the way, but allows them to walk in front of him and lead him to the boardroom. Appearances are everything in this game. Jell mistook the brief and changed his spots, all Spaz does is disguise his to an extent. He knows the value of the long game. He also knows the value of appreciating the strengths of one's opponents, and out of the whole board, he has only the one real opponent. He strides up to Connaught Yar as he enters the boardroom. Yar's as tall as he is, with olive skin a shade darker than his own, and straight black hair. His eyes are black as CO Stark's, and he hides the restrained demeanour of a hunter well beneath an icy smile and a silk suit. If Yar knew what they were planning, he'd kill Bone, which is why he won't know for as long as Spaz can keep it under wraps.

"Connaught," he says, and they exchange a firm handshake, neither too soft nor too hard. They both know the value of holding back.

"Eadin."

The use of his birth name makes Spaz smile, as ever, reminding him of his mother. Reminding him why he's playing the long game. Connaught uses Spaz's birth name as an insult because, although Spaz is the gang name he earned for less-than-sensible exploits as an unruly teen, it's also his honorific, and to use it is a sign of respect. Not one of his people would dare call him Eadin. No one but his mother, who always called him the name she chose for him until Connaught's war stole her voice by ending her life.

She gave everything she was to protect their people, and Spaz honours her memory by giving no less. He takes his seat, his mental focus needle-sharp. These men are living on borrowed time, and Yar lives only because Spaz allows it. When he decides Yar's time is up, he'll end it personally, with his bare hands.

CHAPTER 40

ress gasps a bolt of air, bracing against the weight of hurt her body has become. Somewhere out there, in the cold dark of these never-ending tunnels, he's come at last. He must have because everything's changed. The air feels charged with purpose, a purpose that only ever comes with him. Tress begins to sit, levering herself up on shaking elbows. Her clothes, though no longer filthy, chafe against her raw wounds and she moans. She'd expected soreness, but this is awful.

Straining with every ounce of strength, she pushes herself up in small, wincing movements, each one wringing another moan from deep within her chest, and the occasional liquid belch as she fights down the urge to summarily eject the paltry contents of her stomach. Once upright, she leans forwards, allowing her legs to drop off the side of the shelf she's been given for a bed. A strangled yell escapes her mouth as her muscles shriek defiance. She's so weak and feels so helpless. It's not just the pain, it's the memories of what she faced in that tunnel drilling gaping holes in her strength, her will.

The attack made her feel helpless for the first time since childhood, cutting deeper wounds in her confidence than those carved into her flesh. A sick sort of dread dogs her thoughts, ebbing and rising in waves. She can't fight it, she has to work around it, and

Tress can do that. She's not a quitter. She's a street rat, just like Stark, but she came up from the Rat Gulley, from the down-belows, not the streets of the Gyre as he claims to be.

He's hiding the truth of his past of course, but she's got too much respect for him to snoop. Wherever he's from, it's got to be the gang territories, the hard places, he's too much like her for it to be anything other. This, however, is her place, her old stamping ground, or enough like it for comparison. She can do this. Stark's depending on her. So is Burneo.

Tress lowers her feet to the floor, hissing as they flatten to the rough surface of concrete. If she'd thought the pain of sitting up was bad, she was kidding herself. This is pain, it's fucking horrendous. She doesn't know whether to puke, scream, or surrender to unconsciousness. She chooses to wait, instead, and breathe through it, though her lungs appear to be stuffed to the rafters with barbed wire.

Eventually, as she knew they must, the motion sickness and the hurt pass enough for focus, and Tress launches off her hands, throwing her weight onto her feet and screaming at the pain of it. She throws up a little and sways, in the grip of profound giddiness. Teeth clenched together so hard, her jaw feels misaligned, she leans her weight onto the wall and begins to walk, forcing tired, pain-wracked legs to obey.

Step by step, the pain ebbs to a dull throb and the weakness shifts, replaced by a crazed sort of energy. It's only adrenalin, but she welcomes it like an old friend. It's enough to work with, enough to hold her solid for a while. Hopefully long enough. She's got to be able to reach Burneo, somewhere out there by what he calls his "river." That's where he's going to bring Stark. And she's got to find a way to tell Stark what happened in that tunnel, no matter how much it scares her.

It's so important that he knows there are monsters in the sewer.

CHAPTER 41

*S*tark leaps across another sewer threshold, the impact of his landing echoing a ghostly accompaniment. He holds up one hand to stall his team and walks forwards a few paces, his footsteps hollow tolls in the darkness like warning bells. He sweeps his torch around, searching every hidden inch. Stark's hoped at every step that this might be the one that brings them to Burneo, or Burneo to them. For every step that's failed to summon him, the tension wound within rises by one unbearable notch. Though he's hiding it, he's in an absolute state. And this, this is not helping. It's all wrong. This is not a tunnel at all, it looks like the terminal they've been searching for. But it was supposed to be far further on than this, the map indicating another two or three miles of narrow sewer tunnel to traverse. That singular fact unsettles him deeply.

He recalls what happened after they lost Tress, how far they came in so short a time. He hopes to hell it hasn't happened again, taking them away from where they need to be, to some other terminal, hidden deep in parts of the sewer they'll never find their way out of. If this *is* a terminal though, there should be lights. So, why this darkness? Stark looks up. Fitted into the high arch above are wide, flat bulbs filled with coils of fibre optics to filter light from way above at street level. The delicate bulbs, protected by dense, round cages of grimy alloy, look undamaged. He frowns and follows the thick, black wires running between with his torch. They're vulgar and ugly things, like swollen veins, and they end in a bulbous loop, spewing ragged filaments of frayed white. It's not rat damage; it looks like purposeful, frenzied destruction. He moves his torch to illuminate what lies beyond, a featureless wall. He can't tell whether it's supposed to be there or not. Dirt accumulates rapidly down here, borne on the feet of rats and growing like fungus in the dark and the damp.

Stark motions Suge forwards. "That new?"

Suge's eyes become lambent, he shakes his head, "No, boss, it's as old as it looks."

Stark nods and continues to sweep with his torch. Along the sides leading to the wall, spaced wide apart, are a series of ominous archways. Gaping mouths filled with profound black. Five altogether. Two on the right. Three on the left. There's a rancid breeze floating in from the tunnels on the left, bringing a heavy waft of the usual sewer stench and the slightest aroma of sulphur. He doesn't like this, does not like it at all. Stark rubs at his chin and tries to dampen his unease, to rationalise it, but his gut is not going to back down. He opens his mouth to air his concerns to Suge, but a voice from behind fills the silence before he can.

"This is wrong. Something's wrong, Stark." Nia's there, behind him, rubbing her arms. The sewer's been hard on her, but she's battled on without any complaint. Already high, his respect for her has skyrocketed.

He reaches out and places a hand on her shoulder. "I know it, sister. You okay to move on?"

She visibly pulls herself together. "Well, I'm not going back, if that's what you mean."

"Then let's move."

They take the central tunnel of the three on the left, which should lead to an area of the sewers underneath the left arm of the River Head, deep in Burneo's territory, the most likely place they'll find him by Stark's reckoning. Stark has them all switch to low beam on their torches, keeping the light squarely on their feet so they won't trip and Suge takes the lead, acting as their eyes. A tangible field of apprehension surrounds them, makes the rats brave, forcing them to use their torches as batons in an attempt to keep the continuing attacks at bay. Pushing through water and hitting at rats becomes an endless routine until Suge stops without warning, blocking the whole tunnel. Stark and Nia careen into him, a snarl of limbs and torches, sending slops of water splashing into the tops of their thigh-high rubber wading boots. Nia cries out in dismay.

Fighting the rise of temper as his feet soak through, Stark grits out, "What is it?" Suge is absolutely rigid, like a bloodhound on a scent, his every bone frozen to position. Stark grabs his arm and yanks him down to eye level. His voice is a warning, "Suge."

Suge blinks, the lights at the backs of his eyes briefly hidden. He says, "There was something huge up ahead. *Someone*. Never seen anyone that big. Didn't think it was possible …"

Stark experiences a rush of elation so sharp it's painful. "You certain?" Suge tips his head, just once, and Stark takes in a breath that feels like a cry of victory. "Weapons out," he says. "That includes you, Nia."

There's a brief scuffle as they all take out their weapons. Stark takes a moment to show Nia how to hold her gun and the torch in two hands, one above the other.

She gives him a grateful look. "Thank you."

He leans close. "Remember, we're not here to kill Burneo. Weapons are a precaution, at this point, just in case I'm wrong. If we need to engage him, try to remain calm. The torch will high-light your target. Go for the largest areas of skin. No kill shots. We're not here for that. And wait for my signal. No popping off all trigger happy, okay?"

Nia jerks an affirmative and Stark signals to Suge that they're ready to move. Suge leads them on to the accompanying roar of water, catching up with whatever it is he saw. After a moment, Stark, too, catches sight of Burneo, or rather his shadow on the tunnel ahead, a moving shade of immense size and startling grace. His alien disproportion, in comparison to how he was when Stark knew him as Aron, makes Stark realise at last that this is not the man he knew. He's known this intellectually, but to *see* it is to finally understand it as reality. Burneo is a stranger, and Stark has no idea what he'll say to him, what he'll feel in his presence. He's too numb to know what lies in his heart. So much has changed since they were young. Only his pain hasn't, his anger. They're as fresh as they were the day he shot Teya.

Up an incline and through an archway, they enter the confines of a conduit reservoir, where faint light from up ahead filters through, lending the walls a bluish glow. Suge leads them around the sides. Stark holds Nia steady as they go. The ledges are narrow and the reservoir's scary deep. Under its dank, yellow surface, the shadowed circles of conduits emit occasional bubbles and the dark fleeting forms of rats. Stark glances ahead, trying to keep track of the hulking silhouette. No longer entirely in shadow, now, thanks to the vague light, Burneo's a jumble of flesh colours interspersed with the flat gleam of metals. A hiss of vapour fractures the air above him like heat on tarmac. Recognising the configuration of this tunnel, Stark moves up and touches Suge's shoulder.

"Let me take point," he says.

Suge nods and Stark steps past. As he does the light of Suge's augment flicks off. In the semi-dark it resembles the abrupt dulling as life deserts the body. The image brings Stark a wave of unwanted distress. Reminds him too acutely of the very real possibility that they've already lost both the people they've come to save. The roar of water grows ever louder until it's all that fills his head, a boiling torrent of sound. White noise.

"Boss?"

Suge's voice cuts through the roar, and Stark begins moving. The blur of flesh and metal, paused to wait for them, flits out of sight, fast as a rat under water. Slow and easy, Stark follows until a flood of glaring brightness all but drowns their vision. Cursing, he stops for a moment, allowing his sight to adjust before leading Nia and Suge through a steel doorway onto the side of a canal filled with a rage of water. Black bridges span the watery turmoil, leading to a caged walkway identical to one they're stood upon. It's not the place Bone was given his gift, but it's an extension of the same network. This is Burneo's territory. This is where he will wait for them.

CHAPTER 42

*B*one jerks in his bonds and comes half-awake, ragged nails of dream still sunk into his eyes, gouging holes. They strike out of nowhere, unconscious or awake. Snippets. Tendrils. Grabbing at him from the darkness and from the deep trenches of his subconscious.

Scattergun explosion of glass … Muted ringing in the darkness …

His teeth chatter incessantly. Ahead of him, along the two ropes rising away from his shoulders, black diamonds glitter. The eyes of his ever-present companions. Rats. Their fat bodies wobble as they run towards him and he screams to frighten them away but his voice is reduced to whispers and they simply scuttle on past. Just a highway. They're not after his flesh. Not yet.

He moans, closing his eyes. Better to die of cold than to be eaten alive from the inside out by rats. Behind his lids, vague flashes flicker to greater speed, swooping swift as bats across the fabric of his mind. Whispers skitter amongst the glass. Shadows of red circles multiply into one another in endless hypnotic patterns. They know something he doesn't.

Bone snaps his eyes wide to drive them away, but in this relentless darkness they linger on the retina, taunting him. He tries to replace them, thinking of his mortuary, of Nia, but the weight of their volition outdoes his own and more scraps from his dreams lash out hard as hammer blows.

Sharp searing in the skull ... The world zooming in ... Zoning out ...

Desperate to escape these incoherent scraps, he's saved by the unexpected, the skin of his back beginning to tingle, clear and very sharp. The tingles sink deeper, curling in towards his spine and he realises what it must be: the tattoo, the nanites in the ink. Some-when in this darkness, this cold, these unending visions, they must have completed their connections. Has there been time? It's like Lever all over again, lost hours he's done nothing to welcome upon him.

The thought fills him this time with helpless rage at the theft of his choice, his time. So much taken without permission. As it reaches his spine, the tickle of nanites becomes a cooling tide sweeping upwards against the pull of gravity, suffusing each vertebra in turn and flooding into the base of his skull, into his brain. There's no pain, nothing but that glorious sensation, akin to dunking his head in cool water on a boiling hot afternoon. He sinks into it, allowing it to lap over him. It doesn't matter now what these nanites do, he's dead one way or another. Either Rope will come for him, or time. Either one will be enough.

The cool escalates to cold, then prickles of startling heat. They spark in his brain like faulty wires under water. He laughs, the sound ragged, and from the whirl of red circles a shred of clarity rises with such speed it blacks his vision, and sight becomes words. It's a form of synaesthesia. Words seen as images. They take him over until they find what they need, the will to be spoken.

"*The wrong skin,*" they say through his mouth. "*He was wearing the wrong skin.*"

CHAPTER 43

Stark follows the curve of the wall until the walkway opens to a platform where the massive bulk of the man-machine waits. At the sight of him, Stark stumbles to a halt, the shock of recognition intense and bewildering. The grief that follows too raw to bear. This is not the stranger his glimpse in the tunnel gave him leave to imagine—it's Aron, altered beyond comprehension. The damage to his body is catastrophic, an endless catalogue of modifications so extreme, Stark's gut contracts to knots in sympathy. This Burneo his old friend has made of himself, this man-machine, is nothing but an ugly ruin. A mangling of scar-tissue, half-healed wounds and steel, driven by clattering pistons producing heat that even from this distance warms Stark's face.

How does the flesh not melt? How does he stand the pain? And where does that astonishing grace come from? Nothing so awkwardly, ruinously mechanised should display such elegance of movement. He can't understand how Aron lives, how it is he's survived such appalling self-harm. The will behind it must be terrible, indeed. It robs Stark of his breath, brings tears to his eyes, stealing his anger and replacing it with a weight of sadness so dense, he feels it pressing against his spine. He tries to see Aron's eyes, to see if he knows him in return, wanting to reach out to him, somehow, but they're obscured behind a fall of dark hair, bedraggled and damp.

"*He is lost in the dark and the glass.*" The deep voice is not Aron's, as Stark recalls it, but a lifeless monotone resonating within his chest, as if he's being spoken into, the words imprinting on his very flesh.

"Who's lost?" Stark calls out.

He'd like to say more, but he doesn't know how, or what to say. He can only watch, impotent and voiceless, as his old friend lifts his head in a slow movement that looks painful, as if he carries an intolerable burden. The dark mass of hair falls away. Behind it, Aron's eyes are closed. Not as if he's sleeping, but as if he can't bear to see, and another immense, unexpected surge of grief hits Stark's solar plexus, sickening and all-encompassing. Shaken to his core, he's unprepared for the shock of the small, ragged figure that steps out from behind Aron on unsteady legs.

Stark's gun drops from senseless fingers. "Tress?"

He takes a step forwards, but stupefaction's stolen the function of his limbs and he can go no further. It's Tress. Safe. Alive. She's gaunt, though, and frighteningly frail, her clothes tattered, her body marred by vicious wounds, sewn crudely shut with thick, black autopsy thread. Too dark against pale skin, they riddle her torso and face. Stark hears the unmistakable cocking of Suge's gun.

He raises his hand to command a hold of fire as Tress spreads her arms in front of Burneo and shrieks, "No! Please don't hurt him."

Her voice is a cracked husk of such desperation, Stark snaps out of his stupefaction and strides across to her, pulling her into a long, hard hug until she squeaks pain. He pushes her back, then, and takes in every millimetre of her features, feeling every raw scar like a wound on his own body.

"*How?*" he asks.

She lets out a frazzled little laugh. "He saved my life."

Stark looks up at Burneo, wanting to thank him, but the words lodge in his throat like shards. There's such distance in his old friend and it feels like a reproof. Makes Stark feel small and petty. Ill at ease with himself.

He turns back to Tress and gives her a shake. "What happened? We thought Rope had you. We were coming for Burneo to make him take us to you."

Tress touches the tacked seam on her face, covers the ragged wound from her throat to her chest with a shaking hand. "He did. He had me," she says, and her eyes brim with remembered terror, unshed tears. Stark's hands tighten on her shoulders. He can't help it, despite her wince of pain.

"Why didn't you call for us?"

Fierce rage—so very Tress, he wants to laugh, to give way to tears—flashes behind the pinched look of pain. "He attacked before I knew he was there, the fucking coward, I didn't even see him at first ..." She falters to a stop and her anger disintegrates to childlike sobs, taking over her whole body.

Stark holds her shoulders, utterly helpless. He's completely distraught, her tears more than he can bear. He allowed this to happen. "It's okay," he says, knowing it's not, but needing to reassure her, to reassure himself.

She looks up at him, her pupils dilated to pits. "No," she says. "It's not *okay*. He's not *human*."

"Not ...?" Stark shakes her a little again, gently this time. "What do you mean?"

Tress struggles for calm, but when she speaks the words tumble over each other and her breath hitches and snags, the muscles of her face slack with remembered shock. "Rope's a monster. Sharp bones. Wet flesh, writhing like snakes. So strong. He was twisting around me, choking me. Cutting me everywhere. I couldn't defend myself."

Stark shares a glance with Nia. "Lever again," he says.

Nia comes over to place a gentle arm about Tress's shoulders, her lips pressed to a thin line of outrage. She nods. "I think it has to have been. It sounds similar to what Bone described. She must be strong, if she can break through a ceiling like that anyway. Could Lever be Rope?"

"My gut says no. I think she's the thing that got loose in the lab. If she's transmog on the scale we think, she could look like anything. Could have hidden anywhere and not be known. I reckon this scheme's been years in the making. Reckon they were waiting for Leif's death. Not much that man wouldn't do to keep the truth from sullying his good name. Listen to me," he says to Tress. "Whatever you saw Lever do, it's just gen. She's a genuine modified monster, but that's it. Was she trying to take you away?"

Tears slide down her face. "No, I don't think so," she whispers. "She cut me all to hell with blades growing out of her fucking body, and she wasn't going to stop. If Burneo hadn't come for me, I'd be dead."

Stark takes a few deep, unsteady breaths, racked with fury and guilt. "Rope was onto us, onto Burneo," he says to Tress. "Maybe he thought we needed punishing for not playing by his rules. I'm sorry. I shouldn't have dragged you into this. I should've gone alone. It should've been me."

"Don't be fucking stupid," she snaps, wiping her tears on a ragged sleeve. "There's no way in hell you could've kept me out of it. And if you'd been hurt instead of me, I'd have come after you. You need to quit the self pity and you need to listen." She sways, and he tightens his grip again, holding her steady. "Time's running out. Burneo's on the wrong side of crazy, and he doesn't talk much, but since yesterday evening, he's been driving me fucking spare going on constantly about some man in dark and glass. And he knew you were coming, he's been waiting for you."

Stark's shocked out of his misery. "Bone was taken yesterday evening," he says. He looks up at Burneo, still gone from the room, his body left behind like some vast, ancient artefact. "Burneo," he says, then louder, when there's no response, "Aron."

Burneo's lids slowly rise. One eye is a ball of liquid mercury, blind and alien. The other, recognisably Aron's, is luminescent as amber, but empty, as if he's a puppet of flesh driven by arcane energies far from the human. Gradually, awareness rises in the depths of that amber pool, drawn from a place too far away for sanity. What comes is more frightening than nothing at all, a barely hinged glint of humanity that sears through Stark like a blinding white light, bleaching his innards.

"Reinhart."

There's the impression of a question being asked, an inflection akin to bewilderment. The sound of it echoes around, multiplying within the expanse of the canal walls and mingling with the sound of water until it swallows the name back to silence. Stark's jaws grind together. Hearing that name from his old friend reduces him to points of acute agony, because it isn't true anymore, not for either of them, and there's no way to make it right. They've both come too far, lost too much.

Stark shakes his head. "No. I'm not Reinhart. And you're not Aron."

Burneo blinks in slow motion. "No," he replies, and the sorrow in it reflects the sorrow grown like a wall of granite in Stark's chest. "I am not Aron." The life in his gaze flickers out. "You're late to my playground. The game is near to ending. He is lost in the dark and the glass."

Stark sighs, and there's a world of weariness and pain in it, some twenty years' worth. "Just help us," he pleads, hoping to get through, somehow, hoping they're not already too late for Bone. "Don't let me be too late this time. I can't do it again."

A glimmer of something like the old Aron flits swift as a fish across that amber surface. Burneo speaks, and the words are not meant for Stark, but for Reinhart, Stark knows it as soon as he hears them. "There was time to take her down until you came."

A red tide of rage and fear crashes through Stark's chest. He sees Teya's face, that mess of blood and bone. Watches again as Aron runs away, driven by his bullets. He doesn't know how many times he hit his old friend before Aron finally turned to run, how many clips spent, only that there was a single bullet left for Teya. Aron had begged him to listen, to understand what he was trying to do, but Stark could only see her face, could only hear his pain. He doesn't know how often he's wished there were two bullets left. He knows it's too often, and that it never stops hurting. And he wishes every day he'd been able to stop, to listen, because he'll never know if Aron could have saved her. He'll never know if that bullet was mercy or murder.

Stark tries to talk, but there are no words left. Nothing he can say will make it right. Nothing he can ever do. Burneo stands still as an oak, his presence solid as the metals wound throughout his body. He tilts that great, broken head to gaze at Stark, nothing of Aron flickering within, as though a flame has been snuffed. Savage shadows roil there instead, such plaintive ghosts Stark can hardly stand to witness them.

"He is lost in the dark and the glass," Burneo says, and there's unimaginable agony in it. Words like blades are tearing his mind to shreds, forcing their way out of him, whether he wants to speak them or not.

Desolation, pure and absolute, is all Stark can feel. It's not losing the chance to ask forgiveness, he doesn't deserve that. It's the finality of the loss of Aron within this brutalised mess of modifications. Looking at them, at each irreversible strike against Aron's humanity, Stark sees them for what they are. Self-inflicted punishments. They are for Teya. Like him, Burneo has never recovered from the loss of her. He probably blames himself. But it wasn't his doing. It was Stark's. All of it. Stricken, he looks away from Burneo's gaze and meets Tress's eyes, forced to bite back tears at the empathy in them. He doesn't merit her empathy, but he welcomes the fierce glare of reprimand that follows.

"I don't know what the hell is between you two, but you better get a grip," she whispers furiously. "Rope's winding down to some big fucking finale, and if Bone's his centrepiece, we need to find him *now*."

"I know," he tells her wearily. "But I don't know how to reach him, Tress."

"These visions are hurting him," she says softly. "But he can be reached, he *is* in there. Talk to him."

Stark sketches a terse nod. If Tress says he's in there, then he's in there. "Burneo. The man in the dark and the glass, do you know where he is?"

Burneo blinks. "Lost," he says.

"We need to find him, do you know how?"

Burneo inclines his great head. "Follow the ropes."

Stark ignores the huffs of annoyance from Nia and Suge. They see a madman talking in riddles and nonsense, he sees a man in dreadful pain, and he realises that, whatever happens after they find Bone, he'll have to let Burneo go. It's more than a matter of a debt owed. Burneo's broken, and pulling him up into the world to subject him to the insanity of a media circus and a public trial would be an injustice. More than that, it would be cruel. He still believes Burneo's victims require justice, but he no longer sees the end result in monochrome. There are different types of punishment, and some can go on for far too long. He reaches out, placing a hand on Burneo's massive, ruined shoulder.

"Take me to him," he says.

CHAPTER 44

*D*arkness, pain, cold. The shatter of glass.

Bone wrenches awake, exhausted. Every inch of his body hurts, and the bombardment of dreams has become too much like memory to dismiss. He's tried to rationalise the deluge, but there's no doubting their vivid quality, the physical weight of them. They're bodily recollections of something buried, kept away from him. From the pattern of recovery, the effect on his mind, they have to be coming from behind a failing memory patch.

Emptiness. Cold. Darkness. Screaming. Explosion of sound. Roaring. The pounding of feet.

Bone claws to consciousness. Why would he have a patch? The first thought is Leif. Leif did something to him. Shoved something he didn't like behind a wall, so he'd never have to deal with it again. Is this where Bone's will has gone? Or is it something worse? It feels like something worse. Memories so horrifying, he'd do almost anything to escape from them, but he's trapped here, he's got nowhere to go but inwards.

Lights. Blinding. Searing his eyes. Jabbers of words, jumbles of colours, hands on his body …

He snaps out again, battling hysteria. The patch isn't merely failing, it's fracturing, disintegrating. He's going to drown in these memories, if he can't figure out what they are, why they're hidden.

He has to try because if he dies here, he wants to die with his mind still his own. He looks desperately into the darkness, feeling the cold and the constriction of ropes binding him. This is so similar to the memories leaking from the patch. The events are connected. It must be Rope. Rope is the connection. But how? He tries to remember what happened before waking in the darkness, but it's blurred behind the oily remnant of some sort of drug. He needs to start further back, with the last things he recalls before the swallow of darkness. What were they? A faint image slips across the edge of his mind. He grabs for it and holds on until it sharpens to focus.

"Snow."

Insane, hypnotic patterns of tumbling white. They mesh together, forming a door in his memory, the entrance to Willough Block. 328 Willough Block, the Rise, Kirk Falls. The address rolls heavy across his mind, dragging other scraps of memory behind like boulders. Willough Block wasn't locked. But *her* door was. He'd forced it open, fingers burning as it pulled against them. He remembers softness under his shoes. Her apartment was carpeted. So expensive. She had so much. And computers, too. He sees a revolving spiral, concealing a map, a stream of mail hidden in a tear. He'd taken out his cell to call Stark, the slender shape of it cool in his palm. But something stopped him. Prickles. Prickles on the back of his neck. Once. Then again.

"The drug. It has to be." He strains harder, fighting through the murk brought on by the drug. But all he can recall is a peculiar sideways view of the room and warm rain falling on his face. "Rain?"

His breath hisses out because it couldn't have been rain. Not inside. He closes his eyes, pushing at the memory, testing the reality of it, but it's undeniable. There was definitely rain. Warm rain falling on his face, and even on the carpet, blurring in fading sight. Bone's eyes snap open into the darkness, recognising the colour even through the blur.

"Blood."

Drops of blood like rainfall on the carpet and on his face, but there was no sky, only ceiling. And he's seen blood like that before. Thick, fat drops slapping to the ground, a blood music that fell to the soundtrack of his screaming.

"Lever," he whispers. "She was there." Understanding creeps in on the back of remembrance. "A trap. Lever and Rope, working together." Rage and misery flare like fire within. "Lever was sent to catch me. *Why*?"

Bone scans the pitch-black surrounds, willing his eyes to pierce the shadows. He knows she must be close because she was there with him. She did this to him. Brought him down here into the familiar darkness, the agony of ropes and the cold. He wants answers, and Lever has them, just as he thought she did.

He yells into the dark, the ropes cutting into the flesh of his chest, "Where are you?"

And a voice responds from everywhere and nowhere at once. Low. Scathing. A whispered accusation. "Do you remember what you have done yet, Bone-Man?"

Almost unwilling to believe it, despite all he's remembered, Bone breathes out her name, "Lever?"

A soft laugh ripples through the darkness, and something moves towards him. It's the eyes he sees first, an intense green— bright pools of colour floating in whites pure as new snow. Her pupils are wide and black, an abyss to consume him. They cut straight through him. Lever. Irrefutably her. She steps forwards in measured strides, the delineation of exposed musculature glistening even in darkness. Naked and skinless and perfect, she moves closer to him, scouring him with that verdant gaze.

"Lever," she repeats. Her voice is flat, musical, hard with amusement, and as husky as he recalls. "Is that what you think?"

The eyes change, then. They're still Lever's eyes, but he no longer sees Lever in them. They've become devoid of life as the black hollow of her pupils, avid and leached of emotion, pure intent without the handicap of conscience. There's too much intelligence in them, all of it cold and rational. Nothing of madness in them. Nothing to explain the total lack of humanity. Bone's skewered, stripped bare and vulnerable. He'd rear back from that gaze if he were able. Run till his legs gave beneath him if he could. But ropes hold him here—Rope has him here, and Rope must be Lever, nothing left to deny it.

"I think you're ..." he begins. Then those memories resume behind his eyes in starts and flashes, each a jolt pure as lightning, and he finds himself murmuring, "I've been here before."

Lever bares her teeth in what looks like the hungry expression made before consumption of prey, and drifts closer to him, a mere hand's breadth from his face. "You have. As have I. I played this game to bring you back, so you'd know what you've done. We'll untangle the web they built in you, together, and make you remember. I was forced to wait so long for this, but here I am. Here we are." That smile comes again. Calculating. Animal cunning. "It was so simple, in the end. I used her. Took her skin and wore her like a suit to get close to you, to see if you'd know me. But all you saw was her, and I knew I had you."

"What?" He can't pull his mind wide enough to grasp what she's saying. "Her skin? Whose skin?"

"Lever. My little helper." The smile remains as if fixed with glue. A rictus. "When we were fucking, you and I, I told you my name. Did you hear me?"

"Your name?"

Pain slams into his skull. A fierce itch builds in his forehead as images peel out of his memories: Lever's bright gold skirt, her fingertips reflecting shards of neon, the splash of peacock-blue hair. He watches like a voyeur as they race through the night, Lever's hand tugging him along. He feels it then, re-living it. Mouths devour as the elevator softly chimes floor after floor. They tear clothes like skin. Limbs mesh, entangle, and drop them to the round rug in amongst shapes like leaves. And they fuck as if nothing else matters but the grind of flesh on flesh. Her gold tips rake channels down his chest, drag and burn. Pure white-hot pain. Unbearable. Unbelievably good. An orgasm begins to rise inexorably through his body. She whispers a word into the hollow of his ear. And time stops, a splash of freezing water to the face. He's thrown back to reality, to the cold green eyes before him, but sees nothing to explain this.

"*Your* name?" he asks.

A burgeoning sense of unreality cocoons him. That name can't be hers. Impossible. Lies, then, all lies. This is Lever and she's lying to him, fucking with his mind sure as she fucked his body. He's certain of it, as certain as he is that what he fucked was definitely a woman. It must have been. *Has* to have been.

The thing called Lever inclines her head. "Did you not recognise my name?" she asks him with dangerous softness.

"Bone Adams is *my* name."

"No." The reply is pitiless. "It's not. You stole a life, and the time has come to return it."

With that claim, that accusation, he *feels* the patch rupture—it's raw, like fingers tearing at a wound, and cavernous roaring erupts inside his head as torrents of black memory flood from behind the patch. And from the flood comes something attached to the name, latching into recollection like a hook into the soft matter of his brain and he sees …

Lights. Blinding. Searing his eyes. Panicked voices throw words, questions, between them like blows. There are hands on his face; rough hands prying apart his eyelids; the action causes an abrupt cessation of noise. A single voice speaks. One he knew then and knows now: Leif Adams.

"It's not Bone," Leif says, his voice coloured with puzzling disappointment.

Bodies jostle too close. Another voice speaks, "Oh, hell. What do we do?"

"He's in bad shape, he needs immediate attention."

"What about Bone?"

The response is spat out, as though each word is a bitter mouthful. "I suppose we have to assume he's made use of this as a disguise."

There's an uneasy pause. "I'm sorry, Leif. Bone's gone too far. He has to be held accountable, you have to see that."

A new voice interrupts, clipped and icy, filled with authority. "He'll be caught and held accountable. However, this is potentially disastrous for us all. It has to be buried. Do you understand, Leif?"

"I understand, Connaught, all too well," *replies Leif, and the edge to it slices at his ears, hurting them.*

Hands take hold of his chin, gently this time. He's trying for words, but they're trapped behind dry lips, a deadened tongue. The hands cup his head, so careful, too tender to bear. Then a trickle of water pours between his lips. Glorious. Unspeakable heaven. His stomach cramps, hurling the water back up and choking him.

Behind the water, the words he's been trying to say rise fast and bitter as vomit.

"The wrong skin. He was wearing the wrong skin."

The present crashes in, bright and shattering. He hangs there, disassociated from himself. His thoughts are chaos, haemorrhaging under the weight of escaped memory. He can't feel his body. Only his mind fills him like broken glass, all sharp edges and pain, and the red circles rise behind his eyes like seeping blood. From within them come snatches of disjointed memories, brutal as shark bites, memories of then and now merging into one vast lump. Indistinguishable. *Dark. Cold. Pain. Ropes tight as a fist. The soft scuffle of rats.* The red circles wheel faster and faster. They throw another memory from the chaos hard as an uppercut, whole and absolutely clear ...

Walking in the snow, in the muted light of street lamps, hands deep in his pockets. A door slams in the distance, the sound of muffled laughter ripples across the air. Leaves like fire fall slowly within the snow, a stop-motion counterpoint, their soft touch a caress upon his head. Then glass shatters, resounds in his ears loud as a car crash, and a bolt of pure white agony shoots through his skull. The world tips towards him, and before his staring eyes, red circles form, seeping through crisp, new snow: red in the white, fading as he loses consciousness ...

He's choking on tears, they spatter to the floor like bile and the itch at his forehead becomes untenable, an aggravating crawl, as if his skin is stuffed with spiders. It's driving him insane. If he can't itch it, it *will* drive him insane. He has to itch it. Has to stop the spiders. He pulls at his hands, but they're trapped, tied fast behind his back, and he panics, wrenching at them. Ropes tear into his skin, deep wounds he can barely feel, and blood pours hot as boiled water over the backs of his hands, pooling in his palms. In response, a scalding flash fire leaps from his spine to his arms. As it reaches his hands, the bones of his palms and his fingers explode apart, flesh stretching and twisting about them as they shift within the grip of ropes. Metallic stomach acid spurts into the roof of his mouth as the pressure on his wrists goes slack, bonds falling away to dangle against the small of his spine. His arms flop to his sides, joints burning, muscles cramping, pins and needles rippling from his shoulders to whatever it is at the ends of his wrists.

He wants to leave them dangling there, but the urge to look is compulsive. Slowly, he raises them to eye level, too far gone to notice how much it hurts, and yells at the sight of them, a flat sound of denial. Those aren't hands. They aren't hands at all. They're shapeless, blood-drenched tubes of flesh, like amputations, smooth and featureless and too liquid. Worse than no hands at all. Before his horrified gaze, they begin to reform, skin rippling as bones shuffle back into place, and he's fighting for breath, his vision fading in and out. The crawl of spiders at his forehead translates into intolerable pressure and the skin of his forehead splits, just like Lever's did on Rope's body. Begins to slide apart. He screams, a hoarse note climbing ever upwards, and slams those alien hands to his face, holding it together against the slick well of blood, the pressure of heavy flesh courting gravity. Phalanges pop upwards in quick succession, an alien, gorge-rising sensation against his temples, and his fingers snap to shape, pressing into his skull.

"Stop it," he screams at the red mask of a face that's both Rope and somehow Lever, and also something worse. "Please, stop it!"

"Why would I?" Rope asks, matter of fact. "It's mine. I want it back."

Expressionless, passionless, Rope lunges for his wrists and

starts to prise his hands from his face. He shouts at Rope, an incoherent denial, and wrenches away, slapping loose flaps of skin back onto his skull as they peel towards his chin. Rope roars with rage. Under the thick wrap of tendon-streaked red, Rope's bones begin to move, the muscles unravelling, blood stretching between like thick, red membranes, and though he fights it, Bone's powerless to prevent the response of his own flesh, more appalling than the deconstruction of his hands. Joints rupture and separate, his bones beginning a slow migration to new positions, his muscles sliding beneath loose skin. An unwinding that feels like seasickness, riding in the heavy liquid of his own body, the undulation of his innards. It throws his senses into a frenzy of discordant kinaesthesia. His head spins and reels. Harsh ringing resounds in his ears and has the opposite effect it should, bringing all sound to perfect clarity.

He hears bones crack and move, Rope's and his own, the sibilant rush of sliding muscle, of shifting skin, a melody of change, jarring and hollow in the ear. Then Rope attacks, a blur of sharp edges, visceral speed and strength. Slicing through the bonds at his chest, his shoulders and slamming deep into skin, to muscle, and beyond. He howls at the pain and his body replies with a clumsy shield—ribs flared out from his chest, forcing those blades to slow. Striving to push them way. The harsh scrape of sharp edges on rib shafts reverberates through him. He gags at the sensation. Gags again as his body throws out a veil of muscle to cover Rope's rebuilt head, but he's too slow and Rope too expert. Rope ducks the veil and slams those blades between his ribs again with horrendous force, scissoring them apart. With a snapping sound remarkably similar to twigs underfoot, his ribs fracture, and Rope's blades scythe past. Blood spurts into his eyes. He tries to make blades to cut at his lower bonds so he can escape, but Rope's everywhere, a frenzy of fierce rage and unbelievable power and he's forced to curl over, instead, to protect vital organs.

Those blades of bone fall again and again, cutting through skin and muscle, slicing into femur and rib and scapula, breaching his weak defences to pierce his lung, his liver. So many cuts, the pain bleeds together and becomes a wall of all-encompassing agony, every breath like a burst of flame. Bleeding out, he faces Rope head on, to let him see he's not beaten, not even in death, and a percussive burst of pure sound splits the air, half deafening them, making them scream into each other's faces. The back blast of heat from an explosion slams through in its wake. Serrated metal fragments, white-hot, fly against the ropes and strike burning impacts on muscle and flesh before clattering to the floor. The scattergun sound of feet on concrete pounds into the darkness, and from the shadows, two huge arms— steel-wrapped muscle hissing loud as a tangle of angry snakes—scoop Rope into their grasp. Rope fights back with wicked precision, but the arms of metal and flesh are immovable, the mass wielding them absorbing blows as if they're mere inconvenience.

He hears voices yelling, the sound of more feet muffled by the ringing in his ears. Lights flare all around, invading his eyes with the brute force of blades in flesh. He screams again. Rope joins him, a sound seemingly of one voice as they snap their eyes shut. His lids illuminate like stained glass, delineating veins, the deep purple of blood, the orange of flesh. There are sounds of horror, a volley of shouted words, a woman screaming. Across the top, shots fire again and again, their impacts a succession of dull, meaty thuds. Frantic hands stutter across his chest, pushing at his ribs, trying to force them back behind muscle, behind skin and a familiar voice begs him, *"Come back, Bone, please come back. Don't die. Don't you dare fucking die, you bastard."*

He opens his eyes and it's Nia. It's Nia. She's here. And he wants to stop, to make himself normal again so she won't be frightened, so he won't disgust her, but he doesn't know how. In the momentary stillness of his body, he feels the nanites surge in his skull, sinking back down his spine to repopulate the rivers of ink flowing beneath his skin, and some unseen force takes hold of his flesh and bones, re-moulding him without mercy. Despite the fresh waves of pain, he almost sobs with relief, but Nia's hands halt their frenzied attempt to put him back together. She pushes away and stares, disbelieving, as his body remakes itself. Horror contorts her features, followed by revulsion.

"Transmog," she says, barely able to get the word out. She looks up at his face. "Did Rope do this to you?"

Unable to speak, he shakes his head, and her face crumples, eloquent with distress. She steps even further away and he feels it as a physical sensation of loss. He wants to take this back. Take everything back. It's too much, like the vast jumble of new memories inside of him, an uncontainable amount, most of them incoherent, incomprehensible. The entire, garbled life of a stranger crammed into his skull, overlapping his own and threatening to devour him. There's nothing sane in those memories, nothing whole, and he knows he has to fight, but he's so tired and so very lost. Waves of dizziness pass down from the top of his skull, their passage a vibration that shakes him to the core, and there's a strange weight in his chest. Experience tells him what it is: blood beginning to leak into his chest cavity, perhaps his stomach, too.

His vision doubles and blurs. Unable to fight any longer, he slumps in the ropes, falling to hang below his legs. Nia yells for Stark, her hands finally touching his wounded body again, grabbing at him as he swings there like a pendulum, heavy to and fro, his blood drawing abstract patterns on the concrete. Alarm fills the room, but he hears it only as faint buzzing, far off and untouchable. He swings towards what's left of Rope's denuded face. The last thing he sees is his own reflection in the dead gleam of a verdant pool. Bone Adams reflected into Bone Adams—and he doesn't know which one is real.

CHAPTER 45

*N*ia's fingers hover, trembling, over the zipper of the body bag. It looks the same as any other, but it's not. She can't bring herself to face the contents of this bag. She promised Stark she'd be okay, swore upon her life to Spaz. She shouldn't have done that. Fact is, she just didn't want anyone else doing this. It's her job, her burden, because stepping back from Bone's body as it rebuilt itself was unforgivable. She saw it in Bone's face, how much it hurt. The harm she'd done him. Angry she might be; betrayed, confused, and most assuredly still sick to her core at the thought of what he did as a young man, but deserting him when he needed her most was unforgivable. It goes against everything she is. Everything she's always been.

The feel of his flesh though, under her palms. She shudders. Oh dear fucking hell, it was beyond awful. First to see him so broken, drenched in blood and just *ragged*, as if his flesh were a suit half torn off his skeleton. Then, as she'd tried to hold him together, his body began to *shift* under her hands. Things *moving*, things *snapping*, this terrible, liquid *sliding*. Those sensations hit her right below the diaphragm, visceral and raw. She'd wanted to run, then, run without ever looking back. Merely stepping back from him to distance herself had been restraint at that point. But it was still wrong. Nia hangs her head and clutches the edge of the table, just breathing, breathing through the memory. Blue light flickers overhead, lending the mortuary a watery sheen. It makes her skin look anaemic, dead as the contents of this bag. Nia lifts her gaze to it. So innocuous. A shapeless, black mass, more bag than anything else, but there's definitely a body in there, and she can't avoid it forever. She promised, she swore, and she *needs* to do this. For Bone.

Grasping the zipper, she draws it slowly down, keeping well back from the stench that's released. It's been only twelve hours since the sewer, but that's long enough for things to have become very interesting in there. Carefully, she folds back the edges, allowing them to drape down over the side of the table, and takes her first close look at the thing that tried to kill Bone. It's as bad as she feared. Her gorge rises and she has to turn away, gulping air, coughing in the still cool of the mortuary. *Thing* is the only word that fits what's left of Rope. There's little recognisable humanity in this warped, wet mess of muscle, tendon, and bones. Not to mention the sheer amount of damage from bullets. Vast holes torn into bunched muscle, and jagged shards of bone stuck out like spikes, drooling coagulating marrow.

Stark and Suge shot Rope over and over, unsure where a viable kill shot might be found in the woven horror this homicidal maniac remade himself into. It's unspeakably vile. Repugnant. Why would anyone have gen like this? It's not transformative, just hideous. Taking a deep breath, she begins before she can think better of it.

"On. Record. This examination is for Establishment record and identification only. Decedent is male (no visible penile remnants, but visible fragments of pelvis are flat, tests will confirm), age uncertain, height uncertain, weight at time of death unknown. Very few identifying features due to lack of integumentary system. This was not the cause of death. Rigor mortis is fixed. Multiple bullet wounds, too numerous to catalogue, massive trauma to all tissue masses."

Nia blows out and fetches her scalpel, hands hovering again, unsure where to begin. This mess is so ridiculously *unfamiliar*, considering it was apparently a human body.

"Body is in a state of flux caused by transmog gen modification. Significant skeletal disruption has occurred, with unusual reformations of radius, ulner, and humerus … these bones appear to have fused, sharpening to blades. We had to wrap them to prevent them slicing through the bag. Muscular redistribution is equally extreme. Muscles of the arms and upper torso have moved to provide driving power for the bone blades. This is a fixed form. The decedent's passing has not affected it."

She begins a deeper examination with the head, protected under a helmet of what seems to be re-moulded scapulas and more of that strong, fibrous muscle. Her heart begins to beat too heavily, and she tries to breathe her disgust and horror away again. That tissue and bone can be made to do this … it's unnatural.

"Head intact," she says weakly. "No cranial damage. Decedent appears to have constructed a secondary cranium from the matter of both scapulas. There are a few scores from the passage of bullets across the surface."

Nia moves down to what must be torso and slices through shredded muscle, trying to find the organs, finally discovering them hidden in the middle of a dense wall of muscles and reformed ribs. Perhaps half the rib cage bent to form a protective cage. She steps back, blinking rapidly, and clears her throat.

"Internal organs undamaged, but excessive pale hue indicates total loss of blood flow. Decedent bled out rapidly through catastrophic arterial rupturing. Suggests death by hypovolemic shock." Her grip tightens on the scalpel because Bone came close to dying like that, too, thanks to this creature—possibly his own creation. What horrific irony.

"I'll take some tissue slices and samples for testing. Initial blood test results taken en route from the scene by the team who transported the remains are back, as is basic toxicology and full DNA. I'll review now and recommence after. Recording off."

She steps back from Rope again. "I'll only be happy when they put you in the fucking furnace," she mutters as she strips off her gloves, knowing she'll never be able to strip this from her mind.

Nia moves to the screen at the end of the table and begins to read the results streamed from the hospital lab, trying not to look at Rope's remains, but somehow unwilling to turn her back on him, though he's stiff with rigor mortis. She taps into the records dept of the Notary, thankful that this system is the Establishment's. She's family, and therefore permitted top-level access. That means, from here, she can crack into files the Notary, and probably even Spaz, would prefer she didn't. Tough shit for them. She's determined to find out who Rope is. It's the least she can do. She'll deal with Bone's past and how she feels about it later, when he recovers. *If* he does. Worried Spaz may have anticipated her curiosity, Nia takes a moment to program an almost invisible jack, to hide her intentions and allow her search to go on unhindered.

Spaz has probably forgotten she used to stream-jack for fun when she was just a pre-teen. Nothing too serious, she didn't want anyone to think she could be useful. She wanted a different life, a normal life. Stupid, really, because her life is far from normal. Whilst waiting for the search to complete, she accesses Bone's sus unit feed. There's video streaming alongside the readout from his monitors, but she doesn't look. He's naked, therefore vulnerable, and it feels invasive. She smiles at the readout, though. His body is healing well, and there are delta patterns interrupting the alpha. He's dreaming. If he's dreaming, then he's in there somewhere. That's all she wants, for him to come back as whole as possible, even if it means he has to face trial. The screen pings. She looks across from Bone's feed to the results of her search, and stands there, staring, her mouth working stupidly. She scratches her ear too hard without thinking, grazing the skin, and leans in for a closer look.

"That's not right," she mutters.

Meticulously, she rechecks the results used for the search and frowns so hard, little bolts of pain shoot through her temples. She turns back to Bone's feed, tapping to bring up his medical notes, and compares those to the results from the search on Rope's blood. Her jaw drops. There's little doubt in what she's seeing, but she can't quite make sense of it. It's not possible. How is that possible? It takes a moment for the shock to hit. When it does, she presses a hand to her belly, feeling decidedly ill. There's no way of getting around this. No explanation other than the obvious.

"He's not Bone," she mutters to herself, and laughs, disbelieving.

Dizzily, she triple checks the information, but it's still the same. A secured file pulled up by her jack, rather than her access, one she should definitely *not* be looking at, the results matching the birth of one Bone Adams, son of Amiela and Leif Adams. His blood type and DNA both a positive match for *Rope*. Bone's results don't match. He's B negative, when Bone Adams is recorded as being A positive. But it's the DNA that makes it irrefutable. Her Bone is not a match to the Bone Adams on record. He's not even close. Not even a distant relative. She looks at the mess laid out on the table beyond the screen, but it still won't quite register. *That* is Bone Adams? How? And *who* is her Bone? Or rather, who *was* he? She steadies herself, but her legs don't seem to want to stop shaking. She looks at the sus feed again. Finally watches the streaming video, because she needs to see him, to know that he's there.

He floats in thick, pale yellow liquid, sporting a mass of tubes and bristling with probes to stimulate his muscles, his blond hair waving gently about his head, obscuring that pretty face.

"Is it his?" She doesn't even know.

Everyone seemed to think he was Bone Adams, even those who'd have known him from when he was a child. Colleagues of Leif's and executives at GyreTech, people who wouldn't have been privy to the deception. So, he must *look* like him. She sucks in hard, her heart pounding. Is that what this was all about? The real Bone Adams wanting revenge on the man they replaced him with? And what of the patching? Rope wanted to break his patching. If he's not Bone Adams, then what is it exactly that the patch is covering? And what did Rope say to him down there in the sewer, before they arrived? Before he attacked him? Nia recalls Bone telling her about Lever's skin, the way it fell off, and remembers his skin down there, sliding loose from his face. Nia moans as she finally understands what she's seeing here.

"*His* skin. That's *his* skin."

There's Rope, skinless, and her Bone, wearing a face that isn't his. She covers her mouth, holding in a cry of horror. Does he know what's been done to him? Does he *remember* losing himself? Hot tears begin to crawl her cheeks, spattering her scrubs. Bone's such a mess of wounds under those tubes and probes, his torso criss-crossed, his face, thighs, and arms savaged. He looks so vulnerable and so small, despite his height, like the Bone she's always seen beneath the snark and spark, a wounded animal hiding from daylight. From the whole world.

"Who *are* you?" she whispers.

CHAPTER 46

*U*sually buzzing with conversation and the hum of computers, Stark's floor at Central is a wall of silence. Dressed with his usual cheap panache, Stark weaves between desks, paying no attention to the stares. Of course, they're all fascinated. He's a titan about to fall, and whilst some dreaded this day, others have awaited the fall of the axe with anticipation. Stark's gone his own way, done his own thing. He hasn't made enemies as much as created tides of resentment that swelled and ebbed in his wake. But he's never concerned himself with the opinions of others, and he doesn't now. This is between himself and Burton, and he's made his peace with it. Made his peace with throwing away his career before he went down into the sewer. After leaving Burneo down there, and leaving a whole hell of a lot more besides, some twenty years of basic personal dishonesty for a start, he's come to realise the badge should never have been his. He's not about to decry two decades of righting wrongs, but he's ready to start righting the wrongs he created, to pay for his mistakes.

He arrives at Burton's door, does his usual double tap, and goes on in. For once, Burton's not on the phone. He's stood there, looking out of his window across the Central Mace skyline, his shoulders set into a solid line of pure tension. He doesn't turn around when Stark shuts the door.

"Take a seat."

Burton's voice is not the usual bellow, nor even imbued with any hint of vitriol. But Stark expected neither; he expected disappointment. He obeys without his customary flippancy. He's not feeling very flippant these days. Hasn't felt that way since leaving the sewer almost three days ago. He's so different to how he was, he almost doesn't recognise himself. Burton turns to face him. His hands are rammed in his pockets, and his entire body language speaks of defeat. He's looking creased, his face worn and tired, and a few millimetres of stubble mar his jaw. It takes Stark aback. Burton's never been one for failing to groom properly, that's usually Stark's brief. He can't count the amount of times he's been hauled in and bawled at for not presenting the proper Central image. He's never paid attention. What you look like is only important if you're dealing with surfaces. Stark's always had to go deeper, deal with the shit where it arises, and wearing your Sunday best whilst shovelling the shit is plain ridiculous.

"I can't believe what you've done," Burton says tiredly.

"Really?" Stark was not expecting that particular admission. Burton's aware of how he is, what he'll do.

"You're one of the best defences I have, for fuck's sake," Burton snaps, flaring anger. "There's very few I can trust to do what needs doing. You were my number one for situations that needed handling without bullshit, and now I have to let you go." Burton shakes his head, the anger dropping from him like snow from an overburdened branch. In its place, disbelief and bewilderment cloud his face. "You have no idea how little I want to do this. I understand what you did. Hell, I even understand *why* you did it. I couldn't applaud it more. It got the fucking job done. But the Notary is holding me to my word and that's that."

Stark frowns. "Hold up, you just said you can't believe it and reamed me the hell out for making you take my badge, but you *understand*? I don't get it."

Burton huffs out a tired laugh. "No. I'm not making much sense. Not a bit of it. Let me make the distinction. As your *boss*, I cannot fucking believe how stupid you've been. It's recklessness beyond any kind of idiocy. You just threw it all away, and threw me into a right mess, to boot. There were options: you could have approached me, I could have given you leeway. You *know* that!"

Stark shrugs. "I knew. I didn't want leeway, I wanted to save my teammate, retrieve Bone Adams, and stop Rope, and I did. Any later to that sewer, any waiting on *leeway*, and I'd have lost Bone for sure, and maybe Tress, too, because she sure as hell wasn't in any shape to be down there much longer."

"Which is why, as your *friend*, I applaud it."

"I see. So, what now?"

Burton finally takes his chair, collapsing into it as if his muscles have all ceased to work. "Well. You get one week to wrap up the loose ends of the Rope case and sort the rest of your case-load for handing to other detectives, and then you hand in your badge. I'm going to flout the recommendations of the Notary and give you a final paycheque. I'm also going to free up your retire-ment fund. If you're quick and access it before your badge is gone, you'll have enough to live on for a while. Won't be much, but it'll grant you some space to find another way to make a living."

Some of the stress tightening Stark's chest, stress he's been trying to ignore, fades away. "I appreciate that. You didn't have to."

"No. No, I didn't." Burton's mouth turns down and he glares at Stark, simmering with rage. "I was told not to, but fuck that shit. Kicking you out is one thing, something I can't damned well avoid. But I won't let you starve. That's fucking immoral after all you've done for Central, for the goddamn Notary, for this city." He sighs, and it sounds like the world coming down. "I'll warn you, Stark. Connaught Yar is extremely interested in this case. He's arranged a meeting, wants to *talk* to me about it. If I were you, I'd make whatever it was that tipped you off disappear." Burton pins him with a meaningful eye. "Whatever led you down there to Rope, I don't think you saw it in a goddamn dream, or had some massive gut instinct spark you in the right direction, but I am going to make pretend I do. Understand?"

Stark understands all right. "I owe you one."

"You don't." Burton stands up. "You owe me nothing, not a damn thing. Don't you dare try and pretend you do. I still remember when you were just a bad tempered prick, who got the *both* of us into too much trouble. I've seen you covered in goddamn blood, your nose smashed to one side, and still swinging at some fucker three times your size. You could never have sat in this chair, and I could *never* have stayed out there to do what you've done. It scared the shit out of me."

"Notary meetings scare the shit out of me," Stark replies with a grin, standing himself.

Burton laughs, shaking his head. "Me too, my friend, but it's a clean, bloodless sort of terror. Beats the hell out of street fighting."

"We agree to disagree on that."

"Somehow, I knew you'd say that," Burton says, reaching out and shaking Stark's hand. "Take it easy, huh?"

Stark walks to the door. "There's no easy left in me," he says softly, and leaves without any further words. There's nothing more to say. He's done, and he doesn't care.

He heads out through the resonant silence of the office. They're disappointed to have been denied the shouting and the drama, but that's their fucking problem, he wasn't here for their amusement, or their satisfaction. There's some staring in the hopes he'll get uncomfortable and rush on out of here, but they've underestimated his significant lack of give a shit. He takes his time, walking slow and easy, shaking the hands of those who've shown him support. He's not ashamed. He's done nothing wrong, not in this case at any rate. The only real decision he has left to make is what to do with Spaz's file. No matter what Burton said, he's got to consider what it could do. How it could be used. His old self, the more reckless, bullish Stark, would've used it without a second thought. But he's not that man anymore, and he has serious reservations. The file could do irreparable damage to Bone, who's been punished severely as it is, and to the Spires, possibly starting that war he's been fighting to keep at bay. That doesn't seem worth the benefits of exposing their lie, not even if the Notary suffers.

He heads out, wanting to get to his HQ and get started on sorting files. There's no point in stalling, and he's not much of one for dragging his heels, anyway. As he hits the door and exits to the street, his cell vibrates in his pocket. He slides it out to check, hoping it's from the hospital, maybe some good news about Tress. She's been bad. Not just touch and go physically, but struggling mentally, as well. But it's not the hospital, it's a mail from Nia. He's not been to see Bone, hasn't spoken to Nia since they parted ways at the hospital after she promised to autopsy Rope and try to uncover his ID. He should see her, to congratulate her. She's been promoted to Head Mort at Gyre West, the first woman to make that leap. That's one hell of a mountain to climb against significant, prevailing winds, but she'll make it. He's certain of that. She's got steel, and she's dependable, too, someone to be relied upon. She's certainly come through for him. The mail contains test results for both Bone and Rope, alongside other, less legal information.

He scans it through and stops dead. Reads it again, more slowly this time, and then takes a seat because he finds he needs to sit down. He's outside Central and there are no benches to speak of, so he just sits against the side of the building. After a moment, he stares up into the cold, grey sky and begins laughing. Once he starts, he can't stop, hunched over on his knees, his shoulders shaking. The street, as ever, heaves with bodies, but they push back to the sidewalk edge as they reach him, to give him a wide berth. He must look insane. Crazed. Sat there, laughing and laughing, tears streaming down his cheeks. But he's not crazy. He's relieved. And shocked. More than both of those, he's just goddamn delighted. He couldn't begin to explain it because it's awful. Nia hasn't said as much, but she has no need. Stark's made a living building conclusions, and this one's clear. Just as Lever shed her skin, so must Bone Adams have shed his to become skinless Rope. Their Bone, whoever he was, was forced into that skin, into a lie, and by that simple act, became the target of Rope's fury, baited and terrorised and almost killed for something he very likely had no say in. All that is dreadful beyond words. No doubt about it. But here's the thing: he's *not* Bone Adams. He's innocent.

Stark's never understood how a decent man managed to exist over the hidden wreckage of a psychopath, and Nia's theory of the patch replacing Bone's personality felt too much like vain hope. What happened in that lab was not scientific curiosity, it was psychopathic impulse, just like Rope's recent killings. A patch couldn't change the man who did that, and he could not see that man in Bone, because Bone was *not* that man. It's a burden of doubt lifted, and even better, frees Stark from having to think about that file. The file is just another lie, some cock and bull they've concocted for official record, and you can't use a lie to expose the truth, that doesn't work. His laughter finally winds down, and he sits there, mouth rested on his knuckles, smiling. After a moment, he gets up and carries on walking, making his way to his HQ, his head not precisely at peace, but filled with purpose.

The important decisions are made. The file is going back to Spaz, back to safe keeping, and Stark's report on the Rope case is going to be one unholy, great lie with no mention of transmog. He discussed the report contents with Burton on the phone two days ago, and now Burton's left it to him. It's still his case, and if Yar has interest in the case, then Stark wants to crush it. Bone doesn't need Yar sniffing around him. The Notary Chair is downright crooked, and Stark has never trusted him. If his final act as a CO is one that blocks Yar, then he'll consider it a job well fucking done.

CHAPTER 47

Grey lights erupt in his skull and pain ignites across his body, a great mass of it all at once. At the centre: noise. Seething and incoherent. Heavy liquid presses him into place, hard as ropes, part of the pain he can't escape, and something's pulling where his face should be, a frantic scrabbling like rats trying to burrow down towards soft innards. It reaches his mouth. But there's no mouth. Only this hard lump. And he's screaming, the sound dulled and obstructed. Those scrabbling paws are pulling at the thing where his mouth should be, and with a knifing sensation that splits him from throat to gut, it's gone and liquid's gushing in. Flooding in. Nothing to stop it. He's drowning, filling up with liquid. His body slams against hard surfaces. He's trapped. He's trapped in a box, and he's drowning.

§

Bone's drowning. He's torn the tubes from his mouth and he's slowly going blue. His wounds are sealed, but the violence of his early movements, his battle to escape, send tendrils of bright red through the pale yellow liquid of the sus unit. Alarms blare through the room. The specialist sus team fight to drain the unit as swiftly as possible and get to Bone before it's too late. He needs to come out as he went in. Being put in a suspension unit is a procedure, and removal is the same. Only this small team is qualified to do it, but despite their skill and the speed with which they're working, the process is taking too long. Bone's gone limp already, his limbs twitching in movements that look too much like the last nerve-driven motions of death. They're shouting and half-panicked, but they don't stop working, and with an insanely loud rushing noise, the liquid finally drains away. The various tubing and needle-probes automatically disengage, storing themselves away, and one of the team stabs in the code to open the unit.

The sides hiss as it unseals, and in one smooth movement, yawns open, releasing Bone into their arms. They lower him to the floor and inject him full of a mixture of fairly brutal accelerants because, at this point, CPR won't work. They need to kick-start his body from within, and the range of drug-carrying nanites in the injection stimulate organs directly. His eyes pop open as the nanites hit their targets, and he jackknifes off the floor, sending the nurses flying. He starts coughing, choking up sus liquid in great gouts, and screaming. The noise is hideous, like an animal in pain. He scrambles back against the wall, incoherent, wild eyed, and moving as though his limbs are half-paralysed. It's truly horrendous to watch, his horror leaking into the room and infecting the small team. But they have more to do. They lunge for Bone and he shrieks, high-pitched and piercing as a drill, as they wrestle him onto a gurney.

He's delirious and that screech goes on and on until one nurse slams the injector against his neck, firing in a raft of sedatives and relaxants. For a moment, Bone strains up against the straps, his back an excruciating curve, then he slumps, pale and limp, onto the gurney. The team finally relaxes, smiling at each other. Daina Uri, the ward sister assigned to his post-unit care, waits by the door, her arms crossed. She raises a brow as the sus team wheels him out.

"That was clumsy," she snaps.

The doctor heading the sus team shrugs, unrepentant. "He almost fucking killed himself, there. He's been lucky."

Daina sniffs, unconvinced. "If you say so."

She takes over, then, wheeling Bone to a private room on the upper floors as per Spaz's orders. There, she and her team try and dress him in soft pyjamas, but even unconscious, he resists, pushing the clothes away and making distressed sounds that cause one of the younger nurses to cry. In the end, Daina gives up, covering him with a light blanket, instead. She hooks him up to various monitors and leaves him to sleep.

§

It's nearing evening when he finally wakes. Nia came straight from the Mort, when she heard he'd come out of the unit. Visiting hours are long since over, but she's Establishment family, and for once she's glad that rules don't apply to her in this place. She's sat next to him, her tablet on her lap, going through the giant caseload she's inherited and feeling just a little over-whelmed, when she looks up to find him watching her, his eyes solemn.

"Hi," she whispers, smiling at him.

He blinks slowly. It looks like it hurts. "Hi."

She puts the tablet to one side and takes his hand. "I'm here. It's okay."

Those solemn grey eyes of his, dark as stormy weather, fill with tears. "It's not," he tells her, in a voice that cracks dangerously and he catapults up from the waist, as if yanked by unseen hands, and vomits so hard over his blanket, the tendons on his ribs pop.

The monitors start to blare and Nia leaps up, looking for the nurses, but Bone grabs her. "Toilet. Please," he gasps out, vomit dribbling from his nose as he fights frighteningly strong heaves, his eyes blank with panic.

She whips off the monitor hooks, flips the blanket into a neat heap at the end of the bed, and supports his weight as he stumbles to the bathroom. He collapses in a heap in front of the toilet and throws up, wringing with sweat. He's bringing up nothing but blackish, bile-coloured liquid and coughing so hard his wounds, mostly healed, begin to weep blood. It scares her half to death.

She hears the door of his room slam open and calls out to them, "He's in here. I've got him. He's sick."

Daina runs in. She's taken off the cap and cardigan she was wearing when Nia arrived, revealing hair like spun glass and a see-through implant all the way down her neck to her cleavage of swirling, hypnotic shapes, filled with greenish liquid. Bioluminescence. For some reason, seeing the normality of the woman eases Nia's distress, and she steps back to watch as Daina kneels down behind Bone and rubs his back. Eventually, breath hissing in and out in wheezing gasps, he manages to stop heaving and coughing, and falls back, one arm on the toilet seat, the other braced on the floor. His hair's flopped down over his forehead, lank and lifeless, his mouth's pale blue and his skin's see-through, a ghastly shade of waxy greyish-white.

Nia's mind is wrung out with shock, her lips tingling. "What was that?" she demands of Daina.

"He came out of the tube badly. It's going to be a little rough for him for a while," Daina replies, brushing Bone's hair off his forehead. "I'm Daina, Bone. We're going to get you back to bed, okay?" She smiles at Nia. "Give me a hand, hon?"

Daina and Nia carry him out of the small bathroom, to his bed. He's too thin. It's been five days since the sewer, and even with the nutrient feed from the unit, he's dropped weight. He didn't have enough to begin with. Now he feels so fragile, Nia's scared she'll break him, scared she already broke something in him dragging him to the bathroom like that. They settle him on the edge of the bed and Daina lifts some blue hospital-issue pyjamas from Nia's chair.

"How's about some clothes now, hmmm? I'm all for staring at naked men, especially pretty ones, but we do like our patients to have a little dignity."

Bone throws Nia a pleading look that breaks her heart, and she says, "I think he needs more time." She strives to talk calmly, one professional to another, but manages only to sound as emotionally wrecked as she feels.

Daina sighs. "Fine. But it can't go on indefinitely." She helps him sit, piling pillows at his back, and throws a light, clean blanket over his lower body. "You just keep this on. I don't need any of my girls falling over, trying to cop an eyeful."

Bone sinks into the pillows as if he's not even heard her. His gaze falls to his hands, staring, and the look of absolute terror in his eyes makes Nia's skin contract. Daina's wrong; it's not just waking badly from the unit he's got to recover from. She wonders what it is he's thinking, looking at his hands like that, and aches for him so hard, she has to hold herself in, both arms wrapped tight about her waist. All her edges are cracked and weeping, she's leaking out of herself, and has no means to stop. Later, when she leaves, she takes a moment to watch him as he fitfully sleeps, and tries to secure that image in her mind. To make a solid picture of him she can hold onto. Something real. Anything. But even as she leaves, it slips away, curling into memories of his flesh flared open, his innards exposed, and she understands that this cannot be undone, this knowing. He is not Bone. Whatever happens from now on, they will just have to live with that.

CHAPTER 48

*W*ednesday is the last day before Daina's weekend, and for once, she's getting to leave only a little past her shift, close on for midnight. Mid-week usually gets crazy busy, and she's stunned to be leaving this soon, it's usually closer to 2:00 a.m. Her shoes crunch into a thick layer of fresh snow. It soaks past both trousers and socks to freeze her legs to the calf, making her shiver uncontrollably despite the thick, woollen warmth of her coat. It's the same every year, heavy snows from mid-August all the way through to January. She could move somewhere warmer, go home perhaps, but she likes it here. Her only qualm when moving had been that the job she'd found was based in a gang-run hospital, but it's proven to be one of the best jobs she's ever had.

The Spires is an unusual city, larger than some and more complicated than any. It has a tangled, somewhat evasive history—guards its borders fiercely. When Daina revealed her plans to move here, her friends and family shared all manner of colourful warning stories about the city, the dangers of living here, but everything she was told pales in comparison to the reality. This city is vast and uncontainable. Unhinged and exotic. Brim-full of terrors and marvels alike. It's a clamourous, extraordinary place, and though she's often scared, she'd never leave. There are many reasons for that, but first and foremost is the attitude to mods and modification in general, it's one of the first things she loved about the Spires. Where she came from, mods are just a requirement, as much as a job, a house, or a car. Other cities in the City States Union insist that citizenship rely upon having specific mods. By that simple requirement, whether the mod itself is artistic, surgical, or gen, they're rendered pedestrian, all sense of individuality and autonomy stripped away.

Here, with the riotous insanity of the Zone, mods are more anarchic than obligatory, a declaration of independence instead of compliance to accepted norms, and that attitude prevails even on the streets. Spires citizens actively reject bureaucratic interference in their self-expression, and that's directly connected to the presence of the gangs. To someone from another City State, accustomed to a stifling expectation of compliance, it's liberating. Daina breathes the cold air, smiling. The car park for hospital staff is sunk into the mountains. There's no path out here and most staff use the pods beneath the hospital to get to their cars, but she's got her own light and enjoys the walk through the trees. She's always longing for a bit of fresh air by the day's end anyway, having grown up in a city near the coast with suburbs about as rural as you can get in the CSU. It's ridiculously cold, but it wakes her up enough to ensure she'll have energy to drive home, reheat and eat the dinner her husband will have made.

He's gang. If anyone had told her she'd marry into gang, she'd have laughed, but Hale, though he looks plain vicious with all his implants and scrawling gang tattoos, is the most genuine, decent man she's ever met. A snowy owl drifts overhead, it's wings shimmering moon-bright against the dark sky, and she stops to watch it. They live higher up in the mountains, away from the city, just as most animals have learned to do, and she rarely sees them. As it floats out of sight, pale as an apparition, she hears footfalls crunching in the snow behind her and turns with a smile, expecting to see one of the six groundsmen. Instead it's a stranger. Tall, and as thin as one of her current patients, Bone Adams. So much so, she thinks it might be him.

"Bone? You should be in bed. It's freezing out here."

He's spent the week since he almost drowned in his sus unit throwing up everything he eats. It'll take a while for the sus unit sickness to pass, but she's worried there's more going on. The man is in a state, and seems terrified of his own body. She insisted on psychiatric intervention because she can't see him recovering without it, but it doesn't seem to be helping, and she's at a loss, which frustrates her to no end. In response to her voice, the tall man stops some distance away, silhouetted in the trees.

"Hello?" she calls out. "Bone?"

He doesn't respond, but he no longer *looks* like Bone. He looks like a stranger, and she begins to experience low levels of unease. She's got a gun, Hale insists upon it, what with the troubles coming in from the Outskirts, the Gulley, and the Wharf, but she dislikes using it and invariably ends up leaving it in her car. She wishes now she were closer to the car park, at least then she could run for her car, if need be, and get to her gun.

"Do you need assistance?" she asks, making sure to keep her voice loud and friendly. "Hospital's behind you, it's not a long walk."

"I don't want the hospital, Daina Uri."

Her heart starts to pick up an erratic quality to its beat. His voice is freakish. Melodic and yet dry. Too husky, as though it's hardly ever used.

"How do you know my name?" she asks, still speaking loudly and backing away as surreptitiously as possible. Hale's persistent drilling of how to respond to threat rolls out in her mind step by step, and she makes ready to run.

"Your husband's advice cannot help you here, Daina Uri."

The words are spoken as if they're somehow delicious, and Daina's unease kicks up to full blown panic. Throwing aside caution, she turns and sprints for it, fast as her legs can go in the thick snow, heading straight for the car park. She expects to be chased, but hears no foot falls behind. Perhaps she's been wrong, perhaps he's gang and something's happened to Hale. Daina slides to a halt, thinking of her husband injured, perhaps dead, and then something hits—a mental blow that knocks her from her feet, stealing the breath from her body, the function from limbs and thought.

Hitting the snow hurts more than she expects. A sharp pain cuts through her nose, the crunch of bone loud in her ears, and warm blood spreads out across her cheeks, cooling almost immediately. She shrieks, struggling to breathe as cold flakes fill her mouth. Then a gentle pressure touches her shoulder and turns her over. The stranger looms above her as she coughs up snow, and she finally sees his face, lit by her own bioluminescence. He's an angel. Golden hair down to his shoulders, skin so white it glows in the darkness like an owl's wing, drawn over bones so perfect he could be an IM model. His eyes are a clear blue like fine porcelain, and there's nothing in them whatsoever, nothing in that beautiful face at all. It's blank as a doll's. Empty.

He stares down at her, unblinking. "I'm going to ask you a few questions about a patient of yours," he says to her in that melodic husk of a voice. "You won't be able to scream, so don't try. You will answer every question I ask, or there will be pain. If you behave, I will allow you to end yourself quickly. Nod if you understand."

Something takes her head in a vice-like grip and lifts it up and down, as though she's nodding agreement. But she doesn't agree, she doesn't give permission, and when he begins to ask her questions, it becomes clear that there will be pain no matter what she does because he enjoys inflicting it. Though he never once touches her, there's more pain than she can bear, and yet he forces her to bear every last excruciating second as she answers all of his questions, though she fights hard as she can to prevent herself from speaking. When he's done, he offers her nothing of that swift end, watching her with those blank, beautiful eyes as she squeezes the life from her own heart and slumps into the snow.

CHAPTER 49

*C*old. *Pain in the skull, so bad, the bones shifting around, loose and broken. Endless darkness. He's moaning into the darkness, aware of only pain, dark and cold, when a figure walks forwards, swimming into focus. Skinless, its body is a fluid shape formed of sticky, red flesh. Piercing green eyes float in the midst of it all. So bright. And the white of teeth. Of all of it, the white of teeth frightens him most. The figure lifts something from the floor. Heavy. Dripping. It pulls this weight onto its sticky flesh, smoothing it until it slips into place, fits snug along long limbs, over the red dome of its head. It turns, leans towards him, and he sees his own face. It's wearing his face. And it's smiling. Smiling down at him. The white of teeth gleaming in the darkness.*

Bone wakes screaming, drenched in sweat so cold, he's shivering with it and panting hard, unable to catch a breath. He coughs, trying not to retch, to control the urge, but it defeats him and he throws back the blankets, scrambling for the bathroom just in time to throw up whatever's left of his dinner. This is the third time he's seen this memory, and try as he might, he can't recall the face, though he knows that it was his. It's a torture of the mind, and too frightening because he's not sure he wants to know. He's scared he won't survive it. The nurses don't know how to help him, nor even the psych team. All this recollection is utterly beyond control. It has no limits, no end. There's so much of that other self in there, too much to restrain.

He pushes back from the bowl, feeling vulnerable, trapped inside his head and entirely at its mercy. He's exhausted, and yet filled with horrendous tension, the potential for absolute ruin. Another violent urge to throw up takes over his body. He breathes through it, his head hanging. He's thrown up so much, his throat feels like raw, tenderised steak. If he throws up any more, he'll see bits of torn stomach lining floating in the bowl. He's been there, done that, has no desire to visit it again, and he leaves the bathroom on shaking limbs, flushing to be rid of the stench. The surface of his skin blazes with heat and crawls, it never stops. Feels alive, a separate entity. He doesn't trust it. At any moment, it will begin to peel away again, like it did in the sewer. He keeps touching his forehead, making sure there's no seam, no split, but the relief of smooth skin is only ever temporary. Uncertainty always returns, the fear that he can't hold himself together, that he's not under his control.

Those grey lights hover at his peripheries. Beyond them is fear and darkness and pain, a raging current of memory crashing against the thin walls of his resistance. He's under siege and cracking apart. Too frightened to sleep, Bone staggers to the window and shoves it open, allowing in blasts of frigid air. He's already frozen, but he lifts his head and bathes in bitter cold, wishing this could wash away the transmog, the memories. He leans out of the frame, wincing as his wounds pull, but he can't relax. Everything that defined him has gone, he's nothing left to hold onto. Agitated to the marrow, brim full of hurt and desperate for distraction, he looks out at the view, and catches his breath.

Laid out before him, below the edge of the mountains, is his home, the Spires. Spreading ever outwards across seemingly endless distance, it's an ocean of lights and pinnacles, glistening in the darkness. It looks like a living being, a sleeping behemoth. Out on the cusp, where the city meets the horizon, a thin line of grey dusk bleeds soft ink into the last smouldering embers of sunlight, and above it all, the night is a veil of black, alive with dazzling radiance. Crystalline pinpoints of blue, red, and white float upon the darkness, weightless and luminant, an array of such beauty he's reduced to mere sensation. Trapped in the moment, he's caught like a fly in amber between the earth and infinity until soft footfalls behind him break the spell. He turns too fast. The movement makes him dizzy and he slips off his elbows, begins to fall. A vice-like grip on his arm prevents it. Spaz. Looking so savage that, for a moment, Bone's convinced he's here to kill him. But he pulls Bone up and helps him over to the bed, where Ebony's stood, shoving the few things Nia's brought to the hospital for him into a small, black bag.

"Why are you here?" he asks as Spaz lowers him down, and without speaking, begins to shove Bone's legs into trousers.

"You're coming to the Zone," Ebony says, not looking at him, her bottom lip caught beneath her teeth. But she's not embarrassed by his nudity, that's not her style. Something's scared her. Badly.

"I don't understand."

Spaz yanks Bone's trousers up, his eyes glinting dangerously, tucking him in and zipping him up with the sort of offhand ease that makes such intimacy almost comfortable. "You don't have to understand," he says. "You just have to do as you're told."

Bone frowns. "Why should I?"

"You're not safe here," Spaz replies softly, handing him a shirt. "Rope was only the beginning."

Bone's unable to restrain a half-hysterical note of laughter, considering Rope ended so *much* of him, and damn near killed him, to boot. "You're kidding."

Ebony replies this time, focused on his bag, her movements sharp and harried. "Please, hon, believe him."

Belief is not the issue here. "I do. I just don't understand." He struggles into his shirt, fumbling the buttons closed and trying not to panic at his skin's reaction to the press of fabric, the suffocation of enclosure. He's still not up to this, but argument is apparently not in the cards.

"We don't want you hurt," Spaz says rigidly, standing up and turning away. Closing Bone out.

"Why? Who am I to you?"

The private hospital treatment, and now this removal from danger, are something more than solicitude, more than obligation. He's done nothing to earn this. Maybe it's because of who he *was*. If so, why can't they simply come out and say so? There's so much going on here. Too much. A game in play that he is unwittingly, unwillingly part of, and it all seems to revolve around a life he can't remember. He wants answers, needs to understand why this has to happen. More than anything, though, he wants someone to be honest with him, no matter what it might do to the patches in his head. There's no stopping what's happening to him here. One way or another, he's going to know, but he'd rather have answers *before* he loses his damn mind.

"You're someone we care about," Ebony says, and that's that. She doesn't say anything else, and Spaz remains turned away, closed off, a peculiar tension riding his back. Ebony presses shoes onto Bone's feet, her hands gentle, though she still won't look at him. "He's ready to go," she tells Spaz.

They take him out of the hospital in a private elevator. There's a car waiting that looks a little like Stark's. Nia mentioned something about Stark losing his badge. He doesn't deserve that. If it weren't for Stark, he'd be dead. At least, he thinks so. Nia says there's so much more to it than that, but she refuses to elaborate in case it provokes traumatic flashbacks. She's scared of losing him, even though she knows he's not *him*. How strange. Bone slumps in the corner of the seat, weary to the marrow. He breathes out through his nose, the breath boiling hot on his lips. It seems the world at large feels free to take from him whatever it wants: his autonomy, his truth, his memories, and it's all down to this skin. He's had enough of being at its mercy.

Over the past week, trying to come to terms with what's happened to him, he's thought a great deal about Rope shedding Lever's skin. The parallels are extraordinary. The Lever he thought he knew, however briefly, was a lie, and so is he. And what's underneath his lie? Not a murderer, but that's faint comfort. Instead, he is a stranger. A man he can't remember the face of, let alone the name. Those memories terrify him as much as the transmog does. Alien sensations of otherness, within and without, rendering him incapable of recognising even the smallest part of himself. There seems to be no way of consolidating his state.

Catching the reflection of his eye in the window, he recalls the mirror of Rope's eye, Bone reflected into Bone, and wonders for a brief, mad moment *why* it has to matter to him which one was real. After all, the one who claimed to be real is dead, and all proof of his existence has been summarily erased or hidden. He could just be Bone forever, now, and forget the rest. Go back to his Mort once it's all over and take up where he left off. But the idea is risible. A ridiculous fantasy. His past, much like his future, is in ruins. He can't go back and he can't go forwards, not until he knows who he really is. So, there it is. He has to follow where the path leads, all the way to the end, no matter what he might find. Or lose.

He rests his cheek against the glass. The cold is blissful, if only for a moment. Behind them, the hospital falls away from view, swallowed by snow-capped mountains, and ahead, brilliantly lit, the Spires skyline rears sharp as teeth against the night—a sleeping behemoth, waiting to consume him.

ACKNOWLEDGMENTS

Bear with me on this one, I have a lot of people to thank. First and foremost, and again, Stephen Godden, the wit and wonder who's no longer with us. Thanks for the unflagging faith, for the excellent, insightful beta reads, and for the many, many email rants. I miss you, Welsh Byron. I wish you were here to see this, you were so certain it would happen. You were right. Thanks also go out to Michael Gallant, another grand friend whose input on this one (and others) has been invaluable. You're a star, Mike, and a gentleman. Beers are on me if our paths ever cross IRL, you can depend on it. I owe massive thanks to the irreplaceable, irrepressible Gary Bonn, who made pretty much everyone he knew read this book in its earliest form. Your enthusiasm for this particular book-child has been so wonderful and so warming. Thank you, MooninGary. For everything.

Naturally I can't talk about *Coil* without hollering about Jen Udden, my agent supreme, who offered me representation because of this book. When it didn't at first find a home, Jen made me write another book that did. Thanks for the belief, Jen, for the fierce advocation, and for generally being a badass. Oh, and thanks for not skinning me alive for sending this to an open sub month on the sly. Your patience with my endless reticence is appreciated, as is your immediate, unfailing support.

Huge, undying thanks from the bottom of my cold, dead heart go of course to Apex, to Jason and Lesley, for giving my favourite, slightly strange, and undeniably bloody book-child a perfect home. We promise not to leave too many dead bodies around the place. Honest. We're ever so careful. Waste not, want not.

Finally I want to thank Matt Davis for the pulpy eighties throwback cover of dreams. It's an absolute beauty. You best believe I'm recommending you to anyone who needs a cover, and probably also to anyone who doesn't. Brace for impact!

ABOUT THE AUTHOR

Ren Warom lives in the West Midlands with her children, her cat-pack, a snake called Marvin, and innumerable books. She's currently pursuing a PhD and thinks she may have lost her mind. If you find said mind, please return in a secure, locked box to the address on the collar. Do not, repeat, *do not*, attempt to feed it! Thank you.

facebook.com/ren.warom

twitter.com/renwarom

47553271R00196

Made in the USA
Middletown, DE
11 June 2019